ANGELS AT THE GATE

Sheri Joseph

Regal House Publishing

Published by
Regal House Publishing, LLC
Raleigh, NC 27605
All rights reserved

ISBN -13 (paperback): 9781646036530
ISBN -13 (epub): 9781646036547
Library of Congress Control Number: 2024950300

Cover images and design by © studiochi.art

"The Killing Moon"
Words and Music by Ian Stephen McCulloch, William Alfred Sergeant, Leslie
Thomas Pattison and Peter Louis Vincent de Freitas
C. 1983 Zoo Music Ltd. (PRS)
All Rights Adminstereed by WB Music Corp.
All Rights Reserved
Used by Permission of Alfred Music

Printed in the United States of America
Regal House Publishing, LLC
https://regalhousepublishing.com

PRAISE FOR *ANGELS AT THE GATE*

"Sheri Joseph's mesmerizing *Angels at the Gate* is more than a campus novel, more than a mystery, more than a reflection on memory. It's a deeply-felt story of a young student, Leah, and her friends and classmates, as they begin to create the person they will become, and the choices they make that forever remind them of what they left behind. It's heartbreaking, joyful, and utterly unforgettable."

—Kevin Wilson, author of *Nothing to See Here* and *The Family Fang*

"Sheri Joseph plunges readers into the shadowy fog of tradition-bound Rockhaven University, where secrets, secret desires, and questions of loyalty swirl around cool girl Leah and her friend group of frat boys. With an unerring eye for the complex dynamics of pre-social media campus life, Joseph elegantly captures the '80s, complete with a to-die-for playlist. Compulsively readable and deliciously dark."

—Leslie Pietrzyk, author of *Admit This to No One* and *Silver Girl*

"In the tradition of *The Secret History* and *The Group*, *Angels at the Gate* reinvents the genre of the campus mystery. Leah, inexperienced in both romantic relationships and the privileged world of private colleges, seeks to unravel the mystery of a fellow student's apparent suicide, perhaps in an attempt to find answers to her own mother's suspicious death. Through breathtaking descriptions and witty dialogue, Joseph deftly and convincingly creates the rarified atmosphere of the newly co-ed Southern college on the hill, whose traditions, mores, and secrets remain opaque to Leah, even as she believes that her intellectual capacity allows her understanding. As the danger of the mystery increases, involving secret societies and unrequited longings, Leah realizes that the victim—like Leah herself—like all of us—longed most for unobtainable connection and intimacy. Through Joseph's evocative prose and adept characterizations, this gorgeous novel reminds us, once again, how our earliest relationships may suggest our paths, but our vulnerable early adult years cement our futures."

—Allison Amend, author of *Enchanted Islands* and *A Nearly Perfect Copy*

"*Angels at the Gate* is the Southern gothic stepchild of *The Secret History*, an indelible snapshot of what it meant to be young in a singular time and place."

—Jennifer Haigh

"If you love a campus novel—and who doesn't?—meet Leah, your tour guide through a beguiling mystery set among the lamplit paths and leafy towers of a college as vivid and tinged with melancholy as the one in your memory. Cuskian in the sharpness of its observations of friends, family, and frenemies, *Angels at the Gate* exerts a subtle and haunting power."

—Christopher Castellani, author of *Leading Men*

What is that word honor? Air—a trim reckoning! Who hath it? He that died a Wednesday. Doth he feel it? No. Doth he hear it? No. 'Tis insensible, then? Yea, to the dead.

—Falstaff, *Henry IV Part 1*

BOOK ONE

ADVENT

1

GRAVITY'S PULL

Spring, 1986. In the kitchen of the Gamma Chi house, a boy who will be dead in a few months is mixing drinks. The room is empty but for the two of us, the window light behind him graying with early evening. It's a scene that comes to mind often, though why is hard to say. His name is Brantley Simms. From the next room, a crack of pool balls and laughter, the stereo playing Talking Heads' "And She Was." He measures gin into a row of highball glasses, the ones etched with the university seal, pilfered from the back of a high cabinet. Other pledges would have settled for the Solo cups, but Brantley would like it known he has standards. He's so pleased with the lime I've scrounged from the fridge, desiccated but real, that he kisses me smack on the forehead.

I bring tonic. I bring ice. I'm not actually here.

But with one or two adjustments of history, I could be. Say he has summoned me with a head-tip from the other room: *Be my sidekick*. He's formed a hunch I'm worthy, and in these days I often aim to be what I am not: in this case, the girl who murmurs with him about people just past the door—*Oh, you'd get this*—as he twists an ice tray, saws through the leathery lime. We are hilarious and terrible. He lowers his voice for an insinuation so subtle and dirty it goes half over my head, but I know it's something he shouldn't be saying about a brother. While I'm cringing with laughter behind the shield of my hands, he cuts himself and begins to bleed.

The knife must have slipped. Or a glass in his grip shattered against the counter. Perhaps he cut himself on his own wit. In any case, the gash has opened in a finger. I take hold of his hand to pinch it closed, glad in a way for this task at which I'm proficient. I feel tender toward his wound and its welling blood. I don't yet imagine it won't stop.

And what's the difference, if I am in the kitchen or not? He won't die of this wound, no matter how glary and greenish the light turns, how loud the music. It changes nothing, for him, if I can begin to love him just enough to feel what hurts him.

I've dreamed my way here once or more, to a darker soundtrack: The Smiths, calling young bones to the rocks, or R.E.M. and where gravity will take you. His cut becomes a situation. I apply more pressure, all I can, but the blood must be leaking from elsewhere, unseen; his skin shrivels with its loss, eyes going shocky and vacant. I'm still holding on to the wrong wound, but it's the one I have, and I can't let go.

I know the window light of the Gamma house in its early evening calm, the way it might fall on the shoulders of a boy mixing drinks. But not Brantley's. We were not friends. I was too reserved for his tastes, averse to his barbed comedy and confrontational style. In a tiny, insular school where we all thought we were pretty smart, Brantley Simms was the kind of smart that will make itself a nuisance. I might as well admit I hated him, avoided him by habit, after an encounter that left me scalded though it was half my own fault. *Sensitive*, he would have called me, had I not hidden that wound caused by a few words, and I'll own I was. As an only child, I had yearned for brothers more than sisters, the sort derived from books or after-school specials who would include me in their adventures as one of them. Nonfictional boys, though, were new to me. I didn't yet know I'd have to shrug off a lot or learn to slap back if I meant to keep even the sweetest of them as friends.

The night he cut himself, I was out on the sofas. Brantley was somewhere across the room, orating at his usual volume a few notches louder than the stereo. On any topic, he plumped his humor with brainy references that both irritated and intimidated me, because he and I both held the Harper scholarship. *He's making an impression*, I sometimes remarked, by which I meant he was loud. Like the too-long bangs he let flop over one eye to be flung: too flashy, too blond, a bland face beneath but the hair and its gesture drew the eye, as did the grating pitch of his voice. He imposed himself on the general attention until we all felt slightly deformed with awareness of what was on his mind or, on this night, wrapped around his hand, red and white, a bloody dish towel.

"That'll teach you," one of the actives shouted from another corner. "The glassware is not for pledges." Lime-wedged highballs had been distributed to a cadre of seniors who ribbed him for everyone's amusement.

"There had better not be any of your damn blood in this."

"I'm adding that glass to your dues!"

As an outsider with anthropological interests, I often wondered what sorts of ritual humiliations the Gamma pledges were subjected to in secret. The few I was close to, all Brantley's pledge brothers, were tight-lipped on any matter that hinted of "fraternity business." But I had watched them bask in the playful abuse their elders meted out in public, as Brantley did this night, breaking off his monologue to genuflect at any active's call. *I serve at your pleasure! Yes, sir! Never, sir!*

Surely some of the house girls were there to cringe and fuss as he made his rounds, ignoring his leaky extremity until some new person demanded a peek. Or it's possible that at this haphazard gathering I was the only girl, enjoying myself all the more for it. My friends treated me as a kind of mascot if not one of the guys, and I took care not to assume a place at their house or dining tables—Gamma Wenches, such girls were dubbed. I was merely in the company of these few, who were to me only my friends, incidentally pledged to this particular brotherhood. As usual, our crew was absorbed in our own tipsy bubble of self-reference until half an hour on, when one of the boys noticed.

"What happened to Brantley?"

"Cut himself. Broke a glass, I think."

"No, slicing a lime."

Vince and Jonathan would have been two of those voices as a given, the third probably Pem. The one I'm sure of is Dex, his voice that called out, "Hey, Bran! Is that thing mortal or what?"

Brantley presented himself to our audience, last in the room for the show. "How long do you suppose before I bleed to death?"

Dex nudged me. "Leah, you're pre-vet. Doctor this poor creature."

A joke, since this was still freshman year and I'd suffered through only a couple of science prereqs of a major Rockhaven was too traditional to offer. But I worked at the university stables where now and then I tended to the wounds of horses, and Dex, who'd grown up in Ireland and spoke words like *creature* with a twist of brogue, could have talked me into more for less cause. Thus I found myself holding the hand of a person I had disliked from the start, then had time to grudgingly admire, to find compelling, even to love in a hypothetical way, from a distance, with the quick-born passion we were all prone to in college, before he made me regret it.

My friends circled to gawk as I peeled back the towel. The cut split the meat of an index finger. A tight pinch stemmed the flow. Released, it oozed thickly.

"You need stitches," I said.

"Ugh, the hospital? You can't just fix it somehow?"

Who was I to this boy? He might have had trouble recalling my name, listed with his among the twenty Harper scholars for our class. Over the interview weekend he'd made himself memorable to all of us, dominating every reception and campus tour with his stagy, self-promoting voice. He'd inquired obsessively after everyone's SAT score. He'd shouted his wisdom on topics from Jacobean foreign policy to Greek drama to the arcanery of Rockhaven history, as if every minute were his personal interview. He redeemed himself only in being so easy to mock that I bonded with another finalist by making fun of him. Vince McMillan had sloppy curls the same mouse-brown as mine, so that as soon as we attached and began finishing each other's sentences with all the rest we had in common, we were mistaken for siblings. We were still sometimes called "the twins," since as soon as he arrived on his own scholarship, he'd brought me into the fold with his roommate, Jonathan, and these other charming oddballs from his dorm hall who cluster-pledged Gamma Chi. So I could thank Brantley Simms for the happenstance of steps that had brought me to this exact place, girl-pal at a frat house, summoned to hold his hand.

He could not have known I hated him. I took care to conceal it even from my friends, just as Vince had been required to erase all unkind feelings toward Brantley along with their memory, because they were brothers now. *Brotherhood* had swept the freshman boys into its grip soon after arrival; with a handshake, it superseded all other bonds. The cultish intensity of that belonging, of pledging oneself so fast to strangers, fascinated me. I envied the instant family, having not much of my own, and sororities—their rush delayed anyway until spring—lacked the iron devotion, the love. My guy friends might accept me as their sort-of sister but would never love me in quite the way they loved each other. It pained me that a person like Brantley Simms rated something near that unreachable level just by wearing the same pin.

But suppressing my antipathy took work, and here my enemy had turned his wound over to me with such a docile trust that I felt like Androcles with the lion's paw. So I'll tame you, I thought. We'll become friends. One day we'll laugh about what a jerk you once were to me.

For an hour, I improvised first aid. I made him sit with the hand above his head, holding steady pressure: twenty minutes, no moving, no looking. I tried ice. I tried an ice-water bath, a light tourniquet. "Are you a hemophiliac?" I joked. As the others became bored with the crisis, he and I were left alone, having what amounted to our first friendly conversation, though it centered on the expedient. By the time I summoned some of his brothers to drive him to the hospital, he was worn out and didn't argue. I didn't go with them. Our evening was at an end.

So much blood from so small a wound. No other reason I should remember this hour, among all the other misadventures of college. I did what I could, for a boy who didn't much need my help, let alone deserve it. But I return to it now, replay its altered versions. His hand is in mine. I have this chance, the future unset.

What I wonder is this: Had I changed us, made us friends, would I have turned his fate? At a stretch, my best influence could have held no more power than chance. An alteration in plans, a step to the left instead of the right, caused somehow by me. How could I, how could any of us, know what might have been? This pointless question never goes away.

Few people I encounter in my adult life have heard of the college I attended, isolated on its mountaintop, sunk in some earlier decade's world view. My attempts to describe the culture are met with puzzled squints or open-mouthed disbelief, though for a church-connected university it was not strict. No enforced chapel, no chaperones—*Episcopal* church, as my classmates in the know often stressed, meaning we had in some ways an excess of freedom. That Rockhaven was established to educate the sons of slave owners explained much of what persisted, though this detail had been buried enough to go unmentioned during my time within its gates. Instead we knew it as modeled on Oxford, both in its devotion to the classical liberal arts and, most vividly, in the black academic gowns worn daily about campus by professors and high-achieving students inducted into the Order of Gownsmen. That some of us were women didn't cause any fuss over the name. Cultivating "the Rockhaven gentleman" remained the tacit college priority, so we females who'd been admitted only in the last twenty years, to some outcry about the demise of civilization, would be Gownsmen and freshmen and maybe gentlemen too. None of us minded, as I recall. It was the '80s, when few of us knew to mind.

Us, I say now, as if my belonging were so simple. In truth, I was never sure I'd have tuition for another year. When I was young, eight or nine, my mother went through a phase when she'd pack the two of us sandwiches and spend a Sunday driving around to open houses in rich neighborhoods. Or we circled ads placed by people selling horses, or boats, or twenty acres of waterfront property with a nine-stall barn, and drove miles into the country, idle shoppers of infinite means who were hard to impress. In this spirit, I might drift by my high school guidance counselor's office to pick up a brochure for Davidson or Sweetbriar, some daydream fodder, though I'd never imagined a choice to go anywhere other than a state university—the best, UT Knoxville—where my grades would guarantee free tuition. There was no maybe in view, not a spark of what if, until my junior year awards ceremony, when I was announced as winner of something called the Rockhaven Award for Excellence. The prize was a leather-bound dictionary embossed in gold with the name of the sponsor, Rockhaven University.

At first I suspected my teachers had invented this award to give me, since I'd lost my mother in an accident the previous year. The man who was biologically my father lived several towns away, long remarried with a house full of kids—no room for me there even if I'd been willing to change schools, or live with near-strangers—so I'd arranged to board with a family who kept a horse where I worked and had often served as my sitters when I was younger. This suited me fine but worried my teachers and the counselor I met with once a week during my free period. *Stoic* was the word they attached to me. I had always been a top student, and I found it easier to cope if I kept my attention on class, went straight to my barn job after school, then spent the evening on homework in my borrowed bedroom, and didn't talk about how I was holding up. Fine, was how I was holding up. Better than fine if I didn't have to answer the question. In a year I'd escape to college and then, I told myself, I would become whoever I was supposed to be. Nobody would bother me about my feelings or tiptoe around them or design lighter loads of work for fear I'd crack. My father had agreed to cover my room and board in Knoxville if I lived with his sister, Rose, and this was my only concern—that an aunt might interfere with the shedding of my former life, the process of becoming the person I couldn't yet see and hoped I would like being.

The dictionary, by far the nicest book I'd ever owned, was one of the many life details Vince and I would discover we had in common. Like me, he'd been on the tuition-free path to UT before winning the prize. A subtle, classy advertisement, given out at Tennessee public schools, the dictionary was surely aimed at diversity of at least an economic sort. Yet it was hindered by Rockhaven's lack of a need-based scholarship. There was only the Harper, partial and merit-based. But, we decided, why not try?

For me it had never seemed real: a school with horses to ride—I had assumed college would mean giving them up—and roaming dogs said to be reincarnated professors, a shady campus lawn arrayed in gothic architecture, all crenellations and spires and arches built from local sandstone. A campus small enough to know, where professors in tattered academic robes chalked messages onto blackboards like *We are outside under a tree.* A photographer had captured the blackboard for the brochure, its six words broken neatly across the fold, and on the same whim that made me seal and stamp an application, then borrow a car when summoned to appear for an interview, I studied that chalked message, fronted by a row of empty, historically old wooden desks; I chose the one on the left. When I arrived in January for the interview weekend, the cold prevented any class from meeting outside, though I looked for them anyway under the trees, through a white screen of fog. Here and there, in the cloud I'd ascended into above the solid world, students passed between classes in their black gowns.

Over plates of cheese at the vice chancellor's opening reception, Vince and I found each other by means of an expression no other finalist wore, a bug-eyed *Where the hell are we?* look. To be summoned to such a strange, obscure school was for us like holding golden tickets to the chocolate factory, a desirable but faintly eerie mystery. Quaint, perhaps? Oppressive? The others around us did not seem surprised or alarmed that this school, for starters, had an actual dress code: skirts for women, coats and ties for men. "You are looking at my only skirt," I told Vince, brushing cracker crumbs from the nubby charcoal fabric, a hand-me-down from the family I lived with so they could take me to church. "You're about to see it for three days."

Vince said, "Well, don't be jealous but I have a whole different tie for tomorrow."

We separated, returned to each other, having realized as we made the rounds a feature of our disorientation: we were surrounded by private-school kids. "What's a Choate?" I asked him behind my hand. "Is it something dirty?" Everywhere our peers were talking about one of the application essays, *Discuss a book that has had a significant influence on your life,* and the titles we overheard as choices—*The Brothers Karamazov,* Hegel's dialectics, *Portrait of the Artist as a Young Man*—left us daunted. Private-school books, we decided. And "*that* guy," as we began to call the loudest boy in the room, with his polka-dot bow tie and sun-bleached hair—Mr. Private School. We didn't have to go near Brantley Simms to be apprised of his book choice, Salinger's *Franny and Zooey*: "Have you read it?" came his disembodied voice from deep in the crowd. "Oh, you have to read it. It's *life-changing*!"

Vince and I checked with each other. The Salinger who wrote *Catcher in the Rye*? Wasn't it pronounced *Franny and* Zoe-*y*?

For all my love of reading, I had struggled with the question, none of my favorites feeling weighty enough to call "influential." The harder part was "your life." What was that, other than a hazy destination? Books were what I read while waiting to get there. I'd settled on Rachel Carson's *Silent Spring*, a book I knew the significance of—DDT, eagle eggs—though I had not actually read it. I'd never seen a copy, wasn't sure copies existed, a fact that only now began to worry me. And had my essay been a lie? *Silent Spring* had led to the creation of the Environmental Protection Agency, a legitimate influence on my interest in ecology. The question hadn't specified a book I'd *read*, though the reading part did seem implied.

When Vince told me he'd written on *Hitchhiker's Guide to the Galaxy*, I wanted to punch him. Why hadn't I picked that book?

It's possible the snark that bonded us was all along an effort to resist. By the next day, after muddling through interviews—at least no one pinned me with a book question for which I had to lie or go silent or confess—Vince and I had begun to reserve our scorn for Brantley Simms. The craggy beauty of the campus left us silent, and the school traditions, so many beyond the dress code, gradually charmed us. The guardian angels, for instance: we were told they protected all within the university domain, that students leaving through the stone gates tapped the car roof in order to pick up an angel for the world outside. On return, they tapped the roof again to release the angel back into general service. My dorm host, a bubbly junior named Meredith, confirmed the roof-tapping was not just a pretty story but an actual practice.

And the angels were effective, at least within the gates. The students who dropped by Meredith's room while I was there between events—as many guys as girls, though the dorms were single-sex—couldn't think of anyone who had died on campus, ever. The stories of student death handed down as part of the college lore happened elsewhere, like the boy back in the sixties who drowned while boating on Lake Lanier two months after his graduation, entering the annals as the reason every Rockhaven student was required in freshman year to pass a swimming test. Some quibbled by naming domain overlooks and the drunkards who had fallen from those heights, Rockhaven graced with an excess of both scenic cliffs and alcohol consumption; but others refuted the locations, or whether that particular legend involved an enrolled student or had resulted in death. That no one had ever succumbed to alcohol poisoning, they agreed, proof of either miracle or the iron Rockhaven constitution. No one mentioned drugs, and later I learned that almost no one openly did them.

I didn't know what to make of the drinking, having minimal experience there. But in the students' shared history, their enjoyment in so many odd traditions that set them apart, they seemed like the sort of rangy, mutually adoring family I'd always envied. They claimed to hold the school honor code so sacred that no one locked dorm rooms, bikes, or cars. No one stole, no one cheated. (Would they think I had cheated on my essay? I decided not to ask.) The apocryphal accounts of students dismissed from school—for lying to the Honor Council, for removing a library book without checking it out—belonged to the lore of long ago and not in their ranks.

"We," they kept saying, so I thought they were joking when they mentioned their own separate fraternities and sororities. But they assured me the Greek system, too, was different here. Because Rockhaven had no town or night life aside from a campus pub, the Greeks had evolved locally as a way to create parties, to pool money for kegs and a house to tap them in. Almost everyone joined.

"People have their own circles," they said. "But parties are open. We all go to each other's."

And everyone knew everyone. No off-campus housing or alternative to the meal plan meant all students lived their four years in a dorm. All ate in the dining hall with everyone else. You got close. Sometimes too close, they admitted, laughing. Yet no one went home on the weekends, that mainstay of college life elsewhere. Why would they? The school sat on ten thousand acres of Cumberland forest, so go climb a rock, commune with nature. Hike a full day and you could still be on university land, under the angels' guard.

On the campus tours, I passed the time apart from Vince by wondering what it might be like to belong to a "we"—never mind that my father didn't know I'd applied, let alone driven myself here five hours in a borrowed car on the pretense of being someone who might, in fact, attend. I lingered on the stable visit to speak to the school horses, mud-flecked and scruffy in their winter paddock. In the chapel, I stepped around the university seal as directed, lest I be cursed with failure to graduate. I pictured striding across a fog-covered lawn in one of those floating black robes that marked the academic elite. A diversion, I told myself, for the tourist I was.

"But honestly," Vince said, "if you won, your dad would find the money, right?"

Here, I told myself, was someone I might have met at UT. Vince. Why not? But it was hard to see how, amid so many strangers, catching a city bus from my aunt's townhouse to class on the eighteenth floor of some building.

On the final evening, Meredith invited me out to a college hangout in the next town known as The Truckstop. (It was just that, a truckers' diner specializing in late-night, alcohol-absorbing biscuits and gravy.) As the carful of her friends—two boys in front, three of us girls in back—approached the stone gates of the college, Meredith nudged me. *Get an angel*, she mouthed. The car was raucous, the driver shouting over music an animated story from the night before while the other girl hugged the front headrest crying, "No! You didn't!" But as the stone portal flashed by at both windows, every person in unison touched fingertips to the roof, subtle and light, without comment, without pause in the conversation. A half second behind them, I touched too.

The years erase doubt, minor panics, and second guesses, so that what I recall from then on is overwhelming joy: to win a scholarship, to persuade my father to submit the financial documents, to then secure his consent with every promise I could think of. I'd wait tables every break, contribute all I could spare to my tuition bill, and what was left, I'd pay him back later. I was lucky to have only the dimmest sense of Rockhaven's prevailing affluence. I was lucky my thrift-store, cast-off wardrobe appeared just weird enough, beside the petticoated Laura Ashley dresses of my classmates, to be mistaken for intentional, a quirky flair for style. To the boys who became my friends, my bedroom décor read as "edgy": black-and-white posters of Jim Morrison and Patti Smith, a leopard-print comforter I'd pulled from a K-Mart clearance bin. This person, their cool, confident, not-quite-a-girl friend, provisionally in existence, assumed the form of the hazy someone I meant to become. Their approval nudged the girls with frilled bed pillows and Monet prints to find my *outré* choices interesting. When winter forced me to wear long underwear under my skirts, a few girls even swapped their tights for the same.

I surely didn't fool the loftier sets, but—lucky again—I had no aspirations to. While true that open parties welcomed everyone, the Greek clubs, I discovered, were fixed in their order, and if most of us aspired to the rung or two above our own, not many achieved any movement. During rush there might be some jostling, one level up or down, yet in the end it was as if we'd entered with tattoos on our foreheads, preordained. Your own set took you in, and that was who you were. The system appeared less magical to me once I realized, years later, that the upper tiers were determined in large part by the prep school one had attended.

There are parts of this story—Brantley's story, my story—that I intuited at the time and parts I could not know until later. When I arrived at Rockhaven, he was no one to me, a memory of the egomaniac at the interviews who wouldn't shut up. Vince and I had decided that if they chose *that* guy they would not choose us, and vice versa, so we were surprised to be thrown into his pool. In those first weeks, Brantley did not encroach on our immediate circle—Vince's circle, really, which gathered by magnetic force around a few rooms on his hall. Its lodestone was music: some excellent record collections (mainly Vince's), some skill with instruments (mainly Pem's), some talent at song composition (mainly Jonathan's), and any number of guitars. In fluctuating numbers up to ten, they congregated for jam sessions in their rooms, then turned troubadour and journeyed singly or in pairs from one girls' dorm to the next. They serenaded us full-throated on our beds or in murmurs in the stairwell after hours. In those pre-rush weeks, they exuded so much charisma that they briefly drew in a few satellite freshmen who ended up in the high-tier fraternities. One of these was Will Oliver, my first hard crush and the most hopeless. That he was probably the best-looking guy on campus says something about the vastness of my naïveté.

Rush spoiled the truer natural order, according to its design, but in those free weeks before, the troubadours of Vince's hall had bonded as tightly as any frat. Though as individuals they pretended to consider all options, it was clear they'd pledge together or not at all and had pinned their hopes on Gamma Chi. "The Nice Ones," the Gammas were called, in the comfortable middle of the social ladder. Common knowledge held that Will Oliver was the nicest of nice guys (I took the word of others on this, too afraid to go near him), and he was courted hard by the Gammas. He even seemed to lean in their direction for a while, this boy who was nicknamed "The David" in my dorm for his resemblance to Renaissance sculpture—a comparison I found off the mark, too beefy. Still, he would have looked strange in their midst. And he must have been every frat's top pick, so no real surprise he ended up Phi O.

The Princes, Phi Os were called—less for their wealth, of which they had much, than for their leadership roles on campus, their world-stage potential. They were so untouchably lofty they'd been known to flavor the bids with one or two worthies on financial aid.

In hindsight, I seem to remember what had no reason to register at the time: that Brantley was also rushing in the egalitarian way Will Oliver was, as if serious about these lesser tiers, but aiming for the top. He wanted Phi O or close. And he was so full of himself, so preppy—all madras and pink, seersucker and bow ties, the swoop of bangs he continually tossed from his eyes—that I assumed he'd land where he chose, among his kind. If not princehood, then maybe the nearby frats known as The Assholes or The Old South.

Stranger than his being sorted into Gamma Chi was that he betrayed no disappointment. He took to pledgeship with a zeal that outstripped that of my own friends, who held the fraternity in a secondary position to each other. But later I surmised he must have been chafing. A faction of Gamma Chi was determined to elevate their status, and Brantley fell in with this group. To solve the problem that could not be solved, there were only two approaches: raise the caliber of pledges, or raise the caliber of girls the frat associated with.

What did he say to you? my friends would ask, in those rare instances over the years when I let them know I'd had a nasty encounter with him once. I never told them, partly because the words could not convey the magnitude, partly because I believed for years those words might have the power to exile me from their company forever.

It happened a few weeks after rush concluded, a day or two after I crossed a line I should not have: I sat at a Gamma table in the dining hall. Normally I sat at a neutral table nearby, from which freshman girls not yet brave enough observed the dozen or so referred to as Wenches, all upperclassmen, who took seats at the Gamma tables by habit. I couldn't understand why they didn't seem to mind the term, nor to notice that, welcomed by most, they were resented as well. This I knew only because my friends had taken me into a degree of confidence, so that for all their pleasure in didactic refusal to answer my many fraternity-related questions, I had only to keep quiet and details were loosed in my presence.

That night I had come into Maxon with Vince and Jonathan and Pem, who said, "Eat with us! It's fine." During their first month of pledgeship, they privately considered themselves special, and I had taken note of how they shrugged off much of the fraternal dogma. Pem, for a notable instance, had shown up at my door in the past week with his guitar and, of all companions, a Phi O pledge: one Will Oliver. When I'd asked (trying for calm under this visitation that might as well have been an actual angel, seated diffidently at the foot of my roommate's bed) why they were running around together, not off bonding with their separate pledge classes, Pem answered with comic hyperbole: "We are free men! We do not let others dictate our movements or the company we keep!"

So their dinner invitation had the sound of another such scofflaw move. But I allowed them to persuade me.

Or perhaps I am misremembering, and it was Jonathan who expressed misgivings, while I accepted without a qualm. At the time I must have imagined a future place at their table, not as wench, no one's girlfriend, only a kind of sister-friend to these few. *Little Sister*—many years later I would come across this Greek-life term, common elsewhere, that existed nowhere at Rockhaven, where campus culture remained so mired in lingering bitterness over the admission of females that not a single fraternity allowed an official association. And while Gamma Chi was one of the few creeping toward progressive—the first, for instance, to offer bids to students of color—they had their old guard, same as the others.

Whatever the case, I took the seat they offered and enjoyed the dinner without any discomfort. And maybe it had no connection to what Brantley said to me. Maybe I will never know why he approached me in Maxon a few days later, at lunch. He and I had not interacted since the interview weekend, when he'd accosted everyone for their SAT scores at least twice. Vince had told me he'd calmed down a lot, was actually pretty fun to be around. My other friends, girls too, referred to him fondly, recounting funny things he'd said or done, and I'd been intrigued more than once by some overheard wit of his. I assumed he'd taken note of me too, if only for the company that so often included me. Maybe, like me, he thought we should start over with a better introduction.

"You have a big nose," he said.

I was drawing a glass of chocolate milk at the drink dispenser island we called The Cow when he walked up, waited for my attention, and spoke these baffling words. He appeared pleased to pass along the discovery. If we were rivals on any level, I had supposed it academic, so I was unprepared for blunt physical insult.

And was I pretty? I didn't know, but had gleaned from half a semester of college that boys didn't know either, and not just about me. They were in the process of figuring out what they were supposed to find attractive. Their attentions to me, warm and cool and warm again, suggested I drifted in some interesting middle range between gorgeous and repulsive. The deciding factor was the approval of other boys, and it could be swift and final. Only a week before, I'd watched two of these boys circle about a cute, perky dorm friend of mine named Suzanne Clyde, a frequent object of appreciation in the Gamma Chi fraternity until one of the upperclassmen had idly remarked, "She's got kind of a big butt." Overnight, she became discreetly referred to as Buttsy, and the boys who spoke to her after did so only as charity.

Who knew what feature might turn them next? It hardly mattered that I did not aspire to be pursued, since friendship for them seemed to require a girl they could play at flirting with long-term, who could look the part. Not some troll with a humongous nose. The other boys had not yet brought it into focus, but Brantley, as their brother, need only mention it and it would appear.

Since he stood waiting for my response, I said, "Thanks," as coolly as I could, and turned away. Shaking, I took my tray to a seat with some girls from my dorm. I wanted badly to tell them, but I could think of no way to relate the story that would make them turn on him with the unified wall of rage that suited his crime. Which was what? Calling me ugly?

It wasn't that news. What persisted was his calculated approach to deliver it, without even pretending to get a drink. As if he meant to tell me he could snuff out my life, what had come so tentatively, provisionally, to seem my life, at his next whim.

In memory these events fall in order, in relation to each other if not cause and effect: I hated Brantley Simms, and then he died. The truth is, he was someone I barely knew. He died in Advent—as Rockhaven called the fall semester—of our sophomore year, a full year after our encounter in Maxon, several months after the night I tried to save him a trip to the emergency room.

By then I felt enough like a part of the "we" within the gates of our mountain to be shaken hard by what was not supposed to happen to us. Those of us who knew him at some distance felt our various ties to him thicken, resonate like plucked strings. We shared the pang that was like pleasure even in the revelation that our angels weren't so reliable after all. *Et in arcadia ego.*

His body was found early on a Monday in October, at an hour when few of us were stirring. Coincidentally, I was one of those people, and I have often wondered how near I came to being the one to discover him. Mondays I hosted a pre-dawn radio show, though I had no talent as a DJ nor musical knowledge, only a passion born in Vince's room for what was then being called "alternative" music. Since no one with more seniority wanted the slot, I was granted the hour from six to seven to page at leisure through the shelves, slip vinyl from sleeve and drop the needle down on anything I was curious to hear (Jesus and Mary Chain, The Smiths, Robyn Hitchcock, XTC, R.E.M., The Beautiful South, The Church, The Connells) while at the same time offering to those few awake and listening. All it required was the will to drag myself out of bed on five hours of sleep if I was lucky, after lingering past visiting hours in the room of one of my friends.

On a usual Monday, after rising to dress in the dark and splash my face in the hall bath, I would have cut for the station straight over the chapel lawn, steps from where his body lay. But on that morning the fog was dense before sunrise, the hazy nimbus of each street light visible only from one post to the next, and I went by the road to keep from getting lost. He had died around two a.m., they said, so as I passed the bell tower he would have been nearing his fourth hour at its base, attended by no one, dampened with fog.

By the time my show concluded, the sun had lifted into the treetops and thinned the fog. Leaving the radio station, I took the straightest path to my dorm, along the back of Hampsell and the chapel. In an hour the south lawn would be cordoned with the first police tape ever seen on the mountain, but as I rounded the chapel, nothing stood between me and the scene of his death but an ambulance parked on the gravel path, lights flashing, silent. In the mist and shadow where no sun yet reached, several official-looking men stood about, including an idle paramedic. I paused, then kept walking. A priest with chest pains, I thought—some false alarm or ailment too minor for sirens. I could not have imagined violent death, let alone a student's.

Over the course of the day the rumors accumulated by bits, corrected themselves, became the story. He was found outside the chapel, face down on the gravel walkway. He was wearing his gown. It was noon before we could be sure which one of us was gone, evening before voices began to revise the initial report that he'd been beaten to death. What was known was that he'd been up in the bell tower, officially Polk Tower, which was kept locked though keys tended to float about. He had been drinking. He had fallen.

The entire field biology class, out seeking songbirds at first light, had passed along the lower lawn but missed him in the fog, leaving him to be discovered by the carillonneur's student assistant, who arrived at the chapel at a quarter to seven. He was one of the few who possessed a sanctioned key to Polk Tower, where great bells chimed the hour and several times a week the fifty-six-bell carillon was played: high church hymns, haunting melodies of Mozart, Vivaldi, Handel, Bach. So much of the grace and texture of life on the mountain was supplied by those bells, especially on lonely winter afternoons when the fog settled over the lawns and all but obscured the stone buildings. Once in a while, the invisible player at the clavier keys got fanciful and tossed us some Beatles. It should have been amusing, but "Blackbird" on the bells could break your heart.

I never knew that student, the assistant to the carillonneur, but I imagine he was one of those deep-blooded Episcopalians who spent most of his four years in the chapel. Lessons and Carols, weekly services, daily choir practice. Maybe he went on to seminary, our own graduate school, the reason we were called a university and not a college, though most of us would have shrugged if asked exactly where on the domain it was located; seminarians were rumors we never encountered. His pronoun can be assumed. The privileges to be had at Rockhaven still went to the male students. Yet many of us found our way up into Polk Tower sooner or later, and eventually I, too, knew a boy with a key who took me up late one night, at the very hour of Brantley's death.

Positioned at the chapel's south transept, the tower was entered by an inner door. A staircase led to a second door and the belfry. Here the breeze passed through tall, gothic-arched portals, steeply pointed at their apexes and guarded by steel caging. Overhead, cloaked in shadow, especially at night, hung the prodigious rim of the largest bell. Three more stories up, past rows of smaller and smaller bells, perched the clavier cabin, above which the high-note bells climbed on into the rafters. From the cabin level, a gate led out to a walled, four-sided balcony where pigeons nested on the concrete floor and from which, on a clear, moonlit night, one could see the old bell tower, the peaked dining hall, the other campus rooftops not obscured by trees.

From the balcony wall, Brantley had stumbled, into the sky, down to the earth. Or he'd been pushed. Or he jumped. Polk Tower was the tallest structure on campus. A student who had elected this form of suicide and wanted his body soon found would seek exactly this spot. And what else, we wondered, explained the gown?

Brantley had been gowned only a few days before. As had I. The handful of us with the grades to be inducted into the Order of Gownsmen as sophomores tended to be Harper scholars. Each semester thereafter the requirements loosened, until the last slackers were inducted for passing their comprehensive exams and wore the gown for what days remained. Thus only a member of the Order of Gownsmen could graduate, and we earned the gowns in which we processed to the ceremony. The gownings took place on Founders' Day, a gathering in the chapel more weighty than graduation itself. As gowns were not supposed to leave the mountain, seniors by tradition passed theirs down to an underclassman and often returned to perform the gowning, after stitching their own initials and year of graduation into the gown's scapular. Most legacy gowns remained black as new, even those bearing several sets of initials, so there was great prestige in a gown that had gone rusty and ragged with age. The rare gowns fading to brown, if not belonging to the oldest professors, might have initials on the scapular from the nineteenth century.

Brantley's gown sported several sets of initials, possibly the only legacy among the sophomore inductees. The rest of us, like Vince and me, were forced to purchase our gowns new at the bookstore. Strange as it may sound, I didn't know of anyone not yet gowned who wasn't jealous to some degree, who didn't dream of one day wearing the gown in the casual way Gownsmen did by tradition: open, never zipped, thrown on not always but often as an extra layer on a chilly day, a striking black accessory. Brantley had worn his on that final occasion in the customary way, draped open over a coat and tie. But gowns were for class. No one had reason to wear one so late at night.

The romantics among us (hard to attend Rockhaven and not be one) pictured those dark useless wings to attend his plummet, and the choice in the act seemed implicit. But according to his roommate and fraternity brothers, he had given no indication of being suicidal. They argued that in those days after the gowning ceremony—you had to know Brantley—he was merely overly fond of the gown and its status, likely to wear it everywhere.

No evidence of foul play was found, and among ourselves the possibility was dismissed, since we could not conceive of any Rockhaven student committing such an act. Brantley had his dramas and disagreements, like anyone, but no serious enemy. That left accident. The only real clue was his blood alcohol content, .18, what the real world would call "good and drunk" but for us at Rockhaven was just Sunday night. No buzz of that magnitude, on its own, was going to knock one of us over a ledge. But make room for some extra bravado and miscalculation? Accidents happened. Even here, we supposed.

One more odd detail: no one had been able to find the key Brantley had used to enter the tower. Perhaps it had fallen into some ancient crevice or been picked up by a souvenir-seeking student, even a nocturnal animal. Perhaps the carillonneur's assistant had been careless and left the door unlocked. Some surmised Brantley had not entered at all but free-climbed from the outside, a feat rumored to have been accomplished more than once in years past by a known route, and such a madcap act would fit his temperament and allow for the gown. But the most likely scenario seemed to all of us that he'd entered with a key, which had departed in the pocket of someone he had been with.

For all his abrasiveness I came to regret, well before his death, that I had missed a chance to know Brantley, that I had begun missing it when I turned my disdain on the loud boy at the other side of the vice chancellor's living room. I'd tried to rectify it, but not hard enough. He had never rated the time when I had other friends, the ones he'd not stolen from me after all. So when everyone I cared about was mourning him, I was left out.

Recently, going through old boxes, I came upon a photo of him I could not at first recall, neither the image itself nor how I had come to possess it. I had not been present when it was taken. Many of my photos are similarly inexplicable, given to me in the days when those with cameras would order double or triple prints of every roll. In this shot, he is the focal point, reclining but in flight, airborne over the Gamma lake. Though the image doesn't show it, I know he is not jumping but being flung from the dock, "laked," like all new pledges. He is happy. It would have made a fitting shot for the sophomore yearbook, where a full-page photo spread was dedicated to his memory, and I took down the book to tuck it into place.

It had been years since I'd looked at this calculated collage of Brantleys, and I was surprised how many of them radiated a boyish silliness, an innocence I could not have perceived when he was my own age. The snide arrogance was there as well, accurately burned into memory, but also this: to go with his full, wide mouth, he had a strikingly large nose. Had I not seen it? That day in Maxon, perhaps he'd only been saying hello, flirting in a stupid way, the poorly calculated equivalent of noticing what book I was reading.

It's easy to feel gentle toward him now, that boy in the dining hall with no more than a year remaining to his life. Harder to be responsible, true—*honorable*, perhaps, in the way of our honor code—to the storm of emotion he once induced in me. Given the chance, would I have sent him off the bell tower for his crime? I couldn't have pushed him. But I remember being the one who might have wished the fall.

2

He Clasps the Crag

Will Oliver, my first crush, was well removed from my life by junior year. After the one misfit night in our first fall when he'd knocked at my door with Pem, both of them breathless and bashful and lugging guitars, when he perched on my roommate's bed and sang "Pale Blue Eyes" to an audience of me and my pal Jenny Dixon from downstairs, he returned to the Phi O house where he belonged. Thereafter I saw him mainly in daydreams, or across a party, or in our freshman English class where from three rows back I counted the dirty blond curls at the back of his head and did not approach him to speak.

"Good poster," he'd said, in my room, eyes ticking toward the wall above my head: Jim Morrison, waist-up bare but for a beaded necklace, ready either to be crucified or embrace the lot of us. I kissed my hand and patted Jim's sternum, which made Will grin.

The song, I assumed, was Pem's choice, and they'd stopped first to collect Jenny, whose yellow ringlets framed giant doll-blue eyes. Mine were blue only on forms, lake water under clouds. No one looked that close. Certainly Will Oliver had never looked from any distance and from the foot of my roommate's bed could not have guessed a color, though every upward glance while straining for a chord was directly into them. What color were his? They were all lashes, a lushness in his beauty, his shyness on account of the guitar he was only learning. But none of the troubadours had his voice. Brash Pem had the sense to add nothing but a muted harmony and the guitar.

Linger on, my wish for that song in my room so suited to his voice, and later I could guess Will had chosen it. Later it seemed inevitable that Will Oliver should be joined to the prettiest girl in our class, as she'd been decreed, though none of the boys could explain to me what made tiny, intense Anna Vaughn Whitacre superior to anyone else. She just was. It had been decided. Will, I supposed, had noticed her eyes.

They found each other at the Phi O house, which conferred their imprimatur. Yet they sat two rows apart in our freshman English, where

Dr. Parrish taught us poetry scansion on the double dactyl of her name. *Higgledy piggledy, riddle some poetry, Anna Vaughn Whitacre.* A student body deep in southern lineages meant I knew girls called Goode, Wells, Knight, Manning, and more besides Anna Vaughn whose kinder parents had appended a girl name to the surname—Mary Clark, Ann Wright—to be pronounced, always, as one. No one said Anna, ever. For those chummy enough to employ the single dactyl, she was *Anavon*, to chime with *analog, anapest.*

Against the odds, Will retained friendships among the Gammas, and he and Anna Vaughn, the campus star couple, circulated with unusual ease through the various social classes. Their appearance at a Gamma party was like a visit of royalty. Freshman year, when I attended the spring formal as Pem's date, Will was one of the few non-brothers invited as a guest, Anna Vaughn all aglitter in strapless silver on his arm. My crush by this time was cooled, but still, when Pem and I went to chat with them, I felt weird about mentioning Will's visit to my bedroom. Instead I reminded them of our shared class by offering an impression of our professor, one fierce hand aloft as if balancing a globe to declaim poetry. This vision of Dr. Parrish had been my first experience of a Rockhaven classroom—theirs too, since it met first period on Monday. Square-jawed and auburn-haired, draped in the rusty rags of his gown, Dr. Parrish had not crossed the doorway into the room before he paused, raised the claw hand, and began to recite: *He clasps the crag with crooked hands! Bang,* the door slammed shut behind him and he strode the aisles between our desks without a break in the booming recitation for hello.

Close to the sun in lonely lands.
Ring'd with the azure world, he stands.
The wrinkled sea beneath him crawls;
He watches from his mountain walls,
And like a thunderbolt he falls.

In my version, performed often at parties, I gave only the first line, the words *clasps* and *crag* drawn out to three or four syllables.

Anna Vaughn loved it. "Isn't he amazing? Oh, and that gown! It's from when he was a student, you know."

Will said, "Yeah, her father was his roommate."

"*Will,*" she whined in pain, the two of them nose to nose in grinning adoration. After several seconds of this she turned back to me, a confiding hand on my arm. "That is *not* why I think he's amazing."

Even from a distance, I knew she was more than pretty—she was authentically nice, possibly funny, even a little odd the way he was. At the time, love seemed to me this simple, a coordination of personal qualities, reinforced by community approval. I didn't yet guess how hard it must be for love to lock in without some element of the forbidden in the match, if only a slight one, a disparity in social status, an undercutting of the expectations of friends or family. When that person seems not meant to be, somehow inappropriate, the heart clings closer. But Will and Anna Vaughn were perfect for each other. This was obvious, even to me.

Couples were strangely rare at Rockhaven. It was the smallness of our world, perhaps, the pressure of being so closely observed from all sides. In my own orbit I could name half a dozen pairs who had chosen each other seemingly on day one and would be married four years later, never a wobble visible. Most of us yearned and stayed single. Our cultural talent was concealment and misdirection, a shell game in which desires were made undetectable or projected elsewhere than their actual mark. Even our most intimate friends were best not told. We'd seen the ones who made a try at love sooner or later wounded in public, their flaws and failings picked apart all over campus by people known only by name. And worse for girls, since in most instances a girl once claimed in a serious way was taken forever: no other Rockhaven gentleman would touch her.

But Will and Anna Vaughn, matched with each other, how could either be unhappy? The rumors of discord began in sophomore year, though we hardly saw them anymore, together or separate, and forgot to wonder. Then on our return for junior year, over Welcome Back keg beer on the Gamma balcony, I heard someone ask was it true, Will Oliver and Anna Vaughn Whitaker had broken up over the summer? Was it possible? What went wrong?

That fall I had moved into Benson, where Anna Vaughn lived at the other end of the hall, so I began to see her regularly, always in a skirt no matter the hour, always fresh and lovely even on her way in from field hockey practice. (She was surely the smallest girl on the team, not much bigger than her stick.) In the bathroom on my end, which she never used, I once or twice caught a whispered question at the sinks. They broke up? That's what I heard. Wow, so sad. "Who did the breaking?" I asked, and got a shrug for an answer. No one in Benson would speak a word further, even to pronounce the breakup as definite, since any detail might come across as malicious, and no one was willing to be hurtful to Anna Vaughn.

I must have noticed Will's curly head in my Shakespeare I and Modern American Poetry, but we had separate zones in any room, his crew seated near the door while mine (Jenny, Pem, Dex, Emery, and me, with various associates) homed for the far back corner. Will and I might not have exchanged more than a few words for the rest of our time in college had he not turned up in my Trail Riding class. On the first Friday, when I arrived at the gym to catch the shuttle van to the stables, there stood Will in breeches and boots. The rare sight of a boy forced into skin-tight breeches always made me smile—we sometimes had a boy or two on the equestrian team, and more who would show up for Trail—but one as well-formed as Will Oliver delivered a jolt, even before I'd quite registered who he was.

"Leah! You're in this class?"

Surprised to be so warmly recognized, I cried, "Darling, I teach this class!"

"You do not."

So there I'd gone and called Will Oliver *darling,* and he hadn't flinched. Which meant I was stuck here, hands on hips, three notches sassier than my usual. "'Teach' is a little strong. I'm the leader. You have to do what I tell you to."

"Well, yes, ma'am. I look forward to that."

While we waited, I explained how I'd come by the position called, in fact, "Instructor." I had started out as the Saturday feeder and stall-mucker, a work-study job that came with riding tuition—the only way I could ride—but the job required me to walk out to the stables and back and killed the whole day. With regret I'd requested a transfer to the Commons front desk where I could study on the clock. Then the riding director offered to cover my fees with this additional job that could hardly be called work: leading a two-hour trail ride for PE credit over some of the most gorgeous unspoiled forest in the nation. Students had to know in advance how to catch, groom, saddle, mount, and control a horse, so I just led the way and kept the line in order. "As your instructor," I told Will, "I promise to teach you the least you will ever learn while receiving credit at this institution." A few others arrived then, and I added, "Don't tell these guys."

With another boy and four girls, we loaded into the shuttle van and bumped out the stable road. Will ignored the others and went on with our conversation, mentioning the two classes we shared. "Guess you're an English major too?"

"That wasn't the plan." Matchless, I decided, the school's tallest and handsomest hunter, would be Will's mount. I'd grab Jojo for myself, an appaloosa jumper too high-strung for beginners. "I was aiming for biology but I think our freshman English class with Dr. Parrish did me in. I just fell in love."

"I know that feeling. How do people at Rockhaven major in anything but?"

I asked why he was taking the shuttle instead of his own car, a green Saab I was used to seeing around campus. As we were then arriving at the stables, he grimaced and said, "Long story."

We unloaded, and I sorted everyone for horses and helmets, then delivered my first-day lecture on trail safety (how not to get kicked in the kneecap or fall off a cliff) before we mounted up. However laughable my freshman crush now seemed, I was aware that if I had any chance to make an impression to rival Anna Vaughn's, it would be at the head of this class. My splashy horse helped: Jojo looked like a handful and a half, bit-chomping, neck bowed, head-shaking and snorting, but was secretly simple. For the slightest rein he collected; for a touch of leg he bent his prance sideways and proceeded down the trail in an impression of a dressage half-pass, while I turned back to address my students.

With Will riding second behind me, maintaining proper distance, it wasn't easy to converse, but on the walking stretches we managed a few exchanges. He asked how I had learned to ride, and I said, "Very randomly, speaking of long story. We'll have to trade long stories sometime. What about you?"

"I rode some as a kid." A glance back showed him sitting his blaze-faced chestnut in good form, his reins shifted to one hand in mirror-image of mine—trail English as long as we were walking. "At our club."

"At your what?"

He thought I couldn't hear him. "Our club. Country club."

"With a stable. Okay, wow." Around the barns back home, I'd known some moneyed types, show-hunter people. But I'd never come across anyone whose country club was so posh it had horses. I hadn't guessed such a place existed. And now it occurred to me: Anna Vaughn Whitacre probably had horses at her country club.

The trail's variation allowed only brief questions, one-liners. At a trot, his voice turned breathy, like his laugh at my jokes. Once or twice we were having so much fun I forgot he was Will Oliver. He seemed in fine spirits, not heartbroken, and I tried to come up with an innocent question or remark about Anna Vaughn, who after all lived on my hall. But to bring her up at all seemed risky.

Remember this for Jenny, I kept thinking. She was my closest girlfriend, but our friendship had grown thorns due to her tendency to fall in love with one or another of our mutual guy friends, then fail to hide it well, a big reason they came to me and not her with the bulk of their philosophical musings and existential crises. She was cuter and inclined to flatter them, but I was more trustworthy, endlessly patient and, in my demeanor of impervious celibacy, far safer. They learned they could throw all their flirting and earnestness at me, fill the summer mailbox of my aunt's townhouse in Knoxville with witty oddball postcards and long, platonically intimate letters that flung around the word *love*, as if we were denizens of the nineteenth century. If I was not always immune to falling, they could not have guessed for whom. Jenny had taken to calling them "Leah's boys" in sneering tones—meaning the English majors in our crew plus a few others she cared less about, like Vince and Jonathan. So I looked for stories that didn't involve them to appease her, like one of trail riding with my long-ago, ludicrous crush who had never been to Jenny's taste—*too pretty*, she called Will. This was perhaps only her way of saying he wasn't available to us.

I wouldn't see Jenny until dinner, since she and I had learned early the wisdom of separating our lives in the only way we could, by living in different dorms. I showered after Trail and then followed the sound of The Cure to Mitzi and Carolyn's room two doors down. As a rule I tried to keep some distance from girls who did not mind being called Gamma Wenches but made an exception for these two fellow juniors who were my sorority sisters first and also took my side against a faction of the sisterhood that had decided to make me a pariah for a very dumb reason involving my date to the Gamma formal the previous spring— just a friend to me, but the recent ex of a sister.

"Why are there tampons stuck to your wall?" I asked Carolyn.

"Because Mitzi said our décor wasn't feminine enough!" They both fell on their beds laughing.

"You have to take them down," Mitzi said. "I have suitors coming!"

"Suitors?" We descended the stairs and began the stroll toward dinner, all of us in shorts and sandals, warm light flickering in the leaves. I knew Mitzi had one suitor, a blandly good-looking sophomore named Steve who had written her summer letters and since our return had been knocking at her door with candles and wine, kicking poor Carolyn out to the commons room. But they had news for me: now a second Gamma had come knocking, with flowers. And poetry.

"Don't tell her who!" Mitzi said. "She can guess."

From other corners of campus, voices animate with other drama reached us now and then through the treetop whine of cicadas. "No idea," I said. I hardly knew most of the Gammas, any one of whom I could imagine being drawn to Mitzi's coltish, awkward beauty, all lips and legs. I especially didn't know the sophomores, so recently wide-eyed pledges and thus, I supposed, the more likely to decide a particular wench one class up was "girlfriend material."

But she meant it was one of mine. That narrowed it to half a dozenish options, all juniors, most of them far too dorky and virginal or at least respectful of their brothers' territory. "Oh, lord. Quinn Cooper."

I wasn't sure I counted Quinn as one of mine, but if so he was the newest, the least known, a person I'd avoided until the day he declared us friends. It was obvious, in fact, that he'd pursued my friendship for nearly the same reason he'd come knocking at Mitzi's door: because he'd watched a brother aim that way first. Vince and Jonathan—the most moral and earnest of my friends, roommates now for the third year and functionally one person—were on chilly terms with Quinn, less for the fraternal strife he caused than his habit of seducing virgins he pronounced sluts the next day, loudly and in detail. Since I wouldn't be seduced by an inch, he was nice to me. Relatively. And I enjoyed scolding him. But I didn't trust him very far.

"He's kind of hot," Mitzi whispered. Quinn, fascinating to many with his Porsche and his mean streak, missed the mark on good-looking in any definite way. High forehead, pock-marked skin, some quality to the bone structure of his face that made you see the skull. Girls spent time trying to figure it out. "And they're saying all the time how he needs a girlfriend, so..."

Quinn needed civilizing, went the consensus. "Scorpion," I said. This was only a reminder, since I was known to hand out recitations of "The Scorpion and the Frog" to any girl in Quinn's vicinity.

"Told you," Carolyn said. "Leah is a wise counselor. And Steve is cute!"

"But…" Mitzi said. "Scorpions are hot." Didn't we all think it would be different with us?

"And who are you lusting for?" Carolyn wanted to know. Our steps slowed as we neared the dining hall, where students gathered on the fieldstone steps or sprawled in the grass, delaying dinner in the fine weather. "Surely at least one of those boys of yours, all writing you this summer."

Mitzi said, "Yes, pick one, let's all get boyfriends! Look, there's one."

In the buttery haze of falling sunlight, Jonathan Pitts, who wrote the longest letters by far, stood talking to people I couldn't quite see. Over the summer, his hair had grown out into a dark wing that dropped down the side of one eye. The Calvin Klein Model, he'd been dubbed by my freshman dormmates appraising the Meetbook photos, which made me laugh to recall, since in person he was so prickly and off-key that his attractiveness was either knocked down to average or just erased. Mitzi was joking; she thought he was so awful. Knowing him as I had from day one through Vince hadn't helped: on top of a stiffness that led me to assume he disliked me and a general fidgety oddness that earned him the early frat nickname Twitch (a name he refused to be called), he was also deeply into Jesus. He was so conservative he believed married women shouldn't have jobs, among other intolerable beliefs. It had taken me weeks to get past wary and repulsed, months to decide we were actually friends, and well over a year to begin to understand I loved him more than I loved even Vince, and that he loved me, in an erratic, ardent, soul-killing, impossible way—a feature of which was his mood on this evening, which I'd been clocking for the past thirty-four hours, the icy one in which he and I were not acquainted.

"I don't do lust," I reminded them. "Or boyfriends." What I had was enough, so much already. Sometimes I didn't want to breathe and risk losing it.

The beginning of Advent semester, just ahead of fraternity rush, was packed with open parties, the boys all over campus preening their tail feathers for the notice of other boys. The business of parties was to lure the girls first, the freshmen boys after once the party was crammed and roaring. To make an appearance at each was felt by most of us as a social duty: push through to the keg, fill a cup, begin a slow wandering in hope of spotting someone with whom to stall in conversation for a while. When the Gammas weren't hosting I could expect to see many of them out making the same circuit, but they tended to be homebodies. Thus, after a few stops, the dilemma was how to get to where my friends would be in a non-wench-like way.

Jenny had the same problem, a large part of what kept our friendship intact. Fortified on dining-hall coffee and layered shots we concocted from the random booze in her room, we hit two houses and then ditched our beers when we ran into Pooh Barrow, a Gamma sophomore with a car. The sophomores were useful this way, conditioned as pledges in reflexive accommodation of older girls with any house attachment. As we arrived at the house, I was fighting a case of hiccups and a speck of crud in my contact lens. And no fun stumbling through the doors near midnight when the party had gone elsewhere, leaving a few sulky brothers on the sofas discussing Kierkegaard and displeased with invasion. But tonight, Yaz blared from the stereo and most of the frat waited with pitchers of punch to cheer the arrival of more girls.

All night I'd had to pretend I wasn't seeking Jonathan in every face. So the instant he abrupted into view—with Vince, by the pool table, in the midst of some cringingly inappropriate comedy routine performed for a bubble-cluster of girls—I spun for the sofas, where Pem and Dex presided over the gathering of English majors. With Jenny and me added in, the crew was complete but for Emery, my ex—our trial month the closest I'd been to having a boyfriend—who often reached his limit of our particular energy and took himself apart. He never went home though. It was unclear if he ever slept. If he wasn't revolving on the dance floor, I'd find him by the smoke of a lonely cigarette wafting in from the balcony. Where he was tonight. I stopped by the sofas for a minute, then went out.

The balcony overlooked a small, sacred lake into which the Gammas threw things: pledges, dead furniture, an old wood stove, other items of significance submerged at various spots they could all name. They had constructed a floating dock outfitted with sofas that was generally moored but might at any time be spotted adrift in the water with some private party aboard. Tonight the dock was missing from its berth, invisible in the watery dark. "Who's out there?" I asked Emery, through hiccups.

"Quinn." He passed his cigarette my way. If the smoke didn't get rid of my hiccups, I'd try kissing my ex for a cure. He was a good kisser and very accommodating for someone who wasn't really into girls. This was a fact about Emery that everyone knew and no one did—not even me, since it could not be discussed.

"And who else?"

The interior light glinted in his cross earring and the bleached spikes of his hair. He didn't go as far as eyeliner but could have—it was the '80s, even on our ultra-conservative mountain. "I don't know. Chip, maybe. Some girls."

"Mitzi, I assume?"

He turned with wry query. "Do you have a story for me?" He loved stories about Quinn. I filled him in on Mitzi's suitor problem, the dueling candles and poetry, which got him grinning. "Well, of course she thinks he's hot. It's all that heat he's giving off for Steve! He needs to just fuck Steve and get it over with."

None of the Gammas were treated to these crass tidbits from Emery, who saved them for me. "Be *careful*," I warned him, hiccupping a laugh and checking to make sure no one was close. If Quinn in particular overheard talk of that sort, we were in for a fair chance of violence.

He blew smoke through his nose. "Well, better theories? He's your pet."

"I don't own that." I strained to see or hear where the dock had drifted, but it might as well have passed through a portal to another dimension. "Do you remember this is exactly what he did last year, chasing after Wendy Sharp all because Jonathan decided she was cute for a second? And who was it before that? Quinn and somebody, both lusting after that freckled girl who went Kappa Psi... Was it Dustin?"

He looked at me for a time in silence. "That was Brantley."

"Oh. God."

That name, so rarely spoken, always caused a chill, a needle skip on the groove of time, especially at the Gamma house where it was shrouded in a reverent hush and brought forth only on the high holy days. In the festive hours when I was in attendance, we all spoke around him, as if the fraternity were intact, no reason not to feel lively. And it always happened this way, one of us spooling out some anecdote and oblivious until far gone that Brantley would be there in it, require his name to be said, and then all breath stopped at once as we waited for him to move past us again.

Killed my hiccups, at least. Back inside, I refilled my punch and wandered into Jonathan's zone, noncommittal, on my way elsewhere. When he was in this mood, elsewhere was the place to be. Ignore him back, I told myself, and he'll turn sweet again—as if it were somehow under my control.

He and Vince had broken into separate conversations one pool pocket apart—generally their maximum distance—competitively entertaining girls. *This* year, they had sworn to have girlfriends, and as long as they were dreaming up what would never happen, Vince's would be an undiscovered Playboy Bunny with a hankering for scrawny nerds, while Jonathan would settle for a svelte Bambi-eyed Christ-loving virgin homemaker with enough of a dirty side to be enchanted by his vulgar stand-up routine. The longer they were deprived, the more attributes their girls acquired. It was their only real shallowness, exacerbated by their constant feeding off each other. I did not see either of these girls in the room and had wasted much breath in gently coaching them on how to improve their chances, girlfriend-wise. Vince stood by their standards—what you find attractive, he contended, is not a choice—though he teamed up with me in efforts to convince Jonathan that female people tended to be repelled by grossness or misogyny, however hilarious, and that most people, but especially the female ones, drew the line when he veered racist or mocked the disabled.

Jonathan was our comedian, funny because he was appalling. I forgave him on the grounds that he had no meanness in him, and also he was passing on two relevant counts. He didn't lie—polite Southerners didn't ask—or go in fear of exposure, exactly. A handful of us knew he was adopted. Vince and I had cobbled together a little more: the "sickly baby," as he called himself, of unknown origin, adopted in Oklahoma and raised as white, same as he'd been raised Christian and conservative and neurotypical, so that was what he considered himself to be. Saved in all the ways. People admired his tan, his gift for physical comedy marked by stutters, strange postures, and rapid blinking. He'd become so deft at covering that, in my opinion as an aspiring Jonathan expert, he was no longer aware he was doing it. He was my second minor, my independent study, so I could measure his awareness to the decimal, or spot from across a room what cringeworthy territory his performance had drifted into.

But he'd flipped, gone deep into serious mode. "You wonder," he was saying, to the devoted upturned faces of three sophomores, "when you're living it, what's going to matter in ten years. But any one of us could die tomorrow, and then who *were* we? What will other people take with them of us?"

Jonathan, the most obtuse person I had ever met, was also the deepest of thinkers. He'd written me pages of this topic over the summer, when his father had been ill, so I could have mouthed the words along with him, guessed the next line. "So I'm feeling the need to be more deliberate..." The sophomores hadn't heard it before or didn't care, he was so mesmerizing to look at while delivering a speech.

I weighed moving on to Vince. But a girl stood smiling while he spoke, conditions under which I tried to keep clear. In the doorway beyond, Quinn had arrived to survey the room—no more Mitzi to chase by his irascible expression. He'd be seeking somewhere else to make trouble.

But I'd paused too long, and Jonathan turned my way. "Leah's tired of hearing me go on about this."

Who's Leah? I wondered. "No, I'm not," I managed to stammer.

He extended an arm, until I stepped up and into his body. A sidelong hug, more than I could have hoped for, but next he tumbled off the beam and kissed me on the head, in front of other girls. "I'm lucky to have you," he said, to me only. "Some people you know you'll keep in your life."

This was Jonathan, boy of the paired extremes: the hottest and the coldest, the most irreverent and the most sincere. I never knew which way his switch would be flipped. He'd freeze me out in the morning and in the afternoon declare his love in the same full-hearted way he'd offer it up for nothing to Vince or Pem or any number of random brothers, irony-free. In sweeter moods, he shocked us all speechless. We tried to give it back and never came close.

As soon as his hand dropped from my shoulder, while I was still failing at a worthy response, Quinn's voice in my ear said, "I need you." He took me by the arm and extracted me.

In dense gatherings of male people, especially of the sort who called themselves brothers, it happened with cyclical-seeming frequency that through no act of my own I lit up as a target. Such events were a queasy rush, not unpleasurable, and though I never learned to expect them I'd begun to notice that Quinn Cooper, for instance, who ignored me with ease when I was alone and lonely, needed me with great fervor when I was occupied. Dragging me off by physical force—out onto the balcony, down the stairs, all the way to the dock—wasn't his usual style. But Jonathan had always been one of his triggers.

The dock dipped, shifting wayward in the water as he deposited me at one end of the sofa and climbed up with his head in my lap, face to the stars. "Headache," he said. "It's killing me." I finger-combed his bristly hair, fascinated by his primate efforts to mimic a phenomenon he'd observed between me and his brothers: friendship with a girl. He took my hands and pressed them to the hollows of each temple, where a ropy coil of blood vessel pulsed. "Push hard."

I resettled my thumbs at his temples and applied a circular pressure. He released a long breath, eyes closed. Dangerous, I knew, the zing of ego that came with Quinn's whole head offered into my keeping, the same one I got from riding a horse like Jojo: that he was too much for most people, that I was the special one who could handle him. We all thought we were that one, until we weren't.

"So," I said, "what have you done with Mitzi?"

"Bottom of the lake."

"Scorpion!"

He laughed. "I sort of love how you think I'm evil. Makes me want to outdo myself." He searched my face with a melting concern. "You really think I'm so terrible?"

"That and then some."

"She hates me! One day you gonna hurt my feelings." This he spoke with a little of his Alabama twang.

"Please. First of all, you don't have feelings. Second, I think you're aware we've got the opposite problem here."

In fact, I doubted he was aware or even curious. But in certain minutes, in fiery fleeting bursts when I didn't want to strangle him or put him in a cage, it was true: I adored him.

He only scoffed. "Aw, listen to her. Such a fucking tease."

For reasons I thought not altogether Machiavellian, Quinn had deemed me smarter than the average female, worthy to receive his private musings. Tonight he wanted to rail about Mitzi, about Steve, about his authentic feelings for Mitzi, and Steve's stupidity and failures of taste and observation, and about the very specific qualities that few people noticed in Steve and that might redeem him if he would stop being such a fucking cunt all the time. Up on the balcony, a cluster had gathered, Jonathan's form visible in it and looking our way, though no one up there could see anything but whether the dock was in place.

The Gammas, more than most, had internalized the ideal of "the Rockhaven gentleman," a concept touted from orientation onward and taken as seriously as the honor code. In their pursuit of gentlemanly conduct in all matters, the Gammas enjoyed some drama, all the more if it came with a project. After some conferring, they determined that an emissary was in order. Anyone but Jonathan. So Vince was drafted to wander down and ascertain whether I needed to be rescued.

From shore, holding a cup, he called in a tone of blind innocence, "Leah? Who's out there?"

"Me and Quinn. Just hanging out."

Quinn said nothing, daring Vince to come closer, and Vince, who was only giving me the chance to invite him aboard if I needed a buffer, went on his way. Quinn resumed mid-sentence. I reminded him that Mitzi was my friend, meaning I wouldn't put up with him hurting her or using her for sport, but as he talked it became harder to accuse him, to present him with his past crimes. Wasn't it possible he was sincere? He almost argued me into rooting for him: of course he deserved happiness more than Steve, who wasn't *that* good-looking or interesting; of course if dreams were at stake, maybe even love, I'd want Quinn to have his before Steve.

I was yawning after half an hour, when he began to repeat himself. Had he railed this way about Brantley Simms, I wondered, back before I'd really known either one of them?

Not that I'd ever known Brantley.

Not that I really knew Quinn.

Twice when I glanced up into the bleary light of the balcony, Emery's silhouette stood there smoking. I would have waved but I knew he couldn't see me.

3

AND COMES THAT OTHER FALL
WE NAME THE FALL

Cutting the dock loose from shore was a commitment saved for festive occasions. The first time I'd been invited aboard for a float around the lake, my pleasure in the privilege had been enough to let me abide what I later almost forgot: the company of Brantley Simms. Dex, our captain that day, had filled a cooler with bottled beer and chosen the passengers, more or less those who happened to be nearby when the idea struck: Vince and me, Brantley, a pair of my new pledge sisters. We were freshmen. The dogwoods were in bloom. Dex used the long pole to shove us around the water. Out at the far corner, Brantley slouched in a plush chair, one skinny leg in acid-washed jeans draped over the arm, and I remembered the contented way he tipped his face back to the sun.

A few months had passed since our encounter at the Cow, and he had not yet gashed his finger, so I enjoyed the day by pretending he was someone else—not hard to manage when I was glad to be anywhere with Vince and Dex, and still enchanted with the idea of having sisters. Brantley and I interacted only as part of the group, but I laughed at his wisecracks, hoping to let go of rancor. His usual comedy took the form of argument, and that day he'd been on a tear about shadowy government operatives with ties to Rockhaven, the assassination of JFK, UFOs hidden at Area 51. Paired with Dex, he was especially funny, and the more he insisted on his theories, the more they seemed a joke.

How the day ended, I'm still not sure. Probably we lingered until we ran low on beer, then poled back to the house. Brantley and Dex shot a game of pool, and the kind of impromptu party accumulated around us that tended to arise on these fine-weather planless Saturdays. It may have been later this very evening, in fact, that Brantley cut himself.

I asked Vince, "Do you remember that day we went out on the Gamma dock, out on the lake with Dex?" For the free hour we shared twice each week between classes, I took the chance to steal his company sans

Jonathan. Sunny days found us seated back to back on the quad grass, using each other for back rests with our gowns spread beneath us. I was reading *A Midsummer Night's Dream*; he was reading *Decline and Fall of the Roman Empire*.

"Sorority Shake Day," he said—which would have made it February.

"No. It was later. Spring, I'm sure." I hoped he'd remember and thus break the taboo of the name before I had to. "Brantley was there."

"Oh." He sighed, laid his head against mine. "Brantley. Sure, I remember."

None of my friends had been close to Brantley, really, except through those mysterious fraternal bonds. I might have gone along with them to the funeral in Charleston but for some silly reason—a paper due? In truth, I couldn't find enough personal justification to be there. That his blood had once been on my hands? That I had passed his body as it lay beneath the bells? That I loved people who loved him?

"He seemed happy that day, didn't he?" The words he'd spoken, a story, a punchline, drifted at the edge of my memory, just past recall.

"I think he was a pretty happy guy in general," Vince said. "Why are you thinking about Brantley?"

I shrugged against his shoulders, gazing up into the lacy light of an oak where yellow began to speckle the green. "We're coming up on a year. Don't you wonder how it happened?"

He sat facing the bell tower, and I knew by the angle of his head he was looking up at it. "We're pretty much done wondering, I guess." *We* meaning the Gammas. "Nobody gets anywhere with it."

Down along University Avenue, a sparkle caught my eye. Two sparkles: Will Oliver, dressed for class, striding the sidewalk with Anna Vaughn. They were back together, I'd heard, but as they passed in the distance they didn't look at each other, didn't speak. "Oh, there he goes, my Will Oliver," I recited, facetiously. Once I'd outgrown my freshman love, I'd offered it to Vince and the others as a distraction, a disguise, one they made endless fun of.

"*Willoliver!*" Vince wailed in forlorn *sotto voce* at Will across the quad. I was dredging up a choice trail-riding anecdote from our few not-too-eventful weeks together when Vince added, "Brantley's roommate, speaking of."

"What? No. Brantley's roommate was that Delt, the big guy."

Together we said, "Dukey Clark." Dukey was glum, overweight, and

semi-famous for having lost two roommates in one semester. The other
had only left school for a family emergency, but still, no one would
room with him after that.

Vince continued. "But freshman year, it was Will."

Had I known this? I seemed to recall thinking of them as a pair
during rush, both flirting with the Gammas while destined for other
houses—though of course I'd been wrong about one. I watched
Will and Anna Vaughn march on until they had disappeared behind
Killern-Bennett. "Did you know Will's crazy rich?"

Vince said, "That doesn't surprise me."

It continued to surprise me. My misreading of him seemed linked to
one of my earliest memories from freshman year, a campus-wide event
when we'd all packed into the auditorium to see a hypnotist. From the
stage this man had mesmerized the entire audience into our own peaceful paradises, then told us to press our hands together. "There is a drop
of very strong glue between your hands," he said. "The seal is becoming
stronger. It cannot be broken." After we opened our eyes and returned
to the room, he called up onto the stage anyone whose hands would not
come loose. Mine dropped apart, to my disappointment, while thirty
or so helpless souls, hands locked before them, made their way to the
front. One was a cute guy I had noticed at the welcome picnic, whose
artfully tousled blond curls made him the easiest of my new classmates
to spot from a distance. The hypnotist told these people they were at
a dance party; he told them they were surrounded by dinosaurs; he
put them to sleep in chairs. This happened before I had learned his
name, and when I mentioned it months or years later, people said *Will
Oliver? Really? He was one?* as if the hypnotist had scrubbed him from all
memories but mine.

By junior year I had determined that the best roommate was one whose
social path I almost never crossed. Sarah Beth James, my latest, was often
out, and when home, she was funny and tolerant of the boys who called
me past midnight with an emotional crisis or installed themselves on my
bed for hours of backrubs and talk. Her sorority, Pi Alpha, was the one
I sometimes pictured myself fitting into better than my own, though
it probably wasn't true. They reminded me of the people I had met
in Meredith's room during the interviews: scintillating extroverts without visible awkwardness who appeared to be actual friends. Plus, they

seemed to take the whole sorority idea, with its pressures and anxieties, less seriously than mine or the more elite ones did. Sarah Beth had grown up with Pem, which put her on friendly terms with Pem's pals, and when they showed up in bunches—a likely occurrence since at least two of them had a crush on her at any time—and she happened to be home, she accepted the spillover onto her bed and joined in the massages.

"Wow," she'd said to me once. "Those boys are like your *job*. How do you ever study?"

It was not in the job description, however, to return from a lingering lunch and find a boy-sized lump under my leopard-print comforter, between my week-old sheets. Tuesday afternoons Sarah Beth was in geology lab, hiking down some remote hollow or cove of the domain, a detail Jonathan had gleaned only the week before.

"Come take a nap with me," he mumbled, dozy and child-like.

Though never unhappy to see him, I was as close to it as I could get. "Jonathan, Jonathan. What are you thinking?" Had it been Pem or Vince in there, I'd have taken it for randy silliness and jumped on top of him. But Jonathan meant something less simple.

Once, and forever, on a drive back from Chattanooga in a car full of boys, "Good Advices" on the tape deck and me in the back seat, mishearing the words and transfixed by the edge of his face. Spring peepers out the windows, the lights of lonely houses. The setting sun shining in the curve of his lip, he was talking to Pem in the driver's seat, turning to grin back at Vince beside me. Before Rockhaven I'd never had anyone to love, and I marveled less at this one heedless boy than at my own exquisite misery, my capacity for love, like a creature with a separate life grown somehow bigger than the car. All of us together ascended toward our home on top of the mountain, darkening all around us to silhouette, and how could he not feel what was bigger than the mountain?

"Change clothes," he said. "Just a little nap. Aren't you tired?"

"I have riding at two." I sighed. "Turn around." He flipped to face the wall while I kicked off my shoes and traded skirt and blouse for a T-shirt and boxers, and when I said okay, he turned back to wrap me in. Entwined—he was down to his underwear—we closed our eyes nappishly for a minute and then his hands began to roam under my shirt.

"It's okay," he said, shaking from his knees to his breath in my ear. "We won't go too far."

"Oh, you got that right."

Jonathan's curse was worse than Vince's, though they both suffered from a kind of idealism. Vince merely pined for girls too hot for him. Jonathan was saving himself for the flawless and fertile homemaker angel decreed by God to be his bride. Now his body was pushing hard against his beliefs, and I was not the girl to be helping him out. We each could have used someone who knew how to go about whatever it was we were trying not to do.

The kissing had started back in the spring—covert, drunken, fretful, and just generally unpleasant. Even with my minimal experience, I could guess I was his first attempt: it was not possible to be a worse kisser than Jonathan. For me it was easier to shut it down on pleas of friendship—we had no business kissing in the first place—than to risk hurting his pride with a suggestion. The latest venture had come about rather innocently the week before, on top of the bed, the usual friendly back rub and cuddle progressing by inches, stop and start, try, try again, until he'd pushed up my bra and had a breast in his hand. No longer much point in halting progress in that direction, or even keeping shirts on. And what did I care? I begrudged him nothing. The trick—the insoluble conundrum—was figuring out how far he could go, how much I could allow him to take, before his brain cracked in half and he never spoke to me again.

This was Jonathan, the puritan hysteric hoping to fake himself a loophole. "Well, he's from Oklahoma," Vince and I would deadpan to explain all strangeness, yet his controlling neurosis must have been part of what called him to our remote mountain in Tennessee, last bastion of the Old South with its tendency toward asceticism and shame. Not that sex wasn't happening on campus. Not that most of us wouldn't have laughed to hear spoken that a mutually pleasurable act could amount to damnation—unless it was social damnation, which applied only to girls. Yet the undercurrent was pervasive, as if our elevation, nearer to God, combined with the observant eyes of our close community, pressured us to aspire to purity.

I had no such aspirations, on my own account. I aspired only to keep my friends. But I was beginning to feel a cornered frustration that doing so seemed to require my purity, that maintaining it was my duty, that if I lost it I would become trash and my friends would back away, including this warm, very troubled, half-naked boy fumbling about in my bed.

"You know, I think the right side is bigger than the left. You have good nipples. Does this feel okay?"

"Um...softer."

Ground rules, unspoken: I didn't touch him. The fingertips nudging into my underwear, the oops-it-got-loose penis poking damply against my thigh: I halted him. This was a loan, just some body parts to handle within limits, under the expectation that he could tuck them back in place afterward without anyone's notice, including our own. As much as the skin access, what he needed was for me to find the line and hold it, but I had no guideposts to know where it was. Whenever possible I made him look me in the face, so he wouldn't forget I was there, so he'd have a chance of grasping that I was ready for whatever he wanted but less turned on than miserable with dread.

"Please," he said, his downward-pressing hand caught by the check-point guard, "just a little. A tiny bit." Well...*please* was about what it took. In all blunderings, Jonathan was rigid, forceful, and quick, the reason kissing was a nonstarter, and I warned him: soft, slow, and released the hand to creep beneath my waistband. We watched this event transpire in each other's faces until he'd worked a finger inside me. For a moment the act seemed commonplace, close to funny. Yep, that's where it goes.

He grinned. "Am I the first one who's done this?"

I nodded. "Let me show you something. Relax your hand." I slid mine down over his, drew his finger back outside and up.

He blinked at me, then caught on. "That's...? It's not on the inside?"

I didn't have a lot of actual information to share on this, but it seemed my body could answer without me. A few seconds and I stopped him. Who was this lesson for, anyway? Some other girl I already hated.

At some point Mitzi came tapping at the door with a singsong, "Leah! I know you're in there." We froze as if a rustle would give us away. The next knock, half an hour later—I had definitely missed riding—the low, playful, lips-to-the-jamb call of my name, was Vince. Jonathan turned to the door, his roommate standing eight feet away past that slim barrier. Had I locked it? I was sure I had but ducked in terror, fingers digging into his shoulder, because Vince would try the knob in the right mood.

"He's gone." Jonathan drew me into his arms. "Don't freak out. Would the world end, if he walked in on us?"

"Yes."

"Leah. You don't have a lot of faith in your friends."

"I know my friends." He looked hurt, and I sighed. "You're so intro-spective, and I love that about you, but still. I know you in some ways you don't know yourself. Or him." I propped myself over him, and his eyes dipped to where my breasts grazed his bare chest. "*Listen* to me. I am willing to let you pretend this never happened, but he's not. And you're going to want to tell him."

"I'm not. I won't." He frowned, toying with a nipple, then pulled me up tight again. "No, you're right. And this is really dumb of me. I shouldn't be here, it's just wrong on every level. And you're the last person I should… Really, are you okay?"

"Sweetie, I'm fine. You can't hurt me this way." I knew where his mind had gone. In his belief system, I was the orphan he wasn't, he having both parents while I'd been deprived of one in a car wreck and the other by elective removal. If I talked about my situation to anyone, it was usually Jonathan, whose endearing, exasperating habit was to coddle me like a trauma victim, reducing three-fourths of everything about me to a single cause.

A disproportionate number of my friends boasted two living, loving, still-married parents, and I often wondered if this condition was what made them the people they were, the ones I was drawn to. Almost always they took my deprivation harder than I did. Jonathan took it ten times harder. As much as my mother's death, he couldn't stand that we hadn't been close, that I'd spent half of childhood dumped on other parents until I was old enough to keep myself, after which she and I arranged almost separate lives, like roommates. This story I'd told him was true, but in the way a single color on the spectrum is true, a simplification I could manage and contain. The brighter and darker memories that didn't fit within gradually fell away, to my relief. I could have soothed him with additional shades of truth, but then we'd have to talk about it.

He glared at the ceiling. "Do you know how much I hate it that you think you don't want kids? If you'd had a better home life, you'd feel differently. I know it."

"Yes, I know you think so." On many of his pet topics, including his personal Savior, the woman's place in the home, and the inborn desire of all women to procreate, I had learned not to engage: he'd go on worrying the thing for an hour and never hear a word. But now and then—especially now, his dick against my leg—I could trick myself into thinking his project of convincing me to bear children shifted to the personal. Which was crazy, because make me over from the ground up into his ordained bride and I still wasn't pretty enough.

So: for what possible purpose had I gotten myself into a bed with Jonathan Pitts? Lucky for both of us he had neither the skill nor the will to get me all the way to sex, because I'd have gone anywhere with him. So easy it would be to forget, in the moment, that he wasn't equipped to handle it. While I was mourning our lost friendship, he'd be taking his lash into the closet, if not jumping off the bell tower.

"Let's erase all this," I said, once I'd convinced him back into his clothes. "Didn't happen. Nothing changes. Promise me."

On the way to Modern American Poetry with Jenny two days later I spotted Will Oliver framed in a stone arch of the Killern-Bennett arcade. He stood face to face with another boy I recognized but didn't know, a blond, gowned Phi O a head taller than him, and they were arguing. Their voices weren't loud enough to hear, but the shade of crimson burned into Will's cheeks was startling. Had I ever seen him angry at anyone? He looked as if he might throw a punch. When the other boy—Dalton Gibbs, Jenny reminded me shortly—walked on, Will, from the shadows, caught my eye and turned away fast. I almost considered waiting for him, since he was going where we were, but he didn't look as if he wanted company.

"Yikes," Jenny said. "That looked like a scene out of *Hamlet*."

"Or *Macbeth*," I said.

"Nah, too pretty for *Macbeth*."

Will was becoming a curiosity for sure. If he and Anna Vaughn were truly together again, I had not yet seen him in the halls of Benson to visit her. When I glimpsed him around campus he was often alone, which for Will verged on bizarre, or he was with people he looked odd with for no reason until I noticed that they were not Phi Os. Maybe, as I'd heard Gammas predict, he was becoming disenchanted with his fraternity. And if he was toying with deactivation, that could have been enough to cause a rift with Anna Vaughn.

I wondered, too, what the trail-riding class was about. If he had signed up with some cohort along for the fun, it would not have seemed strange. But alone? He certainly didn't need the PE credit. He was on the lacrosse team, and I had seen him show off some flashy skills in intramural basketball and football games, playing for the Phi Os. When

I asked one Friday, he told me an earnest story about wanting to expand himself, to take all the interesting classes he could while he was at Rockhaven—the same story I liked to tell myself until registration came around and I realized I was too busy for elective self-improvement. Will confessed he was also taking kayaking and rock-climbing, the limit of PE classes his Advent schedule would hold. He was taking a guitar class. He was thinking of volunteering with the local Big Brothers program.

"It's too much," he admitted, when I expressed my jealousy. Yet on trail rides, if I halted at a fork to ask the class preference, Will always voted for the longer route. One day, sloshing through a light but steady rain, he said, "We're already wet. Let's keep going."

Though time had passed since my crush, he was altered from the Will I had studied over so many distances. Subdued. He'd smile, chuckle at a joke, but he didn't engage with people in the way he once had, drawing clusters of buddies or fascinated listeners. In class he was in a fog, one our Shakespeare professor in particular might puncture whenever he spotted it—"What can we make of these particular repetitions, Mr. Oliver?"—showing Will at a loss for even the lecture's previous few minutes.

In Mod Am Po, my friends and I sat in the far back corner as usual. Will arrived with the bell, looking calmer, and took his seat near the door, amid people I thought of as his—drinking clubbers, ribbon society members, the elite. Drinking clubs were for guys and involved wearing either capes or kilts on game days; ribbon societies were mixed gender and more secretive, though they printed their names in the yearbook. I didn't know much about either, since none of my friends were in them. I supposed that at the upper levels, they needed these extra categories for sorting themselves.

After class, my crew adjourned to the Commons to check our mailboxes and debate whether to trek to Maxon for lunch or join the line at the Commons cafeteria upstairs. The SPO was packed at this time of day with students twisting the tiny combination dials on their mailboxes, standing about reading letters from home. I never had real mail, no care packages full of cookies or clothes, but I pulled out some party fliers and a folded note, the paper stamped *From the desk of Jonathan Crowley Pitts* over a pictograph of a hand writing with quill and ink. Of the rather lengthy and formal-looking note itself, I could decipher nothing but my name and his signature, the rest being in Latin.

Classics major. "Dork!" I said to the note.

I looked around for someone to show it to and my glance fell on Will Oliver, reading his own mail with a glower of concentration. The color was back in his cheeks, and as he lifted his eyes toward the crowd past my shoulder, he crumpled the paper in his fist.

Because he blinked at me then, taken by surprise—we were only a few feet apart—I said, "Are you okay?"

"Yeah." His mouth twitched into an embarrassed smile. "Just some stupid crap. From home." He shoved the page into his pocket.

I played along, my curiosity a weak opponent for my need to put him at ease. "About your car?"

"More or less, you could say that." He'd told me he was in trouble with his father for wrecking the Saab on his way back to school. Pure stupidity, he'd called it, fishing a cassette tape off the floor while climbing the mountain's steep, tight curves. He was lucky he'd hit a low table of rock and not sky and treetops. The story had chilled me, despite Will's droll attitude. His father was having the car repaired but considering whether his errant offspring ought to be carless for a while.

"Are you getting it back?"

"Yeah, tomorrow, actually. I can give you a ride out to the stable if you want."

"Well, I don't know if I ought to accept rides from daredevils. What if a tape falls on the floor?" We had arrived before my friends, who stood waiting by the door, and Will exchanged greetings with them. "Lunch?" I said to Will, pointing us all toward the stairs, a nonspecific invitation that would allow him to break off from us once we were in line or after we had filled our trays, join some other group that beckoned to him.

Will looked doubtfully at the stairwell door, then toward the pub at the end of the hall. "I think I'll get something at the pub instead. Anyone care to join?"

My friends looked at each other, thought about it. "I think we're just going upstairs," Emery said. In this group, he and I were the two reliably lacking in money, though he also resisted interlopers and any form of change.

Pem clapped Will on the shoulder. "Come eat with us, man. We never see you."

Jenny and Dex chimed in with more encouragement but Will looked reluctant, glanced at me with raised eyebrows.

"I would love to," I said. "But sadly penniless."

"I'm buying."

It's worth mentioning here that the Commons pub offered some of the most mouth-watering fare in existence, an opinion I'd come by while starving at tables full of other people's food, praying someone would insist I share, and when I was fortunate enough to be gifted with half a cheese stick fresh out of the grease basket I would dream about the rest of that damn cheese stick for a week. Never once at the pub had I simply ordered what I wanted. Yet still, because lunch with Will might be stressful or awkward, because my friends would have fun without me, I hesitated.

Then I was shrugging my farewells and following Will toward a Granger (bacon, cream cheese and swiss nuked on a bagel), cheese sticks, and curly fries. He talked me into a pitcher of Killian's—after all, it was Thursday noon, the start of the Rockhaven weekend, and a frosted pub stein was hard to turn down. We carried the brimming pitcher and glasses to the only empty table, a two-seater tucked away behind a post at the back. "This isn't weird, is it?" I said, feeling it only then. "I mean, is your girlfriend going to see us and go bats?"

He tipped the reddish beer into our mugs. "We're sort of taking a break. Don't spread that around. She doesn't want people to know."

"I'm not people?"

He grimaced, abashed. "Sure, but…I think that's literally the first time I've said it to anyone. And it's no big deal. We'll work things out, I assume. Probably."

While we waited for the food, we talked about Mod Am Po. My crew was crazy about the class, recited lines of Eliot, Williams, Stevens, and Pound whenever we could fit them into a conversation. We loved Professor Dunn, one of the younger members of the faculty, a font of cryptic tidbits and repeatable wisdom ("When you don't understand Wallace Stevens, just memorize him"). I gushed and Will nodded, squinting as if to find his way to my enthusiasm. He confessed he hadn't been doing much of the reading. Of my friends, he said, "I always really liked those guys. I should have spent more time with them these past couple years."

"Gavin!" was called—he'd given my name—and Will fetched our

food, a ridiculous plenty even with the cheese sticks and fries shared between us. I asked how he'd come to be an English major, and he said, "Always had this idea I'd be a poet. Or a scholar, maybe Renaissance or eighteenth century, teach literature at some little school like Rockhaven. You?"

"I like to read?" Truthfully, the idea that school would one day end ignited in me such a phobic denial that I'd thought very little about what I meant my major for. Without this place and my friends, I had nothing, the blank of nonexistence. "Your idea sounds pretty great, actually. Rockhaven forever."

He shuddered. "God, not here. Not me. I'll do it in California. Or... Australia. Don't tell my dad that part. He's not thrilled with the English major, but he doesn't fight as long as he still thinks I'll take over the business."

"What's the business?"

"Dream Cone." He spoke the name tentatively, as if it were some obscure company I might not know, rather than a gourmet version of Baskin-Robbins with nationwide stores.

"So you're the *actual* Emperor of Ice Cream."

He laughed. "Yeah, I suppose. And that one I read. I'm a big fan of Stevens. Of all the Modernists. Read a lot of it in high school. Prufrock, that's what started me writing poetry, some very pretentious stuff. But I guess I have a few things that don't make me cringe. And forms! God, I love the forms. How awesome is a villanelle?"

"The most awesome! Except for a sestina."

"Pound... I don't know."

I recited some Pound at him: "Damn it all! all this our South stinks peace..." He countered with Elizabeth Bishop: "Lose something every day. Accept the fluster..." The villanelle was more fun as a form, simpler to recall—I was done with the Pound after a line or two—and together we pieced together "One Art" and most of Roethke's "The Waking." Sonnets, he said, were pretty cool too. We'd been covering Frost's "The Ovenbird" that day in class, but we jumped over to Shakespeare, where I knew he'd been spacing out, yet he matched me sonnet for sonnet, each of us calling up lines the other had misplaced. *That time of year... My mistress' eyes... Let me not to the marriage of true minds... When in disgrace...*

"Well, damn," I said.

He smiled. "I should hang out on your side of the room. Not too many people on mine will play dueling sonnets over a pitcher."

"We've got poets on our side too." The greasy paper-lined baskets held only crumbs. Will divided the last of the pitcher between our glasses. How had it become almost two o'clock? I'd expected to keep him company while he hid from whatever he was avoiding, but he was attending to me more closely than required. A dozen times, as we parsed the poetry, he seemed about to speak in a more personal vein, then bit his mouth shut and didn't.

"So what's going on with you?" I said, just enough beer in me to feel bold in the knowledge that I had nothing to lose. "Aren't you a proctor?" He nodded—not many juniors were chosen as dorm proctors. "Mister Responsible, and a budding poet, dare I say scholar, and here you go blowing off your coursework and driving your car into rocks."

Caught in sunlight from the window at my back, his irises shone in eight hues of bottle glass, browns and ambers at the center, greens and teals out toward the edges, but the sclerae were pink with blood. He hadn't shaved. "I'm dealing with some things," he said slowly, watching me. "Some pretty messed-up shit you don't even want to hear about."

I waited. He said, "Not Anna Vaughn. But I guess in a way she's collateral damage."

He stalled out again, and I leaned a fraction closer. "Look. I'm a pretty good listener. I should probably get my license as a professional listener. And I'm a vault." I sipped my beer. "Also, we run in different crowds."

"Meaning?"

"Meaning, I don't think that letter you were reading in the SPO was about your car."

"Oh." He looked caught, even fearful, searching about for what to deny and what to admit. But I could see him now, not the angel or god I'd made of him. He was just another boy having an existential crisis.

He said, "I'm getting gowned this semester."

Founders' Day, October twelfth, when we'd all gather in the chapel to witness the Advent gownings, was a few weeks away. "Congratulations. This is what's troubling you?"

"For starters." He shook his head, chuckled without amusement. "Look, are you busy this afternoon?"

"Well, studying's out. I'm toasted."

"All right. If you're up for it, I have something to show you. But I have to warn you, it is fucked up in the extreme. Whatever you've guessed about me, this is worse. Can you handle fucked up?"

"Um...sure?"

"I really"—he paused, drawing swirls with his thumb in the condensation on the table—"would not mind, I think, showing someone."

Will was proctor of Stirling, a small dorm I'd always thought wasted on boys, with its fieldstone arches and long, cool porch lined with rocking chairs. The porch doors stood open to the commons room. Will led me inside to a solitary door at the right, the dorm matron's suite. As he turned a key in its lock, a pair of boys passed through toward the stairs, and I wondered if Will and I were doing something illicit. He flicked on the overhead light, ushered me in without hurry and shut the door behind us. We stood in a living room—stuffed furniture, a TV—backed by a kitchenette with an island.

"Why are we in the matron's suite?" I asked. "She's not here?" The place showed signs of a recent party, cups and beer bottles on the island, dishes piled by cereal boxes on the counters, the faint sour-hops aroma of a frat house.

"Oh." Concerned, he looked around at the framed art and bookcases, the wool blankets folded over sofa arms. "This is my room. Sorry, it's kind of a mess." He retrieved a bottle of bourbon and several cups from the coffee table, stuffed the cups into an overflowing trash bin by the island.

"Your room? Are you kidding me? Okay, that *is* fucked up."

"It's just a weird accident. Because Mrs. Peebles retired, and they couldn't hire a new matron in time. I was supposed to live upstairs, but they just moved me in here. Surprise. It's temporary, I'm sure."

"I'm going to have to kill you if you have a bathtub."

He had one. Clawfoot. And a shower with a matronly bench, his own long sink and shelves. Could the heir-apparent emperor of ice cream buy himself such a room? But it seemed to embarrass him. "The room isn't what I brought you to see," he said.

I followed him back to the bedroom—a double bed!—where he snatched up cast-off clothes and pitched them into a closet three times the size of mine, then dragged the bedcovers into a smoother state. With the bed at his back, he faced me.

"There." His eyes flicked toward the closet door, where an academic gown hung from a hanger. "My gown. Take a look."

A normal gown, it seemed, not polyester like my own but a cotton legacy, with a column of initials and dates sewn down the left scapular. Yet I must have begun to guess what it was from the wary distance he kept. At the bottom of the stack of initials, in thread a shade whiter than the rest, was stitched BAS 89. The date of our class, still two years in the future. *Brantley's gown?* One's own initials were never added before graduation. But in locating the aberrant detail, I understood it was more than his gown. It was the gown he had died wearing.

Will waited, seated on the bed. The braced dread in his posture made me think for some reason of the questions I'd despised at my mother's funeral and after, when I'd wished people would speak only in quiet, neutral statements of fact. I said, "Brantley was your roommate."

Will scrubbed at his eyes. "Sorry. I've been looking at that thing for two weeks. You'd think I'd be used to it by now."

I sat beside him. He said, "You knew him. I figured you would."

"Sure. I did." Had he brought me here on this assumption, my visible Gamma connection? "Not...real well."

"We were pretty close. You know how it can be, with your roommate, even when you don't hang out much outside of the room. I got to know his family. His folks would come up and take us both to dinner. But I don't even know who his friends were—like, of the Gammas, who he was really close to. Do you?"

"I know the ones he spent more time with." From my vantage, he'd appeared attached to an older faction I generally avoided: the hard-drinking right wingers, the old-money Southerners, likely originators of the term *wench*. Its current leader, a senior named Parker Battles, was the jovial voice in my memory shouting, *There had better not be any of your damn blood in this.* "I could ask, but...no, I don't know a particular person."

"Brantley was so into the gown tradition." Will's breath had loosened, past the threat of tears. "He got his dad all into it. So of course Walter, that's his dad, thinks a gown shouldn't leave the mountain. And he's probably right, that Brantley would want it to stay here. To be legacied to someone."

"To you?"

"He asked me. Walter. If Brantley would want it to go to me or someone else. I didn't know anyone else to…" He shook his head, both hopeless and ethereally calm in his acceptance. "It's okay if it's me. I'm probably as near a choice as anyone. And Walter says it's up to me whether or not to wear it, that he'd understand if it's too uncomfortable and…you know, maybe it really shouldn't be worn at all."

Maybe? That anyone should think of wearing it struck me as nauseating and wrong. Will went to the closet and I followed a little behind. "We've talked about it a lot," he said. "Like about the initials, whether to put in the graduation year or not. His mom did the stitching. It's been cleaned, obviously. Sewed up." He lifted a lower fold, where a jagged scar had been stitched so neatly it was invisible at any distance. To touch it, stroke the seam, seemed necessary, ceremonial, and I did so.

He returned to the bed, and I sat in a leather armchair facing him. "So what are you going to do?"

"Wear it." His red eyes drifted to the ceiling. "I'll get used to it. Right? Everyone will just get used to it. I mean, look at those other initials. Some of them are dead, I'm sure. A lot of us wear dead men's gowns."

"But, Will." I searched his face, hoping those two words could suffice. "None of them died *in* it. Horribly. On campus. In front of us. At the age of—"

He held up a hand. "Got it. You think I shouldn't."

"I'm not saying that."

"Would you?"

I drew a long breath and considered the gown, zipped on its hanger. Say it had been Jenny who'd died. Or Jonathan. Vince, Pem, Emery. Framed that way, the question seemed oddly less gruesome, the gown more tolerable as a presence.

"Well," I said, "I guess I'd ask what he would want. Now, if he were sitting here with us. Would he want you to wear it?"

"That's easy. I know he would. He was kind of an asshole that way."

I couldn't help smiling. "Sounds like the Brantley I remember."

"Warped sense of humor." He stared at the wall. And did Brantley happen to die in that gown, or did he choose to die in it? Not a question I could ask yet, but one that seemed relevant here, and on which Will would have an opinion.

He stood abruptly and left the bedroom, calling, "Hey, you want a beer? I've got a fridge full." I followed to the kitchenette, where he was jacking open a Red Stripe. "Or something else? Martini? Maker's Mark?"

"You got water?"

"Leah! What kind of Rockhaven student are you? There's no water on the mountain."

In his rush to recover I sensed something false, or omitted—a gap between the *fucked up* thing that had rattled him earlier and the one he'd revealed so quietly. But maybe telling someone had answered the need—a simple cure for what an hour before had been overwhelming. "Okay, fine," I said. "A beer."

"Atta girl." He opened another and we took seats in his living room which, despite its film of party spillage, was classier and more comfy than the commons room of any dorm. I did some quick calculations for all the reading and paper writing I'd need to squeeze into other spaces of my already crowded weekend. At least I had managed to arrange a schedule free of Friday classes.

"So," he said, "the other problem, which you picked up on in the SPO today, is much more stupid on the surface. It's that I already have a gown I'm supposed to wear, a pretty fancy legacy that Anna Vaughn's dad got for me. See, Ransom Whitacre was a Phi O, which means now some guys in my frat think they have an opinion on what gown I wear. I know it sounds lame, but it's more complicated than that. They actually think they're looking out for my best interests. As does Anna Vaughn. But I get so tired of the bullshit. Fucking tons of it." He took a long pull on his bottle.

"Is it that they have a problem with *that* gown?" I pointed to the bedroom.

"Yeah, but there are factors I can't really explain. A big part of it is that they didn't like him. Anna Vaughn couldn't stand him. Not that they—I mean, they were really supportive of me last year, especially Anna Vaughn. But they're over it and want me to move on, and it just makes me not want to be around any of them. Does that make sense?"

"Sure," I said. "Of course."

"I should have spent more time with you guys last year instead. I just couldn't…be around his friends. It was too hard. I wanted to forget. And I did, to an extent. Kind of went around in a fog."

I thought back to my few memories of Will the previous year, his absence from the social scene. I had never connected it to Brantley.

"Now," he said, and took a swallow of beer, "I think I want to re-member."

4

The Voices Dying With a Dying Fall

Where's your boyfriend? Vince and Pem thought this an amusing question, regarding Will Oliver, to shout at me across the sunny Gamma lawn as I arrived for their pre-rush party. In this last weekend before formal house visits, every frat had scheduled a party as a last chance to show off, but no evening bash could beat an afternoon on the Gamma Chi lake with a band from Chattanooga and fruit-laden grain punch dipped from hundred-quart coolers. People were already dancing to the cover band's "Alex Chilton," which gave way to "Can't Get There From Here," and I half hoped for a bad song next just so I could get some punch and my bearings, so I could not-look for Jonathan, the last and only person I needed to see. But "Trail of Tears" started, no choice but to lock eyes with Vince and run for the front-yard dance crowd.

We took a spot next to Mitzi and Sophomore Steve, turned into a couple though Mitzi had (*oops*, she said) slept with Quinn. No surprise he was bored with her now, but he'd given me the news without broadcasting it to the room or saying anything too horrible about her, which I called an improvement under my influence. Mitzi looked damp and happy, shuffling her shoulders at Steve. The next song, Violent Femmes' "Add It Up," doubled the crowd and left us all drenched, breathless and hoarse from screaming at each other about needing a fuck. Vince and I were hardly the only dancing celibates who screamed in earnest.

When the set ended, we found seats on the edge of the long front porch and gulped red punch quicker than was wise. "So," Vince said, "spill it. You and Will Oliver."

The night before, Will and I had caused a minor stir by sitting together in Maxon. Will's idea, crossing over from his accustomed right side to join me on the left—his way of taking a step toward the Gammas, I surmised. In no way had we looked date-like, since by sheer force of being Will Oliver he caused other people to materialize until our table had collected a dozen lively and interesting companions of varied Greek affiliations like a mini summit meeting. Still, his company was a spotlight beam, and I couldn't say I minded knowing my friends were intrigued and a touch jealous, even if none would believe for a second that Will and I were getting it on.

"He's in my trail class," I said. "We're buds."

"Mm-hmm." Vince had already moved to the next item on his list. "And then there's you and Pitts. What sort of hanky-panky is going on there?" He waved a pointer finger around my innocently perplexed face. "You are being secretive and weird, the two of you. Do not call me paranoid."

Jonathan seated himself cross-legged beside us, expressionless behind black sunglasses. I said, "Vince wants to know what's going on between us."

To Vince, he deadpanned, "Your mama is going on between us," his latest infinitely applicable, foolproof line to make Vince keel over laughing. He added, "Leah's blowing her."

"Um, blow her yourself!" I cried, good for a charmed smile from Jonathan. Easy enough to predict this one gut-grabbing gleam of his attention would be the last I'd get all day, that I'd spend the rest of the party pretending to be interested in people who were not him.

Some perky freshmen from my hall came to chat: Polly, Kelsey, and a boy named Marcus, who was pursuing one or the other of them so fixedly that I accused him of being their third roommate. While I talked to the girls, Marcus, who had designs on a Gamma bid, set about the transparent task of making an impression on Vince and Jonathan. He struck me as Gamma material—funny, bold, quick, gallant with the girls—and he seemed to be showing well for the actives, except that Jonathan, in aloof mode behind the sunglasses, walked off in the middle of it. Vince shuddered at me. "And there goes Mr. Roboto. See ya later, pal."

That even Vince had to weather these polar moods was a comfort. Jenny took over Jonathan's spot, while Marcus went on gamely talking to Vince, and I scanned the party for anyone but Jonathan, a boy I knew for a fact I didn't want to get naked with, nonetheless a beacon in a hazy sea.

Not far away, Quinn performed a showy rush laugh with a couple of the seniors and some freshmen I didn't know. In aviators, touched in glints of sunlight, his face softened and gained some allure. I could picture him laughing on a prep school brochure, maybe on the deck of a boat. To make up for Jonathan's rejection, I pointed out the group to Marcus. "Do you know them?"

"Uh, Quinn, right? Not sure about the others."

I would have taken him over to meet Quinn if needed, but I wasn't about to insert myself in the process otherwise. I nudged Vince to go make the introductions. Kelsey and Polly hung back, Polly perching beside me in conspiratorial proximity. "You know that guy Quinn?" They exchanged a googly glance. "What's he like?"

"Oh, brother," Jenny said. "Here we go."

"Well," I said, "he's a sociopath, he enjoys long walks on the beach…"

Polly giggled. "Be *serious*! He seems really nice."

I agreed that he did seem so. Jenny swatted my shoulder. "Hey, did you know he's a pilot? As in, he flies *planes*. Dex swears that's true."

"Yeah," I said to her, "he wants to fly fighter jets. My bet is he ends up in law school. But he's an interesting guy. Did you know he speaks French? He laid that one on me the other night. *Physics* major. Plays the freaking violin, which is just weird."

"A polymath," Jenny murmured. "Like Goethe. Or…Thomas Jefferson."

"Mmm, and Satan. A lot of serial killers, I think."

"And he's available?" Polly interrupted.

"Available…" I weighed the word. "Polly, dear, let me answer that with a story. See, the scorpion wanted to cross the stream. So he set out to find himself a frog, maybe a cute little freshman frog—"

"What Leah's trying to say," Jenny put in, "is she just wants him for herself."

I snorted. "What Jenny means is that my entirely selfless purpose is to warn the youth of what they will later regret."

Just nights before, however, while regaling me with his French, Quinn had joked about putting me on retainer. *You keep it up with that scorpion story. You're getting me a ton of tail.* So who exactly was I helping here?

An hour later, refilling my punch cup, I ran into Pem coming up from the lake. Pem was a fourth-generation Rockhaven gentleman—Pembroke Cobb Fuller IV—though he didn't look the part, cartoonishly lanky, chinless, and sweet. We called him The Earl of Pembroke.

He was leaving to write a paper. "Loser," I teased him.

"Escapee, more like it. I'm tired of rush and it hasn't even started." An extrovert, with friends in circles all over campus, Pem was one of Gamma Chi's more reliable rush assets. But he hated ranking people, saying no to anyone. A little drunk, I blathered an idle question about the prospects—Marcus, of course, but who else?

Pem said, "Yeah, don't be too sure. About anyone."

Only then did I realize he was angry, and nothing much got Pem angry. I walked with him out along the road, cutting through the arched gate of the cemetery. In amidst the nineteenth-century headstones and trees washed in their muted early reds, we stopped to sit on a bench of lichen-crusted stone.

"I really can't go into it," he said. "But we're having kind of a freak-out." I was dumbfounded already. It wasn't like Pem to be serious and direct for a full minute, let alone dish about the sacred brotherhood. "A movement, let's say. In that certain people want to keep certain other people out so as not to become known as 'the gay fraternity.'"

"The...pardon me, *what*?" I had never heard a whisper of such a rumor, from anywhere. "And Marcus is not gay."

He smirked. "Well. You know, of course, that I'm not telling you any of this." He waited for me to make the lip-zipping gesture. "According to some, he just sort of seems gay."

"Why, because he's *short*? They're hoping for all lumberjacks this year?"

"Something like that."

This was particularly baffling news because the Gammas were known on campus for an admirable inclusivity. They took pride in it. The previous year, the only two non-white freshmen to go through rush—one Black, one Asian—had both pledged Gamma Chi.

That Rockhaven's few students of color usually skipped rush had not yet struck me as remarkable. I assumed they preferred their own company, like the kids at the Black table in my high school cafeteria. Girls were more likely than boys to give rush a try, and they almost always ended up in my sorority—we were oddballs akin to the Gammas, neither high nor low in the social rankings—though I couldn't say even now whether they chose us for our slight mix of skin tones besides other factors, or if they merely accepted the bid they got. We had a Black member, and one from India, yet these two still fell into the larger group (meaning, all of us) for which I was not exactly aware of anyone's specific ethnicity. Carolyn, for instance, with abundant curly dark hair and an all-season tan against my skin or Mitzi's, was mixed-race Dominican, a fact I knew only after she mentioned it many years later. At the time, no one made such announcements, and the rest of us felt it impolite to wonder. To treat everyone the same was to treat everyone as white.

The non-white boys, on the other hand, must have felt more wary. They almost never rushed. So the Gammas had been pleased for the chance to bring in two at once who were not passing, like Jonathan and others, but obvious.

I found my friends' enthusiasm endearing, though also startling in its fairly direct acknowledgment. I still lived under the assumption that the world was fair and just, that no fraternity or sorority would take race into account at all, and that at a school like Rockhaven, the unbroken whiteness of fraternities might be an accident of circumstance. At least subliminally, I must have known there were forces at play. Years later I was told that for a few Rockhaven frats, *whites only* remained an overt principle clung to from inception, so that part of the Gamma delight over their new members had been in thumbing their noses at these other frats, upsetting the system. Nor would I have guessed that those two boys, who seemed even then pretty brave, had rushed only Gamma Chi, on private assurances of welcome.

But pondering Pem's news, I supposed that inclusivity needed hard limits somewhere or it wasn't a frat. This "gay" business might even be backlash. "Who is making this argument?"

Pem hesitated. "You can probably guess. It's mostly Parker and that crowd."

Parker Battles and that crowd—the ones I thought of as Brantley's friends, though I had not yet inquired—were the expected proponents of an argument I didn't care for. Yet they were caustically funny, generous with the expensive booze, and didn't hate me personally, so I'd had some amusing conversations with them.

"Mostly," I repeated. "And also? Let me guess. Jonathan."

He nodded. "And."

Vince was the standard second to that pair, but this one didn't sound like him. "Well, Quinn. Duh." Quinn ran pretty near Parker's crowd anyway. "So, wow. What even started this?"

Only Pem's anger had allowed him to speak so much that we both knew he shouldn't have, and his expression began to button down. "Supposedly, there are rumors. That's what I'm told."

"That the Gammas are suddenly the gay fraternity? If this is about Emery, I'm going to hurt someone. Starting with Jonathan."

"It's not, I swear. Everyone loves Emery. Who, by the way, is hardly the only closet case we've got in that house."

"Yeesh," I said, at the bluntness of the statement. In all of Rockhaven, I knew of no one who was openly gay. The word came near enough to a slur that to label even Emery so frankly was not how any of us was accustomed to speaking. Had I given it thought, I might have picked Emery as the only truly closeted student on campus, in that he'd taken the shocking step of private awareness. The others who were gay, who must have existed, had fed so thoroughly on the culture of repression that they effectively blocked their desires from their own knowledge. They behaved as such, at least, and we treated them as unaware from politeness, the way we treated everyone as white. To become aware of one's own improper nature was to suffer a great misfortune, to be ashamed, or—as I imagined the case for Emery—to keep silent and set the fact aside until some future date well past graduation.

But now that we were counting closet cases, I supposed a few members of Parker's crowd, besides Parker himself, might easily qualify. I'd heard hints about unnamed members engaging with each other in unspecified ways they considered not gay but almost the opposite: an extreme brotherly intimacy, a manly privilege, kept scrupulously secret less because it was shameful than because it was a form of fraternity business. But this sort of culture attached by rumor to all frats. I'd never thought of it as particular to the Gammas. And I didn't see how Marcus Langley "seemed" more gay than half my friends, than any number of unquestionably straight actives, if viewed on some outsider scale of perception.

Pem made me promise to say nothing. "Especially to Jonathan. Or, God forbid, Quinn. It may blow over and affect no one."

Back at the party, I couldn't help veering in Jonathan's direction, just close enough to check on his tics since Vince wasn't near. Only one worried me enough to bother with in today's mood, and it was hard to detect: an extended pause, a stillness. *He zoned out*, others would joke, but the first time I heard Jonathan say it—"Did I zone out?"—I knew he'd been lost in more than thought. Vince and I had tried on the term *absence seizure*, but only with each other. If we spotted one in public— or was he only thinking?—we readied ourselves to step in, to subtly distract all the surrounding attention while getting a hand on him. We wanted him to feel us there, if only after he came back.

But half a year had gone by without a hint of blankness, my cherished secret excuse to keep near him, even when, as now, he was talking to girls and didn't want me around. I looked past him and kept walking. To shake loose of my obsession was beginning to feel urgent, my best protection against losing him.

Inside, I joined a crowd of sofa loungers presided over by Quinn. "You know what's a travesty around here?" His mood was merry, drunkenly declamatory, his feet crossed on the coffee table. "That I'm not pledge master! Who better, I ask you? Next year, I swear to God it's gonna be me. Y'all better look out."

Dex, from the perpendicular sofa's corner, leaned to reassure a standing trio of freshmen boys. "We would never elect him pledge master."

Quinn bellowed, "Oh, we'll see about that! Bring back hazing, I say. You should have to work to be one of us."

"Suffer, I think he means," a sophomore said.

"Hell, yeah, brother, like Christ on the fucking cross! Get rid of the damn pussies around here."

"He's kidding," Dex said to the freshmen, who were grinning broadly and laughing like the rest of us. The promise of torture became enticement when everyone was taking it in stride.

The band packed up around five, and people began to move toward dinner, banking stamina for parties later in the evening. Jonathan had vanished. The sofa crew made plans to drive down the mountain for pizza, and since someone would always offer me a slice—a less painful sort of charity than the "loans" at other restaurants—I waited around for them to clean up and fetch cars. The house was nearly empty when, heading toward the bathroom, I heard a confab of hushed voices around a corner: Parker and company, discussing rush. I flattened to the wall. They were being so cagey that I couldn't pick up much: "He'll be okay"; "We'll need to address that"; "I talked to that one, totally see what you mean." Quinn was with them and sounding truculent with an agenda, saying, "I told y'all not to—" and someone else said, "Calm down." Then one of the seniors—Matt Stafford, I was pretty sure, mild and a bit of a lunkhead—said, "I mean, really, the last thing we need is a repeat of the Brantley situation."

This was met with a collective hiss of objection and a roar that made me flinch: "Don't you *fucking* say his name!" Quinn.

"Enough of this," Parker said, clipped and firm, and I knew my cue to scoot out of there.

All the next week, "the Brantley situation" echoed ominously in my head, while I wondered which friend I might dare approach. Nobody, not even Pem, would respond well to a direct inquiry about fraternity business.

Whatever it was, I told myself, my own friends would have had little to do with it. Brantley was their pledge brother. This year's seniors, or the classes above them, would have been the ones to designate one of our class a "situation." Ballsy of Quinn, in that case, to stand up to a senior over it.

Maybe. And "situation" could have meant almost anything—unrelated to his death, unrelated even to rush. To speculate on an overheard scrap of Gamma business was folly. I wouldn't have tried, except that Will Oliver had come into my life with that gown, if nothing else reminding me that a year had passed and we still didn't know what had happened on the night of its last wearing.

Whatever his issues with the Phi Os, Will couldn't get out of house visits every night that week. So we made our plans for the afternoons. I went to his suite with my books and we sat in the luxury of his living room to read Shakespeare aloud, assigning ourselves the various roles of *Much Ado About Nothing*. This, I had decided, would be helpful not only to Will, who would not otherwise read it, but to me, since after lunch I could rarely get through an hour of reading without falling asleep or giving myself a break to visit a friend. For instance, Jonathan Pitts. Studying with Will would serve as my enforced restriction.

After we'd traded a dozen lines between Leonato and the messenger, Will said, "Ugh. We need a beer for this."

"No drinking. Reading of the play."

"But—"

"No. Nada. Zero beers. Let's say if we get all the way through Act Three, then we can have a beer."

"Yes, ma'am. Reading of the play." His smile was only a pretense of snide. I had figured out a couple of things about Will, and one was that he was a boy in desperate need of someone to tell him what to do. For now, at least, the director he'd settled on seemed to be me.

Another was that he was not hurting for non-Phi O friends who would be happy to help him kill time and brain cells. He had no need of an additional drinking buddy, and he didn't need to be drinking as much as he clearly did. What he needed, essentially, was a study partner: some-one to keep him from failing out, but also with whom to be quiet and sober through the long hours while, in the background, he contended with the gown in the bedroom. A scholar's gown, one that Will would receive only because the gowning tradition included dorm proctors, so I fancied that finding his way back to his studies might be another way of moving closer to Brantley.

Much Ado turned out to be an ideal play to launch my experiment, since it became hilarious a few lines in. Because it was written in prose rather than iambic pentameter, I could deliver Beatrice's face-slap lines with saucy energy. Will, of course, was Benedict, but also Hero, the sec-ond female lead, whom he read in a wispy falsetto. We cracked ourselves up repeatedly, and re-read lines, and paused to check footnotes or to remind ourselves who was who.

"Maybe we should invite Pem and all them," I said. "It would be easier to keep all the roles sorted with more of us reading."

"Nah, that would just turn into a party, wouldn't it? Two works."

I was shocked that in the end it did work, that we survived three acts without a beer, that Will wanted me to come back the next day to finish the play. The reading had seemed to relax him. If I'd insisted, he might have pushed on through the last two acts, but it was a respectable four o'clock, so I packed away my *Complete Shakespeare* and said he could have a beer.

"And you," he said. "You'll stay, right?"

"Sure, I suppose."

He opened a pair of bottles. I was still in a skirt from class, my bare feet tucked under me in a corner of his love seat. He resumed his place in the armchair, also barefoot, tie pulled askew from the open collar of a white shirt. Outside the sky was musing on rain. In the distance, the carillon played what sounded like a waltz in a minor key.

To be in this room, relaxed with a beer, made me feel the purpose in the privilege. I'd be the one he could speak to. "Tell me something about Brantley," I said.

"Like what?"

"Anything."

"Okay. He was crazy about *The Black Adder*. You know this show?"

I didn't. Head tipped into one hand, he said, "No one does, it seems, except the two of us. It's British. We could quote all the lines. The hero, who calls himself Black Adder, has a sidekick named Baldrick. So me and Brantley, we called each other Baldrick. He was mine and I was his. So stupid."

I clapped a hand to my chest. "Will. That might be the cutest thing I've ever heard in my life."

He chuckled. "No, it's moronic."

I wasn't buying that he thought so. It was very much the kind of dork-o-rama dialogue Vince and Jonathan would concoct over some equally obscure subject only they had heard of.

"Tell me something about him," Will said.

"Oh, gosh." What would I know that he wouldn't, that he would want to hear? I sipped my beer, sorting through the bits in my possession. "I know his favorite book. Do you?"

"That would depend on when you asked him."

"Oh, right, figures. The one I know is *Franny and Zooey.*"

"That's an early one. It was probably our first night in the room together freshman year, he was talking about that book. I think he wanted to be a Glass kid."

"What was your favorite?" I asked. "Not now, but that night, when you had just gotten to campus."

"*The Last Gentleman,* Walker Percy. Know it?"

"Sure. Nice choice." It was Pem's favorite—I had read it the summer before on his recommendation. Now *that* was a book for boys suffering from existential crises. It should have been all my boys' favorite, especially the Southerners. I had since read Brantley's book as well, though I had failed to find what he might have considered life-changing about it. So much of the book was about being too smart for one's own good and jaded with college. How had Brantley connected to jadedness before he'd even started?

"Two books about suicide," I ventured, perhaps unwisely—Will stiffened at the word, shifted in his seat. "Sort of, in the background. If you count Seymour."

"Brantley would. For sure. Both about religion."

"Right." I had never thought of the two books together, but the overlap was striking. "Seekers. The struggle against the suicidal impulse. More in the Percy, maybe." I quoted a line I knew because Pem liked to quote it, about the problem of staying alive on an ordinary Wednesday. Then I remembered the speaker. "Oh, that's your namesake! Will Barrett."

"Too true, unfortunately. I read it in high school, back when I went by Willard. Decided to rename myself for college." He gazed toward the window, looking vexed enough that I restrained my gleeful rejoinder. The renaming gesture, I knew, was purely romantic. To know Will at all was to know he had never been teased for what on anyone else might have been a comical name.

"Stupid idea," he said, "since now I'm living his life. He's so passive and...fucking lame. Remember the part where Will is reading about the cigars wrapped with Confederate battle orders that get dropped on the road and turn the whole course of the war? And Will can't stand it, reading the book a second time. He knows they're about to fall and he's trying to work out how to reach in and grab them. That's all I do now. The bell tower. I think: I'll be there, standing there... I'll just"—he opened a hand, closed it on air—"grab hold before he falls. You know?"

My throat tightened. "Will, it's not just you. Everyone thinks that. And you go back further. You think: What led him there? Where was I? What if I had done something just a little differently, at the right moment?" My eyes flashed wet, and I pressed them dry, faintly horrified as always in these unexpected moments when a dead boy I had not fully succeeded in liking made me cry.

"You do that?"

"Some. My friends—probably most of the Gammas—have played it out from every angle. What if this, what if that. Not that anyone quite talks about it. If they do, it's on the assumption that it was just one of those things. An accident." He was nodding, listening, and I said, "Is that how you think of it? Or...?"

His gaze fixed on a spot on the floor as if a film of the event might be projected there. "An accident. I guess."

For the Gammas, this had been true almost since they returned from the funeral, as if by vote. Whom shall we blame? No one, God, fate. An accident. Only now was I beginning to wonder if some of them might know more than they let on. And all I had to go on was *the Brantley situation*, bumping up too close for comfort against *the gay fraternity*.

I said, "He had a girlfriend, right? Freshman year?"

Will blinked. "Yeah. I never met her, though. Carrie? Cara? They were off and on for a while."

"Right. Cara Somerville." A Gamma wench two years older than us, sweet but not pretty. "She graduated last year. I didn't know her that well, but I seem to recall he was not too nice to her."

Girls who didn't mind their boundaries at Rockhaven were asking to be treated like trash. To be treated the way Quinn treated them, after which they were marked for the majority as "not girlfriend material." Cara Somerville should not have been anyone's girlfriend material, yet to some degree she had been for Brantley. I could almost hear Quinn's voice at his ear. *What are you doing with that skank? Do you know where that's been?* The choice, however, did guarantee sex involved, if that was what his brothers had needed to see.

Will smirked. "He said some unkind things behind her back. Not to make excuses for him, but he was actually kind of a romantic at heart. An idealist."

I raised an eyebrow. "You don't say."

"Just ended up a little bitter over the perfect girl he couldn't have. You know how it goes."

"Who was the perfect girl?"

"Franny Glass? Maybe no one. Unattainable if she existed at all. Another unfortunate trait we had in common, pining after the ideal."

Like Jonathan. Like most of the Gammas, in fact. Will would have fit in with them so well. But then what could Will ever pine for, when all was attainable? One lingering look at the perfect girl, Anna Vaughn or any other, a thought, *her*, and she'd be in love.

Shake Day—when the freshmen boys received bids, often more than one apiece, and the brothers of all fraternities waited on their house steps to greet whichever of their choices would arrive—devolved after its first hours into an open party. Thus I was at the Gamma house to congratulate Marcus Langley, to see him treated warmly by all, including Jonathan and Quinn and even Parker. So the controversy had come to nothing. Or Marcus had been only on its fringes, other boys I didn't know at the center.

With the end of rush, Will and I switched some of our afternoons to evenings; we put *Much Ado* to rest, started on Pound's *Cantos* for Mod Am Po. Each day I was surprised to have one more, expecting him to grow bored with me or irritated with my direction, even angry with me for knowing too much. Though we didn't change our established seats in either class, he often waited for me afterward, joining my group of friends or drawing me off alone. I wasn't always eager to go, but my crew would survive without me. Will—whose manner was only friendly, not needy the way some of my boys could be—gave me more reason for concern. He was taking sleeping pills and antidepressants, prescribed by a doctor back home in Buckhead; but still he had trouble sleeping and helped himself to extra pills, which accounted for some of his fog. To avoid Anna Vaughn and the Phi Os, he'd been eating meals in his room or at the pub or off campus. Since he'd gotten his car back, he'd all but stopped venturing into Maxon.

"Just eat on our side," I told him. "Eat with us."

"Yeah, I could do that," he said, hesitant. He offered vague, unconvincing excuses about not wanting to upset people.

Once, after class, my friends talked him into lunch with us at the Commons cafeteria. To them he seemed alert and social, and afterward they snickered or rolled their eyes when I implied he required my attention. They assumed I was chasing him. Jenny offered snotty reminders that I already had enough boys.

Strangely, though, my freshman crush had not returned. Like Jim Morrison who still adorned my wall, Will was a continual pleasure to look upon, but I had long ago ceased to imagine him as someone I could have. Or maybe I was too accustomed to barring myself from boys who were my friends. In any case, he was a fine antidote to my Jonathan affliction, since I had no more time to knock at Jonathan's door and might easily have missed a wayward boy waiting between my sheets.

The week before Founders' Day, descending the Maxon steps for morning class, I spotted Will on a bench outside the chapel, below the bells. "I'll catch up," I told my friends.

He was dressed in coat and tie, his backpack at his feet. As I approached his bench and took a seat beside him, he didn't look at me. "Where are we going?" I asked. "World Religion, right? In Hampsell?" He'd been missing class lately—overslept, he'd say, or unspecifically ill—and getting him there when I could was one of my few self-appointed duties that felt simple and clear. I hooked a hand lightly around his arm, then slipped his hand into mine and squeezed it. "We'll go in a minute, okay?"

He nodded. "You'll be late."

"I can be late."

"Leah, I don't know if I can get together to study today." His gaze drifted to the gravel path where Brantley's body had lain. "There's something I have to do."

Jesus, I thought, and stopped myself from asking what. "Okay. But we'll just go to class now. Right?"

Nodding, he held firm to my hand. In the last wave of students leaving Maxon for class, I knew people would see us and wonder. Nevertheless I drew him to his feet and started toward our destination. Steps later we stopped. Dalton Gibbs, gown billowing, was striding toward us on the path.

Since the day I'd seen him arguing with Will, I'd noticed how visible he was at any distance, one of the tallest students on campus, the motionless shrub of his hair a distinctive shade of blond against tan. Up close—he stopped before Will, whose hand I dropped—his size became almost absurd. He was like some giant, handsome zoo animal, or two boys stacked inside the gown that barely reached his knees.

"Excuse us, will you?" he said in a patrician drawl, directed to me though he did not look at me. His voice carried a lazy burr, as if he'd just woken from an amusing dream.

Will gave me a nod, and I was so unprepared for this turn of events that I began to walk away. A few steps off I stopped, without a plan. Dalton turned to blink at me as if I had just then arrived into existence, confusing him in the process.

"We're actually going to be late for class," I said, in the loud, bright, half-apologetic voice of a person who had permission to argue with Dalton Gibbs, or was too stupid to mind her own business. My urgency to move Will—less to class than away from the bell tower—canceled any other fear. And Will, I felt sure, didn't want to talk to Dalton, needed the excuse. "Maybe he can catch up with you later?"

Dalton laughed, glancing at Will, then folded his arms to squint at me. That Will stood locked in place gave me pause. "Well, you're cute. *Who* are you?"

Though his tone was friendly enough, I wasn't sure he was really asking. And to tell him my name, I felt as it formed, would be to acknowledge I was no one. "Will's friend," I said.

Just as Dalton went to say something sharp that started "Look—"

Will cut him off, stepped between us. "Yeah," he said over his shoulder, "I'd better go. I'll see you after class." He caught my arm and walked me ahead of him in fleet paired steps more graceful than violent, the way it felt to be led by a very good dance partner.

"What's *that* guy's problem?" I muttered, trying for some humor. However relieved I was to have Will moving, we were walking so fast, my arm snugged up under his for longer than warranted. Of course, we were late. Still, I looked back to make sure Dalton wasn't chasing us.

We stopped outside the heavy door to Hampsell, where I would leave him to run down to my intro to film class in the library AV room. "Thanks," he said. Then I really began to worry. "I owe you. But you probably shouldn't have done that."

His face was flushed, two steps above me, and I could hear my own breath. "Will?"

"We'll talk later," he said. "Go."

Rattled, I went on, spent that hour and next in a state of distraction. Outside our eleven o'clock Shakespeare, I waited for him, fingers crossed he'd show. At the opposite end of the hall, my friends snuck looks my way and whispered over my latest weirdness. Lovers of a good mystery same as I, they were hoping for some indication that this was more than drama of my own devising, and Will obliged them by cresting the stairs and heading straight toward me, drawing me to a conspiratorial corner.

"Listen," I said before he could speak. "Whatever he wants from you, you don't have to do it. You don't need to meet him. Okay?" Though I felt half crazy blurting this, he was listening, as if I were not altogether off base. "If you want to get off the mountain, I'll go with you. Whatever you want."

He sighed. "Look, it's not like that. I didn't mean to freak you out. I'm not dying to talk to him, but I can handle him."

I wasn't sure if he was lying, or if he'd know it if he were wrong. I kept seeing his eyes, his posture as he'd stood before Dalton. As if he wanted to leave with me but couldn't. And he'd moved only because I had not, as if to snatch me from in front of a bus. At the age we were, any crisis in a given day could take on the weight of life or death; I knew this well enough, yet the present one was starting to feel literally so. And unlike Brantley's death, or my mother's—a simple car accident of unknowable factors, or climax to a drama in the closed-off world she excluded me from—the outcome for Will might have been in some way under my influence. I clutched the thinnest scrap of his fate in my fist, but there it was.

"But," he said, "I need something from you." Leaning close, he waited for me to nod. "This is important. I need you to steer clear of Dalton. You're better off staying one of those people he's not really aware of."

"Will." My voice cracked; I felt half an inch from bursting into tears. "That is not very reassuring." A knot of KPs, Anna Vaughn's sorority sisters, passed by staring, but Will didn't seem to register them. "You're telling me he'd hurt *me*, but not you?"

"He can't hurt me. I have leverage on him."

At opposite sides of the classroom, we opened our books to the day's chapter and verse. *O that this too too sullied flesh would melt, thaw, and resolve itself into a dew.* Did Hamlet, Dr. Macintosh mused aloud, really declare the flesh must go because it had been dirtied, contaminated by the world? Or was the true word less complicated: not sullied but *solid*? Shakespeare was like the Bible that way, crack the text and point to your own day's tribulation. If only the Everlasting had not fix't his canon 'gainst self-slaughter, indeed. Two hours earlier, in the tower shadow, Will had appeared plenty agonized over his own solidity, yet now, across the room, he sat softly attentive, facing the lines. We already knew Hamlet was all talk. Much ado about nothing, I told myself.

At the end of class, Will was the first one out the door. Ten minutes later, walking down to the Commons with my friends, I saw him get into a car with Dalton Gibbs.

And by the end of the day, I had a new enemy, one Will hadn't seen coming but I sure had: Anna Vaughn Whitacre and all her minions.

5

LEARN TO FLY

On Founders' Day, Will received his gown. We had spoken little since he'd left in Dalton's car—or been kidnapped?—and was gone for days. On the Monday after, I'd spotted him on the quad in cordial-seeming discussion with some Phi Os, as if reconditioned to appropriate behavior. So I had a guess as to which gown he'd chosen. From my place far back in the chapel's crowd, I could see only that the one who gowned him was Dalton Gibbs.

Many of my close friends—Jonathan, Jenny, Emery, Pem—were gowned in the same ceremony, none by me. By tradition we asked someone older to perform the duty, so a number of recent grads had journeyed back to campus for it, some passing down their own gowns. Parent-alums like Pem's dad gowned their kids. Families attended, and afterward the quad lawn was crowded with people congratulating the inductees, taking pictures in their new academic attire.

I was never lonely at such events. A feature of Rockhaven's high percentage of living, loving, still-married parents was their sincere interest in knowing their kid's friends, their tendency to take those friends warmly into the fold. By junior year I'd become a little overwhelmed with offers of adoption. Jenny's, Pem's, and Vince's parents, with whom I'd spent holidays, and even Jonathan's, who knew me only through campus visits, all treated me as something like their second Rockhaven child. Thus Founders' Day kept me too busy for more than a glance over to the far side of the lawn, where Will stood in a crush of Phi Os and others, Anna Vaughn close by, along with a handsome fair-haired couple who must have been his parents. They certainly could not have been Brantley's.

Had I gone to the funeral, I would have met Brantley's parents. Will's references to them—Walter's sweet interest in the gown tradition, his mother's sewing of Brantley's initials—had caused me to picture them vividly enough that now I felt a pang at their absence, these parents lacking a child, as I was the reverse. For their sake, I felt annoyed with

Will. Surely they would have attended the ceremony if Will had elected to wear their son's gown.

But then, hard to guess what stir that gown might have caused, once the campus realized it. "That other thing was a bad idea," Will told me days later when I caught him in the hall of Killern-Bennett, as if the decision had been easy and obvious. "The gown shouldn't be worn." I hoped the shame he seemed to feel in saying it was his main reason for avoiding me, if he was, begging off study sessions, skipping a trail ride.

But it was hard not to wonder if his distance had as much to do with my personal shortcomings, the kind he might not have noticed until hearing them enumerated by Kappa Psis. For instance, I smelled like a horse, dressed like someone's backwoods grandma; my hair was no known style, and maybe I should try brushing it. Oh, and I was a slut. These *bon mots*, delivered sideways into my hearing, should not have stung when I knew the reason was my proximity to Will. My own sorority had charged me with a similar crime, merely for accepting a formal invitation from Ainsley Rowell's recently-ex boyfriend—never mind that we hadn't even kissed—that crime being "Proximity with appearance of attachment." My sisters had comforted Ainsley by telling her I must have used my secret slut-wiles to somehow cause the breakup, but still, their hostility was nothing so insulting as the KPs unleashed, blatant enough that my own friends caught a whiff and stuck close for support. And while grateful for their concern, I couldn't help worrying: Were they *too* close, signifying my sluttish nature? Would they smell the saddle leather that clung to my fingernails an hour after scrubbing? Would they begin to consider my hair and clothes unacceptably odd? The KP opinion, if spread to the right corners, might fell me more swiftly than any opinion offered by Brantley Simms.

A week after Founders' Day, I was stopped in the laundry room doorway by the sight of Anna Vaughn loading a machine, a smile ready for anyone's footsteps but mine. She went flat and turned away.

"Listen," I said, risking words since we were alone. "I don't know what you heard, but Will and I are just friends."

She made a sound in her throat, disgust or disbelief. "How nice for you."

"We've been studying together. He's—" Laundry basket against my hip, I wondered mid-sentence what I thought I was going to explain to this girl about her own boyfriend. "He needs a little help right now. Just, you know, focusing."

"And he needs it from you. You showed up yesterday and now you know so much about him." She shook her head to marvel at the depths of my hubris. "I'm sure you've been giving it your best. But he has bigger problems than you can understand, and you're actually about the last kind of help he needs right now. I'd suggest you leave him alone. You have no idea what people are saying about you." She dropped the lid on her washing machine. "Forgot my quarters," she said, and marched out.

This left me shaking, emptying my basket into the second machine. She may have been a good actress, but a dressing-down from this poised pixie of a girl did not feel like jealousy, pettiness, or spite. It felt as if the Rockhaven honor council had deliberated my case and found me in the wrong—less a slut than a self-important meddler, causing actual damage out of ignorance. And what if she was right? The chance made me feel as if the rest of the school, filled in, would vote in agreement.

In hope of reassurance that not everyone hated me, I hiked over to Gilchrist and climbed to the second-floor hall where most of my boys had congregated for junior year. No specific door in mind, I was headed like a possessed creature toward Jonathan's when I was saved by Emery popping out of the hall bath.

His roommate was in, so we took a walk, passing along the quad and across the main avenue, then down steps into a wooded greenspace called Bishop's Walk. A trail led us through shivering heights of yellow sassafras, red sourwood, melon-tinted sugar maple, all nearing peak color against the cloudless intensity of blue. A chill made us zip our jackets and pocket our hands.

Perhaps it was a superstition in me, that I almost never talked to friends about my own problems. I was the listener. I felt loved for listening when their moods were serious, for laughing when they were not, and that was enough to soothe any ache. Emery was glad to be with me, which relieved me of the need to vent about Will and his imperious ex, and I was content to proceed into Emery's favorite topic: the salacious exploits of Quinn Cooper. We stopped on a stone bridge to peer over the side, where the stream now and then carried a bright leaf along, while Emery relayed a story involving Jägermeister, an impromptu drinking game, and a stray sophomore named Jocelyn

Peters, who found herself off in the Gamma woods with Quinn, out of sight but within the hearing of some amused brothers monitoring the action from the back patio. Emery supplied sound effects.

"Disgusting. And shame on all of you."

"Yeah, but Jocelyn Peters," he said. Meaning: she asked for it; she's expendable. I knew her only by reputation, which included a few one-night stands with Omicrons over a semester. Ergo, none of the Gamma gentlemen would ever notice she was pretty, which she was, nor send an emissary to intervene between her and Quinn.

"Oh!" Emery grabbed my arm. "I forgot the part where he left her in the woods and came to hunt down more condoms."

I pressed a hand over my eyes. "It's good for me to hear these stories. I do forget what I'm dealing with now and then."

"No doubt," he said, grim. Meaning, *back at you double-time, sister,* though how he felt about Quinn was not a broachable topic between us. I often wondered whether Quinn was aware of Emery's interest and had simply chosen to ignore it or grant it an exemption, the way his casual invective against the world's legion of faggots and pussies never seemed aimed at Emery. If anything, I might have said he was fond of Emery, though Emery generally avoided his orbit to observe from a safe distance, like freshman Leah with Will Oliver.

Emery seated himself on the bridge wall and I hoisted myself onto the cool stone beside him. "And extra condoms, really?" I cracked. "Was Steve out there too?"

I expected Emery to fall off the wall laughing, sling back a crass rejoinder. Instead he folded his arms and looked at his knees. "I'm just joking about that, you know. Which I shouldn't, so let's just pretend I never did. It's disloyal."

"What?" His spanked about-face was disconcerting, so unlike Emery that I blurted, "Does this have something to do with a crazy Gamma uproar over keeping out the possibly gay-looking pledges?"

His expression gave away little except that I was right. "You shouldn't know about that, missy."

"I don't," I said, then proceeded to rant about how ridiculous it was, considering who was fanning the flames. But I couldn't get him to take the bait, and he looked more oppressed as I spoke. "Emery. I hope you don't just let them go on like that. If you don't stand up to them, who will, ever? Pem? Dex? I mean, someone should."

"It's been tried." The separate weight he gave each word made my mouth drop open. "End of topic."

"Brantley?" I whispered.

"Leah." He shook his head in warning, patting his pockets. "Where are my damn cigarettes?"

I kept my voice quiet, nearly asleep with calm. "The Brantley *situation*, perhaps?"

"Where did you hear that?"

"Some seniors, who didn't know I was listening. What does it mean?" At his shrug, I pushed on carefully. "I'm not going to say anything, I swear. To anyone. Just tell me. Or I'll tell you and you can nod. He fought back against them. During rush last year, the same dumb argument about who looked like what."

Emery stayed quiet for a while, then choked out a mournful laugh. "Worse, actually. He wanted people in the house to be open about it."

People? Despite Pem's flip remark about closet cases, I still didn't imagine there could be more than one person in the house to whom being open about anything might apply. Emery's eyes widened with the horror of memory. "The way he talked. He was so damn *casual* about it. He made jokes. He wasn't careful with what he said, and he was practically naming names. People didn't trust him."

Then Brantley wasn't gay. Or if he was, he was crazy. In thinking over the rush controversy, I'd already sensed it would be up to someone securely straight to take it on. But someone like Dex or Vince, mellow and diplomatic, as Brantley was not. "Did they...?"

"They put some pressure on him. I don't really know. It was mostly done in private." Emery pulled his feet onto the wall, hugged his knees. I worried he would tumble backward off the bridge, and with the impulse to grab him or brace him I remembered our first kiss, and when it had happened: not long after Brantley's death. No more than a month, on one of the first nights that people had begun partying again at the house, still in plenty of time for us to attend the Christmas formal as a couple. *Pressure* of some sort had been placed on him only recently, for him to come up with that word "disloyal" about a private joke.

"You can't repeat this," he said. "I know some of them are worried they were harsh on him. That it drove him to something. But he never seemed to take it that hard, to me. Around the house, everything seemed fine. He had friends. No big deal."

Some of them are worried... It could explain what I'd overheard at the house, the "situation" no one wanted to recur. The trouble hadn't faded from Emery's expression, though, and I murmured, "But maybe a bigger deal to some people?"

He shrugged. I said carefully, "No one would have gone further. Out of fear or...anger. To get him up there and push him."

In an instant I felt that, as usual, we were talking about Quinn. That Emery's fixation on him might have some other origin than I'd assumed.

"No," he said, "but. Sometimes I wouldn't put anything past certain people."

That Friday, the day after my laundry room encounter with Anna Vaughn, Will's green Saab sat idling outside of Benson. Picking me up there had become our custom, unremarkable until now and probably unnoticed by anyone, but as I ducked into his passenger seat that day at least half a dozen girls must have been monitoring from different Benson windows and crying in unison, "There goes that frizzy-headed slut!"

"Go, fast." I crouched low in the passenger seat, and luckily Will didn't take me literally enough to burn rubber out of the lot, summoning more eyes. "I should not be in your car, you realize. Half my dorm is going to chew my head off and spit it out just for sitting here."

"I'm sorry," he said. "She's usually not a bitch. This has all just gotten her very worked up. She ought to take it out on me, but she won't. I guess you're easier." Rain began to patter against the windshield.

"Why *aren't* you back together?" My tone was crisp. I suppose I was feeling abandoned, besides thrown to the wolves for no purpose.

He drove so long in silence I assumed the question had angered him. I weighed an apology but instead gazed out the runneled window at the green fields, the shaggy retired school horses shaking off rain in their field. Parked at the stable, we sat, the rain falling too heavily for riding any time soon. "I don't know," he said. "To answer your question. I just can't, yet." He turned off the engine, shifted his back against the door. "But she's right, they all are. I need to move on."

Now I could glimpse a more familiar Will, fighting to keep some Phi O-approved mask in place. I slumped against the leather headrest. "Isn't that what you tried to do last year?"

He shut his eyes, kept them closed as I spoke. "Look," I said, "the gown, that's your decision. Probably you made the right one. But I really think it would be good for you to spend some time with his friends. It's not helping you to try to forget him."

"It's this Tuesday, you know."

I didn't like his knowing the exact date, circled on my calendar only because Vince had mentioned it, but I stayed bland. "Yeah, people are doing something at the bell tower, I think. Candles and whatnot. That might be a good start. Maybe you wouldn't resent your friends so much, or Anna Vaughn either, if you just live your own life, don't wait on their instructions."

All about his golden-curled head, the car windows fogged. "You know, you're really a good friend to me."

Unprepared for such a quietly heartfelt claim, I came near crying. If Anna Vaughn hated me, this was why: the chance that her own influence might be the hurtful one, that I might be the one to help. And fixing Will's unhappiness was all I cared about.

I told him about a picnic my back-corner English crew had planned for the next day, assuming the rain let up. "They're not Brantley's closest friends. But they're the easy ones, a good place to start. Will you come?"

"Is it okay with them?"

"Of course. They love you." Actually, when I'd brought up the idea, they'd been a little grumpy and resistant to having an outsider along on this special occasion, for which Pem and Emery had composed a sonnet invitation placed in each of our SPO boxes. But they had agreed. "Just, if people ask, say it's Pem's party, not mine."

"Come on," Will chided. "You're tougher than that." At my comic look of surprise he said, "No, you are. To me you've always been this self-possessed, kind of edgy, in-charge, no-nonsense girl."

I coughed. "*Really?*"

"Oh, sure. I've always liked that in you. You have no reason to let anything those assholes say get to you, for a second." He bumped me in the shoulder with a fist. "You know, live your own life and all?"

"Right, I'll just go do that." But I was enchanted by the quick portrait he'd sketched of a girl I wanted to be, all the more if he was the one who saw her.

This conversation caused the dramas around me as well as my own to recede by a few turns of the microscope. I even allowed Will to drop me back at the dorm. At dinner that night—easy enough anyway on the dining hall's left side to forget the existence of the right—Jonathan, Vince, and Pem made an occasion of my persecution to bolster me at a neutral table and keep me entertained. Our remaining seats filled fast until the ranks over at the Gamma tables looked comparatively thin.

From behind came a surprise massage, and I tipped my head against some belly to identify the masseur. Quinn. "I need to talk to you," I said.

He dipped his mouth to my ear. "That sounds serious. Be at the house tonight?" Vince beside me and Jonathan and Pem across the table spun up the volume, as if too engrossed in their comedy routine to pause for Quinn, while over at a Gamma table, Emery lifted an eyebrow my way.

"Nope. Hot date with Ezra Pound at the computer lab."

Quinn made a retching noise in my ear. Yes, I was a nerd for writing a paper on a Friday night, the only way to clear my Saturday for our wine-and-cheese poets' picnic on a rock. But rather than pursue the topic, he said, "Come use my computer."

"Oh yeah? Sounds dangerous."

He chuckled. "If I were there, sure. But I won't be. Chip will be out. You can have my boudoir all to yourself."

I turned around on my bolted stool. "You trust me alone in your boudoir?"

"Well, there will be punishments if you're bad. For instance." He bent to grip me at the pressure points of both knees, hard.

I retaliated at the cartilage of each ear, until we had *ow*ed our way to a truce. Now his brothers at the table couldn't help granting their attention, which was nine-tenths of Quinn's objective and provided me a brief span during which he would stand on his head if I suggested it. I rose and plucked a pinch of his sleeve by which to lead him to seats at an empty table a few yards off.

"Seriously." He leaned back on his elbows against the tabletop, while I tucked in toward it, murmur-close. "Come use my computer. It'll be quiet over there."

I searched his eyes for an ulterior motive. No matter how convinced I was that I had this boy's number, he still managed to stump me with overtures that might have passed for genuine friendship. "Thanks, sweetie. Maybe I'll do that."

"Ah, you won't."

"I might! You don't know everything. Hey"—I backhanded his shoulder—"I heard an appalling story about you taking advantage of a poor drunk girl."

"Who, Jocelyn Peters?" He grinned with wild wicked delight as if I were not scolding him but dying for the details. "Sure as hell wasn't her telling you that. And she wasn't all that drunk, either."

"No?"

"She wasn't sober, but who is, ever? You know me, Gavin. I don't like a pushover. It's no fun." With one finger he lifted a piece of hair back from my ear and leaned in to speak. "Better if it's a challenge."

"Ha ha," I said, as usual treating any hint of a reference to me as a joke. Most of the time it was. What I enjoyed about Quinn was walking this edge, a flicker of risk always present while at the same time he spoke to me as if I'd passed his coolness test, only nominally a girl.

"But listen," I said. "I have a serious question for you. It's about Brantley."

Since growing accustomed to speaking the name, I'd been bringing it up with the other boys. Most of them balked at the subject. No one would come near the question of whether he was gay or even rumored to be. Between Jonathan, Vince, Dex, and Pem, I'd satisfied myself that none of them knew more than I did about what had happened on the bell tower—that they, at least, would never keep that kind of secret in the name of brotherhood. Vince, the only one who allowed me to fold Brantley into our standard analysis of everyone we knew, had told me Brantley and Quinn had been a close pair for a while, then had "some sort of falling out." By the way he talked around it, I could guess he knew the reason but didn't want to say.

To test Quinn with the name in the middle of Maxon had not been my plan. But in that moment, all the eyes he was performing for seemed better than privacy for keeping him in check and responsive. And coming from me, I thought, he might receive it softly.

Quinn said, "What about him?"

"You knew him pretty well, right?"

"Your point, Leah." No change at all in his half-bored, quiet immobility. It was my name—Leah and not Gavin—that made the pulse of his anger palpable. He was too volatile to play the sphinx.

I dropped my eyes. "I've just been thinking about him lately."

When I looked up, too soon, his face was an inch closer, all steel.

"Well, don't. You didn't know him. You're not going to now. Don't go acting like a wench. It doesn't suit you."

Even in my shock, I had to admire his precision: legally a miss on the W-word, but closer than I'd tolerate. And on the pretense of a compliment. "Okay. Fuck you."

As I stood to go, he leapt in front of me. "Sorry, I'm sorry. Jeez, calm down." Hands at my shoulders, he forced a smile while steaming some mix of emotions none of the others had shown me yet—guilt among them, and a guard dog's focused rage. But who knew what Quinn Cooper would feel guilt over? Maybe only being mean to me.

And how might I, in the middle of Maxon, explain what had seemed a minute before my perfectly reasonable intentions? *I actually believe in you, you dolt. I'm trying to give you a chance to prove you didn't murder someone.* No way out but to toss up a dismissive hand, push past to my original table.

"It's okay," I said firmly as I sat, the human equivalent of *down, boy* to Vince, Jonathan, and Pem, my protectors ever on alert to "deal with" Quinn the instant he did me any sort of wrong. Vince closed me in an arm as Quinn departed in some direction I didn't look up to note. That they would beat him up was hard to imagine. But I took them as serious about throwing him in a sack, yelling at him on a cliff edge, one of those apocryphal punishments meted out to keep the brotherhood in line. If one took a notion to go after him, they all might.

Roark's Steep, our grandest and dizziest vertical cliff, was one of those Rockhaven wonders not included in standard tours of the domain. Reached by a drive and a half mile of rocky hike through the woods, it often remained unseen until one's geology lab—geology the elective almost all of us signed up for eventually due to its famed hikes. On a football game day, my friends and I could count on having Roark's broad table of rock to ourselves. The weather was ideal for a clifftop picnic, the leaves at peak. Through the woods the trek had been chilly, but on the rock the sun stripped us down to T-shirts; a breeze tempered the heat.

Will had said he would meet the rest of us there, though I wasn't sure I expected him to show even before Pem said, "I doubt he'll skip a football game. Isn't he a Dragoon?"

The Dragoons were one of the drinking clubs, ostensibly a secret society but easy to identify on game days, roaring from the home fence in kilts. As far as I could tell they were more elite than any one frat, skimming the cream from several. "Oh, of course he'd be one," Emery said as we unpacked the cheese and bread and opened the wine. "I'll bet he's even a member of that *super* secret society, the one no one knows the name of."

"Are you making that up?" I asked.

"Very old, very twisted gothic shit. Supposedly it still exists. Dex, tell her."

Dex laughed. "That's some Rockhaven legend, I think. Like the drunk ATP who did a nosedive off this very rock."

"It was a Phi O," Pem insisted. "And that really happened."

We were deep into speculation about how one went about forming an exclusive order, like a ribbon society or drinking club or any number of strange, small, oddly named others that got themselves acknowledged in the yearbook—and why couldn't we, the Backrow Poets, do the same?—when Will appeared at the trail head. In that instant I may have regretted inviting him, forgetting that Will Oliver was no slouch at fitting in. He'd packed out two jugs of wine, along with some fancier cheese and bread than any of us had bothered trying to find at the Piggly Wiggly. The offering greased the rails, and then he was so deferential to our ways that not even Emery could hang on to his reserve.

Soon we were all buzzed and writing sestinas on a passed notebook, each adding a line in turn. The braver among us—me, Will, Dex, Pem—crossed the handspan of vertical fracture that sliced between the mountain and the farthest shelf, then crept out on our bellies to peek over the edge. Several hundred yards down lay broken slabs of former shelf, once joined at the edge we clasped.

"We're clasping the crag with crooked hands!" I cried. But no one present, not even Will, could help me remember the rest of Tennyson's "The Eagle." None of the others had been in Dr. Parrish's freshman class with us. Back on the safer side of the fault, we folded *the crag clasper* and other allusions into our expanding sestina.

Jenny, unwrapping new cheese, shrieked as a beetle charged through toward the cliff's edge. I scooped it up and held it between thumb and forefinger, glossy and black, mandibles thrashing. After dropping pre-vet, I had kept taking biology classes and thus could name the order of this particular arthropod: Coleoptera. Only Will, though, would pretend any interest, the others having grown weary of my schooling them in the identities of every vulture and warbler that wandered our way.

"Want to see some cool evolution?" I picked at the back of the carapace. Will peered close as the beetle's hind legs grabbed hold of my thumbnail and shoved it away. "You know how most beetles are split down the back, so they can open their wings and fly around? Like ladybugs, june bugs. On Coleoptera, the carapace is fused shut. See? He doesn't fly." I got enough hold to lift the rigid carapace by a millimeter. "But look, he's still got a full set of wings underneath."

"No way. Actual wings?" As gently as I did, Will lifted the shell to peek from his side, a half-second's glimpse of the crumpled translucent tissue of forever-folded wings. But with a sickening snap, the carapace split up its dorsal seam.

Will gasped. "Shit, we broke it."

"Oops." The mandibles continued to gnash, the legs to churn. "Maybe we fixed it." Released on the rock, the beetle staggered on, its gait somewhat drunken. Will watched until it had crawled past the fracture, out to the edge and over, as if he were waiting for it to fly.

Of that day on Roark's Steep, moments like this one endured in memory, intact but isolate, packed in fog. Too much wine eroded the rest, though by group effort we wrote three sestinas, a sonnet, and a villanelle. This record survives. Emery typed them into a chapbook for each of us, so in reading I could no longer judge by handwriting whose lines were whose. They were all of a piece, pretentious or silly poetic riddles constructed to impress each other or raise a laugh or simply to make sense. I could guess as Will's contribution one sestina line, *When fall of man becomes another fall,* since I'd studied the framed print of William Blake's "The Fall of Man" that hung in his sitting room. And hard to blink away the final word, the one to be picked up and echoed by those who followed.

Dr. Parrish's eagle remained elusive until near day's end, when Will and I, quite trashed—someone should have stopped us—crawled out toward the sunset in search of our broken beetle. Broken or restored? Once, in the deep of geologic time, those wings had carried his ancestors into the air, until unknowable forces determined that body armor would serve him better than flight, and he marched forth wedded to the earth, wings imprisoned. He arrived in our time as a being in need of a fable to explain his punishment, his gift.

My attention was on the rock, and then—mindful of the drop—in the seams and miniature shelves just over the edge where the beetle had seemed to crawl, when I noticed the mud-rimmed soles of Will's hiking boots planted just beside me at the cusp of the world. Above the shoes, he stood looking off toward the sun as if on solid earth. His face was a golden red in the light. His loose thermal shirt and the sweater knotted around his hips rippled in a gust of wind.

"Will," I said, "I've got it, I remember." I was assailed by a drunken vertigo, though my ear was nearly on the rock. He didn't hear me. Probably a good thing, since all that had returned to me of Tennyson's poem was its final line.

6

AND LIKE A THUNDERBOLT HE FALLS

Ringed with the azure world, he stands; he falls. *Finis*. But Tennyson does not watch the eagle long enough. Or, trusting, he does not need to keep watching to know the fall is not the end of the story. The wings open, of course. The eagle flies.

Dr. Parrish didn't much care for my interpretation of the poem, offered up in the first short response paper he assigned us. Though he gave me an A-, he wrote *But why does the eagle have hands? Without the title, would you think it was a bird?*

Rockhaven, our Camelot, did not wish to summon us across the chapel lawn with carillon bells to commemorate the one-year anniversary of a student's death. It would have preferred the day not be remembered at all, and certainly not with a sea of candlelight beneath the tower at two a.m., while the carillon played, let's say, "Blackbird," and then, with a dying fall, held silence. We who knew our lost member through our various slender ties to him sympathized with the institutional resistance. Whether this one of us had died by choice or accident, he had done so by following an impulse others of us might have dangerously shared, one we hesitated to celebrate.

To be, at the least, drunk and reckless in high places.

On Roark's Steep, amid our picnic haze, I felt certain Will had mentioned plans to mark the day. "I'll wear the gown," he said. "I'll do it." His voice strained with insistence, as if to appease me, and looking back, I wondered if he'd been saying it to Brantley. But on Monday, when I offered him my company at the tower, he told me he was driving home to Buckhead for the day. It couldn't be helped. He had to see his doctor.

Among my friends, there was talk of gathering Tuesday evening at nine, the date of his death if far past the hour. But the Gammas had planned their own ceremony, held in secret away from the rest of us, and by their muzzy expressions at Tuesday breakfast I could assume the time they had chosen. From what little they would divulge, I deduced that the rituals had been confined to the house and hadn't involved Polk Tower, where overnight the south transept steps had sprouted a cluster of candles, some with folded notes weighted beneath, interspersed with flowers and crosses and one stuffed bear, a meager version of the memorial we'd all been too stunned to think of the year before. Most of us gave it only a solemn glance as we passed, but all day people would stop there, usually alone, and stoop to add a candle, or relight the ones blown out by the wind, or sit on the stone bench (dedicated to a departed priest of decades before) that happened to face the spot. By dinner our commemorative energy seemed drained, and by the next morning the candles and notes had been cleared away. *Et in arcadia ego*, sure, but now please return to feeling immortal within these gates.

And most of us preferred to do so, with Homecoming mere days away. The previous year, it had fallen a week later on the calendar, but still, none of us had been in the mood for parties. The alums had proceeded with their university-hosted fetes, the pre-game parade in which they lined up behind the banners of reunion classes dwindling in number and increasing in age and soon all male, all the way back to one relic wheeled in to represent the class of 1911, celebrating his seventy-fifth reunion with no one. Our players took the field. But for the rest of us, Party Weekend had been all but canceled, subdued if not sober, and no one was eager to see that turn into a tradition.

To that end, fliers collaged every wall and filled SPO boxes for themed frat parties starting Thursday and packing the weekend, the biggest ones co-sponsored by sororities. On Saturday night the university itself meant to aid our revival with kegs and a bonfire and a real band, Uncle Green, at Lake Patterson. My sorority, besides co-sponsoring an open sangria party called "South of the Border," was throwing an invite-only Friday red-eye breakfast, the kind of event planned to ensure that one did not lose one's buzz between Thursday night and Friday afternoon, as well as to allow those with Friday classes the hard-core boozer's pleasure of donning shades and attending class while sipping bloodies from specially printed stadium cups. The red-eye was one of those nutty debutante concoctions for which, once we'd committed to printing cups, one was required to dress and ask a date. I'd been on inactive status for three semesters, unable to pay my dues, so I took no part in the planning, but I was still invited, nay, obliged to attend, lest I look like too much of a jerk.

Being in a sorority meant that much of my life at Rockhaven was threaded with the anguish of borrowing a dress and locating a date. For the red-eye, I'd winnowed my escort options to precisely two, at which instant, in our campus game of musical dates, the needle scratched from the groove. Jenny grabbed Pem, Carolyn snapped up Vince, and I was left chairless, moaning to Jenny as we collected trays in the dining hall that maybe I just wouldn't go.

She sighed, with what I could stretch to imagine as remorse for stealing Pem. "Ask Dex."

"Oh. Okay," I said, shorthand for *We all know you're hot for Dex and only asked Pem out of sudden-onset anxiety of looking too interested, so let's not pretend you won't sulk for days if your beloved escorts your best friend while calling her* m'love *in that sexy brogue.*

"No, really," she said.

Some boy's hands clapped over my eyes. "Um...Jonathan?" I tried, enough evidence in the hands, the posture, and the gesture itself to tell me it was him or Quinn. And if it was Quinn, my guessing Jonathan would nettle him as he deserved.

It was Jonathan, holding up the salad bar line to embrace me while pouring off a flood of wounded, smitten sincerity. "I've missed you. Where have you been? You're ignoring me!"

"I would never," I said, my chin mashed to his chest. "In fact, I was just going to see if you wanted to come with me to my dumb red-eye on Friday."

"Really?" he said. "I'd love to."

For this sweetness I could thank Will, since on my own it wasn't possible to ignore Jonathan enough to move his switch, let alone transform him into a reasonable date. My usual rule was "Never ask Jonathan Pitts to anything"—doing so opened a fifty/fifty chance he'd turn into a granite slab of cold and even hostile impenetrability from the hour he was asked until a week after the event. But now I was wishing I had something better than a red-eye to use him on. Assuming he could maintain for two days, he'd make an excellent impression on the chilly faction of my sorority, since he was beautiful to look upon, charming when he needed to be, and few of them were likely to know what an utter headcase he was.

When he arrived Friday morning, though, it was my own mood that had crumpled. He knocked, holding uncalled-for rosebuds just opening, and told me my dress was pretty. In fact, my shapeless black-and-red sweater dress was hideous and cheap-looking, because it was my own.

I said, "Liar. Let's not go."

"Lordy, stop it," said Sarah Beth, in the midst of snugging a fat plaid bow into her hair. "A boy in a tie bought flowers."

"I'll go to *your* red-eye," I grumbled. She was in jeans and a Pi Alpha sweatshirt and looked ridiculously adorable. In her crowd "fancy" meant adding a hair bow.

"Good luck with that," she said brightly to Jonathan on her way out.

He reexamined the dress. "Didn't you wear that to a formal once?"

"Don't remind me." Somehow in the mirror it had seemed to me classy and svelte, passable for a formal, and no one said a contradictory word. But after that, girls leapt to save me from myself before I could ask, until I got in the habit of knowing who was my size, asking to borrow. Since few of them would wear a dress a second time, fresh options abounded. But this time I hadn't found the energy to let it be known in the enemy territory of my dorm that I was in need once again.

Jonathan extracted the tall cup of a past formal from a stack on my bookshelf and took the roses from my hand. "It's not like you to want to skip a party."

"Can we skip the whole weekend? I can't face it." A good portion of my self-pity stemmed from the oppression of girls, the understanding that I'd never have real female friends and would forever be pelted with their active suspicious sniping enmity simply because I had real friendships with boys. *Real*, that is, for a girl; less real than what they reserved for each other. But I couldn't talk to Jonathan about that. I said, "Last weekend I drank, let's say, dangerously too much. That I didn't fall off a cliff is a miracle. And then…Brantley, I guess. The memorial."

"Yeah. Rough week." He sat beside me and handed me the cup.

I stroked a fleshy petal, brought the roses to my nose. "I know you guys did something, but I feel like the whole day just passed by. I don't know what I expected."

Answers, maybe. An angel to appear on the rampart of the bell tower and trumpet the truth. The light of heaven to fall on Will, who wasn't there.

Jonathan gave me a chiding headshake. "You didn't even like him."

I had to acknowledge this. But in my growing attachment to Will I had entered a strangely unoccupied middle ground between him and the Gammas, these separate pieces of Brantley's life. No one else stood here, with access to both. The position seemed to carry some responsibility, to Brantley himself or only to the mystery, to that part of the mystery that began to feel vaguely like a danger to still-living people who were dear to me. But responsibility to uncover or conceal? My protective instinct had been trained toward the latter.

"I could have liked him." I laid my head on Jonathan's shoulder. "I was going to. Then I ran out of time." My regret over the missed chance of our friendship ached especially when I held Brantley up to Jonathan—this boy who had such capacity to repel people if they met him at the wrong moment. "Did you like him?"

"Sometimes." He leaned his head against mine. "He was funny. I'm sorry I didn't know him better." This was more than he'd been willing to share with me yet. As I went ticking over my questions for one he might answer, he said, "Leah. Do you think all this concern of yours is really about Brantley? Or is it about someone else who died who you're trying not to think about?"

His meaning lost me for several seconds, his target so distant from where I'd aimed. "Jonathan. Do not psychoanalyze me, please. I will beat you with these beautiful flowers. Which totally look like vaginas, so let's talk about *your* issues."

He laughed, then squashed me in a violent hug. "Let's just go to this thing. It'll be fine once you're there." He released me. "Tiffany will be there, right?"

"Tiffany Dean?" A friend of Ainsley Rowell's, though one of the nicer ones.

He squinted as if at a menu, considering whether he was hungry and what for. "I might have a crush on her."

At "South of the Border," I sat with Mitzi and Carolyn on the front steps of the Delta Lambda house, sharing cigarettes and scoping out the crowd. Mitzi, who had brought Steve to the red-eye but now declared herself single, was a crimson-painted grin under the awning of a mammoth blue sombrero.

The yard teemed with people. Over half looked like Imports, lured up the mountain from hours away by the legend of Party Weekend.

"There's my imaginary boyfriend," Carolyn said. "Brown shirt, five o'clock. *Yum.*"

"Oh, there's mine," Mitzi said. "Scott Wyatt. Come to mama. Y'all wait here, I'm gonna go down on him." We all giggled.

"Let's get Leah laid," Carolyn said. "Imports are freebies, since they're gone in two days. Pick a yummy one, girl, we'll hook you up."

"I wish." I tried mentally undressing a few yard boys. "All of these are gross and boring," I said, not wanting to confess that boys I didn't already love were invisible to my libido. The last stranger I'd found compelling at a distance had been freshman Will Oliver.

"What you need is a change of perspective." Mitzi hefted her sombrero onto my head.

Half blind in its vast shade, I felt my way inside to the sangria, mixed in a row of coolers with spouts. Mitzi was right: the sombrero compelled a festive mood. I stretched my arms full-length past its horizon to top off my cup, and next I was turned by the brim to face some slim, toned male torso in a green Henley shirt, snaps half open below the throat. *Yum.* For a panicky moment, I was sure Mitzi and Carolyn had spotted my type in the pack of Imports and sent him my way.

That stranger's face, dipping under my hat's brim to remark on the handy privacy it made, would have been less alarming than Quinn's. I slid the sombrero to the back of my head, restoring the light. He pursed his mouth in half a pout. "So are you planning to go on forever not speaking to me?"

"I haven't seen you to not speak to you." I turned to wander clear of the sangria path, the equator of my hat thunking people on all sides. "Oops, sorry," I said. "Lo siento. Perdóname, señor, muchacha."

"No problemo," some guy answered. Madonna's "La Isla Bonita" played over the speakers, and I danced and sang a little as I walked.

Quinn reappeared before the hat's flank. "Can we talk?"

"I don't know, can we?" On tiptoes, I gave a cartoonishly goofy wave across the room to Vince and Jonathan.

"Now you're being a bitch."

I wasn't trying to be. I was only distracted, unready to think about him, not caring too much for that swoony thrum I'd gotten from his unpersoned torso either. I faced him with a look of weary maternal disappointment. "Now you're being a person I'm not speaking to."

"Oh, bite my ass. Here's your rescue party, m'lady." Vince and Jonathan had caught the cue to ford the crowd and save me, all smiles, their attention on me. When I turned far enough to check around my blinders, Quinn was gone.

"Is he being an asshole?" Vince asked.

"He's fine. Just sitting in time-out for a while."

"Are my eyes working?" Jonathan nodded to the stage, which was full of Delts and some of my sisters dancing in a sloppy conga line to Menudo.

Vince scoffed. "Um, yeah, spaz, they do that in the dining hall. Have you never noticed?"

"Oh," I said, slow to catch that they meant not the dancers but the Renaissance club members, a subset of the theater crowd, seated at one edge of the stage. They were all Greek like the rest of us but of the lowest echelons for each gender, a kind of untouchable caste to some. You got used to guys invoking *Beta Nu,* the sorority, as shorthand to say a girl was a dog, no matter that many were prettier than any number of KPs. Their sector in the dining hall was often lively enough to draw attention, people wearing random pieces of costume, hugging and dancing and sitting in laps. On the stage, a boy perched on a boy's lap, a girl on a girl's. One boy played with the other's hair. The girls kissed on the mouth repeatedly, smiling. The foursome sat close, often turning to kiss or touch one of the other pair. Another girl danced up and stooped to tuck paper flowers into the hair of all four.

I had seen this sort of display before and never thought much about it. I suppose I assumed they were just goofing around, being provocative theater-types. Jonathan had surely taken in some similar if less-obvious show in the past, and after a moment's befuddlement he turned his back. "Okay, then," he said, more cheery than disgusted. "Just keep the AIDS out of the sangria, please." And on he sailed to the next crass topic of humor.

Only now did it occur to me: if rumor was going to point to "the gay fraternity," wasn't this it? But the answer was simple, known before I could form the question. This bunch didn't count. So far down the social ladder they weren't even on it, they were free to be and do what they pleased. Even a knee-jerk homophobe like Jonathan Pitts, ready to drum up a mob against any whiff of gayness in his own fraternity, could watch two boys all but make out and shrug it off. *It's just them.*

Across the room, Quinn had a pledge in a headlock, snarling something lewd-looking into his ear as two other actives looked on. I thought of Emery on the bridge in Bishop's Walk, telling me Brantley had *wanted people to be open about it*. And Emery, of all people, had sounded appalled. He had sounded like any sane Rockhaven student who cared a jot for his social standing, facing a threat to it so unreasonable it could only be banished.

Saturday afternoon, hungover and trying to read Shakespeare, I could hear the loudspeaker from the football field through my window. The day was cold and brilliant, the leaves beginning to crunch underfoot, and the echo of faraway words I could not quite discern brought the ache of knowing happy people gathered somewhere without me. Not that I cared for football. Amidst the debauchery of the weekend, I was always glad for the few hours' respite provided by the game. Strange to think that for many of us, the game was the central event. *You have to go to the football games.* This was the only thing I could remember my mother saying on the subject of college. She'd attended Ole Miss for a year, maybe part of another, I wasn't sure. I suppose I never asked. I was a teenager before I realized she'd left when she became pregnant with me.

"No more that thane of Cawdor shall deceive our bosom interest: go pronounce his present death..."

But I couldn't concentrate on *Macbeth*, and a nap was likely to put me out for the night. A walk would perk me up, I thought, and instead of jeans I grabbed my long black wool skirt—suitable, I supposed, for somebody's backwoods grandma. The boys, when I wore it, called me Hester Prynne, Goody Woodbine. But it was warm, and a football game, in case I felt moved to stop by, was one of those dress occasions.

The road ran close to the end zone, easy from there to see the scoreboard. Rockhaven was up by ten. Along the home fence, more than a dozen Dragoons lined up in their tartan like beefy Catholic school girls, bellowing, fists pumping in unison—so far from my type, my station, and yet, *yum*. Hairy-legged boys in kilts, the embodiment of masculinity, surpassing somehow even the players on the field in their own extreme costumes. Of the crowd, the Dragoons were the most visible element, and as I looked for Will among them, it occurred to me that Shakespeare as much as my mother had summoned me here.

I wandered in through the groundlings, keeping a little distance. At the far end of the Dragoon line, the brushy blond head of Dalton Gibbs rose above the others, most of whom I'd never spoken to though I knew a few names. Behind them, Anna Vaughn stood in the bleachers, in a snug-belted pink wool coat. One petite hand in a cream-colored glove made exuberant gestures to attend her speech and the other wrapped a cup. Like most of the dressed and drinking crowd, she looked toward the field only when something happened.

Will would be nearby, then. The day before, he'd caught me at lunch to make sure trail riding was canceled, and had confided that he and Anna Vaughn might try a reconciliation, on rather remarkable terms: "She has to be nice to you," he said. "She has to understand I'm going to have friends apart from her." It was hard not to wonder if he'd acquiesced to her in order to make this bargain on my behalf. Still, I wasn't eager to be spotted lurking in her territory. I marked where her sisters stood and tried to keep the bodies of others between us. My thrift-store peacoat had a heavy, draping hood, which I lifted—though whether this helped to conceal me was a toss-up. I was now in head-to-toe black down to my lace-up granny shoes and would have looked less weird in jeans.

Nearer to me along the fence, a Dragoon cluster formed, chanting. At its center, one had another in a headlock to drain a flask down his throat. I could see the edge of a swallowing jaw, a hand strapped across a forehead. When the chanting crested and the drinker was released, it was Will who stumbled loose. Two of his laughing brethren steadied him at the elbows and parked him back on the fence between them. His back to me, I counted those dirty blond curls as I had in Parrish's English, observed his bare legs in wool socks and hiking boots that buckled and swayed, straightened again. He would, I knew, have friends apart from me and mine as well. Here, he was with his kind, a creature I had nothing to do with, could not save.

After watching the game for a few minutes, I was ready to leave when a husky voice close by said, "Girl looks like a witch." Two Dragoons were passing toward the exit with Will sandwiched between them, head hanging toward the grass. The one who had spoken looked straight at me and said, "Hey, you a witch?"

I froze, then realized that his speaking to me, noticing me, was only a moment's drunken wit between the two, not meant for my response. "Maybe she's Amish," said the other, not caring what I was. But Will's head bobbed up like a cork.

"Hey, hey, leggo." He veered my way, then pulled loose of one cap-
tor to seize hold of my hand. "Leah!" He stared hard into my hood, his
face a lopsided mask of fear, then awe, then delight. "These are boot
police. You all go none in, it's fried."

Or something like that—he was slurring. I glanced at the boot police
to see if they would clarify. They gave each other a narrow look and fell
into conversation behind their hands, freeing Will to take both of mine.
"Hi, drunkie!" I said, wincing with worry as he attempted to balance
against me that we'd both hit the ground. His breath was monstrous.

"You sound like Brantley." He spit the words with a force like anger,
but instantly looked ready to cry. Or vomit. "Let's just go. Done with
this shit."

My sobriety surely enhanced my sense of his drunkenness, but I'd
never seen him sloppy. Odds on, he had not told the boys who were
force-feeding him booze what sort of pills he'd gone home to refill. But
for this thought, I might have handed him back over to the boot police,
who were far better equipped than I to keep him upright. "Can you
stand up?" I asked him, parent to toddler. "Do you really want to go?"

Breathing hard and slow into my face, he nodded. His legs straightened, his back straightened. I could feel him concentrating, trying very
hard, the way he did with me sometimes, to follow my instructions. But
why? Why did he even see me there, seek me out, let alone listen to me,
among so many friends? "Well, then, screw you all," I muttered—to the
Dragoons, Anna Vaughn, the football team, the entire Homecoming
crowd. *Looks like he's mine now.* Even these people, to whom I was as
invisible as the Renaissance club was to my set, would have to see the
evidence before them.

Will, somehow, was in range of vertical with an arm around me. One
of the boot police, half amused and half weirded out, said, "Witch put
a hex on him." The other one handed me Will's car key and pointed.

The road was chock-a-block with parked cars, which Will used for
balance, but it was slow going. Fetched up against a tan Mercedes to
rest, he hauled me into crutch position and we stood like that. To brace
against his weight, my hands were at his sternum and back. Even with
him wasted beyond sexiness, I felt the privilege, so like being serenaded
in my bedroom freshman year. How few Rockhaven girls got to put
their hands where mine were now? Was there any boy on the mountain
even half as beautiful?

He peered down at me and sputtered a laugh. "You're not my date."

"Oh yes," I groaned. "I suppose you ditched your date. Fantastic." I patted his ribcage. "Good going, drunkie."

This was thoughtless banality, an attempt to keep the mood light, but he let out a kind of wail and grabbed me tighter. "I'm sorry," he mumbled, his mouth mashed sidelong against my scalp. "God, I'm sorry." His voice came cracked and breathy as if he were crying.

"Hey, okay. Easy there." A bit alarmed, I shook him straighter. No telling, this drunk, if he was reacting to me or just off on some addled jag of his own. "Will." I waited as he blinked tears, gathered himself, began to look semi-cogent. "Why are you sorry? What did you do?"

He shook his head. "I can't. *Told* you."

"You didn't tell me," I said as casually as I could. "You said I sounded like Brantley. Why did you say that?"

He stared off toward the trees. "Classified," he said—so slurred I had to make him repeat it. "I can't tell you that. I can't tell why or what or…anyone, any thing, ever."

I rubbed the center of his chest as if testing reflex on a coma patient. "Why can't you? Who says?" He pressed his lips shut, done talking.

We soldiered on. As I spotted the Saab a few cars ahead, Will took a lurching step and tumbled head first into the roadside ditch. He went down so fast that for a panicky moment it seemed deep, and I thought he'd break his neck. But the fall had been a neat one, and I found him on all fours in soft grass, one hand planted to the wrist in a leafy trickle of stream into which he vomited, and went on vomiting.

I stooped to rub his back. "So is it true," I asked, "y'all don't wear anything under those kilts?"

I didn't expect him to answer. "That's it, there you go," I said, and all the other things you say to sick people who are going to feel better soon.

Nothing like a few bucket-loads of bourbon puke to put me in the teetotaling mood, even for the last night of Party Weekend. My plan had been to stay in with my charge for the evening, make sure he was okay. But he'd emptied himself enough to get into bed under his own power, and once he'd passed out I knew he wouldn't be rousing for small talk or further imbibing anytime soon. Besides, I expected Anna Vaughn or some Dragoon squadron to show up every second I lingered. So I left him to his dreams and crept out.

Later, after finding the dining hall all but deserted and Benson too, I walked out to the Lake Patterson bonfire—Vince would be there if no one else, since he owned the Uncle Green album and had played it for me more than once. The stage was lit in blue-green hues, the lakeshore all darkness away from the fire, and I wandered up to some of my sorority sisters, of the set that formerly hated me but had been pleasant enough at the red-eye breakfast, so maybe they were over it. "I hope you didn't think I was stealing your date," Tiffany Dean said.

She had spent fifteen minutes or so of the red-eye talking to Jonathan, while I was engrossed with Pem and Jenny. "Not at all," I said.

"I mean, you're just friends, right?"

"Very serious, long-term friends. You're welcome to him."

"He is *cute*," she confided behind her cup. "But. I dunno, kind of odd?"

I smiled. I hadn't overheard much of their conversation, but I knew for damn sure she hadn't seen anything yet. "Actually," I said, "he's great." What other answer was there, when being forced to picture that wingnut with a real girlfriend made me want to swallow arsenic?

Vince stood in the crowd at the stage, but I headed up the hill past him, to where Dex and Pem perched on a picnic table near the woods. Quinn stood with a group farther back toward the trees, and I sent him a smile. I'd been mulling that *Can we talk?* in the middle of the Delta Lambda house—very unlike Quinn, to approach me with a direct, human request, or ever when I was alone. Probably he'd come with something to say about Brantley, if only to make clear why I should quit prying. And curiosity aside, my day with Will, all the inarticulate grief welling up through his stupor, had made a spat with Quinn feel trifling. I didn't want to take a chance on losing a friend, not when one of us could die tomorrow, as Jonathan would say.

At the picnic table I said to Dex and Pem, "Y'all haven't seen Anna Vaughn Whitacre around here, have you?"

"Oh god," Pem said. "What have you done now?"

I gave them the capsule version.

"I'm afraid we're going to have to ask you to hide out in some other group of people," Dex said.

"His friends are trying to kill him!" I declared—a piece of hyperbole until I heard myself say it. Could his friends be *trying* to kill him? What had Will said about Dalton Gibbs and leverage? Nothing I had witnessed fell outside the Rockhaven code of manly conduct and reckless consumption, but suddenly I was sputtering mad. "I hope Anna Vaughn does say something to me. Because I have something to…say to her!"

"Easy, tiger," Dex said. "Who got him hammered last weekend on a cliff?"

Pem snorted. "And then spent the whole time talking about 'let's fly like eagles.'"

"Fall like eagles," Dex corrected.

"I did not! And, okay, we drank a little, but that was a sweet baby buzz compared to what I saw today. I think we were all forming sentences."

Before I saw him coming, Jonathan hurtled onto the table and tried to crawl inside my coat. "Let me in there. I'm frozen."

"Hey, sugarpie." His hair smelled of woodsmoke, his breath of beer. Dex and Pem took their leave. "Bonfire not working for you? Tiffany's right over there, you know?"

"I saw." He buried his nose in my neck. I would have taken this for display aimed her way except that she couldn't have seen his cold hands sneak up under my sweater, adhere to my skin.

"Be good," I warned him.

He grinned, eyes shut under my chin. "I'm always good."

When I glanced up, Quinn stood before us, hands pocketed in his bomber jacket, a sardonic eyebrow raised at Jonathan. "You two need some privacy?"

Too soon to ditch Jonathan; I patted the table on my other side. "Come sit here and see if you can do your impression of a gentleman."

Quinn looked skeptical. He tipped a high-noon gaze to Jonathan, observed the idle play of my fingers through his hair, and slowly moved to sit without unlocking his gaze. Jonathan went on clinging like a koala on a tree trunk, eyeing Quinn over my breasts.

"I didn't mean to blow you off last night," I said lightly.

Quinn took a minute to ease back. "Does that mean I'm forgiven?"

"He actually knows how to apologize," Jonathan offered. "I'll bet he could do a nice job."

Quinn leaned in past my head to breathe into Jonathan's face. "I'll bet you'd do a nice job sucking my cock, Twitch. You want to take a walk and see?"

Not far away, Gammas were looking in our direction. I braced for anything, but Jonathan lifted only his volume.

"Please keep your faggot fantasies to yourself and apologize to the lady."

"Okay, whoa." I threw hands out to both of them before Quinn could gather himself. "You're supposed to be brothers, and…" My speech was going to be something about life's unpredictability and what might happen to any of us tomorrow, but I lost the thread and turned to Jonathan, perplexed. "The *lady*? Are you serious?"

"I'm serious that he owes you an apology and that I'm fucking tired of him." A whine crept into his voice. We'd tumbled into a private conversation while Quinn was on his feet. Here and there around us, Gammas were inching in.

"Okay, just…" I took his face in my hands. "Don't try to teach him manners. Not on my account. Let me talk to him."

Vince, dusting his palms together, stepped up and parked an ambassadorial foot on the bench before us. "Hey, folks. What's shaking?"

"Nothing much. Little drama. Will you take him?" I squeezed Jonathan's shoulder. "You two go get a refill at the keg."

Jonathan acquiesced without a word, went off with Vince into the shadows that flickered about the bonfire. I waved Quinn back in. Pem, Dex, and the hovering others pretended to turn back to their business.

Quinn stood before the table, arms crossed, fidgety inside a nearly visible fog of testosterone. Lately he'd seemed more wound up than usual, complaining of a headache at least once a week. By report, he'd gone begging at the house to get punched on more than one occasion.

"Now," I said, "try to say something to me like I'm a person and your brothers aren't standing right there looking at us."

"I'm sorry. I really am." He sat meekly on the bench at my feet, sincere until he couldn't stand it anymore. "Please bestow the blessing of your forgiveness upon me." I did so, releasing him for a woe-is-me sigh. He collapsed limp over the table, his face cradled on one arm and mashed into my thigh. "God, what a shitty day."

I nudged him an inch off. "Believe me, you can't top mine, so don't try."

He cracked an assessing eye to peer up at me. "Can we get out of here, please? Truckstop. I'll buy you a biscuit."

"Hmm." While none of my friends would be thrilled at the idea, getting Quinn clear of them for the night was probably wise, even if all he wanted was to make them watch us leave together. We had never actually gone anywhere before, just the two of us. "Maybe. If I can drive."

"Uh, that's a no." He hopped up, offered me a hand I declined. "It's a Porsche, darlin'. And a stick."

"So? I drove Will Oliver's Saab just today, *darlin'*. It lived."

As we walked off with our hands in our pockets, I had no real worries over what some of his brothers would assume, what Quinn might tell them later to help with the sensory details. He wouldn't do that to me, I was sure. What I wondered instead was whether anyone watching us go, anyone at all in the frat other than Emery, harbored a doubt that Quinn had limits. That he would not in any way force himself on me; that he could not have murdered Brantley. It was strange to imagine that my own faith in him might be stronger than any one of theirs.

The Porsche's throaty vroom at start-up was drowned by the stereo blast of baritone-voiced electronica: Depeche Mode, "Fly on the Windscreen." Quinn popped out the cassette. "Aw, I like that song," I said, turning us out of the Lake Patterson lot, first gear, second. He hesitated, then poked the tape back in, lowered the volume.

My few blocks in the Saab had given me no chance to notice how the engine responded. All my attention had gone to keep from stalling it. In the Porsche, I tried the tricks the Saab had liked, mashing the clutch hard to the floor, light and steady on the accelerator, and three times in a row we purred away from a stop with hardly a jolt.

If the storm-dark seduction issuing from the speakers could be translated into a look, it might be the one I was getting from the passenger seat. I wouldn't have picked him for a Depeche Mode fan, since it fell in with the music—New Order, Yaz—I liked to dance to at the house with Emery or Vince, a turn of the evening that tended to elicit groaning objections from Quinn. *This shit again?* and next: *Gawd, Gavin, what is that you are doing? You're hurting my eyes.*

"Awfully quiet over there," I said. "Aren't you going to warn me not to ride the clutch?"

He chuckled. "No, I think I'll just let you ride what you want, girl. Go nuts."

On the main road, I gave it more gas than was strictly legal, enough to feel the engine jump up under us and surge. "You know, in riding competitions," I said, "we ride school horses. We draw from a hat, you ride whatever horse you draw. School horses are like plain old cars, kind of pokey, need a ton of leg, usually a crop." I tapped the roof as we sped through the domain gates, half ready to bet Quinn wouldn't. But he did. "A show horse though, say a warmblood jumper, that's a whole different machine. You feel it right away. You just think *go* and the horse is all collected up and moving under you."

I glanced over at his peculiar silence, the roadside lights passing over his watchful face. *"That was a long story about horses,"* I said for him in his snide drawl. The Smiths were playing now, Joan of Arc with flames climbing up toward her Walkman, me and Quinn alone in a space capsule hurtling into our headlights with our angels on strings.

"Mixtape?" I asked.

"Yeah. How'd you learn to drive a stick?"

"My mother's boyfriend." I would have left it at that, but he gave me silence to fill. One night the previous spring, Quinn and I had bonded over that Rockhaven novelty, our broken homes. It was one of those boozy late-hour conversations, tricky to recall in its details, except that his parents' divorce had been rancorous enough that he'd been "shipped off" for two years of boarding school. Now and then, in larger groups, he alluded to our bonded status: no one understood Quinn's special pain, except maybe Leah. But in truth we knew little of each other's lives, and since then I'd sensed his hesitance to share too much, or worse, inquire too much about mine, for fear my sad story would overshadow his.

"She never kept them very long," I said, "but now and then there'd be some guy with notions of being my dad. This one, Eddie, he taught me to drive on a stick when I turned fifteen. Then they broke up. But he'd still come by after, to finish my lessons."

I trailed off in a way that brought a grunt of disdain. *"Lessons.* And what all did that involve?"

I shook my head. I hadn't thought of Eddie in a long time. "Nothing like that. Just remembering he was at my mom's funeral. He'd always wanted to get back together with her. But he was too nice for her, I guess." Though not an especially emotional disclosure for me, this felt more personal than what I usually allowed Quinn, and I stepped back toward firmer ground. "He said no one who learns on an automatic really knows how to drive."

"Sounds like my dad. Automatics are for pussies." Mentions of his father always carried this note of resentment. "He has to have a new Porsche every three years. This is a leftover."

"Poor you. Who's this?"

The song was minimalist, all thwanging bass and echoed staccato male singer, only slightly familiar.

"Joy Division. You've heard it before."

I turned into the Truckstop lot, thinking he must be right though I couldn't recall when or where. It would be a bleak choice for the Gamma house. "I like it," I said uncertainly. "Can I borrow this tape?"

"No. It's Brantley's."

I turned off the ignition, dropping us into silence. Quinn didn't move. "I had it when he died. I just kept it. Sometimes I can't stand it, switch to something else. But lately it just plays in here all the time. Round and around and around." With a glance to check my reaction, he opened his door.

I'd been unable to draw much from my own memory on how close he'd been with Brantley and when. But in replaying those flashes of rage, at me and others—*don't you fucking say his name!*—I had surmised they were based in grief. Or I wanted them to be. Entering the bright-lit shack by the door he held for me, gentleman-like, I wondered if I was stepping into a ruse.

It was early enough that the Truckstop was only half full, more truckers than Rockhaven students sipping coffee, smoking, dunking biscuits in gravy. That would change the instant the Party Weekend taps began to dry. Quinn headed for a four-top near the back, while I went to the bathroom. In the mirror my face was flushed and bright, my hair a fetching array of unfrizzed curls—prettier than usual, or I was only buzzed from the day's adventures. I felt powerful, a girl who hexed Dragoons and drove imported sports cars and caused boys to fight over her.

A biscuit, at forty cents, was my usual Truckstop order, grilled cheese when I was feeling rich. Hungry people with pocket money went straight for the chicken strips with biscuits and white pepper gravy. By the time I got to the table, Quinn had put in two orders, and the waitress was setting down coffee for him, a sweet tea for me.

"The lady will have the chicken?" I mocked, taking the seat opposite. "Will she not?"

I couldn't argue. "And sweet tea. How did you know?"

"I pay attention now and then." His expression was a Quinn standard, halfway between choirboy and *the better to eat you with, my dear.*

I unwrapped my straw and took a long sip. "I wish I'd seen you earlier this week. I don't like you thinking we're having a quarrel."

"A *quarrel*." He emptied a sugar packet into his coffee and clacked his spoon about. "That's adorable. You're adorable. Really, I mean that." When he gathered his energies and kept his anger in check, he could maintain this enigma for quite a while. It was usually for other girls, though. If I was getting it now, maybe he was regretting what he'd said in the car.

"Joy Division," I said. "Ian Curtis. Committed suicide."

"So you do know them."

"I remember hearing that somewhere." I set my chin on my knuckles, examined his face until he looked away. "Brantley was into them?"

"Doesn't make him suicidal, if that's your angle." With a restless shuffle of shoulders, he scanned the room behind me, and I gave him silence to fill. "He was into all kinds of things. Started me listening to The Smiths. He got very involved, intense, about his obsessions. Knew a ton about music. Fucking waste." He sipped his coffee, the vein pulsing high along the bone of his forehead. No anger, though, that I could see. He seemed to want to speak.

"Is that tape all you have of his?"

He shook his head, thinking. "I have his pledge pin, for some reason. Not sure how. A shirt. Bunch of photographs, some other things."

The waitress brought our piled plates with two bowls of pasty speckled gravy and a third brimming with jelly and butter packets. As we unwrapped silverware and broke biscuits, I asked, "Why do you listen to that tape so much? It must be like having a ghost in the car."

"Exorcism, maybe. For the music. Like when you take one word and just repeat it over and over until it becomes meaningless?"

"Does that work?"

"No. But I'll wear out the tape and it will break any day. *Then* it'll be gone."

I ate, feeling an ache of sadness for the impermanence of this thing Brantley had made. *Gone.* Even this moment—Quinn and me at a Truckstop table, reaching toward each other in some tentative way— already gone, passing into the next.

"So." He dragged chicken through his gravy, took a bite, and spoke around it. "Nancy Drew. What exactly are you digging for? Will Oliver sent you to investigate?"

I'd been braced for the shift in his tone, but not for the reference to Will. "No. I told you, I'm just thinking about him lately."

"Because of Will. You got the hots for *Will fucking Oliver.* That's so sad. I mean, you've seen yourself, right?"

Given the callus I'd grown by listening to him trash the looks of a dozen girls all prettier than me, that slap smarted more than it should have. I'd hoped being chosen his confidante had meant I was cute enough by his standards, or at least exempt from critique. His eyes, though, were sparking with anger and swimming in guilt. By the time he made himself look at me, I had the upper hand. "Go on, what else? Just so you know, if you want to make me hate you, it's not going to be that easy."

He swallowed, looked down. I tried not to soften too much, though Quinn's remorse, a rare and rather lurid creature, affected me more than most. "Want to know why that is?" I said. "One is I think you're about seventy-eight percent bullshit." I dragged chicken through gravy and bit.

"What's two?"

"Well. I once decided to hate a boy who said something mean to me, and he fell off a bell tower and died. So. You reap the benefit of my past mistakes."

His eyes lifted to the fluorescent panel above us. "I'm sorry. Honestly. I'm a jerk and I suck."

"You are and you do."

"But you love me."

"Yeah, hold *that* over my head."

He twisted his mouth dubiously askew, never sure if he wanted to take this love idea seriously or make a joke of it. "What did Brantley say to you?" There was a soft curiosity in the question. His reflex was to lash out, guard the gate, but he seemed past it and returned to his need to talk.

"I'm not telling you that." Tables nearby began to acquire familiar faces, though no one yet who would take much notice of us. "So you and him. Pretty close?"

He went back to eating. "We had our moments. Won't say he never pissed me off."

"I heard you had some kind of falling out."

"No." The word was clipped, frosty. He put down his chicken.

"Look, some douche says that, he's got no idea what brotherhood is. There's no 'falling out.' You fight, you make up. You settle your issues. You're in it." He shook his head, some qualifier being raked over in there as he went back to his food.

I thought of something Vince or Pem had told me freshman year— about Brantley, not Quinn—that he was one of "the ones" who got overly invested in the concept of fraternity. To me, they all seemed so; but most of my friends, I was assured, weren't about to sink their whole identities into it or rank it with God and country.

"It's hard," I observed, "if someone dies and maybe you haven't finished settling your issues."

"I wouldn't know." He tried to rest on that claim, press it into place, but it wouldn't go. "It wasn't just me, you know. Brantley pushed a lot of people's buttons. Now and then, someone like that needs to be set down…" Sorrow passed over his face like a wave, vanished. "But then it's done. We're good as new." He sat back and fiddled with his napkin. "Now you want to know if I killed him, right?"

I was genuinely surprised—if the question was out there, I hadn't thought we were close to it. Before I could form a denial, he said in a fervid rush, "God, why are you looking at me like that? Fine, I've done some shitty things. But brothers… We love each other, we hate each other. I—" He shut his eyes, swallowed, began again. "I've wanted to kill him. I'd give anything to bring him back. That's how it goes."

The starkness of this admission was more than I was ready for, and I blinked, processing. Quinn said lightly, "Well, Jesus, don't cry about it."

I pressed at each eye with a thumb. *I'd give anything to bring him back*: a fiercer grief lurked there than I'd heard anyone else express yet. Unless it was Will, who just couldn't get the words out.

"You didn't want to kill him." I would make it true if necessary. In a sidelong way, I felt the too-familiar danger that I might gentle this boy into speaking, and then he might tell me something I didn't want to hear. "Not really," I said. "You wouldn't."

But to be the one who might have wished the fall…

"You think you know that about me." His expression betrayed nothing but curiosity, a faint pleasure.

"Yes. I do."

Ripping chicken, he said warmly, "You know, sometimes I feel like you're the only person I can really talk to. No one else gets me."

I smiled, only a little. Anyone whose guard didn't creep up when Quinn dumped a can of sincerity straight onto the table hadn't been paying attention. "Why did he die? You all must have an idea about it."

"I have an idea. Or two."

"Not suicide."

He shook his head. "Not our Bran. And what about you? Do *you* have any ideas?"

His pointedness threw me. "No," I said, without enough force. *Why would I know anything?* Casual denial should have been easy. But what ideas I had, embryonic as they were, clustered too closely around Will. In all my careful handling of Quinn, I hadn't wondered whether he was engaged in his own investigation.

A professorial pity shaded his gaze. "Here's your problem, Leah. You take on these, let's say, intimacies. You trust people you shouldn't. You get all wound up in their little universe, and you want to believe it's all secretly good and beautiful and worthy of your loyalty, no matter how fucked up it might look." He broke a biscuit and buttered half. "Then, there was Brantley's problem. Well, two problems. Care to guess?"

I shook my head.

"I have a hunch you could." He studied me as if he were really wondering. All that saved me with Quinn was his suspicion now and then that I might be smarter than he was. "Okay. For free. One I just told you. He was obsessive about his interests. Two is he had a big fucking mouth."

I felt the buzz of truth, my hands shaking on the table, because I did know this. This was Brantley. "His interests being what?"

"Like I said, all kinds. But toward the end there were a couple I'd have to call *fixations.*" He was enjoying himself now. "Did you know he was a conspiracy buff?"

"Quinn, c'mon. What fixations?"

He steepled his fingertips and drummed them together, evil-scientist style. "Patience, m'dear. I might tell you if you're good, but not tonight. No matter how good you are." His tongue slipped up to suck his teeth. "It's the kind of thing I really ought to keep to myself. Or maybe we figure out what you're willing to trade for it."

"I know you're joking," I said. I didn't—far from it. I was trying to pretend his eyes hadn't just gone dead cold and slid down my collar. "But can we please go back to talking like people? Like friends?"

He made a sad clown face. "But so boring."

"Seventy-eight percent bullshit," I said. "Keep trying."

"Yeah, well. Watch out for the other twenty-two."

Whatever his intentions, I sensed we were at an impasse, and little frogs who went looking for a way around the obvious were the ones who got stung. I pretended interest in my food while picking my way backward over all he'd said for the thread I'd dropped, the question I could pin him with. But the one that came jumped back from earlier in the night. "What was that with Jonathan anyway? Why are you picking fights?"

"*Me?*" If I'd meant to knock him off his game, this did the job like a two-by-four.

"Yes, you. Purposefully."

"He started it!" He slumped and scowled. "Go ask him what it was. That self-righteous tool. I'm sorry, I know he's your baby, god knows why. The hair, is that what you like? The pretty eyes? Fucking *girl* lips." He mimed a smack, then spoke what I was about to. "*Ease up, Quinn.* God, if anyone needs to ease up, it's him. I've never met a tighter ass in all my days, fucking virgin."

"Yeah, *enough*." This was worse than he'd been giving me on Steve.

He relaxed. "Well, see. Brotherhood. Love, hate. Sometimes more of one than the other."

He paid the check. I returned his car key without argument, exhausted, ready to be in bed hours ago. The tape that would soon break played "This Big Hush," Shriekback's bass-whispered underwater lullaby, an eerie beauty that slowed every light passing over Quinn's face. *What sort of trade?* I pictured asking there in the car, even knowing the way he'd turn to look at me. One question, and I'd be one step out on the ledge, less safe.

7

SLEEP WHERE WE FALL

In freshman year, I took zoology with Dr. Crocker, one of the few female members of the faculty. She was a specialist in prosimians and, though it was somewhat outside the course parameters, she hauled us all off on a field trip to the Duke Primate Center, which housed the country's most extensive collection of lemurs. A small woman with close-cut hair and rhinestone glasses, she exuded a breathless enthusiasm for her work that I got wound up in, until I was sure, for a month or two, that my own calling would be in zoology, even primate studies. Or, if I could overcome my morbid dread of physics enough to stick with vet school, I might specialize in zoo medicine.

For the most part, it took serious trouble to make me brave enough to visit a professor's office. While I was the kind of student who never let a morsel of professorial wisdom go unappreciated, uncollected in a notebook, class time gave me enough to ponder. Who was I, with my inane little question, to interrupt the mind on its elevated plane after hours? In most classes I felt out of my depth and feared a one-on-one meeting would show too much the mistake made in choosing me for a Harper. Vast numbers of my non-scholarship-holding classmates appeared far smarter than I was, in class and out. I counted myself only more diligent, one who struggled daily while people like Jonathan or Pem breezed, studying here and there, and still-ungowned closet geniuses like Quinn didn't crack a book until breakfast before an exam.

Dr. Crocker, though, struck me as approachable. She was younger than most of the male faculty, mid-forties, and more recently hired. She followed Rockhaven form and addressed her students as *mister* or *miss*, but seemed to do it wryly, as if she found such formality amusing. She used the overlong sleeves of her gown to erase the chalkboard, turning them to tatters the color of weak tea. I hoped I could be special to her, that she could be my mentor, and I began to show up at her office hours once or more a week. Generally I could find a class-related question to justify the visit, but soon we were talking about her graduate work at

Duke, her travels to Madagascar and the Comoro Islands. Back in my dorm, I began to devise independent studies I might propose for her to direct, then a senior honors thesis for which she might be moved to take me, her star pupil, to Madagascar on a bit of excess grant money. I pictured the two of us trekking through forests with our guide, cooking beans over a fire beside tents. But I hadn't polished any of my proposals enough to feel confident in revealing them, and when I asked about the possibility of an independent study with her, she said, "Wait until you're a junior, at least."

As my drop-ins became more about my larger interest in the field, I found it natural enough to bring in pieces of context from my personal life, about the riding team or my work-study job or my friends. When the topic of spring break arose—a bunch of us were going to Pem's beach house on Tybee Island—I even mentioned, hesitantly, the fact that I didn't have a real home to go to, that for holidays if I didn't tag along with friends, I'd have to catch a ride off the message board to Knoxville to stay with my aunt.

One day, while we were walking together across campus—she must have excused herself to go home and I followed after her—I blathered some piece of appreciation for our not-yet-existing relationship. "It's really wonderful to have a woman I can talk to as a mentor. I've always wanted that kind of professor who really cares about her students as people, about their lives—"

"Miss Gavin, let me stop you right there." We stood under a great spreading oak by the faculty lot, she half a head shorter than me. "You may have mistaken me for someone else. People make assumptions of this sort more often than they should, and surely there are female professors in this world who are nurturing and maternal. But being a woman does not make me one of them. That's just not what I signed on for, getting into this profession. I'm happy to talk to you about the course, or lemurs, or graduate studies when the time comes. But I'm not your friend. I can't be your mother. I'm sorry to be blunt, but I want you to understand how it is."

Looking back on this episode, I felt more embarrassed over my own naked need than resentful of the rejection. Had I really chased after her and just *said* all that, straight out? I'd told the story a few times, but in abbreviated form, simplifying my end of it considerably. It became an anecdote about the hazards of seeking closer relationships with professors. At first, I thought it was about the inherent perils of doing so with a woman. Years later, I realized a subtle distinction: it was about women at Rockhaven and the mentor deficit, poor me with no one and poor Dr. Crocker accosted every semester by some new crop of needy girls. And, of course, she was right: a mentor was probably not precisely what I was after in the first place. Privately, at the time, the story of Dr. Crocker became my own personal object lesson on not wearing your heart on your sleeve.

It came back to me one afternoon when Will and I were in his room, having returned to reading Shakespeare aloud together, and he mentioned he might be having dinner that week with our professor, Dr. Macintosh. "What?" I choked. "Why?" All I could picture was the white-maned lion of Shakespeare sitting Will down for a stern talk about the C on his last paper. But over dinner?

Will shrugged. "He might not be there. It's at Edelman's house."

"Edelman? You take art classes too?"

"I took a drawing class once," Will said, as if this were a strange question, unrelated to having dinner at the man's home. "He has students over from time to time. It's no big deal. Though when Macintosh comes he'll sometimes bring Myron Bell along."

My mouth dropped. Myron Bell was our single local celebrity, an elderly emeritus professor and former poet laureate who had been a force in the Southern Agrarian movement back in the 1930s. I had seen him only once, when he came to give a once-a-decade reading on campus. He moved slowly with a cane, and word was he didn't often leave his house in Alston Cove.

"Will Oliver, please tell me you are kidding." Clearly he was not. "How often exactly are you having dinner with *Myron Bell*?"

"It's just been a couple times." Casually, then, he listed the other professors, about eight of them, with whom he'd had dinner, or coffee, or played poker. Part of this, he qualified, was related to the Dragoons. "A drinking club thing. A bunch of professors are members."

"Dr. Macintosh and Myron Bell? Is that drinking club stuff?"

"No. That's just…Edelman."

I told him I had never been invited to a professor's house for dinner, that it would never cross my mind to hope for such. I related my condensed version of attempting to get personal with Dr. Crocker. Boiling up under all of this was my indignation that I was a Harper scholar, a gownsman since sophomore year, an A-average student, and Will was none of these. Quite beside the point that an invitation to dine with a professor would intimidate me so much I might look for a way to decline.

Will said, "You should come."

"Excuse me?"

"Edelman won't care. He likes a few extras showing up. Though"— this seemed to occur to him only as he spoke—"the guest list tends to be pretty heavy on guys. In fact, I'm not sure I've ever seen a female in attendance."

I laughed. "And you think if you bring me, he won't care?"

"No, wait, there was a girl once…" He puzzled over this, then said with finality, "You're coming. He's told me before to bring along a friend or two. If he forgot to specify a gender, I guess that will be his problem."

Dubious as this prospect sounded, he convinced me, or I convinced myself, that if I was lacking in opportunities I should take the ones I could get. And what person, arriving at the side of Will Oliver, would not be welcome anywhere? In the end I felt more emboldened than if I'd received a personal summons to attend without him. Only as I was walking over that evening to meet Will at Stirling, just ahead of people on their way to the dining hall, did I realize I was about to accompany him to a function that had managed to exclude Anna Vaughn Whitacre.

According to Will, she was not enraged over my stealing her Home-coming date from under her nose and putting him to bed; it seemed she'd not been aware of my involvement until later. But he'd been sparing with the particulars. And what would he know anyway of the nuances of Anna Vaughn's moods—especially now that he'd charged her with being nice to me?

"Was she mad you drank so much?" I asked, when he called the next day to apologize.

"Probably. But she pretends not. She's just glad if I don't kill myself, I guess." I wasn't sure if he heard himself the way I did, his voice weary and soft through the line. "Party Weekend," he added with ironic cheer, making light, the way we all did often enough. While our rarefied drink-ing etiquette called for excess combined with decorum (you should *always* have one more, yet remain poised enough to kiss the bishop's ring), it was also true that if you managed to graduate without a single story of your own that involved puking somewhere inappropriate or the hilarious/awful things you had slurred or done in a blackout, recorded by your friends for posterity, you had missed something of the full Rockhaven experience. I didn't try reporting to him all he'd slurred. None of it made enough sense to me to turn into a question, and then I was leery of the sense it might make to him.

Dr. Edelman, professor of studio art and art history, lived at the bluff edge north of Alston Point, in a fieldstone house that seemed to merge with rock shelves and hang over the sunset. He met Will and me at the door with a cocktail in hand, peering at us over large tortoiseshell glasses: an attractive, long-nosed, bearish man with shaggy dark hair, wearing an apron that invited us to Kiss the Cook. "Willard, my dear." He spoke with a comical pointedness.

Will shuddered. "Do not call me that."

"You've brought more of that Bordeaux, I'll bet. Come, come." He ushered us into the entrance hall, taking the bottle Will handed him and setting it onto an antique-looking hall table backed by a gilt-framed mirror. "And who might *this* be?"

Will tipped a hand toward me. "Leah Gavin, another accursed English major. Leah, the esteemed Dr. Lucius Edelman, of the Paris Edelmans."

Dr. Edelman gave Will an eyeroll as he set his cocktail beside the wine, then swiped the apron before taking my hand in both of his. "Delighted, my dear, and please call me Lucius if you can stand to. I'm not all that esteemed." As he was speaking, Will moved on into the house. Dr. Edelman—I doubted I could call him Lucius, hoped I could skip calling him anything—watched him go with consternation, confiding to me in the droll tone that seemed his habit, "He knows where the *bar* is."

We followed Will out to a glassed-in porch, aglow with the pink and orange of sunset, the bar to one side and to the other a sitting area occupied by two young men who lounged tieless in khakis and sockless boat shoes, same as Will had worn. I knew them vaguely, Charles Guillory and Davis Cheek, nearer to Will's set than mine except that Charles was a Harper scholar: both were handsome, athletic, upstanding types. Dr. Edelman murmured our introductions, then hollered past my shoulder to Will, who stood behind the bar with a cobalt bottle hoisted. "Put that down! As Charles and I have already discussed at length, it is not gin *season*."

"Doesn't apply to martinis." Will pulled stemmed glasses up onto the bar, squinting at Edelman's drink. "What is that thing, a greyhound?" Not waiting for an answer, he called to the others, "What are y'all drinking?"

"Rusty nails," Davis answered.

"Who are you, my grandfather?" Will lifted eyebrows brightly at me. "Leah"—he held forth one L-shaped hand as a partial frame—"I'm picturing you with a Manhattan. Gotta use these glasses and I'm not allowed gin. Plus he's got smoked cherries. They're kind of excellent."

"He'll end up a *bar*tender." Edelman ushered me to a seat beside Charles and Davis, while Will poured booze into a silver shaker. "Can't you just see it, little tux vest in some classy hotel? Now, my dear, I trust you eat meat. I can't feed these cretins anything but cow or they mutiny."

By the time Will brought our drinks, Edelman had excused himself to the kitchen. Will and Davis fell into talk of the lacrosse team—Davis played, Will had quit after freshman year—including me as they could. Did I follow the team at all? I admitted I'd never seen a game, something it would not have occurred to me to regret until now. The Manhattan's flavor was intense, unfamiliar—I could smell the smoke of the cherry resting prettily in the crook of the glass—and I had never before drunk from such a stylish container. It was, I decided, exceedingly pleasant to hold and sip from while chatting with fine young gentlemen in sockless boat shoes about sports that for all I knew involved riding a unicorn but must have been played at places like Choate.

Charles mentioned an eight a.m. sophomore art history class we had shared, taught by a notoriously monotone professor, in which every meeting had consisted of looking at slides in the dark: tracing chiaroscuro patterns through folds of rich cloth, comparing the manner of representing the Christ child's halo between the Medieval and the Renaissance. "I could *not* stay awake in there," Charles said. "Yet here I am, an art history major." Davis, I assumed, must be one too. But no, he said, poli sci.

Edelman emerged with an empty paper grocery sack. "Can I impose upon a couple of you dears to fetch us some salad before the light fails."

Will stood to receive the bag and said to me, "Come along. Part of the adventure."

"Let's all go," Charles said, in a farcically jovial manner that required a British accent. The four of us trooped outside into the soft gray chill of dusk. We passed through a rickety wire gate into a garden, stepping through loose soil over half a dozen planted rows, down to a section of low, dense, leafy plants, some green, some red shading to blackish purple. "Get a variety," Will told me. "Just rip off leaves from around the outside that look good."

We all squatted and ripped, tossed leaves into the bag. "I just have no idea what we're doing," I said to Will, giddy. "This is nuts." I had never picked food from a garden, never met a piece of lettuce that hadn't been cracked off a head of iceberg or romaine.

Will said, "Just wait."

Inside, Dr. Macintosh was helping Myron Bell into a chair in the sitting area. Davis delivered the bag of leaves to the kitchen, while Will and then Charles shook hands with the newcomers, addressing them both as *sir*. Will introduced me to Myron Bell, who said, "Oh!" and blinked at me, as if someone had brought a pony into the room. "Forgive me if I don't stand, my dear," he said in a flustered way, taking my hand between his.

"It's a great pleasure to meet you, sir," I said.

"And of course, Dr. Macintosh, you know Leah from our class," Will reminded him.

"I certainly do," he said, in a surprisingly convincing way. "How nice to see you." I could never be sure my professors knew who I was, especially the ones like Dr. Macintosh who handed back papers and exams by calling our names, placing each into whatever hand came forward. I had not been in a class yet that required me to speak. Discussion was not the Rockhaven way, and no one complained, since ninety percent of professors had more scintillating wisdom to impart on their subjects than could fit into an hour. We tested our own feeble thoughts in papers. The professors who now and then called on a student for response, like Macintosh, tended to single out only those who appeared inattentive or hungover. While Will took the man's drink order—"One of those, my good sir," he said, waving a finger at the dregs of my Manhattan—I wondered if our professor had picked on Will all those times in class out of a kind of playfulness beneath my notice.

"It is so civilized here," Dr. Macintosh said to me as we took seats. I considered him the Platonic ideal of "the Rockhaven professor," our famously stern, dignified, and passionate professor of Shakespeare, who resembled an elder statesman or Beethoven, his hair dense and white as a powdered wig. We got smiles from him in class, but only when the text moved him. Now he was slouching, almost goofy with mirth. "Mr. Bell, aren't you glad we came?"

"Yes, I've been feeling under the weather, you know," Mr. Bell said loudly and distinctly to Charles and me. He was in his nineties, I knew. "But Richard shows up and reminds me of the salutary effects of an Edelman event."

I had read much of Myron Bell's poetry as well as his book of criticism, *The Devil's Lighthouse*, and earlier in the day, in case he might turn up, I'd reviewed my books, combing for a comment or question I would not feel too foolish speaking. I sensed now that we were meant to be social, not studious; but, I argued with myself, the man could die tomorrow, and I'd forever be the idiot who could have asked him something of import! Will saved me from the dilemma by calling me to bring our glasses.

"Extras," he said, rattling the shaker. "Top us off before we're obliged to switch to wine." He plucked the cherry from his own glass and ate it. A new Manhattan glowed on the bar top beside a tulip-shaped glass of milky green liquid over ice. "Pernod," Will told me. "Edelman stocks it for Mr. Bell."

I extracted my own fleshy, near-black cherry before the shaker arrived. "Make mine very petite, please, my dear." Will poured me a generous half and emptied the rest into his own, dropped in two more cherries while I ate the first. The smoke flavor was pronounced, followed by sweet. "Interesting."

"Brantley liked those," Will said. His face was soft, unreadable, as he closed the cherry jar and set it away.

"He came here?"

"Once or twice. His kind of scene." Will settled a hand on the stem of Macintosh's glass, gazing into its amber light, then nodded to the Pernod with a hint of a smile. "Why don't you carry that one to Mr. Bell?"

Dinner was laid in a formal dining room closed in red velvet curtains: disks of rare, herb-crusted beef; roasted fingerlike roots from the garden I would not have guessed were sweet potatoes; beets, also from the garden, roasted and tossed with pecans and fluffy white dollops of what I had to be told was goat cheese. I'd finished my first helping before I caught on that it was literally cheese from a goat. *Stop asking questions that make you sound like a hick*, I would have told myself if less buzzed, but instead I announced perkily to the table, "I will now stop asking questions that make me sound like a hick." The party was talkative, free with laughter, and everyone seemed to find this a hoot. There were fat sourdough rolls with salty, pale spheres of butter (goat butter?) and the salad we had picked, tossed with a champagne vinaigrette, dried cranberries, more toasted pecans. Edelman presided over one end of the table and Myron Bell the other, while I was placed between Will and Davis. Bottles of red wine were passed around to fill the glasses that sparkled beside the cocktails we had all carried in. Will and Davis got into a dispute, settled by Myron Bell, over which of the wines paired better with the beef and should therefore be the one poured into my glass.

In response to compliments, Edelman insisted all this sumptuousness was quite simple. "Listen to him," sneered Dr. Macintosh, across from me, his mouth half full. "Miss Gavin, for your benefit, let me assure you that you are eating one of the finer meals to be had in this world."

While I consumed what must have been an impolite amount, far past comfort, the conversation ping-ponged around me. Though its rhythm faltered somewhat in deference to Mr. Bell, who was hard of hearing and slow to contribute, it leapt from gardening to opera to the Sorbonne to High Church theology, Edelman and Macintosh taking the lead and the boys chiming in often on what was clearly a shared context of people and events. It was all I could do to look alert and offer a word or question now and then.

Edelman made fleeting references to a Parisian woman, Solange, who seemed to be an artist or collector or importer, who hated the curtains, who was engaged in various dealings with the Paris art world, and who, yes, was presently there ("again!") because she went stir-crazy on our mountain. "Oh!" I said finally. "You have a wife?"

"You're surprised?" Edelman said, round-eyed with delight.

"I don't believe in her either," Charles said to me in dry aside, and got whacked with Edelman's napkin.

"I don't know," I said, flustered, surely blushing. "It just didn't occur to me." The gathering was so male, with Edelman in charge of the kitchen and garden, that I had attached maleness to the glassware and the drinking porch and the entire lavishly furnished house. I felt welcomed into it as some kind of alien specimen, an entertaining fancy of Will's, and from the first step over the doorsill had harbored no illusions I would be asked to return. But perhaps I began with the assumption that most of my professors, Macintosh included, were bachelors, cohabiting with nothing but books and perhaps a roaming Labrador, simply because they never mentioned wives.

At dessert, a flan on which I could only nibble, Myron Bell's head nodded toward his plate. "I hate to run," Dr. Macintosh said, rising, "but I'd better get Mr. Bell back home." I had gathered by now through the slimmest references that Dr. Macintosh did indeed have a wife of his own, and that Myron Bell had a live-in nurse.

Dinner had lasted nearly two hours. The boys and I carried plates to the kitchen, where we wrapped and put away the food and, at Edelman's insistence, left the dirty plates and cookware piled. "Verna," he said, "will be by in the morning." To me, he added, "I don't need much help around here, but I simply can't face the kitchen after one of these soirees."

I expected the rest of us would make our departure shortly, but instead we adjourned to a lamp-lit den where the boys arranged themselves on furniture of fawn-colored suede. I took a spot on a short sofa with Will. Brandy and port had been laid out on a silver tray with glasses, and Will poured me one of each to try. Chet Baker crooned from the stereo. Cigars, now, perhaps? If other ladies were present, I imagined I would be shuttled off to join them in a separate room—if not the kitchen, then the parlor for tea and what…petit fours? But when Edelman brought forth a wooden box of smoking materials, he pulled from it a plastic bag packed densely with pot.

He passed the bag to the boys, who each inhaled from it like connoisseurs. "Leah," Edelman said, "I hope you won't object if we indulge a little. And join us, of course, if you care to at all."

I looked at Will, whose brow lifted with mischief. "I told him you were cool."

Marijuana was a sort of exotic vice on our mountain; I had yet to witness a single person light up. According to alums I met in later years, it had been plentiful a decade earlier, but a change of administration in the early eighties had shifted the whole culture, to the extent that when classmates of mine mentioned their pre-college or off-campus sampling of any sort of narcotic, they were not boasting but sheepish.

The stoners collected in a single fraternity, Zeta Nu, to which I was sure neither Charles nor Davis belonged. I had once tried a few hits in high school, sitting around a tack room with some show hunter people, but it hadn't affected me. Since then, having communed with enough cigarette smokers, I was aware I had learned to inhale.

While I attempted to compose myself in the bearing of a person who thought getting stoned with a professor was no big deal, Edelman rolled a pair of fat joints. When Will passed the first into my hand, I managed to suck back the smoke with what felt like a proper burn in my lungs and minimal girly coughing. Will slumped in an attitude of decadence, his brandy snifter cupped in one hand against his belly, and I mirrored him with my own, grooving to Chet. Each time a joint arrived, I managed to not blurt out my lack of familiarity, but Will wasn't fooled. After my fourth hit, he said, "Let that sit," and stopped passing to me.

Edelman lounged in an armchair perpendicular to Will, his eyes half closed, a faint, sensual purse in his mouth as he examined his guests. "I beg you, look at the two of them."

"Two of who?" I asked.

"Why you, my dear, and Will, together in this light, you look like something out of Rossetti." Edelman chewed his lower lip in avid study that settled on Will.

I laughed, beginning to feel my high pin me into my cushioned corner. "Him, sure. Not me."

"You're the image of Beatrix," Edelman declared, abrupt, having none of it. I glanced at my art history classmate Charles, who squinted back doubtfully through a haze of smoke, while Edelman continued. "But *this* one, my god. What creature is he? Adonis."

"Narcissus," Charles cracked, getting a snicker from Davis but a rise neither from Will, who leaned his beautiful face on one hand, eyes half-lidded in the lamplight, nor from Edelman, who said, "Oh, precisely. Though Narcissus would let me *draw* him."

"You need to grow your hair a little longer," I said to Will. "Doesn't he?"

Edelman either ignored the query or was caught in indecision about it. "This boy refuses to sit for me. He has been torturing me for years. One session, Will, I beg you. You can keep all your clothes."

"No," Will said, smiling to himself, not quite with us, nor of us.

"These two as well."

Edelman waggled a pair of fingers at Davis and Charles.

"Watch out, Leah," Davis said, his eyes closed. "He uses nude models for drawing classes. One male and one female. He'll try to recruit you."

"Damn, I sort of want to draw him too," Charles said, examining Will in the clinical manner of a guy who'd never been visited with a homoerotic thought. That all of us who had chosen Rockhaven were uncommonly susceptible to beauty was a given; it might as well have been inscribed in Latin on the cornerstone.

"I can't move my arms," I said. "What Greek myth am I in? I'm turning to stone. Or growing roots. I'm not kidding. I'm stuck to the sofa. Am I talking?"

By the end of the evening, I had risen back out of that pleasant pit, so that all my limbs were functioning again as Will drove me home, past midnight. I felt dozy and sated, trying to recall which painting was Rossetti's Beatrix. I'd have to look it up in the library, since I'd sold my art history textbook back to the bookstore. Though it strained credulity that someone might look at me and see a pre-Raphaelite painting, I knew for certain that Anna Vaughn Whitacre, the prettiest girl at Rockhaven, even lounging on that sofa beside Will, would never have called to mind such a picture. She was too prim and tidy; there was nothing sexy about her. In such light, she and Will were discordant images.

In the night shadows of the driver's seat, he was fully human again. I teased, "Why don't you let Dr. Edelman draw you? Do your part for art."

He chuckled. "I don't even think he's serious about it. He just talks. His way of being social."

"So is he...you know, um...?"

"He does enjoy entertaining the male students. As far as I know, that's the extent of it."

Even this bare suggestion of unsanctioned desire carried an interesting shock, baroque in its possibilities. As if all night some door to ancient Greece had been waiting beneath the den's rug to be opened, not by us but by a convergence of planets, the right combination of guests, a more potent drug. The idea of Edelman mooning over boys in his own home horrified me less, strangely, than if I'd learned any Rockhaven professor at all had ever felt similar stirrings for a female student. The latter failing hardly seemed possible, beyond the rectitude of our elder gentlemen who were charged with not just educating but protecting us. The boys needed only educating.

I leaned back in my seat as we turned up University Avenue. "I cannot believe I just got stoned with a professor. I had no idea you were such a bad influence, Will Oliver. Oh my god!" I grabbed his sleeve. "Do you get stoned with Myron Bell?"

He laughed. "No. Not so far."

"Dr. Macintosh?"

"No." The Saab pulled up to stop at Benson. Will turned to face me. "You know you can't tell anyone about it, of course. Not a word. Not to anyone, ever. You're a vault, right? I spoke for you."

"Yes," I said, concentrating. "Of course. I'm a vault."

When I crept into the dark of our room, Sarah Beth turned in her bed with a rustle of covers. "Where have you been, young lady? Edelman's all this time? Lordy, what smells like a Grateful Dead concert?"

"No, we," I faltered, "went somewhere later." I realized that in my years at Rockhaven I'd grown rusty at lying on the spot, if I'd ever been much good at it.

"You little burnout. Are you stoned?"

"No!" I hissed. "Go back to sleep."

8

What's Left to Hold On To

Most afternoons that week, I had to forgo studying with Will in order to ride. The coming weekend was our final equestrian team trip for the semester, two back-to-back meets in Kentucky just before the Thanksgiving break, and I needed saddle time if I was going to be worth anything. Often, a competition looming, I considered dropping out, hating to miss a full weekend on campus. But I was the sole rider representing the team at novice level, and at present, getting off the mountain to clear my head seemed prudent.

More than a week had gone by since our Truckstop trip, and I hadn't spoken to Quinn. Just seeing him in the distance made me nervous. But our friendship, such as it was, had always happened on his approach, and I knew his games well enough not to change that now.

The day before I left for Kentucky, he showed up at the stables. I was in a pre-meet tutorial, out in the arena with our coach and two other riders. My horse of the day, a black-bay draft cross called Ajax, was heavy on the forehand, a puller, and a pain in the ass to keep collected. We were working on flying lead changes, and I didn't see that we had an audience until I'd finished my turn at the figure-eight cross, badly, the coach yelling at me through it to keep my fool *heels down* and *shoulders back* and *what lead are you in now, Leah?* Ajax, in a counter-canter, was steaming on into battle on giant hooves like he was pulling the cannon, and I hauled him back to a trot at the arena's far end, where Quinn hung on the fence. No one else at Rockhaven had that brown bomber, the leather scuffed all to hell like the toes of the motorcycle boots he wore everywhere in winter. I coveted that jacket and still needed three looks to realize it was him.

"Big horse you got there," he said, once I had wrestled Ajax into proximity.

"What are you doing here?" Gasping from the ride, I was too surprised to settle on whether to be amused or flattered or annoyed.

"Spectating." He tipped his head to frankly examine my ass in the saddle. "Don't your friends come out to watch you ride?"

"Not a single one, ever, in the history of all time." At the arena's far end, my coach glared, arms akimbo, the other two riders halted beside her. I had ten seconds to make the horse pick up a left lead before I got yelled at again. "Or *their* friends either. I can't even talk. You need to go."

"All right." He made no move to leave. "You got me kind of turned on the other night, all that talk about horses moving under you. Thought I'd come out and see for myself."

I took that in, bewildered. "You're incorrigible," I said. Then, because it was one of his easier tricks, I gathered up Ajax and put him straight from the halt into a left-lead canter. When I looked back from the arena's other end, Quinn was gone.

In the soporific back row of the riding team van, where on road trips I camped by habit on claims I meant to study, I had always been prone to drift off in unproductive reverie starring some boy. Same story in the Dixons' spare bedroom, where just after the Kentucky trip I spent my third Thanksgiving holiday, feeling guilty for hiding away to study while neighbors and extended family dropped by—always a party at Jenny's house. I should have been social instead of reading the same lines a dozen times, distracted by gothically elaborate erotic scenarios. Especially if the boy in them had somehow become Quinn.

Jenny was exceptionally pleasant company for the holiday, since Dex had agreed to be her date to our sorority's winter formal. This good fortune granted her extra capacity for interest in my life, and I had to take care with what I divulged. About Dr. Edelman's dinner party, for instance: just enough that she talked me into considering Charles Guillory as a formal date. The idea had appeal. Bringing in new blood, besides fun in itself, would exempt me from the usual battle with half my sisters over the same small pool of escorts. Charles struck me as the sort of gentleman who would provide a first-rate evening, stress-free if I could keep him from imagining I had a crush.

But even simpler would be Emery. I needed simple.

Trying not to think about Quinn only intensified the problem. Trying not to talk about him to Jenny compelled me to stumble through pale recreations of scenes between us—the Truckstop, the stables— that couldn't achieve full sense when I left Brantley out. Creepy, she conceded. But wasn't creepy Quinn's specialty?

True, but I couldn't explain how his recent escalations struck me as something else: background noise, a diversion, analog to the same maneuvers all of us at Rockhaven were obliged to go through in order to block our friends from too much access to our true obsessions. And whatever Quinn was diverting me around surely came back to Brantley.

The Thursday after the Thanksgiving holiday marked the end of classes for most of us, so the Gammas bucked up for a pre-weekend keg. At ten o'clock, Jenny picked me up at the library, ultra-sweet ever since Dex—from politeness, perhaps—had turned around and asked her to his own formal. I had snagged Emery for ours, so at least I was set for a fun and stress-free date, maybe with enough snarky distraction for me to survive a night spent wondering if Jenny and Dex might upend all our lives with coupledom. Let alone having to watch Jonathan in a tux with Tiffany Dean.

In the Gamma living room, Motown was playing and the shaggers had cleared a dance floor. With the osmosis of competitive males in small spaces, over half the Gammas had mastered this dance, which they all called the shag though it was more of a local swing variant. Once a few of them got going, the rest would start grabbing girls right and left, throwing them into pretzels and turns and dips. Hoping to sneak past to the beer before some forlorn sophomore spotted me, I had started in through the crowded furniture when someone grabbed me by the wrist and yanked. But instead of being rubber-banded onto the dance floor—shagging tended to be violent this way; a girl was lucky to keep her arms in their sockets—I was snapped in the opposite direction, back over a chair arm and square into the lap of Quinn.

He guffawed with open-mouthed astonishment. It must have been an accident, to catch me at that instant of perfect imbalance that allowed him to flip me to him like a yo-yo. A few of his buddies, seated nearby, hooted appreciation as he closed his arms around me, a soft trap. "Aren't you a light little thing. I can just throw you around."

The fury I should have felt at being manhandled was delayed and distant, a train idling in some far-off station. Could it be so wrong, to melt a little into the arms of the devil? But with Vince and Jonathan looking on from the far wall, I tried to appear stern, control my gasping into Quinn's over-close face. "Okay. Bravo. Now help me up so I don't have to scream."

He answered in French, a coddling and agreeable sentence or two I couldn't guess a word of. "But let's talk later. I've got things." He boosted me up.

Not glancing at another person, I concentrated on navigating with poise out to the cool dark of the balcony. "Beer me," I said to Emery, who held the keg tap. "Goddamn, beer me twice. Did you see that?" He hadn't, and I didn't have the energy to describe it.

"You look like my mom with the hot flashes," he teased, while I sucked night air and fanned myself with my shirt. "You got the change of life? Is it the vapors?"

"Let's see who's in the kitchen." I took him by the arm for a shield and steered him inside, inserting us into a fresh crowd.

Within ten minutes, Jonathan arrived, sounding far too serious for the situation. "Can I talk to you?"

I went with him to the downstairs room, where he found a pillowed corner of the fireplace hearth for us to sit. He took hold of my hand, struggling with the eye contact until I grew alarmed that he was about to tell me someone had died. Someone was dying. Jonathan was dying. Jonathan had a brain tumor, which would make so much sense… "I want to ask you to be my date to the formal."

"Um. What?"

He took a breath. "Will you go to the Gamma formal with me?"

"Honey, I heard you. Aren't you asking Tiffany?" Once she'd asked him to ours, the reverse seemed a given.

"I'm asking you."

Despite the work we all went through at Rockhaven to disguise our true intents, I'd figured out by now a thing or two about formal dates. Girls asked friends, willy-nilly, all the time. And boys were happy to accept an invitation as such. But boys did not ask friends. Except in particular cases—laziness, lack of specific interest, the unavailability of the true object of desire—if a boy asked you to a formal, you were either the girl he was pursuing, or you were some girl at least two levels out of his league, one he didn't have a chance with but who would impress his friends, look gorgeous in pictures, and be nice enough to accept. Needless to say, I was neither of these two people.

I made prayer hands under my nose. "Is this about Quinn?"

"Are you *going* with him? Leah—"

"Oh my god no. Are you insane? Why would you think that?" His shoulders slumped, and I said, laughing, "First of all, he would never ask me."

"Oh, really? Now who's insane?"

"So, what then? You're going to run over here and ask me first?"

He rubbed his knees in rhythmic thrusts, one of his tics when stressed. Every pair of corduroys he owned, like the coffee-colored ones he wore now, was worn smooth at the knees. "Obviously, I...don't have a say in who you go with. And I'm fine with anyone else. Anyone." I set my hands lightly over his, stilling them, and he lifted his eyes. "Just not him. Please don't."

As much as I wanted to kiss him for the concern, this was painful. I could concede Quinn wouldn't kick me out of bed. Quinn wanted to have sex with most girls, maybe especially me. As a conquest, I rated pretty high on his scale. But a formal date was an almost opposite category: someone he wanted to be seen with. How to explain this to Jonathan?

"He won't ask me," I repeated. "He'll ask, I don't know, some random KP babe like he always does."

"He did that *once*—"

"He thinks I'm a dog. He basically said it to my face."

I hadn't meant to voice this, wanted to snatch it back. But at least it would serve as a bleak debate-ender—one I prayed Jonathan would immediately forget before it began to eat away at his attachment to me like acid. He rolled his eyes. "*No one* thinks you're a dog, Leah, and by the way, that's a tactic." He smiled grimly at my surprise. "You can add that to your list of Quinn Cooper atrocities. He says if you make a girl feel a little insecure she's an easier mark."

"That evil shit." Aghast, I wanted to stop time and go back over every word Quinn had ever said to me, or to any girl I knew, but I ran the eraser of a hand through the air. "Doesn't apply in this case, because the context was...something else. And I'm not a mark. He's knows I'm not. It's the only reason we're friends."

Jonathan sighed. "I do want to go with you. I don't care about Tiffany. I'd *rather* go with you."

For the first time since he'd started to speak, I attempted to take this in. It had been over a year since I'd last entertained the hope that this boy could feel about me the way I felt about him—just that much, never mind the twenty other obstacles that made us impossible as a couple.

But with those earnest eyes so close, I couldn't sort it through. And I knew the answer. I had to shut it down. My stupid heart didn't have a clue the mess it was asking for. "You know I'd love to go with you," I said, "but let's both see if we're sure. There's time, right?"

Not really—the formal, he reminded me, was just over a week away.

And if he really wanted to go with Tiffany, wouldn't he have asked her by now? I squelched this voice and insisted on a day. Twenty-four hours to think, and he agreed.

Nobody thinks you're a dog was ringing pleasantly in my head half an hour later as I waited for the bathroom. Meaning nobody in this house? On this campus? How were such questions decided? Quinn sidled up and stood second in line. "Hi," he said.

"Hi. You have things?" In our few conversations since the holiday he'd been almost disturbingly un-Quinn-like, all neutral topics and lack of innuendo, until I'd begun to feel he must be working his way up to something about Brantley. Down the hall behind him, people milled around the entrance and back to the kitchen. No one appeared to be monitoring us.

"I do have things."

"Catch you in a minute," I said, as a girl exited the bathroom. Quinn pushed in behind me, locked the door.

"Oh, come on, really?" Annoyed, I set about checking for mascara smudges and fluffing my hair as if he weren't there. He stood with his back to the door, looking as if he regretted the decision. I turned and sat on the counter. He wore the same green Henley shirt that fit flat to his abdomen, the sleeves rucked up his forearms. He stepped closer and his hands, accustomed when chance presented to a vise-grab at my knees, planted instead on the counter edge, one at either side of my thighs.

Bent over, eye to eye, he said, "Do you know you're driving me a little bit crazy?"

I stayed small, still, rational under the span of his arms. "I'm not doing anything like that."

"Trust me on this."

"Said the spider to the fly." I was furious at him for being such a jerk, for making me think about him too much, for being such a jerk while making me think about him, but I couldn't get any force behind my voice. I was trembling, already half caught. If he'd kissed me right then, I would have let him and then some.

Fog-clearing seconds ticked by: one to regret my hypothetical folly; two to find it strange he'd missed the opening; three for the creeping understanding that Jonathan was right. Quinn Cooper was going to ask me to the formal. He was about to ask me to the freaking goddamn Gamma formal. "Go to the formal with me," he said.

"No."

He stood back, blinking. "No, *really*. Like when I put on a tux, and you put on a pretty dress, and I buy us a bottle of, I'm guessing, Jim Beam—"

"Stoli," I said.

He smiled. "Stoli." He leaned in, his cheek's heat brushing along mine, to speak toward my ear. "And we're gonna dance and have a fantastic time."

"And then what? Go on."

"Then whatever. Up to you." He studied my expression. "Believe this, okay. I have no expectations. I'd like you to accompany me to a dance, and that is all."

Someone knocked. "Just a minute!" I called. I took hold of his head, gentle reminder that I was his buddy Gavin, and he was my pet. "Stop," I said, with a firm pause on the word, "messing with me. I mean it. I'm not your toy. Ask someone else."

Stricken, he stepped back. "Look, I don't think you're getting this. I *really* like you. All I do lately is think about you. There's no one else I want."

Part of my confusion, trying to piece together his angle, had to do with whatever he meant to tell me about Brantley, and how we had gotten from some kind of sexual *quid pro quo* to this raw and courtly sincerity. But if there was one thing I'd never given Quinn enough credit for, it was the authenticity of these emotions. I dismissed them as feigned, when most of them were only warped. When he'd been pining for Mitzi, for instance: he really felt that. His agenda came to me then on a beam of light, simple and obvious. He was telling the truth. He wanted to go to the formal with me, not with some easy lay or KP beauty queen. I was the girl in all of Rockhaven he wanted to be seen with.

It wasn't about Brantley at all. It was about driving Jonathan Pitts the rest of the way out of his mind.

"Okay, I've heard you," I said. "I'm not answering you in the bathroom. Now see if you can make a discreet exit and let me pee."

I locked the door behind him, then hurried to use the toilet before half of everyone in the house gathered outside to call my hypocrisy to account. No way could I go to a formal with Quinn. Maybe I needed to let Jonathan save me.

Quinn, I realized, had missed a crucial detail that might have saved us from this. The one he should have been picking on was Tiffany Dean. Had he spotted her in time, imposed himself there to wreck Jonathan and Tiffany before they ever had a chance, I sure wouldn't have been crying about it. I would have scolded him, and let Jonathan vent all he needed to, and watched from a little distance as Jonathan and Quinn fought and made up—*settled their issues*, as Quinn would say, those of his own creation—as Jonathan inevitably let Quinn have the girl he didn't want so much anymore, right about when Quinn would have dirtied her up enough to not want her either.

And now that girl was me. Too late to point Quinn in the right direction, and in the state he'd worked himself into, he'd be difficult to reject. Next he'd be at my door with the flowers and poetry, deaf to logic.

On our last day of Trail for the semester, an arctic cold arrived, and no one showed up other than Will and me. "We can skip it if you want," I said. "Or we can go and have a real gallop."

He wanted to try Jojo. But Jojo hated to follow, so I put him up on Ajax instead, who had a wonderful rolling gallop on the trail. On our first attempt down the firebreak road, easing from a canter into a hand gallop, Will had less trouble controlling Ajax than expected, which gave me an inspiration: we doubled back and cut over to Lake Patterson, where we could race the horses over open fields.

"Don't tell anyone we're doing this," I said, as we picked a starting line at the field's edge. Though I'd never been told not to race over these fields, I was reasonably sure I was about to cross the line of good judgment and would be in major trouble if caught. "It's dangerous," I told Will. "Mainly because I don't know the footing here. But I know you go for a risk, right?"

The sideways glance we exchanged at that, the horses dancing under us in anticipation, was the first with Will that had felt a little erotic. "And you can keep a secret," I added. "I mean, you're cool, right?"

Will laughed, his cheeks and nose flushed pink. "I'm a vault."

Gouts of fog issued from the horses' nostrils. "Ready. Set." We blasted off, thundering side by side over the soft, grassy earth. Half to shield ourselves from the icy wind of our own speed, we leaned into the horses' manes like jockeys, down around the lake, up the hill at the far side to our finish line where the trees thickened and the driveway cut through. Both horses loved to race but Jojo loved to win, and he paced Ajax until I let him know the finish line was near; then he dug into his quarter-horse roots and shot into the lead.

"That was fantastic," Will said. On loose reins we walked down through the woods, over a wooden bridge, a cool-down that completed the lake's circuit.

"God, I haven't raced like that since high school." I grinned at him. "Our end-of-class party."

I didn't think of it at the time, but this ride shared only the exhilaration of speed with the racing I'd done in the past, over known ground in the owner's company. I had never before taken such a risk with expensive animals that weren't mine, never accepted for myself so much casual privilege, and it could only have been Will's presence that brought it into imaginative reach. Will was allowed anything, I merely his lucky companion, partaking of his spoils.

We had come back to our starting line. "One more?" Will said. "You gotta give us a chance to defend our honor." Though cold numbed my fingers, toes, and face, I couldn't resist. Couldn't say no to Will. Off we went again.

Maybe I'd been craving the risk, the reckless abandon, as much as the gallop itself. But it didn't cure me, and as we were walking back barnward, Will asked what I was busy thinking about.

"Oh, it's the usual. Too many dates to the Gamma formal." It wasn't the first time in recent days Will had witnessed some of my distraction over Quinn, but I'd held back before from speaking that name. "Jonathan's one, and then, Quinn Cooper—you know him?"

"Somewhat."

"Actually, he was one of Brantley's closer friends."

Will nodded, flushed with the cold and attentive to the horse beneath him, so that I didn't detect a reaction. "Who's the lucky guy?"

"I think neither, unfortunately." I'd promised them both an answer that night and was still puzzling over it, the how and the what, exactly, I might say.

"Want to go with me?" He waited a beat, and I laughed. "No, I guess I have to take Anna Vaughn, don't I? I already asked her and all."

"To the Gamma formal?"

"Pem invited me. I think it will be good."

More reason, I thought, for me not to go. Though it felt strange, too, if Will and Anna Vaughn were poised to recover their visiting royalty status without me there to see it.

At the end of dinner I slipped into Maxon for a sandwich, then hiked over to Gilchrist to face my dates. Upstairs in Jonathan's room, only Vince was in, writing at his desk while the new Smiths album played on his turntable. It was thanks to my hours in this room that my radio show had been elevated to passable. Jonathan was down the hall somewhere, in Dex's room or Pem's.

But Vince would do. Safe to assume they'd hatched this plan together anyway, flipped a coin for which one would ask me. I sat on the cozy tartan at the foot of Vince's bed. "Will you please tell him to ask Tiffany? Or whoever. He needs to."

Astraddle his chairback, Vince assessed me. "Does that mean you're going with Quinn?"

"No. *Not* that I can't handle him, and at a formal, for god's sake. But I realize this is all a twisted game of his, and I'd best not play it."

Vince rested his chin on his arms. "Want to go with me instead?"

"Yes! That would be perfect, thanks. But I'm guessing you already have a date."

He waved a hand. "Technicality. Jonathan, too, actually."

"Get out."

"He'd already asked Tiffany." He pressed hands over his ears. "I know! So now he won't have to go through ditching her, at least."

I had to laugh. "That sweet...idiot. And you, who allowed it."

"Not always in my control."

From the stereo came *I started something*... I wondered if every time I heard The Smiths from now on I'd think of Brantley, who would never hear this song, this album, their latest and reportedly last. "Make me a tape of this?" I said. "I can't believe they broke up. Is that real?"

"That's the word. Sucks, don't it?"

I listened, delaying the inevitable, until the album ended.

Quinn lived in the Gilchrist basement, where larger, high-ceilinged rooms compensated for the bang and gurgle of pipes overhead and the persistent smell of mildew. I'd been to his room a time or two, always in the company of some group that ended up there. As juniors, top of the lottery for double rooms, he and Chip Esterhouse shared one of the few rooms on campus large enough to host a party and secluded enough to evade Rockhaven's strict quiet hours—a fact I forgot because he and Chip both seemed to spend every night at the frat. The door stood open as I approached, U2's *Joshua Tree* issuing forth as it did from so many rooms that semester. One of the Omicron jocks who lived on the hall was crossing over from another open door, four beer bottles hooked by the necks. I crept up to peek in. At least a dozen guys and a couple of girls sprawled about on sofas and chairs or stood at the stereo, Marcus and some of the other pledges among them, no one I really cared to talk to.

Chip spotted me from just inside the door. "You looking for Quinn? He's back there."

I wanted to leave but worried doing so would imply I'd come on business too serious for a party. Chip wiggled a frosted bottle of Falstaff through the doorway like a lure. "Just opened this for you, I swear. Come on in, join us." Reluctantly, I stepped in and accepted the bottle. He cocked a thumb toward Quinn's end of the long, narrow room.

A central party area was furnished with sofas and chairs, bar tables and minifridges, with the beds curtained off at opposite ends. Chip's curtain at the shallow end was open, the party spilling onto his bed, while Quinn's at the deep end was drawn. *He's back there with a girl*, I thought, checking as I went to see if Chip was setting me up, but he had turned back to his conversation.

No way to knock, I called his name, moved the curtain with a finger. He lay atop the bed covers, my freshman hallmate Polly curled up at his side. "Oops." I bit my smile at her pop-eyed horror as she whipped her hand out from under his shirt. "No, don't let me interrupt."

In a way, it was pleasant to be right, to be handed the easy reprieve and also have a reason to stand there sipping beer while he hauled himself upright and muttered something to Polly, and she hopped up to skitter out past me, cringing. Better by far to return him to his place as

pet, to resume my license to scold him for appetites I knew too well to
be wounded by.

"I can go," I said, "if you're busy thinking about me."

He rubbed his eyes. "That was nothing. She just invited herself back
here."

"No need to explain. I am not your girlfriend. And how would I
know I had the right room if there wasn't a mortified girl running out
of it?"

"Ha-ha, so funny. Will you come over here, please?"

The space was dim, the only light what penetrated the curtain, nowhere to sit but his bed where Polly had been. The walls were covered
in concert posters, formal photos, framed fraternity composites, draped
in Mardi Gras beads. Within the curtain, the room's sour air became
diluted with a spicy incense and the warm smell of his skin. "It *was*
pretty funny," I observed, stepping closer. He didn't move, slumped
against the headboard, eyes half shut. "What's wrong? Headache?"

"It's better now. I just had to lie down a minute." He reached for my
beer, helped himself to a few swallows. "You've come to give me your
answer?"

I sat on the mattress, accepted the bottle back, and drank. It felt like
one of the more intimate acts we'd ever shared. Past the curtain, the
voices of the gathering buzzed under Bono's desperate wail of *hanging
on*, a loneliness in it that stabbed me in the heart every time, like a flash
forward to graduation, like impending loss. To whatever, whoever, was
left, hold on. It made me want to stay beside him, at least until he'd
recovered. I'd expected to be stuck here a good while regardless, fend-
ing off eight kinds of counterargument with the quiet refusal I'd been
rehearsing in my head, but he didn't look ready to fight.

In fact, he looked so pliant, sapped by the headache, that I said, "I've
come to talk about Brantley."

His eyes shifted to the wall where, amid the photos, I saw Brantley's
face, and another, a cluster of Brantleys gathered at the center as if
by design. For major Greek events—shake days, formals, the fancier
parties—we hired a photographer from whom we later ordered prints,
so I'd seen many of these exact white-bordered, titled-and-dated
photos on other walls, like the ones of the full fraternity crowded
on the porch in tuxes, or of the pledge class in their red and gold
shirts. Quinn had more: of himself posed with Brantley alone, both

of them looking drunkish in tuxes; in foursomes with their dates; in small groups with other Gammas. I stood to examine a candid shot of Brantley extravagantly mud-splattered with a yellow bandana around his head, an intramural football game. Was this boy gay? He must have been, I'd come to believe, when none of his brothers would linger at the topic long enough to say emphatically he was not. Beside the muddy ball player, a shake-day snapshot had caught open-mouthed, newly pledged Brantley in the air, being thrown from the dock into the lake. How much had he known, a month into freshman year, about himself? Of all the grinning people gathered at his back, none touched him. Only air touched him. He seemed to be rising through the arc so that when the shutter snapped, catching him forever, he had not yet begun to fall.

"Looks like we were best friends, doesn't it?"

That was, in fact, what it looked like. Vince and Jonathan displayed as many of each other, and in the past year every Gamma room I'd been in had featured at least one photo of Brantley in a prime spot. They were shrine-keepers—Quinn more than others, perhaps. I went back to the bed, folded a knee up on the mattress edge. "You said he had fixations."

He glanced at the curtain, marking the party sounds, then sat forward, cross-legged. "The Order." He watched me for a reaction. "Ever heard that name?"

I shook my head.

"That's what he called it. A Rockhaven secret society. Supposedly. You'll hear rumors about it now and then. Nobody knows who's in it or what the actual name of it is. Brantley was obsessed with it." He lifted the beer from my hand, took a slow drink. "He'd been collecting evidence. I don't think he told a lot of people about it, but he told me."

"Why you?"

He shrugged. "It was before things got a little ugly between us. I don't know what he found, though. He didn't tell me that."

His expression was wistful, almost inward, as if he had no agenda in offering up this story. Which wasn't possible—not when he wanted something from me. But that didn't make it not true. "You're saying someone could have killed him over this?"

"I'm not saying anything. I don't even know if the Order exists. All

I know is he was serious about it, more than he was about who killed Kennedy. Still, not exactly the kind of thing you go tell the cops."

I recalled Brantley's opining about conspiracies, enough to grant some credence. "What happened to the evidence?"

"Not sure. But I have an idea where we might look for it, if you're interested." He handed me the beer but kept hold, reached to stroke the back of my hand settled around the bottle above his. "Are you interested?"

His fingertips made a slow circle that radiated heat all the way up my arm. "I might be."

"Are we going to the formal?"

I sighed, hoping to sound exasperated and not despairing. I'd been kidding myself, plainly, to think I could walk in here with my carefully prepared arguments and say no. "Why don't you ask Polly? Bet she'd love to go. And probably be a lot more fun." He only waited, as if to be entertained, and I leaned closer, severe. "You are not even attracted to me. The only reason you're asking me is you think it will piss off Jonathan, and this is fun for you."

He didn't scoff or twitch, only looked back at me so steadily that I felt it in my gut. "Let me worry about who I'm attracted to. Maybe ask yourself who it is you're attracted to."

His fingertips had shifted to the denim seam inside my knee, and watching them there delayed me in catching his meaning. With one finger I scooched his hand back to his own lap. "The truth is, I'd like to keep you as a friend. Which I'm a little worried about, with you… whatever this is. So just go be attracted to some *other* girl you haven't defiled yet. There must be at least twenty."

He broke into a chuckle, shook his head. "Gavin, you kill me with that shit. Fine, we'll go as friends. I know you do that."

No, no, no. For Jonathan's sake if not my own. To buy time, to regain some control, I said, "Let's go see that evidence, and then maybe I'll think about it."

"If you want, once you put on that pretty dress, we can go look for it. We'll just duck out from the formal for a bit." At my dubious look, he said, "It's probably the best time to do it. You'll see."

I took a big breath. "If I go with you, *as friends*, will you stop playing games about Brantley? Just tell me what you know?"

"Um." His eyes narrowed. "That would depend on what it was."

"You know what I mean. Don't be a *tease* about what you can tell. And don't lie to me. I'm not interested in chasing all over for 'evidence' if you're making it up."

"I wouldn't do that. Look, you want honesty? The idea that what happened to him had anything to do with some secret society is far-fetched. There's a reason I haven't said it to anyone. Or even gone looking myself. It's because I don't actually think we're gonna turn up jack shit. But you got me thinking about it, and if there's an answer, I want to know it. Lot more than you do."

This far, I believed him. "And why are you telling me? Not"—I tipped my head toward the party—"one of them."

"Because you asked. Because we're friends." He said the word as if it were a weird-looking rock he'd found, one to be turned over and examined.

"Because you want me to go to the formal with you."

"True. But there's another reason." He peered down into the bottle we'd emptied between us, his voice soft. "I'm telling you because of Brantley's other fixation. Obsession. Which you forgot to ask me about, didn't you? I said he had two."

The word *obsession*, near whisper, sounded in Quinn's mouth like pure sex, and I stumbled trying to say it back. "What was his other... fixation?" Then, too late, I didn't want to ask, didn't want to know.

"That very pretty and well-connected roommate of his. Your new friend."

9

THOU WILT FALL BACKWARD WHEN THOU HAST MORE WIT

Over the next several days, mired in dread of the formal, I once or twice came to the verge of backing out. Jonathan gave me reason enough, with his anguished *Please don't*, and now he wouldn't meet my eyes or walked away when I approached. "I'll talk to him," Vince said, more forgiving of my weak will than I'd expected. "It's your business. And we'll all be there, so it's not like you'll be in some kind of danger. Just that, well, that's where the trouble comes, right? That we'll all be there."

Eventually Jonathan knocked at my door. I was studying for my microbiology final on my bed. In place of words, he crawled up and laid his head on the mattress at my hip like a sleepy child. His hair had gotten long enough for me to finger-comb almost to his jaw. "I know you're just worried about me. You don't need to be."

"I'm going to be watching."

"Oh, honey. Please, do the opposite." I meant this, though one of the conditions I most aspired to was to be watched by Jonathan. Perhaps Quinn and I were conspiring together for his attention. "You know he's only trying to get a reaction from you."

"He'll get one, too, he does anything to you."

This gallant claim made me wince, that he could allow no room for me to want Quinn to do something to me. Worse, he was right to leave none. Sex with Quinn would be throwing my whole social life into the garbage, and for what? Probably not even a pleasant experience, let alone a second night.

My frustrations might have been boiling too near the surface as I got ready Saturday night. I had borrowed a dress, a classy beaded black number, slim fitting with a scoop neck and short sleeves. It was flattering on me and, I could guess, expensive, more than appropriate for a formal. Fully dressed in black hose and pumps, ten minutes before Quinn would arrive to collect me, I shimmied the zipper back down and slipped from the dress, took off my bra, went into the back of my closet for a dress of my own that I'd bought at the Salvation Army store the previous summer: scarlet, lace overlay, sweetheart bodice, a flared skirt that ended above the knee. Strapless. I'd tried it on for kicks, knowing I'd never have the guts even if it had straps, and it turned me into a tiny-waisted, bosomy, red-hot bombshell. For fifteen dollars, I couldn't not buy it. But even with Emery at my own formal the night before, I hadn't summoned the bravery to wear it in public.

On the hanger it looked even cheaper than I recalled, mostly elastic, some trailer-park prom cast-off. To be dressed if nothing else, I put it on, zipped up the back, hoisted it into place, fluffed out the skirt, and there was the bombshell again. Snug, it required some gut-sucking, but a built-in corset kept me well bound. Though my décolletage was moderately out there, propped on the dress's structure, I seemed to be covered. I lifted my arms, shimmied and jumped, and the bodice did not creep down. I looked at my watch. Five minutes. *Decide fast.* Sarah Beth would have been no help—I could have put on a leather teddy and bunny ears, and she'd have said, *You look fine.* Mitzi, the one I needed, was already out the door on the arm of her latest sophomore stud.

To Quinn, the most superficially judgmental person I knew, the dress would matter a great deal, color his attitude for the night and, later, about the night. He'd be thinking about it even now, on his way to me, poised to pass judgment the instant I opened the door. Either way, I'd lose. To be classy and prudish, or trashy and hot? I put on the string of pearls I'd borrowed from Sarah Beth to wear the night before, which didn't suit the neckline of the black dress. Not bad with the red.

But I'd forgotten the scuffed edges of my shoes. In the midst of re-blackening the bare spots with a Magic Marker, I recalled that my hair wasn't curling right and I looked like a sheepdog. While attempting to rack the offending curls back into an ugly but serviceable barrette, I remembered that Anna Vaughn would be at the formal, with a judgment perhaps fiercer than Quinn's. Black dress, no question. But as I reached for the zipper of the red, Quinn knocked. For a few seconds I stood staring at myself, witless. Then I futzed my hair into place without the barrette, exhaled, and opened the door.

"Gavin," he said. "Well, look at you."

"And you," I said. He looked, in fact, rather dashing in a classic tux, black coat and tie, though I wasn't capable of seeing much as he stepped inside, examining me up and down.

"That's a dress with something to say."

The upside of the existence of Anna Vaughn Whitacre was that she made Quinn Cooper less formidable. As with a willful horse, the trick was to never let him sense insecurity. Hands on hips, I inquired, "Does it meet your standards? There's also this one." I lifted the black one on its hanger. "I'll let you choose."

"Uh, no. This one will do."

The black dress would have been better armor, a good defense, but the red one, I felt now, was power, offense. It knocked him back a step, maybe for no more reason than the confidence required to wear it.

"No coat?" he said, as we started out the door.

"Is it that cold? We're driving, right?"

"Yeah, but bring one anyway. Might need it."

"Okay, Mister Mysterious." I grabbed my peacoat but only carried it, stuffing my lipstick clutch into the pocket, and accepted the arm he offered. Always a jittery moment, taking the arm of a boy in a tux who had been so recently a buddy, now subtly transformed into this sturdy, dapper something else. In every case, I had to remind myself we were playing dress-up—and how different was this evening? *Just friends*, as he and I had agreed, as I still felt to be true beneath all the layers of recent strangeness.

We could count the couples already arrived by the "38" the seminarian hired as a bartender markered on our bottle of Stoli and the backs of both our hands. He broke the seal and mixed a pair of vodka cranberries in green stadium cups printed with *Under the Mistletoe* in gold letters. The cup was a thrill in itself—to be at the Gamma formal, chosen—brimming and heavy on the vodka, and I warned myself after a first sparkly sip not to suck it down too fast. Easy to get sloppy at a formal, even under normal stressors.

One of the first people I saw, as Quinn got pulled off into a group of seniors, was Jenny, wide-eyed and already half smashed. "Whoa!" she cried, and slapped a hand over her mouth. "That is not the dress we talked about. Hubba-hubba. Somebody's getting some."

Dex, bless him, said, "You look great." I was secretly relieved to note that Jenny was flushed for the second night only with hope, while Dex exuded an easy, immovable friend-vibe. Still, Jenny could go the whole night unkissed and have more fun than anyone, because Dex was a famously good date. He and I had danced at the sorority formal while

Emery danced with Jenny, and I'd had a hard time resisting the urge to lay my head on his shoulder, make him mine for one song.

Quinn, from a circle of seniors, was looking my way, talking about me, and I excused myself to join him. "There's my date," he said. The sleeve of his tux brushing my bare skin as he set a hand on my opposite shoulder gave me shivers, like a heavy silk bedcover under which we were naked together, and I amped up my smile, dove into conversation with one of the girls about our drinks. As we circulated from one group to another, all his friends from outside my crowd, he guided me at the waist and returned his hand to my back or shoulder, a thumb idly stroking as I endeavored to be scintillating to near strangers. It was hard to block out the fact that he was always touching me somewhere. When he meant to address me, his fingertips went to my neck. The small-talk conversation was a hum tuned softer than what was said with one hand—speaking as much to those around us, I assumed, as to me.

Here and there I noted other girls in strapless dresses who didn't look as naked as I felt or tug at their tops as if they were always falling off, and I tried to emulate their ease, or at least keep my hands off the thing. The photographer snapped photos: Quinn and me alone; in groups of six and eight; just the guys; just the girls. Jenny, Dex, Quinn, and me. Far through the crowd, as we arranged our shots, I spotted Jonathan and Vince with their dates and then, coming in at the front door, Will and Anna Vaughn.

"Put down that drink," Quinn said, when the band started up with "I Heard It Through the Grapevine." On the crowded floor of the living room, emptied of furniture, lit by constellations of white Christmas lights, the shaggers shuffled to the beat, while Quinn led me in a languorous, possibly ironic half-time. As he turned me so that my arm went behind my back, then spun me out and back to him, I recognized a shag move in slo-mo. Like a lot of the house girls, I didn't actually know how to shag. I depended on being led skillfully enough that my feet landed where they were meant to, my hands primed for the next turn. The good ones—Parker Battles, for instance, with whom I'd danced once—could make a girl feel all the fancy steps and triple spins, arms every which way, release and catch, were somehow her own doing. But the good ones were few and picky about their partners. The rest approached the shag like a game of speed and would crack a girl around the floor like a whip, trapping her in knots or leaving her stranded, empty-handed, then have to catch her back and start over. Carolyn had once been knocked unconscious when some boy dropped her on the floor.

Quinn wore a little smile that mocked the popping and flashing dancers around us. Did we look bizarre? My feet kept moving where they were meant to, at least, even through a triple spin dizzying enough that when my feet stopped, I didn't fully realize I was being kissed. He pointed to the doorframe above us—mistletoe—and spun me back onto the floor. "Smooth," I said, as if I'd watched him do it to someone else. Good bet Jonathan was somewhere near, though I was too disoriented to look for him. And mistletoe meant I was not even allowed to be annoyed.

For "Tracks of My Tears," the rest of the floor slowed to Quinn's pace. I spotted Jonathan back by the pool table, Tiffany in satiny blue laughing with a wide, red-painted open mouth—but at what? Something Vince's date had said, maybe, because Jonathan was stiff and grim-looking, gazing off over her head. Poor Tiffany. No one was more difficult than Jonathan in the wrong mood, and the previous night I had sensed him cooling on her, more than he might have were he not committed to the next night as well. Had I been the one on his arm tonight—always that place I longed to be, half because it was bound to include Vince and my other friends—he might actually have had more fun both nights.

Quinn and I stepped off the floor to revisit our drinks, then got caught talking to more of his crowd, including Mitzi and her date. All week she'd been teasing me about having the secret hots for Quinn until I finally confessed with dismay, "What if I do?" And then, not meaning it, "What if I just have sex with him and get it over with?" Mitzi, a proponent of ditching the burden of virginity, cheered the notion. Doing so hadn't hurt her, she argued. But beautiful girls got away with more. And she didn't trouble herself trying to sustain actual friendships with boys the way I did.

"Use protection," she burbled now into my ear—a joke, since I had withdrawn my hypothetical and vowed abstinence.

Quinn, into my other ear, said, "Look who's here. Your friend Will. We should go chat."

"Should we?" Queasy at the prospect, I rattled the ice in my cup. "I need a refill."

I hoped to finish that refill before we ventured in any such direction.

But as we turned away from the bar with our fresh drinks, Will hailed me, approaching through the crowd. By the hand trailed Anna Vaughn, caught in the press and turned back to shout pleasantries to people she passed. "Hey!" I called brightly to Will, grabbing Quinn around the waist with my free arm—partly to alert him to our audience, partly for defense.

Anna Vaughn arrived at Will's side in wine-dark, floor-length satin, profuse gems of a diamond nature—were they real?—at her throat. "Oh, hi, Leah," she said with unfaltering breathless poise. We had not actually spoken since our meeting in the laundry room, but she seemed to have called off her minions and had once graced me with a passing hello on the dorm stairs. I still hid in my room if I heard her in the hall. I wondered if Will detected the hatred I felt seething from her even now, capped under such a pretty smile at his insistence.

"Y'all know Quinn Cooper," I said.

"Of course." Will shook his hand, while I took a double gulp from my cup that nearly sloshed down my cleavage.

"Anna Vaughn," Quinn said. "You look stunning as always."

She curtsied, giving her skirt a flourish over the toes of matched satin shoes. "Oh, go *on*. You will make me blush!"

"And you look lovely," Will said to me.

If anyone in our foursome was blushing, it was surely me. "Oh, shut up."

With the arm clamped around my date, I was rubbing his side with some vigor, and he took the hint. "*You* shut up," he said, mouth at my temple. He shifted me in front of him, one arm looped with casual ownership over my collar bones. "She pretends she doesn't know she's hot. Drives me nuts." To me he said, "Don't you?" and bit the air next to my face.

I snorted an involuntary laugh. "All right. Down, boy." I hoped Anna Vaughn might assume Quinn was my boyfriend. If she already knew he wasn't, then I'd at least make the point that Will was not that special to me, only one of several close guy friends.

"Good to see you at the house again," Quinn said to Will. "We were starting to wonder if you might be avoiding us."

His tone was so genial that even I couldn't tell if he meant anything by it. Will blinked, taken off guard, then smiled. "Just busy, I guess. Took a crazy course load this term, Leah can attest."

"That you did," I said, feeling summoned to rescue him. But my gaze shifted to Anna Vaughn, who tipped her head at me with mock interest, and my mouth fell shut.

"Good to have you back." Quinn's fingertips tapped keys over the top of my shoulder as he spoke. "Last time I talked to you must have been...what? A year ago. Little more." His voice remained friendly, even warm, but Will's smile fell. "We were all glad to see you at the funeral, you know. Decent of you to come."

Will swallowed, nodded. He tried to speak but couldn't, and I felt so distressed on his behalf that I said, "Quinn."

"What?"

"Let's not talk about that."

"No," Will said, clouded and earnest. "I... It's strange, I guess, when your main friends end up being the people in your frat, after... Sometimes I think it was just an accident. That we, that Brantley and I, ended up in different fraternities." As Will rambled, I caught Anna Vaughn in an eyeroll that she pretended was someone through the doorway catching her attention. "And I had to be kind of an outsider at the funeral."

"Naw, man," Quinn said. "Not to us. You're like an honorary brother, almost. And not just because you and Bran were so close." Will opened his mouth to say something, but Quinn went on as if struck by his own words. "You know, you hardly ever see freshmen roommates who stay together sophomore year. Most of us get itchy, want a change. Not you guys." Before I could think to interject—common knowledge that Brantley's sophomore roommate was Dukey Clark—Quinn went on, tapping my shoulder in time to his words. "And pledging different frats? I mean, *no one* stays together through that, right? Plus, you've got that Dragoon thing going on." Looping both arms around my neck, he leaned on me like a table across which to address Will. "Brantley had to be jealous of that, I'd assume. Seeing as he was so into secret societies. All kinds. Wasn't he?"

"Yeah, I guess," Will said, cautious.

Though I couldn't see Quinn, I felt his attention fixed like a laser on Will, and they were about the same height. Surely he'd missed what I caught: tiny Anna Vaughn at "secret societies" going rigid and pale. She broke in with a daffy, beaming sigh, slipping a hand through Will's elbow. "Sweetheart, we ought to get *going*—"

Quinn went on, chummy and jocular. "I'm sure you heard plenty from him on that topic. His so-called investigation, like it was scientific curiosity. But I think what he really wanted was to join one. Figure out how to get himself a *bid*. You ever get that idea?"

Will only now looked down at Anna Vaughn, who showed him her watch. "Remember, we promised Lawton and them? I am so sorry, y'all, but we have to scoot."

He turned back to Quinn. "That was probably true."

"Hell, he must have bugged the shit out of you about it," Quinn said. "He could get so...fixated. Like a broken record. You miss it now, of course. I always wondered if that had anything to do with you guys splitting up. Like a month into sophomore year, didn't you change rooms?"

Will looked as stunned as I must have. Anna Vaughn laughed and said, "Oh, gawd, that was so nutty! Just because Dukey Clark's room-mate left school." She petted Will's arm. "You remember. And you were the assistant proctor on the floor, so they put you in the smaller room by yourself. Really it was crazy, changing everyone around like that mid-semester."

Will shot Anna Vaughn a look that could only have been annoyance. To Quinn, he said, "Actually, I had filed a room change request. Which I later withdrew, because I decided the reason was stupid."

"You *what*?" Anna Vaughn said. Will ignored her.

"Just petty, ridiculous nonsense. But this room came up and they decided to move Brantley anyway." He gave Anna Vaughn a dark look, and I recalled him telling me how she couldn't stand Brantley. So much that she'd insisted on a room change? "It was pretty *nutty*," he said.

"Sorry, bud," Quinn muttered. "Didn't mean to stir up anything there."

"No worries." Will tipped back his drink and swallowed it empty.

"Sweetheart—"

"Can you give me one goddamn minute?" Will's voice wasn't harsh, only tired, soft, and, I noticed now, creeping up on a slur. He looked at me with immense sadness, as if asking me to save him from Anna Vaughn or grant him patience, then turned back to Quinn. "It feels good to talk about him. It's just hard. I don't get a lot of practice. Except with Leah sometimes."

I expected death rays from Anna Vaughn, who was no longer smiling. But when I checked, she was looking past me, fighting tears. It surprised me so much I said to Will, "We don't mean to keep you. If you have to get somewhere."

He smirked at Quinn. "Here I go wrecking another perfectly good party. But it's good of y'all to have me around now and then. Will you pardon us?"

As they threaded the crowd back through the hall, probably straight out the door if Anna Vaughn had a say, I turned to gloss for Quinn what seemed visible enough on its own: how Will was grieving, hurting for an outlet, how Anna Vaughn tried to thwart him. Before I could get out a word, he poked me in the forehead. "*J'accuse, ma cherie.* You were helping him."

"Helping him *what?*"

"Wiggle off the hook. That was halfway to a confession, of some sort." He chewed his lip, set his back to the wall.

"Are you cracked? And were you paying any attention to Anna Vaughn? If I was helping anyone, it was her, god knows why. She was about to lose her shit."

"The room," he said, not looking at me. "The room is weird."

"Her idea. She made him do it. That's obvious, right?"

"But why?"

"She hated Brantley. Will told me so, ages ago." I felt, if possible, more wound up than Quinn was. In the pressure of the crowd, I backed up to the wall beside him. "And you're right about the secret society, but Will's not the one who flipped when you brought it up. It was her." Friends were wandering our way from two sides, and he stepped in front of me close, a hand parked on the wall beside my face to prevent interruption. "I was watching her. She looked like—"

"Like what?"

I clapped a hand over my mouth. "It's not funny. Oh god, why am I laughing? She looked like Lady Macbeth."

Quinn checked over both shoulders as if for anyone close enough to overhear. Some new idea or revelation, I expected when he leaned in, and got his mouth on mine instead. I glanced up to the ceiling—no mistletoe—and went to register a complaint, which caused our mouths to open. In an academic way, I had surmised he'd be a good kisser, besides master of a few other skills I might in theory be interested to try. But I had not expected this personal thing, tender and electric at once. He felt even better than kissing Emery, who had no flaws in that department aside from the sour taste of cigarettes and lack of palpable desire. Balancing my drink in one hand, I lost full sense of our surroundings, so that some passing voice jibing, "Get a room, Cooper" broke through as if into a dream.

Without a devil's grin, without a word, he took my hand and led me to the teeming coat closet, went in, and fished out my coat. I was not quite with him, trapped a minute behind in the kiss, then in the public nature of the kiss, then in Jonathan's eyes, which I caught in a backward glance as Quinn led me on all acquiescent. To the front door, I expected, but instead we went down the interior stairs, past more couples gathered in the dim light of the lower room where the furniture had been collected. I spotted Pem, Emery, and Jenny, before Quinn led me out to the back patio dark, where a few dancers were cooling down—boys aglow in white shirts, giggling girls in oversized tux coats. Quinn set our drinks on a ledge and picked up a bag of some sort that he slung over a shoulder. He held my coat open for me. Awakened in the chilly night air, I hesitated before inserting an arm. "What are we doing?"

"Going fishing." It was only the fierceness in his voice that recalled to me Brantley and his evidence. Down the rutted, moonless lawn we went, and he guided my steps from the shore onto the dock. "Off," he barked at some pledge mugging with his date on the sofa, and they scrambled to obey.

He unhooked the lines and jammed the long pole into the shore. "Have a seat, babe." I did, mouthing *babe* as he shoved us off. The night wasn't too cold to rule much out, among his many possible intentions for this trip, though I was glad he'd arranged for my coat. Upstairs, the band started back up with "I Can't Help Myself," and through the wall of windows, fogged at their edges, speckled lights illuminated the shagging throng. I could see no one watching us go.

Quinn worked in silence, levering off the lake bottom with the pole while I lounged on the sofa like a gondola passenger. In the dark I could hear his breath and the slosh of water at our leading edge with the force of each thrust. How many girls had he ferried into this oil-black, watery darkness? Private spaces on our mountain were hard to come by when all of us—apart from Will Oliver, apparently—were compelled to live with a roommate until the luxury of a senior-year single. I was sure this sofa had seen more action than I should have been comfortable sitting on.

From the lake's center, the house's romantic party lights only sharpened and clarified its presence. We could not travel by water far enough. Where did one go for real privacy, besides off the mountain? Out into the perimeter woods, perhaps. Into an empty classroom. Up into the bell tower.

Quinn walked up the dock to my end, where he corrected our course, then paused to gaze down at me. "You look nervous."

I didn't feel it, for some reason. "You must not be able to see me very well."

Another thrust of the pole returned a *clong* of struck metal. "Hear that?"

"The wood stove?" We were floating in the general vicinity where some party of house-cleaning Gammas had sunk the thing years before.

The lake was less garbage pit than time capsule. Besides the detritus of house renovation through the decades, the Gammas consigned to the water's keeping all manner of personal objects: mementos of ex-girlfriends, spurned record albums, failed comprehensive exams, knickknacks with meanings dependent on convoluted stories. My friends were cagey about where and how any treasure of their own had been submerged, though it was the kind of ceremony, whether silly or serious, that called for a witness or two. Had Brantley, out of caution, made the rare choice to venture to the task alone, he would have at least hinted it to one of his brothers.

Quinn called me to take over at the pole, jammed into junk at the lake bottom to hold us steady, while he squatted to empty the duffel bag. Over the boards beside my feet, he spread a blanket and laid out a crowbar, then a wire coat hanger; he flicked a flashlight on and off. "I'd just about decided," he said, as he shucked his tux coat and draped it carefully over the sofa arm, "that a formal was not the greatest time for this adventure. But I swear to god, after that crazy shit just now?" Coming to stand before me, he unhooked his cufflinks, weighed them like a pair of dice in his hand. "Keep these for me?"

He set them in my open palm—heavy for their size, glittering, shaped in Greek letters I could guess—and closed my fingers around them. He unbuttoned his cuffs, folded the white fabric up his arms. "See what a gentleman I can be? You're already half naked. I could be sending you in."

The gravelly intimacy of *naked* brought back the shiver of his tux jacket across my bare shoulders. He knelt on the blanket at the dock's edge and reached into the water with the crowbar. Muffled metal banged metal, and he hooked the crowbar to some part of the stove and hauled the dock over by a foot. Flat on his chest, he stretched one bare arm into the water. I slipped his cufflinks into my pocket, and only afterward thought to run a hand along the lining to check for tears.

"Hand me that hanger." It was no longer a hanger but a disassembled wire hooked at the end. I squatted beside him, one hand braced on the anchor pole. He inserted the wire and fished about—inside the mouth of the woodstove, it seemed—his arm nearly to the shoulder in the water. "Fucking freezing," he grumbled.

"Hope there's not a snapping turtle in there."

He soaked his sleeve, cursed some more, grumbled over his stupid idea. Then he went silent. Thirty seconds later he reeled in and landed beside my shoes a slimy piece of garbage. He clicked on the flashlight, illuminating what proved to be a gallon-sized plastic bag. "Wait." He stood and used the blanket to dry his arm and press his wet sleeve. Then he scooped up the bag with the blanket and took it to the sofa. I laid the pole on the dock and joined him.

Inside the bag was a smaller bag, and a still smaller one, each zip-locked. Quinn's fingers shook as he picked apart the seals, while I aimed the flashlight. Inside the final one was a square wafer of blue plastic: a floppy disk. "Shit," he said. "It got wet." The label had bled; the plastic appeared mottled, faded, the metal shutter at its edge foxed with rust. I took it and scraped at the rust with a thumbnail, buzzing with elation and fear. Could this be Brantley's? I hadn't expected to find something real, something that might hold answers. It felt so inexplicably dangerous, to all of us, to Will, that only shock kept me from flinging it away into the water.

A piece of plastic, adhered to the back, came off in my fingers: a laminated card the size of a driver's license. Black mold bloomed over part of the type, printed from a computer in a tiny font, but I could read the words "The Order," which seemed to be followed by a question mark, and then "code." Below that, a series of letters and numbers arranged in short, uniform lines.

Quinn was busy with something else he'd pulled from the bag and was rubbing with the blanket. "This is his. Holy shit. I know this." He held a cookie-like object, round and flattish and lumpy, metal. "An ashtray," he said. "You know those foil kind they put out in fast-food joints? But all crumpled up like a piecrust around the edge. He was a compulsive ashtray crumpler, always exactly like this. He kept one on his dresser. Said it had sentimental value. This could be it. I picked it up once and started to mess with it, unfold it or something, and he wigged out."

While I took that in, he picked at a red splotch at the disk's center. "But this thing shouldn't be here." He aimed the beam at it and laughed. "Sealing wax. That's Bran. He actually sealed his letters with wax. But that's not his seal. Too small for a seal." Pressed neatly into the wax's center was a round, coin-like mark. Some detail was visible within it but I couldn't tell what.

"Like a cufflink," I guessed. "A signet ring."

"Maybe. Or a pin." By the flat face of the impress and the size, I knew what he meant. A pledge pin. But not Gamma Chi, not one I recognized, though it was hard to make out any detail. He took the laminated card from my hand and examined the type, his breath shuddering all the while as if he were on the verge of sobbing.

The dock had drifted back into range of the house, so that the regular snap of the snare drum inside gained some brass melody. "Let's go in," I said. "We can look at it later."

"This is it. I don't know what it is, but we fucking found it." Our treasures gathered in his hands, he looked around for somewhere to stash them and chose my coat pocket, sliding them all in carefully together. Then his hands, one cold and the other colder, were at each side of my neck. "God, can you believe it?"

From the moment he'd taken my hand in the house, I hadn't fully stopped wishing for him to kiss me again. But now his question echoed as real. *Could* I believe it? How convenient, how simple, that he'd known precisely where to look, that he could verify the source. A lot of work that would have required, all to get me out here.

Unless it was to manufacture some case against Will.

And if he'd meant to seduce me, he seemed too shaken now to try. Strange to be huddled up with him afloat on the lake, unmolested in so flimsy a dress. "Let's go get warm," I said, and he nodded.

Coat restored, he applied the pole to the lake bottom. On the approaching shore, in the spill of light below the balcony, many figures stood about in the yard. Jonathan's voice called out, "Leah? You okay?"

"I'm fine," I said, in a tone of bemusement that anyone would wonder otherwise. Once Quinn had roped us back into port and helped me off onto the grass, I spotted Jonathan up at the porch's edge with his back to us, talking to Vince, who was surely urging a nonreactive calm. Tiffany conversed nearby with other girls.

"Nice night," Quinn remarked to no one in particular as we picked our way up the lawn. "Who's next? Didn't realize we had a line forming."

At times Quinn was baldly readable, like a horse that minces one step on a jump course and telegraphs that he's thinking about jamming to a stop in front of the next fence to dump you over it. Lacking a crop to flick him with, I pinched his bicep. "Behave yourself."

"Babe, you got my cufflinks?" He stopped to address me, coincidentally enough at Jonathan's back.

"*Quinn.*" I hoped my annoyance would convey that he knew full well I did not have any piece of his clothing on my person. But Jonathan turned. Quinn leaned to speak into his ear, a report from which he came away grinning.

Jonathan's eyes raked over me. A breath later he launched into Quinn, propelling the two of them down the rutted hill. In the dark, past the surge of late-reacting, intervening bodies, someone hit the ground with a grunt, someone—Jonathan—rose above the knotted form they made to haul back a fist. I stood open-mouthed, a bystander, until some seconds after that meaty punch resounded and I recalled that I was, to some degree, the cause.

Quinn didn't want to leave. His jacket and pants smeared with mud, he insisted on getting us fresh drinks. Summoning a crowd to follow him to the kitchen, to bring Jonathan along, he ordered pledges to assemble ice packs—for his face, for Jonathan's fist—and to set up a pair of tequila shots. "I was just joking," he said warmly to Jonathan more than once, and pasted on a contrite expression whenever he caught my glare.

"Come on, brother." He nudged a lime wedge and shot over the kitchen island toward Jonathan. "Together."

Jonathan, his fist cradled, hung back and sulked. From all sides Gammas looked on, ready to let Quinn direct the proceedings but not yet won over enough to urge Jonathan to pick up the glass—this despite the magenta fist-print blooming high on Quinn's cheekbone, unreturned. I couldn't stop staring at Quinn, who was barely recognizable, a paragon of serenity. He exuded so much love and brotherhood he'd gone handsome with it, his eyes soft with forgiveness of Jonathan's resistance as he toasted him with his own shot and downed it.

When the tussle in the yard had been broken apart, I had gone straight to Jonathan. Quinn, I could already sense, didn't need me at all, even as a prop, but I was the one who could calm Jonathan now better than Vince could. I drew him into the shadow beneath the balcony. "Look, whatever he said to you. Assuming it's about what happened on the dock, you *know* it's a lie, right?"

He was exhaling through his teeth in fierce animal bursts, looking everywhere but at me. "Well, that just makes it worse, doesn't it?"

I had to turn my great sigh of relief, to be believed, into pitying disappointment in him. "I told you. He wanted a rise out of you. And there you went and made all his dreams come true."

He laughed without mirth. "I could hit him some more if he wants." He examined his knuckles. "Don't you want to know what he said?"

I took hold of the hand tenderly, though Tiffany lurked in wait. "Thanks, but I'll pass."

I could see he would have told me regardless but it stopped itself on his tongue, too horrible to speak aloud. "If you knew what he said, Leah, you wouldn't forgive him."

As others in the kitchen began to help themselves to shots from the bottle, Jonathan was induced to leave his corner and shake Quinn's hand. I decided I deserved the neglected shot and swallowed it. It was past midnight, the formal crowd just beginning to thin, the band on break but about to retake the stage for more, and Quinn seemed to have salvaged the evening. Jonathan went off to find his date, while Quinn remained the center of a heavily fraternal side party in the kitchen. I was drawn away to other rooms, called upon to relay the story. Not that I much wanted to do this: declaring over and over again that *nothing happened* on the dock, that my date had merely "said something rude" and almost certainly to the contrary, which made for many more people than just the two thinking about what was going on or not between my legs, besides mulling over the added fact of the two boys who had made themselves overly concerned with it. "It's not even about me," I kept insisting to dubious gossip-curious half-strangers. "It's about *them*."

Quinn found me half an hour later. His manner remained disorientingly gentle, reinforced by more booze. His right eye—Jonathan was a lefty—was beginning to squint.

"God, I thought you'd gone home or something," he said.

I almost had. More than once while waiting for him I had thought of Brantley's treasures in my coat pocket, which Quinn seemed to have forgotten. Safer, I thought, whatever they were, if I took them away somewhere, until I knew...what? Whether they could hurt someone. Hurt the wrong person. But if I learned some damning truth, would I keep it to myself?

Quinn, though, had not forgotten. He wanted to go to his room and try the disk. Would I come? Ten minutes later we were on his sofa, booting up his Mac II. He popped in the disk. After some consideration, the screen said: *The disk is unreadable: Do you want to initialize it?* Quinn clicked the eject button, then pushed it back in.

The disk is unreadable: Do you want to initialize it?

I was surprised how sad it felt to read that disembodied message, despite my relief. Quinn took the disk out, scrubbed a thumb over its blotchiness and rust. He tried it again, failed again.

"It's lost," I said. The light caught the darkening swath along his cheek, and I touched it with two fingers, no more pressure than the air. "Does it hurt?"

"Yeah." He closed his eyes, leaned into my fingers. "You know, I respect him for it."

And what did you say? I would have demanded to know, had the story involved some other girl. Quinn Cooper, crazy and complicated enough in himself without being, also, Brantley, what I had left of Brantley.

"Please don't tell me," I said. "What you said to him. If you said something horrible about me, I don't want to know."

He scooped my face into his hands like something fragile about to drop, bringing me a notch closer to tears. "Listen," he said. "It was inappropriate. And pretty crude. But it wasn't *mean*." I checked his eyes, surprised he'd remembered the word. His mouth began to quirk. "For the record, it was something purely, let's say, complimentary. About you."

"Oh, don't smile." His assurances did, however, make me feel better, since of the half dozen options my brain had devised, none could be stretched into compliments. "But it was a *lie* about me?"

His gaze had become very involved in my dress. "That's the thing, see, I wouldn't know."

And you never will, is probably what I should have said, before he even started kissing me.

INTERLUDE

CHRISTMAS

I had arranged a ride to Knoxville for noon on Wednesday, when only the stragglers from the last Advent exam would be left loading into cars. Of all of us vacating the mountain, I was surely the only one facing a Christmas day alone, my aunt having gone off on a two-week Caribbean cruise that would keep her away until the day after. "We'll do Christmas when I'm back," she said. The holiday between us didn't amount to much: a dinner we cooked together, sometimes with an unattached friend of hers, a present apiece. My father would call—or, more precisely, his wife, Gretchen, would call, and then put my father on with both Aunt Rose and me. This year that call I didn't even want would be the only marker of the day.

Had it troubled me much—I decided it didn't—I might have gone home with Jenny or Vince or even Jonathan. None of them, nor their parents, would have permitted me to stay away lonely. But knowing the special sanctity they all accorded family time at Christmas, I felt hesitant to impose. I needed to work over the break, and besides, I thought I might enjoy the solitude, the chance to lie in bed and read the day away. My aunt would leave the kitchen stocked with hot chocolate, candy bars, chips, microwaveable meals. For company I'd have her tortoiseshell cat, who would be glad of my arrival as I turned my key on an otherwise empty house, temporarily my own.

Quinn liked the sound of this. "What if you cancel your ride and I drive you?"

He'd been set to leave after his last exam on Tuesday, due at his father's house for dinner that night. His parents, both remarried in Montgomery, had scheduled his and his brother's holiday time to the minute. The chance to screw with these plans and keep his father waiting, I could surmise, appealed to Quinn as much as anything my aunt's deserted house might have in store.

We left on Tuesday, though it meant more people around to see us loading the Porsche's tight back bench to the ceiling with our combined junk. "Jesus, you're going to read that many books?" he asked.

I'd checked out twelve, the holiday limit. "Maybe."

He leaned against the car in his brown bomber, tongue playing in the pocket of a cheek. The bruise below his eye was like some hack movie trick to distinguish the new Quinn from his evil twin. "Not while I'm around."

"You won't be, since you're going to see your cousins."

This was the story he'd spooled off for Mitzi a few minutes earlier in the Benson hall, as we carted the bags from my room: that he was going to Knoxville to visit cousins, figured why not give me a ride?

She'd caught me aside once he was down the stairs. "Convenient," she sing-songed. "*Now* are you getting laid?"

"Ha. Not remotely."

Mitzi had believed my story that nothing had happened the night of the formal, not on the dock and not afterward. Her new mission was to convince me Quinn wasn't so bad he should be rejected out of hand. I insisted that yes, he was exactly that bad. What amazed me was that Quinn, as far as I could tell, had spread no rumors of his own. We were acting pretty normal for us, keeping apart except for a fleeting interaction or two each day, when he would wander over to mutter some usually filthy sentence or two into my ear. Jonathan, who might otherwise have formed suspicions, had started to feel bad about the punch, and lenient, since Quinn was taking it so well.

No one but a few Bensonites witnessed our departure. We lassoed our angels and a few hours later arrived at the curb before my aunt's row house. I hurried him inside—musty-smelling and chilly, the heat turned down—lest the nosy neighbors spot us. "It's not much," I told him, with a stab of late regret for whatever whim had consented to this plan. The house was tight, lightless, and vertical, entered by a foyer alongside of which a living room shot-gunned back to the eat-in kitchen and laundry alcove, a half bath. We climbed stairs to the second floor—my aunt's bedroom, a junk room/office, and a hall bath—and up again single-file on narrow steps to my slope-roofed attic room with its demure, quilt-covered twin. It was five in the afternoon, winter-dark but for the stairwell light through the door.

"Nervous?" he asked. I was, maybe more than I'd been the first time. It had not gone well. He lifted the bag from my shoulder and dropped it, clawed the loose neck of my sweater aside and fastened his mouth where the strap had rested.

Since Quinn was known for never having sex with a girl twice, I was still a little confused over how we had gotten here, ready for a second go; it seemed as accidental, as implausible, as the first. All I had known for sure then was wanting to kiss him. But my dress soon presented a problem, its frothy, weightless skirt offering no obstruction to his hand slipping all the way up my thigh while my attention was elsewhere. One of me wanted to kiss him forever and not think, while the other was scrambling to figure out the brakes. How to be the cool girl, besides the girl he'd still like the next day? I didn't know of any way to say yes, or no, and hope for that outcome. So I started talking. Between kisses, out came a story to explain why we would not be having sex, true enough in its way: I saw no point in my first time being a one-night stand. Why bother unless I could gain some familiarity with the act? I wasn't waiting for a boyfriend, someone special. I was merely waiting for a worthy partner who would do it more than once.

"And I mean a lot," I'd said. The words still echoed in my head. "Like twenty or thirty times." This absurd number, the unprecedented proposal of future bounty to be dispensed in secret and only as friends, turned out to be the magic catalyst that got Quinn intrigued.

Not that I had meant to intrigue him. I had only pitched an idea I thought might impress him and at the same time scare him, make him back off without calling me frigid or worse. *Twenty or thirty times* now struck me as ill-considered, if not appalling, when I wasn't sure I could handle the second.

"So…this just happens right now, I guess?"

"Uh-huh." He laid a row of kisses up my neck to the back of my ear, and my shudder brought his puppet master's smile against my skin. "You have another idea? Want a drink first?"

"No."

Being in the mood wasn't the problem: I was ridiculously turned on, more than I cared to be. This edgy, quivering arousal stood as the sole argument that letting Quinn drive me to Knoxville might be other than a terrible idea. All he had to do was touch me, murmur a vaguely dirty sentiment or two. If he ventured so far as a kiss, I was all in.

But in for what? The first time had borne little resemblance to what I'd expected sex to be. I'd known, for instance, that the act involved making a lot of moany, gaspy sounds of pleasure, basically at the end of things, preferably in the dark. But we'd still been in all our clothes, under the full lights, his hand somewhere farther up my thigh than it should have been but safely blocked by the barrier of formal-requisite pantyhose while we sorted through the terms of a hypothetical contract for an act I was still half-hoping to evade, when my body went through this paroxysm all on its own.

"Wow," Quinn said, after watching this happen in consternation. I didn't know enough to guess that all he'd ever seen of female pleasure had been fake, during the act. Of course I, too, thought it belonged there, that I'd already done it wrong.

And how could I then say I didn't want to move to the bed? I wasn't sure I didn't, wasn't sure of anything except that the light must be turned off, so he would not have another chance to watch me do something embarrassing. But the dark that descended was so absolute I felt uncertain the bare skin that returned to press against mine was his, which made me almost change my mind, about the light. In fear of changing my mind I rushed us to begin—to end, really, so I could begin to know what it was I had done. Some pain at the start was part of what I expected, but again I was wrong. This was pain joined to obstruction, as if he were shoving against a locked door. Baffled by me once more, he withdrew, tried again, slowly, each second more agonizing until I had to cry out—"Do it! Hurry!"—and he complied in what seemed a rending of flesh. My need to stop him was stopped by my sureness that it would be over soon on its own, that I could hold out against whatever this was, which could not be sex, because if it were, no one would ever have it.

Some time afterward—he was deep asleep—I lay dazed and sore, halfway into a pounding hangover topped by an urgent need to pee. I had no choice but to creep out of his bed, into a room so dark I came near hyperventilating tears trying to find my dress in it. I was ready to try a naked dash when I stumbled on my coat, which proved just long enough to cover me for a scurry on tiptoes down the gross hall carpet, onto the chilled, clammy tile of a room used only by boys. A mercy it was empty, the windows black with night.

On a toilet, too stunned to sob, I could only wonder vaguely what had happened, what was wrong with me. Quinn had said nothing much to enlighten me, and now the blood seemed endless, reddening the toilet paper and the water in the bowl, dried to my thighs. I wanted to be back in my own room, in my own bed, and I wasn't sure how I'd get out of the stall.

The hall door opened: Quinn, calling my name. I pulled up my feet and didn't answer, certain at first I could hide there until he went away. But I needed some assistance, and what would I do if he left? "Please," I said, my pipsqueak voice barely rising above the hum of the lights, "will you just bring me my dress and shoes?" Though I'd sworn him to a number of advance conditions—that he'd be nice to me, that he would not talk about me to other people—I could all but hear him carping over breakfast about the clingy bitch who wouldn't get out of his dorm.

He blackened the crack of light at the stall door. "Come out of there, Leah."

"No, thank you. I'd rather just stay here for a while."

Eventually he coaxed me out, huddled in my coat, straight into the nightmare of my reflection over the sinks, pasty and wild-haired and raccoon-eyed, a doll some kid had punched the eyes out of and then lost between the sofa cushions for a month. But I felt distant from any need to appear attractive to him, so sad about it all and embarrassed that I accepted his arms around me. "Are you okay? My bed kind of looks like a crime scene."

"Oh god." It had not occurred to me there must be blood on his bed. No one, I thought numbly, had ever been this mortified in front of another person, and of course that person would have to be Quinn. "Can I just disappear now? Am I gone yet?"

But he had come with a towel and led me back into a shower stall— in a boys' dorm, something I would have counted about twelve rungs above my bravery level the day before. Nothing to fear once the last thread of my dignity had snapped. Not fully cognizant, I failed to notice at first that, having joined me, he wasn't trying to get rid of me, that he was smiling and playful. He washed smears of blood from both of us, with amazement rather than disgust, as if we'd come from battle and every new spot we found another proof of valor. Warmed in the shower spray, kissing him again in the sudden novelty of mutual nakedness, I began to feel almost like a human girl. He, at least, seemed to take me for one. And there was really no wound, it turned out, that couldn't be at least temporarily salved by kissing him.

When I mentioned I might still be bleeding, he said, "Wow, really? Light-headed? Do we need to go to the hospital?"

"Oh god, no. Please. I feel…fine." *Fine*, strange word to speak while naked in a shower with Quinn Cooper. "But it's not supposed to happen like this, right? I'm a freak."

"Are you a hemophiliac?"

There was humor in his voice, and I said, "I hope not"—too disoriented to feel the *déjà vu* of the question until later in my own bed, once the bleeding had more or less stopped without medical intervention. Without, what, stitches? And what, exactly, might have been stitched? *It will be way better the next time*, Quinn swore, and I fell asleep to that pair of remarkable notions, the *better* and the *next time*. That I might be some variation of normal after all. That Quinn might keep his promises.

But the next night was far too soon to try again, and in any case I had most of two papers to write. We contemplated waiting out the long stretch of the holidays, until Quinn lit upon the plan that brought us to my attic bedroom. Here, three days after the first time, two since any blood or pain, would be the true test.

"Do you think I'm a slut?" I asked, as he lifted off my sweater.

I felt only curious, testing whether the question might feel sexy, but then his reasonably gentle answer—"Only in a good way"—made me tense enough that he felt it. "Don't worry," he said. "Embrace it. I'm loving this in you."

Because I was so different, so special, so unlike every other girl he'd not only despised but publicly destroyed for the same reason. I couldn't possibly believe this, yet belief was the only way forward. "No," I said, as if he'd misread me, "I just need to shut the door."

He held me back with a shake of his head. "Let me lead. You said you wanted to learn some things, right? So now we'll learn the beauty of a little light."

"What do you know about light?" I quibbled, while he unhooked my bra, began to undress the rest of me. "How much is there out on the dock or in the woods in the middle of the night?"

"Shh. Less talking. Unless it's obscene and specific."

In such terms—that is, obscene and specific—Quinn had given me to understand our two anatomies might not be sized for an easy fit. The idea served to dull my obliterating humiliation just far enough to deliver me, now, into a more animal fear.

Whatever my body thought it wanted, sex would murder me, like one of those arthropods driven to copulate when their mate is clearly going to eat them mid-act. Once he was ready, I clenched up so tight I couldn't fake my way past it.

"How about you try being on top? Then you can control it." He moved onto his back. "I'll just lie here and you can have your way with me."

This was the reason I was here, after all, to learn new skills. To expand myself with an exotic PE elective. But the still-present fear combined with him supine and watching made me chicken out before I had a chance to fail.

He switched our positions. He kissed me and went slow. And it hurt. I felt the disappointment more sharply than the pain. Yet it was a blunter, reasonable kind of pain, a tolerable pressure and friction.

"You look amazing," he said. "Open your eyes." I made myself do it, intending, for the duration of this adventure, to try any reasonable thing he suggested.

Afterward, we got under the covers. He murmured a story about camping in the Smoky Mountains with his father and brother as if we were sitting around the frat house with beers, as if lying naked together in my aunt's attic were not the most bizarre state in which we two could find ourselves.

We returned to our clothes and went out for burgers at a pub down the street. We'd become suddenly strange to each other, forgot how to talk. I imagined him busy thinking of ways to leave. Ordering a pitcher, he got carded—we forgot, on the mountain, that this happened in the real world—and presented an ID he told me he'd had since he was sixteen in boarding school. When the check came, he put down a credit card before I had to think too long about how to chip in.

If he'd walked me back to my aunt's stoop and gotten straight into his car, I wouldn't have been surprised. I felt ready, in fact, for him to go. But he followed me inside. We watched some TV. Upstairs, he drew me into my aunt's room, chased out the cat, and tossed me onto her queen-sized bed: number three, not bad. And from the lazy tangle of morning in a bed we should not have been in, four, better still, with sunlight pouring in at the window and nobody's teeth brushed. The cat meowed at the door.

"It's weird I've never tried this," he said to the ceiling, hands behind his head. "I mean, even in a bed is kind of rare for me. But doing it with the same person. Waking *up* to do it with the same person."

"That's crazy," I agreed, settling myself against him. "You're like a virgin."

His brow folded, musing. I withdrew my hand from playing through his chest hair, over his nipple, rationing touch, and he grabbed it back. "Don't stop."

All my desire just then was concentrated in stasis: to lie draped along his side until he booted me out like the cat. So I was relieved in a way that a lunch shift would force me up and out. Stella's, the diner where I'd worked since the summer before college, employed enough UT students that I could count on being called in the instant the holidays began. Too long with him in that bed and I might start feeling too much, or worse, saying it. I would ask for more than I should, like *stay one more day*. Measuring every word against the loop of *it's just sex* in my head, I'd become quieter with him. The image of myself taking this leap into liberation, having a wild side, having fun, was like a snow globe to turn over in my hand and admire. I wanted it to go on, for him to want the same. But I couldn't let myself start to need it.

As I hurried to get ready, Quinn still in bed, it struck me that I hadn't thought this through, that I should leave in street clothes and change at Stella's. But I didn't have time to dress in other than my uniform, a turquoise polyester shirtdress with white trim, hideous enough to make me cringe even when no one whose opinion I cared about had to see me in it. "Don't laugh," I warned him.

He examined me from the bed, half draped in the sheet, propped on an elbow. "Now that's hot."

"Ha. You're kidding, I assume."

"Not even a little bit."

I looked down at myself, wondering what he could see in the uniform that wasn't the opposite of hot. "So I work until six. Will you be here when I get back?"

"I don't know. Maybe." He studied a fingernail. Impossible to tell if he was being coy, or if he'd given it the first thought. His body had all the stark, pale beauty I recalled from a painting, some languid and velvet-draped young poet or philosopher, possibly deceased, projected onto the wall-sized screen of my sophomore art history class.

I set a spare key on the bedside table. "Stella's on Cumberland. If you leave, lock up and bring me this. Okay? I need it." I was aiming for cool, nonchalant, but maybe this had sounded cold. I smiled from the door to soften it. "And be nice to the cat, or I will fucking kill you."

He turned up in a booth that day, and the next, and the next, this facsimile of Quinn who had followed me home. Every time I expected him to hand me the key, but instead he sat for an hour or two over coffee, reading an aeronautics magazine or a book on chaos theory he'd bought at a street stall. When I got off, he was waiting back at home, and we'd go out to dinner or order in and watch TV, trying to delay sex, to hold ourselves to twice a day to stave off soreness. I waited for some indication he was leaving. I never asked. In clothes, he tended toward detachment, as if present not by choice, just waiting out the time; yet he slept wrapped around me, his face in my neck or my hair. *What have we done?* I kept thinking, the two of us wound up and dozing.

Regular sex unwired him. He surprised me with long bouts of mellow sweetness, of not seeming to mind lying around naked and idle, talking about nothing, or about the guys who'd sat alone in my station that day—every one a creep or a weirdo, according to him—or about my father, whom he called "that shit," based on his notion that the man had to be forced to call his daughter on Christmas. He surprised me, too, by never pushing sex beyond a variety of positions he'd toss us into; he seemed to consider acts past a certain line to lie in whore territory, impolite to expect of a person he meant to eat dinner with later.

Meanwhile his parents must have been having fits. "They're fine," was all he told me, after at least one phone call I wasn't present for. Much as he liked to pretend his father was a brute, I'd deduced from his stories that the divorce and ongoing hostilities had left Quinn in position to be coddled from both sides while he did essentially what he pleased. And often what he pleased was to test their limits.

"What did that asshole tip you?" he'd mutter, at the exit of a solitary customer who had spoken maybe a dozen bland words and done nothing more than eat a BLT, but probably had a look on his face Quinn didn't care for. Any tip amount was damning. For a standard fifteen percent on a larger check, he'd say, "Two bucks? Are you serious? What does he think you're going to do with his crappy two dollar bills?" Less, and he'd spin fantasies of violence. More, and it was: "Told you he wanted to get into your pants."

"Your boyfriend," my manager, Marty, called him.

"Just a friend," I said.

Marty was tall, dour, mustachioed, married. "Looks like a jerk," Quinn decided.

Though self-conscious at first, I felt competent enough at the job that I began to enjoy his watching, finding the whole enterprise down to the smiling slice of pie on my nametag somehow sexy. I kept his coffee warm, brought him random plates of food he hadn't ordered, and when Marty made me kick him out, he left a twenty for a tip.

In the dead of mid-afternoon, when there were no solitary patrons for him to snarl over, I would sidle up to ask in my waitressly way what I could bring him besides coffee. By day four, it had become a little scene we enacted, and I knew he wouldn't ask for food.

"Your panties," he said, deadpan. "Go take them off and bring them to me." Normally I'd laugh in mock disgust or swat him and turn heel toward more respectable duties. But as his requests went, this one was the first I could grant on the spot without being arrested. I ducked into the ladies' room, shimmied out of my underwear and stuffed them into an apron pocket, then carried the coffee pot to his booth. When I thought no one was looking I dropped them into his lap.

He left Stella's soon after but was waiting just inside the door when I got home, not a word before he pushed me back against it and began pulling up my skirt. He wasn't usually rough, impersonal, unreachable in his self-containment, but it wasn't the first time I'd felt that blankness pass over him like a cloud shadow. As long as he wasn't hurting me, I let him go. I liked knowing he was turned on. I liked being the cause of it all by myself, even if I sensed I was no longer fully there for him, that I could have been a stranger, anyone. Go along, I thought, and he'd outrun that cloud of toxic frustration that followed him. This time, this time, maybe I'd be what he was seeking.

Afterward, sliding back into his shorts, he said, "Are you aware that your underwear is ridiculous? Seriously. You need to do something about that whole situation." He held up the panties I had taken off at Stella's, hooked on a finger. They were one of my better pairs, in that they were pink and satiny rather than white cotton, and relatively unstained, but holes were opening at the seams; the elastic sagged and frayed into fine, catchy threads. "I mean, have some self-respect, really." He dropped them on the coffee table.

I stood blinking, slashed open by a few words, as undefended as I'd been with Brantley in the dining hall more than two years before. Was he disgusted that they were rags, or that they were briefs, or that they'd come in a bag of six from K-Mart? All three? My bras were as bad or worse: once white, worn soft and puckery from too many washings, without frill but for maybe a faded pink rosette between the cups. I had never paused to consider their appearance—and this was the failing that blindsided me. That even after a boy had started seeing them, and I was fully aware which boy it was, I hadn't formed the first notion that what I was taking off anyway should matter. All at once I understood that any other girl, even a very stupid one, would know better than to subject a boy to ugly underwear. And yet I felt rage too, that these were *my* things, parcel to what I thought I'd been so brave and generous to give him.

I picked up the panties he'd dropped. "I can arrange for you not to see them again."

"Oh, come on. Admit I have a point."

As I yanked my uniform back into place, it occurred to me this was one of the few pieces of my clothing he found attractive. The strapless red dress was another, of the same order: costumes for some trashy fantasy. But when I dressed to go out for dinner he'd say, "Is that what you're wearing?" "Is that all you've got?"

I fled upstairs, where I shucked the uniform and put on my flannel robe, another rag he was sure to hate. My anger had seeped away into a threat of tears, a frantic need to remake my entire wardrobe with a genie's blink. But the truth was that even with a pile of money, I wouldn't have known what to buy. What was the right sort of underwear? How was the right kind of girl supposed to dress? I knew a piece of this feeling from battering myself against Jonathan. With Quinn, I was a different sort of wrong, but all the same, the wrong sort of girl.

He leaned in the doorway. "You're being kind of insane right now."

I wanted to scream whatever magic string of obscenities would make him disappear in a puff of smoke. But I wouldn't be anything he said I was. "Right," I said, as close to placid as I could will myself to be with blood burning my cheeks. "I'm insane, so I guess that means you don't have to apologize for being a jerk."

"Are you crying?"

I touched an eye to check. "No. And fuck you." I moved around the room picking up clothes, mine to tuck into the laundry basket, his to pile at the mouth of his open duffle bag.

He sighed, oppressed. "How about if I rephrase? I'm just trying to be helpful. You wanted to learn things, right?"

True, though I'd already wished more than once I hadn't told him so. I did want to learn. I just didn't want to be taught by him, nor have him watch while I blundered through the lesson. I had to stop myself from granting him the point about the underwear. In a voice gentle and reasonable, if wounded, I said, "You're the one with the credit card. My daddy didn't send a check this week, so if you need to see some pretty underwear, maybe you could go get some. I'd wear it."

This was a little unfair when he'd been paying for dinner every night besides grossly overtipping me, and I'd wondered if he might be making some trouble for himself, overusing his father's MasterCard. But I hadn't spent these years holding the orphan card up my sleeve without learning how to play it in a pinch. And Quinn was a pinch, all the more once our few days together had rendered my habitual concealment of the poverty more or less futile. He'd watched me pick coins from sticky tables and attempt to smooth crumpled dollar bills into a stack. Often I'd perceived my terrible mistake, though less profoundly than now: I'd let our bouts of intimacy trick me into exposing myself in ways I couldn't take back. I should have made him sit at home while I worked. I should have changed into the uniform after leaving the house. I should never have told him where Stella's was, so that he could invite himself there to sit in audience while I degraded myself.

Then again, I should never have let him into my aunt's house. I should never have let him under my clothes, into my body. Where was the line I had failed to draw? I wanted the mutual vulnerability we sometimes shared, and then its opposite: pure privacy. I wanted to give him everything and then erase his mind, or barring that, make him find every detail of me down to the loose thread of my underwear sexy and endearing and beyond reproach. That I couldn't make him into this non-possible person by clenching my fists and willing it brought me near hysteria with the urge to kick him out and bar the door, leave Rockhaven, change my name, and start over somewhere else.

"Look," I said wearily. "I don't know why you're still here anyway. Just go. Go home. Your family is waiting for you."

"That's what you want?"

I meant to say something poised and dismissive, but it wouldn't come. "I don't know what I want. But it's for the best." This sounded, as I said it, right, final, maybe a reprieve for both of us. I knew not to let him go without talking through the terms of our return to school, but already I was choking up and couldn't risk getting into it. "I'm going to take a shower," I said, and crossed the hall, shut the bathroom door.

He was gone when I got out, by which time I had convinced myself to be relieved. I would call him before Christmas to laugh about those four crazy what-were-we-thinking days, and maybe I could sway him against telling obscene, specific, and only slightly enhanced stories about me back at school. I was already back there, thinking of Jonathan and what I could salvage, when I went to take out the cat litter an hour later and he was sitting on the stoop next to a Victoria's Secret bag.

"I was just going to leave this for you," he said. "I was deciding, I mean, whether to just leave it."

I sat on the other side of the bag and peeked in, but all that was visible was a wrap of pink tissue paper. "Well, then you wouldn't get to see it."

So he came back in, and we made up by not referring to it. His apology was the bag, besides being careful in all he said, extra sweet and playful, and mine was to model pretty underwear and make another try at some of his more challenging requests, like the dirty talk, or telling him what I wanted, or making the first move. The last was the hardest: to initiate even a touch, a kiss, made me feel clingy, braced for rejection.

The next day, my day off, we went back to the Victoria's Secret store, since the silky, jewel-colored underthings he'd picked off the shelf didn't really fit. He consulted with the salesgirl, a glossy brunette, and she fetched item after item to my dressing room while he waited outside the door for a peek. At the register, he'd gathered an armload of lingerie, enough to bury his face in, enough for every day of the week as well as a few slutty special occasions.

"It's too much," I said. "I don't even need all this." In trying to picture all the underwear I'd glimpsed on roommates and friends, it came to me that the poshest girl at Rockhaven—Anna Vaughn Whitacre?—could not have owned more than a few of these items, a matching set or two. I wondered if I might be the expert here, and Quinn had no more idea of female underwear than he'd gotten from a racy catalogue. "And your dad is going to shoot you."

"I want you to have it," he said, pretending he wasn't pleased with himself. "You deserve it, and it's what *I* want, so shut up."

The salesgirl, dragging our booty over the sensor, said to me in a confidential purr, "You have such a great boyfriend!"

I raised an eyebrow at Quinn, who raised one back.

Farther down the mall, he spotted a pair of black velvet pumps, which he made me try on, and bought, and then we left the mall and went to Planned Parenthood. He had been telling me from our second time on how much better sex would be without condoms, that I should be on the pill, and I didn't have a doctor in Knoxville. We had both assumed a simple prescription would eliminate the condoms. "Bad news," I told him as we left the clinic. "It takes a whole month to start working." We hadn't been talking at all about the future, and I tried not to think about it, resisted all references to Rockhaven and our inevitable return. "We'll be back in school," I said.

"Shit. Really?" But he filled the prescription without me realizing what he was doing until he handed me a bag of three disks. "Start taking them anyway. You never know. I mean, twenty or thirty times might end up taking that long."

We were strolling back along the razor aisle of the drugstore, his hand on my neck. At first, on our holiday, he hadn't touched me in public, but now he would absently take hold of my hand for short spells or put on arm around me. "So I'll take this whole pack, and when I'm finished we'll have, what, that one time left?"

"Yeah, well. Let's hope, because that one time's gonna be worth it."

Over the next couple days, having learned my size in some detail, he snuck off while I was working to buy me clothes: two wool sweaters, a pleated tartan skirt, a rather conservative burgundy dress. He had them wrapped in boxes laid with tissue paper, Christmas presents to open early. To make me over, to show me his wealth, to annoy his father with every purchase or impress him with some image of the goddess more appealing than home: brainstorming for motive didn't stop me from loving each gift more than I wanted to, until finally I had to beg him to stop.

"Why are you sad?" he asked, my head on his thigh in twilight. From the radio, Sting sang in an echoey minor key of Gabriel and Mary and *gloria* that made my aunt's living room feel like Christmas in London in the thirteenth century. The song alone made me want to weep with inchoate nostalgia for a lost faith, or one I'd never had, or something. An ache, yes, but *sad* didn't come near it.

"I'm not," I said.

He'd asked before, and I'd answered the same. We'd fallen into ways of being that seemed outside the bounds of *just sex*, and I spent a lot of time trying to see the line.

"You love me," he said, as if he'd caught me at something embarrassing and was prodding me to fess up.

"I've always loved you. You know that."

He couldn't have guessed how it fed the ache to say it now, to remind him it was all free and not under my control. And did he really want me to feel more than I had in the past? He had a childish tendency to insist on my falling for him, to demand it, until I began to sense in it his new ride across the stream. This was how he meant to win.

And however he might have felt with me now and then, he'd have no real trouble delivering the sting. Buy me all the sweaters in Benetton, I would never be the girl he had in mind. One day, I told myself often, he would marry a pretty-enough girl who came from money, who played tennis and knew how to dress and would keep herself thin while bearing the appropriate number of his children and many years later, drunk at a reunion, he'd drag me aside to gripe about all the ways he hated her without ever forming the first regret over what he might have missed with me.

Not that I wanted it otherwise, really. Once, in the course of our battles over attending Rockhaven, my father had conceded with harried sarcasm that the school might be worth the price if I could use it to find a rich husband. Hearing this enraging piece of news may have marked the beginning of my understanding that I didn't want to be married to anyone, ever. And if by Christmas of junior year the knowledge had not yet solidified, I felt ninety percent sure I'd prefer being Quinn's reunion confidante to trading places with his wife.

Confining myself to closer futures, even while we were laughing or naked, when I was overcome with delirious happiness, I never for long forgot we were in the bubble of another life. This was not the Quinn who would return to Rockhaven, and I knew the other one too well. What would we be once school started again? I wasn't ready to lose what we had, but there was no alternative I knew how to imagine.

He told me nothing of how he'd explained his absence to his parents or how they responded. But the day after our blow-up I overheard a mollifying call, in which he was forced to commit to a departure day. "I should bring you home with me," he said, as we sprawled on the bed with the cat wedged between us. He pressed a finger between her eyes, trying to annoy her away, but she was the sort to settle in and purr more loudly. "I hate you being alone for Christmas."

I wouldn't have considered going even if he'd been serious about it. In his telling, the holidays sounded like constant strife: fighting with his brother, a senior at Auburn, over who got to stay in their mother's pool house; his parents fighting over which one got to take the boys skiing in Vail or surfing on Oahu for New Year's. And yet I could tell he was looking forward to being there, that Christmas and family were at some deep, unmentionable level as sacred to him as to my other friends.

"You can call me," I said. "If you want."

"You don't think I'd call?"

I answered with a look that said the obvious. He moaned, teasing, "God, you think I won't! Because you have no faith in me, and you don't even *care*. That's cold, sister. You're the most brutal, heartless girl I ever met." This was more approbation than complaint, but still strange to hear, since it was how I thought of him. I was the sappy, susceptible one. Maybe he was only providing another lesson, coaching me in how to be. If he truly saw me that way, I must have learned it by mirroring him, as I had mirrored the other boys through those summers of letters, mimicking their moods and attitudes for the right conversational response.

The night before he left, he told me to put on my new dress and shoes: he had a surprise. I could guess where we were going, a restaurant of famed elegance called Antoine's, which I had mentioned as a dream place. And I didn't spoil his surprise, though I debated telling him I didn't feel well. I honestly would have preferred to order Chinese and eat in front of the TV. No one had warned me before I'd started Rockhaven how hard it would be, the exposure to money and what came with it, those various lives not meant for me. So many tastes of what I'd never have again.

"Why are you sad?" he asked, while I tried to puzzle out an option or two from a menu all in French.

"I'm not," I said. "I'm happy."

Later, lying with him in my aunt's bed, I asked, "Has it been twenty or thirty times yet?"

"Well, pick a number. Is it twenty or thirty or what?"

I'd intended to tell him we should call it done, end it while it was good—and it was; we were almost in a place to say so—before school started and the mountain made a mess of it. But his voice was full of play, and I was too happy. "Um. We should say thirty."

"Good thinking. And no, not even close."

He stayed seven days that seemed like twice that, perhaps in the way that days are long for young children to whom everything is new. In that time we spoke only a little of Brantley. But we studied the mark in the sealing wax, tricky to discern until I thought to try a pencil rubbing on overlaid paper: a broad-beamed cross inside the circle, and at the center some sort of plant with wicked leaves and a bulbous flower head in the form of a human eye. While I worked, Quinn visited the UT computer lab, where he found some assistance in extracting the contents of the floppy disk. What it held was no more than the code on the laminated card, a copy in another form, but a small victory since the blurring on the card had left us uncertain of several letters. Over those days, if Quinn was feeling agitated, he would scrawl the code from memory on whatever was handy. He wrote it on blank pages of the book he was reading, on receipts in restaurants, sketched the insignia beside it. I scooped up napkins at Stella's he'd penned with the series:

ANA57
MPH03
REK45
WCW09
WLS59

I kept a few of these. When he was gone I was always finding them in drawers, under the mail, in the odd pocket.

BOOK TWO

EASTER

10

THE LONG WAY DOWN

For spring term, two of my English classes, Southern Literature and Shakespeare II, would be shared with Will. My third he'd taken previously, American Romanticism to Realism—a title with the ring of a Rockhaven inside joke, as if the class were designed to slap us awake from our special reverie. To crown the point, it was taught by the department's lone female, Madeline Mathers. My friends and I chose it despite our half-facetious concerns that we'd be courting danger to take it before senior year, its effect like that of waking a sleepwalker: "Zero-point-five percent chance of permanent zombified psychosis," Pem claimed. Will had survived it, I could have said, except that I wasn't entirely sure he had.

In any case, we hadn't begun classes, let alone cracked the first page of *The Scarlet Letter*, before the rumor about Quinn and me had been passed to the four corners of the domain and back. Somehow I'd returned to campus under the delusion that I could control it. Jonathan had phoned me in Knoxville on Christmas Eve, and for a minute of that call I'd dreaded what might emerge. If he asked the right kind of question, I wouldn't be able to lie to him, and if he were anyone but Jonathan, I might not have minded letting it out. But we had a lovely long talk so full of other matters that Quinn and the formal were never mentioned, or we purposefully talked around him. In the morning, to my father, I lied easily: my aunt's absence aside, all was as usual, and he helped by showing no curiosity. This second call solidified my sense of a dull, chaste, working holiday, so that later in the day when I talked to Jenny and then Vince, either of whom might have led me to a confession, the narrative was already in place, easier to deliver than truth. It felt like truth, even with Quinn beeping in on call waiting.

The fact that he called didn't answer many questions. We had conversations much like the ones girls seemed to have with very new boyfriends: long, languid, flirty, rife with loopy anecdotes, but unspecific. He floated the idea of returning to Knoxville after Christmas, of taking a road trip together since my aunt would be home. I told him I might be able to get out of work for a few days, and he thought he could sweet-talk his father into letting him continue to use the credit card. Finances were no real problem, though, since at the first hint to his mother that he might be in trouble for his spending, she had given him a second card, just in case. "Did you tell them you're spending it on your girlfriend?" I teased, and he said, "They know there's a girl involved." So that's what I was, a Girl Involved. I gathered, in fact, that Quinn had been granted a pass for running off as he had *because* of the Girl Involved. Soon, though, he mentioned his father was planning a family ski vacation; our road trip looked unlikely. Just before New Year's, he left for Colorado and didn't call again.

He was right that checking out twelve books had been excessive on my part. I didn't finish one. When I wasn't dragging myself through the hours at Stella's, I lay in my attic bed composing letters I'd never let near the mail or staring at the ceiling until my aunt wanted to take me to the doctor. I was fine, I insisted, just really tired. And I didn't want to eat—my stomach was on the fritz.

From a phone call or two, she had surmised the Boy Involved, yet her first question caught me unprepared. "You're not pregnant, are you?"

Oh, there it is, I thought. I'm fucking pregnant. I'm carrying the devil's spawn. And my period was complicit, a week late. It was almost funny.

I was on the verge of submitting to the doctor's visit when my period arrived. So it's some low-grade virus, I told myself; it's mono. I am not in love with Quinn Cooper.

I repeated this mantra until I made it true. Adding back in all about him that I'd subtracted, I remembered it was actually true. When it became clear he wouldn't call me again, I got pissed off, not for the not-calling but for the assumption he could hurt me that way. I retroactively decided we had decided to end our arrangement before school started, to call it a fling and go forward as friends despite any eagerness on his part to continue. Once settled in my resolve, I felt cleansed and whole, got out of bed, and started eating. The lingerie, so meticulously selected, was hard to return, but it gave me some pleasure to dump all but one set onto the counter in exchange for cute but sensible everyday underthings I could imagine letting some future boy see. The tricky part was eliminating my anger, which struck me in random, blindside bursts, and I had to breathe and remind myself I wasn't angry at all. There was nothing to be angry about. I was the queen, who on a whim had decreed a little sexual service. My knight had served me well enough, no reason for discomfort between us. If I wanted more, I would have it, but I didn't want more and wouldn't. If I ever felt the urge again, I would summon a different knight.

This was the worldview I'd arranged for myself when Mitzi—if not president of the campus gossip society then at least my personal source for most salacious news—came knocking our first afternoon back. She shut my door behind her and pinned me with a look. "All right, you little sexpot. Talk."

Under a less direct approach, I could have lied for an hour, but at this I collapsed backward onto my bed. "Great, what did you hear?"

"That some naughty girl took a *shower* in Lower Gilchrist, for starters."

"Oh lord…" This was not at all the rumor I was prepared for. "Listen, it's over, so totally over. And kind of painful, so I *really* don't want to talk about it." From under the arm I'd thrown over my eyes I peeked at her, cross-legged on the end of my bed, smiling with equal parts sympathy, guilt, and delight. I groaned. Could I not have invented some excuse for an emergency late-night shower? "Better tell me what else you heard."

It was only that, plenty when combined with the trip to Knoxville, which she admitted was "probably getting around." "I need this to go away," I said. "Do you think we can come up with a cover story? God, I haven't even seen him yet."

The last few words were strangled in a kind of whimper that made her gasp. "Do you *love* him?"

"No!" I cried. "No, no, no, no, no. I'm just dumb. I'm not…crazy."

"Poor little frog."

"Oh, please shut up." I began laughing hysterically, and then Mitzi laughed, and the whole debacle became almost, a little bit, amusing.

She told me a story she'd heard from hometown friends at another college, where boys had taken to rigging tobacco spit cups over doorways. Unquestionably, the victim of such a prank who happened to be in a boys' dorm at two a.m. would need an immediate shower. While we were arranging my excuse, Jenny popped in, then Carolyn came over, both having caught enough of the rumor that I figured I'd better enlist them both. This meant fessing up to Jenny that I'd slept with Quinn, and worse, hadn't told her. But I hadn't told anyone! Or I was *trying* not to tell anyone, but now everyone knew...

One of the smarter things my body ever did without me, it turned out, was to start sobbing right then, before Jenny could work up a snit and storm off. Magic tears: the girls all snapped into line, my hand-maidens, ready to calm me and take up arms against my oppressors. I'd served as a handmaiden before but had never copped to a crisis worthy of my own set. It was almost pleasant, like being Ainsley Rowell or Anna Vaughn Whitacre. Or, come to think of it, Suzanne Clyde, the girl I had attended as handmaiden once upon a time, who had survived being known as Buttsy but left school at the end of freshman year, after straying across the path of Quinn Cooper.

Being attended by handmaidens, one's former pals transformed into these creatures of boundless sympathy, could make one loose-lipped. Worse, they expected Quinn to have done something awful to me, and I felt so miserable and victimized that I had to remind myself more than once that he hadn't. Instead, I spent as much honesty as I could by confiding in some detail how bad the first time had been. To explain our trip to Knoxville, I said Quinn had talked me into a do-over, only once more, to prove it could be pleasant. And yes, I admitted, pleasant. But a giant, glaring mistake. No need for anyone to ever know more than the story we all agreed on: Quinn, to make up for my dress getting ruined by tobacco spit, offered me a ride to my aunt's house. And not even that: my handmaidens would relay only that there was a perfectly good and non-sexual excuse for the shower but one that was too embarrass-ing to Leah to tell. For those few persistent insiders sworn to secrecy, they'd have the spit story, the story that sooner or later always came out, so maybe people would buy it.

But, the handmaidens wondered, what story would Quinn tell? Ah, that was the question. "I don't think he'll talk," I told them. We were all on my bed but for Carolyn in the desk chair, and I sat propped against the study pillow girls called a Husband. "I really don't. But if he does—"

"If he reverts to form," Jenny put in.

"I know he could. But he's a known liar. He already lied about it once that same night."

Carolyn asked, "What made you say yes to him, after he did that?"

Good question. "I'm an idiot?" I buried my face in my knees. "And he's a really good kisser. He's a danger to society, is what he is." I was trying to be jokey but lifted my eyes in time to see them all exchange a look.

They promised to meet me for the walk to dinner in an hour, and then I felt so calm and brave and fortified that I sent them away and called Quinn. Even from Knoxville, I had never placed a call to him, had to dig into the piles of last semester's detritus on my desk to find the phone number to his Gilchrist room he'd once given me.

When he answered, my voice got stuck for only a second. Then I said, "Hi, it's Leah."

"Hi."

His greeting staggered a bit, taken off guard, and I said, "Look, I'm calling because I don't want things to be weird between us, and I gather there's this rumor going around—"

"Yeah. I didn't start it."

"I know," I said, before I knew if I meant it, my voice so serene it suggested the next words. "I trust you. I just want to get our story straight before this goes too far." I relayed the version Mitzi, Carolyn, Jenny, and I had concocted.

He laughed. "Okay. And do they know the truth?"

"Which truth is that?" The question was more for myself and my many versions, but it came out frosty, and he didn't answer. More lightly, I said, "I'm going to assume they know more than I'd like them to. But I really hope nobody else has to know anything happened between us. Can we try to keep it that way?"

"Yeah, but… Yes. If that's what you want."

"But what?"

"We can try, that's all. Secrets, you know, aren't always so easy to keep around here." His voice had fallen to a murmur, a flash of being in bed with him I had to shove away.

"Just watch your end of it."

His voice sharpened as if cornered. "Leah. I want to talk to you."

"We're friends," I said carefully. "We can talk when you want to talk. Any time. Don't worry, though, about anything else between us. There isn't anything."

"There isn't," he repeated. I couldn't tell if it was a question.

"There shouldn't be. There never should have been. It's okay. You don't have to think I'm mad at you for some reason. There's no reason for me to be mad at you." I shut my eyes, tried to stop the tape that had been spooling through my head for weeks. *Why would I be mad? I'm the queen! You're the knight!* "Just, please, promise you'll be my friend."

"Sure," he said, with a note like sarcasm.

I sighed, on the verge of a lecture on the importance of friendship, but found I had very suddenly hit the limit of my control. The rawest pledge knew what I still had to remind myself through multiple drafts of unsent letters: do not let out emotions where Quinn can get at them. Better not to have them at all. "Okay-talk-to-you-later-gotta-go," I said, the words strung together with a high-pitched fluttery note meant to convey my casual good cheer, and flat hung up on him.

"Shit," I whispered, too late to unconnect my thumb from the button. I had to manage him better. Manage myself. Hearing his voice in my Benson room had brought into stark relief that we were back in school, that whatever else Quinn might be, he was first a no-joke threat to what I most cared about, my normal Rockhaven life. If Jonathan and I could wipe a little hanky-panky from the slate, then surely Quinn and I could do the same. I needed him as the friend he had been, only that, and not someone who held a dagger I had to guard against every second.

I went down the hall to wash my face. As I was leaving the bathroom, a bright voice from the hall's other end called, "Hi, Leah!" Anna Vaughn. "You have a good holiday?"

I wanted to check behind me in the empty hallway for someone else named Leah. "I did," I said, near perky with automatic mirroring. Because she was still standing there smiling her pageant smile, I said, "And you?"

"Fantastic." Her voice was animated, confidential, pure Southern deb. She wandered toward me, so that I was forced against my dread to meet her near the stairs. Ordinarily, the rumor about me would not have found its way to Anna Vaughn. Nor would she have cared one jot if I took a shower with the whole Gamma Chi fraternity, as long as I kept to my set. But if she was actively seeking ammunition with which to destroy me… Would she even know how to use something like this, which mattered intensely to my friends and not much at all to hers?

"Will and I went to Martinique," she said. "He may have told you."

"No," I said, surprised. "I haven't seen him."

"Oh, well. He really needed a vacation, poor thing. He loves it down there. My family has a place. Did you do something fun?" The question seemed a thoughtless bubble of pleasantry, without implication.

"Not really."

"Quinn Cooper," she said, so abrupt that I flinched. "Just remembered the name of your date! You two sure are cute together." A question mark of puzzlement screwed itself into her forehead.

"We're just friends," I said, picking up, to my horror, her deb inflection. "Barely. I hardly know him, really."

But before I'd finished, the hint of intent was gone from her face, only my paranoid imagining. "Oh. Well, he seemed to like you a lot." *Lawt*, she said, with a quirk of a smile, only half-attentive. A door opened, one of her friends emerging to shriek as if they hadn't seen each other in a year. I took my leave with a wave and ducked back into my room.

So Anna Vaughn was going to be my friend now? Maybe she'd noticed my subtle assistance with Will at the formal, decided that if I was going to be around anyway I could be a useful ally. Either that, or she was scared of me. Managing me. She wanted me to know she and Will were happy, untroubled. Perhaps, too, she was checking on my communication with him.

Had they really gone to Martinique? It was easier to picture her placing a furtive call to him: *We need to get our stories straight.* But as soon as I conjured lounge chairs on a beach, drinks with umbrellas, I found myself hoping her sunny vacation story was the simple truth, that Will had enjoyed himself and would return to school tan and relaxed. If his happiness was a lie, a construction, so be it. If Anna Vaughn decided to lobotomize him with an ice pick to make him forget whatever he needed to in order to be at peace, I might consider helping her do it.

Except for one thing. I was three-quarters sure that pixie princess was somehow the cause of it all.

At dinner that night, Dex and Emery joined our ebullient and girly table, neither hinting at any knowledge of the rumor. Quinn was in his usual spot several tables away. I kept Mitzi's head between us but also looked his way now and then to prove to myself that I could. *We're friends* repeated in my head, and *This is my normal amount of looking.* Jonathan had been delayed in Oklahoma for another day, but Vince and Pem kept eyeballing me from a Gamma table, and as soon as Emery rose to get dessert, Vince popped into his spot. "We need to talk," he declared, comically scandalized.

The handmaidens exchanged smug, indulgent glances. Before the end of dinner, the boys at my table had been sworn to secrecy on the tobacco spit story, while the circumspect version had been told a few times around the room, since whenever a handmaiden rose to fetch something she was likely to be waylaid. Would I have believed such a story, I wondered, about some other girl? I wasn't sure. Might depend on the girl.

As the girls and I descended the Maxon front steps, wrapping ourselves in scarves and gloves, Quinn appeared at my side. The handmaidens, who would have circled me if he'd done something terrible, could only give me uncomfortable checking glances from a distance. "I'm good," I said to them. "Go on, I'll catch up."

"Let's walk," he said. Side by side in the frigid night, we crossed the road, aiming away from the lit paths others followed back to dorms. I felt only relief to have him next to me, to know he wasn't going to avoid me for days as I'd half expected. We ambled along the back of the chapel and through to the quad, where a few lit office windows and the chapel's stained-glass glow made a bath of ambient light.

"So," he said, hunched with his hands in his pockets, "I should probably explain." He blinked. "What's funny?"

"Sorry, just the way you said that." I wanted to imitate it back to him: his slow, thorough pronunciation on *explain* the way he'd once said *friends* to me, as if it were an alien concept he was attempting to use correctly in a sentence. But I knew it would only sound sniping, and I straightened my expression back to neutral. "No, go on. You were saying?"

Thrown, he had to gather himself again. "I should have called you and I didn't. Things just got strange and sort of complicated, when I was in Colorado." He spoke with some unease, forcing the words. "There was actually this girl out there I kind of got involved with."

This news, at once obvious and somehow unforeseen, should not have stabbed me as it did. While I tried to get a breath, *We're friends* went on looping through my head, and it triggered a reflex that popped up a shield in the form of a word. "So?"

"I...should have told you, I guess." It was nearly a question.

"Quinn," I said, on a great exhale of fog. "We're friends. Tell me, don't tell me. It's not shocking news to me that you fuck other people. You're kind of known for it. If you *waited* until Colorado and didn't fuck three girls in Montgomery before you got on a plane, that would surprise me more. For all I know, you were banging some girl out in your mom's pool house while you were talking to me on the phone! I would not put it past you."

Though he was trying hard to be serious, this very Gavin-esque characterization of himself drew a laugh. "Okay," he said, testing. "I guess I thought you'd be upset. And maybe it would be this whole big thing. That I didn't really want to face."

Bullshit, I almost said in pure sincerity, before I knew why. Quinn thinking we were exclusive, feeling compelled to report a transgression—something was off. And what did he mean by *involved?* In the instant his news had stung, I'd imagined him falling hard for some ski bunny, the right girl, everything I was not. If he was telling me this at all, the girl had to matter. But that picture was of some standard sort of Rockhaven gentleman, Pem or Dex or Jonathan, that I must have let myself forget Quinn was not. Quinn didn't get involved. He merely grew bored enough with one entertainment to be distracted by the next. I saw him then as I should have from the first, standing before me and scrambling about for an excuse that might sound more human than the likely truth: he'd stopped feeling the urge to call. With a girl or not, probably with, he was skiing, entertained, busy. He forgot.

I pressed a gloved hand to my forehead. Calling bullshit, putting him on the witness stand until he cracked, might have been fun but would have made me seem far more invested than I felt at this point. I said, "I don't know why you'd think that."

"So...we're cool?"

"Sure." I sighed. "Look, I'm really glad we can talk. I mean, we're talking, right? We're out here together, and it's not too weird? So we can just erase everything and not speak of it ever again, and we'll go back to the way we were. Like it never happened. Right?"

"Eleven," he said.

"What?"

"You tell me." He smiled and turned away toward Gilchrist.

Actually, I'd worked it out to more like eight or nine. He was overestimating. I scoffed and called, "Make that zero! Not kidding!"

Steps away down the gravel path, he turned and stage-whispered, "Pssst! You still on the pill?"

"Jesus, Quinn. None of your business!"

He laughed in the dark. "That sounded sort of like a yes."

When I asked Will if we were studying together again, he said *God, yes*—the matter, it seemed, was desperate. He'd pulled Bs in his English classes but failed two others including—for the second time—World Religion, a core requirement. He'd been placed on academic probation. Though he'd registered for another term of trail riding, he'd been summarily dropped from his PE classes once his Advent grades came in. He was hauled in for a lecture, in which it was suggested he might face removal as proctor and compulsory leave from his fraternity and other clubs. Rockhaven didn't like to carry out such threats, though, and he was left to remedy matters on his own. When asked why he was passing English, he told them, "I have a study partner." They advised him to find another in religion.

Though the first week of classes hadn't heaped us with work, Will suggested we aim hard for virtue, hole up in his room Friday night. Doing so meant I'd miss a gathering shaping up at the Gamma house, but I decided staying away wouldn't be the worst idea, what with Jonathan in a cold spell of undetermined origin and everyone else looking at me askance. Not to mention Quinn. I expected to find him cranked up for a while, eager to mess with me in any number of unpredictable ways that would only be enhanced by the arena setting of the house, every denizen keeping an eye on the both of us. No matter that our cover story seemed to be holding, I estimated the general assumption that we'd slept together at about forty percent. If I gave him space, let our rumor grow old and dull, he'd eventually be distracted by some new target.

Once settled in Will's room, I began to suspect he was more interested in hiding out himself than in studying. I did most of the work as we labored through the opening scenes of *Measure for Measure*—a comedy, but one Dr. Macintosh warned us we might find more disturbing than the lighter fare of first semester. Will stopped mid-line, claiming the tiny type was too much for a Friday night. He shut his eyes, dropped his head to the back of his chair. "Why didn't I just fail out? I don't want to be here. Yet here I am. Something keeps bringing me back."

"The beautiful scenery," I suggested in lullaby tones, making satiric what I meant sincerely. How could anyone, especially one to whom it was handed for free, not want to be in this place? "Your classmates, who love you and wouldn't know what to do without you." He opened his eyes without lifting his head. His jaw was covered in stubble. I didn't detect a tan. In his oatmeal wool sweater, in which he generally called to mind some robust woodsy sort building a fire in an L.L. Bean catalogue, he looked almost sallow. "I suppose Anna Vaughn wants you here."

He grunted. "Which reminds me, I'm sorry you had to witness that scene at the formal. I have been under strain and not myself." He spoke the last part with rehearsed wooden irony, adding, "This is me making sure you don't think any worse of us. Or her. Or something. We're extremely happy. We're practically engaged." He scowled at the ceiling's fluorescent tube. "Sorry, that light is more than I can deal with. And I'm dying for a drink. Please, can I corrupt you a little earlier than planned?"

A venting mood. I tried not to look too keen. "This isn't good for my reputation as a study partner. But yes, you may."

He headed for the kitchen. "I have to tell Quinn that shit about the formal too. Can you pass it on for me?" Before I could answer, he said, "How was your date, anyway? Love match?"

No surprise the rumor hadn't reached him at all. The pipelines didn't run that way. "No," I said, "but..." With that one unintended, somewhat elongated word, it came to me that I *could* speak, that Will was the perfect audience: insulated, sympathetic, not to mention the only boy in my life whose estimation of me might be improved by the news rather than the reverse. "Things may have happened."

He shot me an avid look without pausing from gathering glasses and bottles. "*Things*, you say? Of a physical nature?"

Already my inner censor was blaring *too much*; and besides, no matter how I wanted to talk, I couldn't risk sidetracking him just now. "Of a messy, complicated, stupid nature. Not to be repeated."

"Hmm. We'll see. He likes you."

This was Will being graceful rather than intuitive. "I think the word you're going for there is *liked*."

He mixed us a pair of Manhattans over ice ("No cherries," he lamented. "No fancy glasses either.") and shut off the lights, all but one lamp. If I didn't know him better, I might have expected seduction by the time he hit *play* on the stereo. And then what came softly from the speakers made me smile: "Girlfriend in a Coma." Not exactly make-out music. He tapped his glass to mine on his way to the armchair.

"So." Still in reading position, stretched sock-footed across the love seat, I sipped my drink. "Should it concern me that this is the song you've been listening to?"

He snorted and spoke quietly—"She's not that bad"—while looking off to one side as if at someone else's argument to the contrary. I remembered him saying once, *I talk to him sometimes.*

"You know," I mused, "everyone has always thought of you as the perfect couple. Me included. But lately you seem to me…"

"What?"

"I don't know. Un-alike." I meant in other ways than the formal had revealed, yet I kept thinking of Anna Vaughn's ferocious smile, Will fatigued and sucking down his drink. "You seem really unhappy, Will. Both of you." He said nothing, faintly nodding, not looking at me. "It's like you're married already and you can't break up. Like you're stuck."

"It's complicated, I guess. She knows what's best for me." He sounded thoughtful, more sincere than when he'd been reciting the lines she'd fed him. "She's smarter than me in a lot of ways. Tells me what to do when I need it. Not that I'm always super eager to listen."

What did that make me? I wondered. The angel he'd placed at his other shoulder? All along, he may have been hoping I'd be the voice to pull against hers. "Like about Brantley?" I said. "The room change? I'm guessing she was behind that."

"We just shouldn't have stayed together sophomore year. It was dumb. We should have split up and roomed with people in our own frats, like everyone does."

"I never do." I shifted into the closer corner, feet tucked under me. "Rooming with someone outside your social group is the only way you get a little privacy around here, I say. Plus you get to know some other people."

"Yeah." He leaned his curly head on a hand. "That part was good. With Brantley. We had this weird little world behind our door, and it was completely different from everything on the outside."

I had pictured them in that room so often and vividly that I felt I'd visited them there: the beds placed at either side of a second-story window with a view of Polk Tower, the two boys stretched out talking, calling each other *Baldrick.* Listening to Brantley's music, as we were now. "I guess I wanted to keep it a little longer," Will said.

From the stereo, "Stop Me If You Think You've Heard This One Before" was playing. "Is he singing about a trust fall?" I asked.

Will listened. "Crossbar."

"Oh."

My picture of their room, though, had gained a new shade: Brantley was in love with Will. He must have been. Quinn still skirted the question of whether Brantley was gay, as if it were beside the point, and maybe it was when it seemed to me half the freshmen boys who might have been randomly assigned to room with Will Oliver would have been in danger of a crush, if not obsession. Quinn's nearest words on the topic, murmured in bed, had stuck with me: *It was the way he looked at the guy. Early on, at least. He was so into him I don't think he knew it.* And it was the way Brantley talked about him, or later, the way he stopped talking about him. It was the way he kept people from their room or protected certain possessions from touch, as if all had been sanctified in the name of Will.

How quickly had it happened? Will had a way of engaging with new people, a soft, unguarded candor about the eyes that made his beauty hard to ignore. Perhaps it had begun the first night, without Brantley's awareness, as they traded favorite books between their beds, and by the time I'd watched him drape a leg in acid-wash denim over a chair arm on the Gamma dock, the dogwoods in bloom, he was in love with his roommate.

Had Will known? I doubted so, when there was nothing reticent in his own love for Brantley. He spoke easily of affection between them. But what had Anna Vaughn picked up on? "So," I said, "Anna Vaughn didn't object until Advent semester?"

"Oh, she did." He glanced toward a hiss at the black windows, the beginning of an expected snow. "She of the definite ideas, especially about the class of people I should spend my time with. To be fair, Brantley didn't help." He shook his head fondly. "Thought he was smarter than everyone. He *was* smarter than most people and didn't mind being a jerk about it, to her especially. He picked on my girlfriend, it's true. But he was aware she considered him beneath us. So I called it even."

"Wow," I said. "I mean good for you. I think most guys would have caved to the girlfriend on that one." And it would have been simple, painless, at the end of the year, when changing rooms for most was a matter of course.

"And then I caved to her anyway, in the fall, when it made a mess." His voice caught, fell to a whisper. "Why did I do that? I can't even remember. Leah, it might be the stupidest thing I ever did." He pressed a hand to his eyes, suddenly wiping tears.

"Why?" I asked, baffled, feeling too late the jolt of alarm.

"He'd be alive. Maybe."

"Why? Why would you think that?" *No*, I meant, in the lullaby tones. *No, of course not. Nothing you ever did was stupid or caused any harm.* "It couldn't have been that bad," I said, before he could answer. "Nobody dies over a room change."

I suppose it had been plain to me for some time that he was tortured by guilt. But whatever he thought he'd done, he had to be wrong. He was missing something. I didn't know how to make him see past his own murky misdeed, all the more urgent when I glimpsed the tiny chance he didn't know that it was really, somehow, Anna Vaughn who had done it. I still believed this, though Quinn had laughed in my face at the idea. I'd argued to him that Will might have nothing at all to do with the Order, that Anna Vaughn was the one who belonged. *Adorable*, said Quinn, that I could imagine a clandestine organization of this sort would admit a girl, any girl.

"Will." He was too far away to touch, slumped in the armchair. "You're hurting yourself, and over nothing. You didn't want to change rooms. You only did it because she made you. If anyone is to blame for anything, isn't it her?" My heart gave a surge that he seemed to be listening, turning this over. "You're not like her. She wants to make you... something else, right? Keep you with your own class." I was grasping, past what I understood. "Like all those special societies. Drinking clubs, things like that." He was watching me, dazed or wary, and I set my words down carefully. "She's the one who cares about those. Right?"

"Right." His red-eyed gaze turned baleful at the word, and for an instant I worried his anger was for me and not her. He took a panting breath. "Sometimes I think I shouldn't have joined a frat at all. Much less the...Dragoons, those other—" He swallowed, shook his head. "I hate the club mentality. I hate the sadism and the conformity, the obsession with control, obedience. The fucking entitled assumption that you submit to this so that one day you rule the world. It's such bullshit. I *hated* being a pledge."

This attitude, striking in its vehemence, was not one I was used to hearing among the boys in my set. I recalled Will as a pledge in my freshman room—often I forgot he was that person—when Pem had declared the two of them free men: *We don't let others dictate our movements or the company we keep!* It was the sweetest sort of freshman naiveté, already a joke.

"Other people say that," Will muttered, "but I really hated it."

Until this moment, I hadn't put the two together: that if Will truly belonged to a society more secret than the Dragoons, then he'd been a pledge in it. And that at the time, against the wishes of everyone around him, he'd been rooming with Brantley, the two of them closed up in their little world behind the door.

Slowly, cautious of any step outside the bounds of what he had put into words, I said, "Did Brantley know how much you hated it?"

Will nodded. "He wanted to help me get out of it. But he envied me, too, for getting in. I guess we envied each other."

He fell to silence, backed by an ominous piano from the stereo. Our glasses were empty. "Only one more," I said, as he grabbed mine to refill, "for *you*, too," and excused myself to the bathroom.

Wasted at the football game, he'd tried to tell me something—to tell Brantley, wasn't that it? But too little had made it into words past the one, *classified*. The items hidden in the lake had led me to assume Brantley's snooping, collecting, had been a covert endeavor someone might have discovered—someone like Anna Vaughn. But Will had told him. Possibly a lot, and far more than he should have. Anything at all would have been too much, knowing Brantley, assuming the degrees of secrecy involved. The notion gave me hope. It didn't seem so much to be guilty of, if it turned out Will, like his roommate, had a bit of a big mouth.

Out in the living room, the lamp was shut off, the only light a weak under-cabinet glow from the kitchen. Will beckoned from the floor beside the stereo, flat on his back in the dark. Through the windows, a fine, swirling snow had whitened the grass but not yet the paved surfaces. "Come here," he said, "listen," and pushed *play*. I looked down at him—his arms spread open like Jim Morrison's, eyes shut—and I lay down in the same position and opposite direction, my head beside his. "This is how I listen to this song," he said. I glanced over at him, then faced the ceiling and closed my eyes.

He had rewound the tape, raised the volume. From the speakers came the ponderous keyboard notes, and between each stagger-step the faint sounds of a throng, its individual shouts swelling, almost discernible, growing angrier. The song would have been merely sad without this lead-in that made it wrenching, the poor soul at its center not just lonely and loveless but hounded by a mob wielding torches and pitchforks, meaning to tear him apart.

The music surged to a crest; the singer rode it down. *Last night I dreamt... that somebody loved me...* Another song from past Brantley's time that he would never hear, that Will had to listen to alone. That we all did.

A knock came at the door. Will didn't move. Another, three quick raps, and Anna Vaughn's voice calling his name. "We're not here," he said to me.

11

Some Rise By Sin, and Some By Virtue Fall

One of the benefits of having no money was my special dispensation to sit out sorority rush. Besides its enforced week of sparkling small talk with a hundred and fifty freshmen girls, rush demanded two to three advance weeks of work. Not that I could claim in the previous winter, having failed to apply for inactive status early enough, to have done much work. Others had been saddled with the all-night sessions of song writing, script writing, choreography, the ordering of punch and cheese trays. I had merely shown up to the many required meetings, strung decorations through our borrowed frat house, and cringed my way through hours of skit practice. At Rockhaven, Greek life for girls did not approach the intensity level the boys suffered or enjoyed, depending on one's perspective. But we far outstripped them in time spent putting on dorky skits.

This January, I'd received a letter in the SPO threatening to award me a hardship grant to cover my semester's dues. I had to beg them not to be so kind, imply I'd be too embarrassed to accept. Just one more semester. I'd get the money by fall for sure.

I did regret, now and then, missing the fun I might have had if I'd ever given sisterhood a real chance, especially now that I was guilty of a more promising form of sin. A dalliance with a semi-famous cad who belonged to no one was just the sort of blunder that might have brought me closer to them instead of walling me off. It was certainly nothing to bond over with boys. Then again, as Jonathan had said, maybe I had too little faith in them. Being granted these few weeks of spare time to drop by the boys' rooms, where female visitors were scarce most weeknights from seven to ten, I found my brothers—even Jonathan—more or less where I'd left them. Was it possible that succumbing to the worst of all ideas hadn't ruined my life after all? Though untempted to confess to them, I felt far more tranquil, after that week of nothing but sex, than I might have been had I made the mistake only once. I'd become near worldly in this one small way, no longer prone to obsess over the act itself or whether my friends could see it on me like a Day-Glo tattoo. They left the topic alone because I did. I fancied myself wiser for the experience, especially with Will, where I needed all the wisdom I could get. And during rush, in certain hours, we could relax without the risk of Anna Vaughn's knock.

The rush weeks passed without mischief from Quinn—mischief, I should say, of a noteworthy sort, since I'd been in his presence more than once, and he'd been breathing on each occasion, which guaranteed something afoot. Hearing his voice on my hall, I had spied him leaning in Polly and Kelsey's doorway to flirt; later, unable to further delay a trip to the bathroom, I caught him rolling around with Polly on her bed in the midst of some very annoying form of tickle fight, from which, as I passed on my way back, he paused to engage me in conversation. Once at the Gamma house he ignored me for an entire night. Another night he suggested we take the dock out and tick off one of the remaining eleven. (*Zero*, I said, *so no, thanks.*) A third night, he inquired what color underwear I was wearing; he asked to see it, just a peek, just a bra strap, *the top of a measly bra strap*—the last of which I might have granted if he'd found the right tone, the edgy-sweet play of our former friendship. He came close, once or twice, to making me miss him, and then he'd flash a sneer that took it all back. The creepy thing about the scorpion was not that, in pleading his case to the frog, he was deceitful for his own ends or unconcerned with the cost to others. It was that sometimes he had no real interest in crossing the stream. He was only a little bored and thought it might be fun to see what manner of stupid thing he could get the frog to do.

Yet he had not relegated me to frog. I knew because he kept his promises, a loyal creature, in his way, to those he considered worthy. Catch Quinn in the right light and you'd see loyalty was his one guiding principle. The problem with his maintaining a moderate level of decorum around his brothers, though, was that it came back to me all the quicker. "All right, what did you do to Quinn?" my friends would ask. "Why is he acting so weird?" Dex complained of missing his stories: "By now we all should have heard at least four conflicting versions of that formal date, with the nasty bits, and every one of them would have been *good*. Some of us around here aren't getting any action and we need stories, damnit!"

In any case, the mischief was negligible until one day in early February, when Will and I were leaving Southern Lit. The class was a senior-level elective Will had picked because the professor, Dr. Beales, was a poker buddy and frequenter of Edelman events, and I had picked because I loved Southern literature and Will could get me in. Since neither of us had much of our own crowd in the class, we'd fallen into the habit of sitting together, then leaving together, strolling down to the SPO to check our mail and making plans as we walked for the next day or two of studying. Coming out the heavy side doors of Hampsell, we were talking, and I almost didn't see Quinn leaning against the building with books propped on an arm, a notebook on top in which he seemed to be writing. When I glanced over his eyes were down, and since he hadn't seen me see him, I went on by with the crowd. Will didn't look his way.

Lately I could stand at the rail of the Gamma balcony, gazing out over the lake, and feel every step as Quinn came up behind me, though sometimes I'd turn and he wasn't there at all. With that heebie-jeebie awareness I sensed him following us down the gravel path, one of the many students passing between dingy borders of old shoveled snow on the noon migration to the Commons, but I had to check. Two steps back, he concentrated on his notebook as if he hadn't noticed us. Will and I were having a flippant and somewhat bawdy conversation about the Walker Percy novel scheduled for later in the term, *The Second Coming,* which featured Will's namesake in later years. "Beales lives to talk about sex," Will said, "whether it's literal or not. He'll make sure we all grasp what sort of *coming* is involved."

"And of key importance, I assume," I said. "Just forget Jesus and all."

Will peered at the gray heavens. "Well, Jesus was a virgin. Not much to talk about."

"*Or* he was secretly getting it on with Mary Magdalene."

My third glance back, Quinn popped his eyebrows at me, and a glower I couldn't keep from my expression made Will turn. "Oh, hey, man. What's up?"

"Admiring your gown," Quinn said.

"It's an old one," Will allowed. In his Phi O legacy, I had to admit, Will was stunningly picturesque, the gown faded pale at one shoulder and worn to safety-pinned scrap at the other, both arms ripped open wrist to pit, one front piece a lace of holes halfway to the tattered hem. Professors envied it. It looked sturdy, eternal, yet as if it might at any moment drop off him in a pile of dust.

"Plainly," Quinn said, as we all went on walking, Quinn between us. I wasn't accustomed to seeing him before noon and therefore dressed for class as he was today, in the same navy coat and gold-striped tie he'd worn the night we went to Antoine's.

"Were you following us?" I asked him.

"Maybe," he said, syrupy, as if he meant only me.

My few attempts at telling Will about me and Quinn hadn't made it past vague: we had a "complicated relationship" that was "emotion-ally all over the map," and were "still basically friends" despite those "lapses of a physical nature." Mostly I grumbled about him, which may have been as revealing as any story. Yet it occurred to me as we walked that trapped within the story I'd withheld was the very part I needed to tell him, now and immediately, the part that had not once bubbled up to the surface to be spoken or suppressed, and it was *Be careful around Quinn.*

As we walked, Quinn spread a bland, butter-smooth layer of ques-tions about the class we'd come from and our reading list and where we were headed. At the Commons, he held the door for me, ladies first, so that I was inside while he turned to Will as if inspired. "We should all have lunch. How about it? Get something at the pub?"

No, I mouthed back at Will with a fierce headshake, and the answer he was about to give stopped in his mouth. We all descended the inner stairs, and I said, "Sorry, Will and I have plans."

"Darn," Quinn said to me. Then to Will, "You know, I really have been meaning to get in touch with you. Get together, catch up." He set a brotherly hand on Will's shoulder. "Do some of that talking you mentioned. Maybe we could hit the pub some night this week, get a pitcher or two."

"Sure," Will said. We pooled through the doors into the SPO crowd. "I'd like that. Maybe Thursday?"

"Works for me."

I was on the verge of reminding Will we were studying together Thursday, but I could see where this was going. "Oh, you know what? I just remembered we *don't* have plans right now. That was a different day I was thinking of." My impulse was to at least ensure my presence between them; but I saw how it would confuse Will, who must have thought I was trying to avoid Quinn on my own account. And I wasn't eager to go blind into whatever trap Quinn had laid. Letting my distress show, I said to Will, "Actually, I have some things I need to talk to Quinn about. Do you mind, if we...?"

Will gave me the *say no more* face, a relief for the few minutes in which we got our mail and confirmed plans to meet later at his room. Then Quinn said, "Hey, Will, I just remembered Thursday might be a problem. Probably fine, but give me your number, just in case."

Will tore a corner from a pale green flyer and turned away to write on a table where Pi Alphas were selling Valentine's Day roses. Quinn twitched his nose at me.

Will handed over the fold of paper and bid us both farewell. He was still in the room, passing out the doors, as Quinn waved the paper scrap in a show-off flourish before my face. "Oh, and look, I got a note too!" He glanced at me over the top of the paper as he read it. "What a sweetheart. You know, I *like* that guy."

"What?"

"What does my note say? I'd tell you, m'dear, but you're being kind of a brat, aren't you?"

"You're the—" I was stuck for a word, seething.

"So angry," he said softly. "Why don't you want me to talk to your boyfriend? Aren't we on the same side?"

This was, I had to recognize, a reasonable question. "There aren't any sides," I said, deflated, anxious. "I don't know why you want to talk to him."

He threw an arm over my shoulders and walked me toward the stairs. "Come see what I found."

Upstairs, I was still headed toward the cafeteria in an automatic way, fretting over the crowded tables and people who would see us. "Screw lunch," he said, dragging me down to a bench along the hall. "Know any congressmen from Mississippi?"

Contemporary politics, not my strong suit. He opened a folder from his stack and handed me a photocopy of a news article, a puff piece it seemed, the congressman in question balding and smiling: William Lee Sewell II. In the text, a line of yellow highlighter marked his name where it appeared in full and "graduated from Rockhaven University in 1959."

"Ring any bells?" Quinn asked. At my confused look, he began handing me more photocopies. "These are from old yearbooks I got in the library." One page showed young congressman Sewell as a sweet-faced twenty-one-year-old, circled on a page of other school portraits, all male. The next pages were from older and older yearbooks—not a female to be seen—each with a single photo circled. On a page he'd marked in ballpoint with "1945," half the boys including the one circled wore military uniforms, sabers sheathed at their sides. The final page, penned with "1903," showed a blurry group photo of that year's Order of Gownsmen, about a dozen in all, with one face circled, the name in the caption highlighted: Martin P. Hill. In the margin under the year, Quinn had written "MPH 03."

He flipped open a spiral notebook to a page on which he'd listed the selected names from each yearbook, lined up beside Brantley's code. Initials, years of graduation. "I mean, obviously," he said. "The only reason we didn't see it right away is the code is alphabetical instead of numeric. I'm still figuring out who they are, who they became, how powerful. But these are the grand dragon wizard poohbahs, or something. Right?"

My heart had seized shut. "Boys and their secrets," I said, not quite achieving a dismissive tone.

"Men," he corrected. "Who don't want to be known."

And if so, if any of this was real, what happened to a boy—an obsessive one, a brash one, an above all loud-mouthed one—who discovered them? Nothing, I wanted to say. Nothing happened because it was a bunch of boys with a secret club. Unevolved upper-crusters who hadn't found enough exclusivity in their frats and ribbon societies and drinking clubs, who needed one more level to distinguish those who mattered. Yet I wanted to clap a hand over Quinn's mouth, grab his pen, and scratch out the names.

"Now look at this." He flipped the notebook to another page, another code-like row, but not the same. It was slanted and sloppy, maybe a dozen sets of triple letters followed by numeric pairs. "What do you see?"

I was too slow, scanning the unfamiliar sets, wishing them away with a sick dread before I really looked. He reached in with his pen to make an impatient box around a single one at the center: WLS 59. The congressman. "And where did I get that from?"

"I don't know, Quinn. I'm not as smart as you."

He gave a grunt as if I were being sarcastic, as if he didn't believe I'd concede a round to him in our long-running contest of who's smarter. "I got it from the back of your boyfriend's gown just now."

My brain was reeling with this for half a minute, and somewhere in there was an alarm voice: *Don't give him more.* But with no clear sense of what mattered, I could at least steer him off Will. "Okay," I said. "The gown is Anna Vaughn's."

"What?"

"Her dad's." I was foggy, trying to remember. "It's, no, not his, but he got it for Will. He was a Phi O. It's an old Phi O gown. That's all I know. Anna Vaughn's father is where it came from."

Quinn absorbed this. While he was questioning himself, I rushed in to dismantle what I could of the rest. I took his notebook, turned back to his coded list, and flipped through the photocopies. "This guy." I held the photo of Reginald Kirkland, class of 1945, against the list. "Doesn't give his middle name."

"I can find that. I just have to check some other sources."

I retrieved the young congressman, who was designated in the yearbook only as William Sewell, two photos down from a young man named Walter Smith. I pointed to Walter. "What's this guy's middle name? And what about the ones who missed picture day?"

"I know. That's why I had to look harder and get this." He rattled Sewell's news article. "Come on, guy's a congressman."

"Okay." I held my hands poised over his, wanting to take hold, still him, the way I had to with Jonathan when he got keyed up. "Do you see you're working toward the answer you want? If I gave you a random list of letters and numbers, you might be able to find them in yearbooks. And even if these are the people, how is it code? Code for what?"

"I don't know that yet."

"And...it's too easy. Isn't it? Initials and graduation dates. Any of us could guess it."

"Don't try to tell me it's nothing!" His voice nearly cracked with the force of anger, but his expression flinched toward a startling devastation. As if he were arguing with himself. "It's a reason, he knew too much..."

His own words stopped him; we'd both heard how crazy he sounded. Like Brantley with his theories. And here was the real weakness in his argument, the soft spot through which he'd let me introduce doubt, though I hadn't seen it to exploit. All along, I'd felt his reticence around Brantley's memory, riddled with what he couldn't or wouldn't tell me. But he had lied—I could see it in his eyes—when he'd told me with such offhanded ease that Brantley could not have committed suicide. *Not our Bran.* He only wanted to believe it. He was afraid of what he'd done. This whole pursuit was about finding something else to blame.

"Leah. Help me." His plea was so naked and urgent with real pain that I shut my eyes to it. He took hold of my arms. "Look at me." I did, had to. He drew a neutralizing breath. "You started this. Now are you going to help me? Or are you going to get in my way?"

"I want to help you." I felt I had never said anything more whole-hearted or true. All I wanted was to put my arms around him and make it better any way I could, yet he cooled and inched back to study me with suspicion.

"I don't know how," I said. "I don't have anything."

And what could I have given him? Nothing that would help, nothing I could parse the significance of. But I was almost sure of what I'd find the next time Will was called from the room by the same Stirling freshman who'd been knocking every other day to complain about the volume of someone's stereo on the third floor. When Will stepped out to intercede—it happened later that same afternoon—and the door closed behind him, I crept back to his closet, snapped on the bulb, paged rapidly through hangers in trepidation of his return, and maybe he'd put the gown away somewhere, stored it. But I didn't think he would take it off the mountain. After all, it, too, was a legacy, as much Will's as the Phi O rag he'd been gowned with.

Just as nerves fired warnings to give up, I found it by feel, tucked askew between sport coats toward the back. I drew the hanger out. Even after I'd seen the code a hundred times, it looked unfamiliar, stitched in white down the gown's left scapular, ordered by graduation year with Brantley's own initials, brighter than the others, added at the bottom as if he were one of them now.

MPH 03
WCW 09
REK 45
ANA 57
WLS 59
BAS 89

Surely I had seen in the first instant, though I'd never registered the fact, that the gown was too black, too new, to have initials that old. I simply hadn't had the space in my brain, when Will had shown it to me, to take it all in. Brantley had gone to the trouble to dirty his stitchwork somewhat, but the yellowing of the thread had a uniform look. I ran fingertips over this thing he had made before I tucked the gown back where it had been, careful to set it at the same cockeyed angle that had concealed it from me. Then I was in the living room with our books for a good ten minutes before Will's return, trying to recall the day he'd shown it to me.

"Look at those initials," he'd said. "Some of them are dead, right?"

Look, he'd said to me, and I hadn't.

You're a vault, right? he'd said.

Though Quinn put some effort into making sure I wouldn't know when he was meeting Will, it was only to show me he could get around me if he pleased. Wednesday night I was at my work-study job at the Commons' front desk, half-asleep over an Emerson sermon at ten o'clock, when a pillow-soft "boo" made me jump.

Quinn planted elbows on my tall counter-desk, close enough that I smelled the beer on his breath. "Looking kind of dead up here," he said. *Up*, the pub being all that was *down* at this hour. "You have to work until eleven?"

"Yes, Quinn. I do." I was careful to choose these dead-hour shifts, when my only tasks were to check out the rec room equipment for students who wanted to play ping-pong or pool, or to place the occasional long-distance call for them on the WATS line, which rang through from my desk to the bank of phones around the corner. The boys considered these my office hours if they needed to talk, but often, as tonight, I might go half an hour and not see another person.

He shook his head, *what a shame*. "We're about on our third pitcher down there. Your boyfriend gets kind of chatty when he drinks. You should come join us when you get off. He'll have ordered number four by then."

Past my survey indictment of Quinn's character, I'd found no real way to warn Will, even when he'd confided how glad he was to have a friend of Brantley's to talk to. *Be careful*, but of what? I still believed Quinn had the capacity to be that friend, that he would grasp Will's innocence if given the chance to know him as I did. I could almost squint into that future, the three of us joined against some better foe or simply accepting a sad truth. But getting Quinn there...I didn't like my odds.

He left me caged at the desk to watch the clock for most of an antsy hour, until I could lock up the main floor, ten minutes early. Down in the pub, Talking Heads' "Stay Up Late" was on the jukebox and a large, loud group played darts along the back wall. The bar was lined with study-break drinkers, and past the empty middle tables the high-backed booths were mostly occupied, Quinn and Will in one. As I approached, Quinn hardly glanced up from gazing with clinical curiosity at Will, who slumped across from him, a sobbing wreck. "Oh god, Leah," he wailed. He tried to right himself, fell back. Now he seemed to be laughing through a stream of tears.

Quinn slid over, pouring from the pitcher into a third mug. "It's a sad song," he explained for me as I sat.

"It's not!" Will shouted into his arms, collapsed over the table in hysterics. "It's about a baby! It's a happy baby, and it crawls..."

Quinn gave me a look that was nothing but somber. "And it's so cute you just want to mess with it."

"That's all it is. A baby baby." Will was slow to choose his words and arrange them for sense. He straightened on his bench and attempted a grip on his philosophy. "Who writes a song about that anyway? And how does that make me sad? Is it because babies need *sleep*"—his voice strained with emotion—"and those people won't leave it alone? But they can't help it. It's the damn baby's fault." He and Quinn locked eyes, sappy and fond; Quinn began singing along, mimicking David Byrne's angst over the baby's smile, too adorable for its own good, and Will joined in. A lip curled back, Quinn looked over at me as he sang with a faint head shake, meaning: are you seeing this?

Will stopped at the chorus, gasping. Quinn filled me in. "The juke-box is stuck."

"Is it?" I knew well enough the song was on Brantley's mixtape. The drive to Knoxville had given me ample time to enjoy it and then some. Quinn claimed he didn't hear it anymore, didn't notice the same two dozen songs going around and around. I had my doubts on that.

"It's probably the only happy song there ever was." Will pressed his hands over his eyes. "I'm just...because of..."

"Give me quarters," I said. "I can find you happier ones."

"We've been reminiscing," Quinn said.

Will remained behind his hands. "I can't say that word. Drank too much." The song started up again, to a groan from the dart players.

"I can say it," Quinn observed, a perky aside for my benefit. "How's it going over there, drunkie? You with us?"

"That's my word," I said, half to myself.

Quinn looked dubious. "Reminiscing is your word?"

"No, *drunkie*." When Will had been trashed at the football game, I'd given myself credit for coining it on the spot.

Quinn met this with a tiny imperious scoff. "I don't think so. That's Brantley's. Right, Will? You've heard it, I'm sure."

You sound like Brantley, Will had slurred at me. And then wept, apologized—had that been why? I couldn't remember. Quinn went on. "Late at night, come home a little smashed, wake your roomie up when you stagger in. *Hey, there, drunkie.* He puts you to bed, takes care of you. He was good at that. Like a nurse."

Will nodded, wet-eyed. "It's true."

I said, "I'm sure you did the same for him."

"No. No, I never did."

"Regrets." Quinn offered the word gently. "This is what we've been talking about, Leah. You have any regrets? Will and I have a few." All his innuendo rinsed away, he spoke slowly, thoughtfully, pausing to drink. Will nodded along from deep in some shared space Quinn had fashioned. "For instance, I was regretting earlier some of the ways I made Brantley miserable just before he died. For expressing an opinion, because I didn't like what was being said. It seemed like a threat to me. And I don't think it really was. If he were here now, we might be laughing about it. But he's not. There's nothing more I get to say to him, no way to atone." The word snagged into a breath. His attention had left Will and drifted into the tabletop. "And maybe he died thinking I wasn't his friend, that he didn't have any friends left."

"No," Will whispered, a word meant to stop, to retract, some terrible event in a story that had already happened. "He didn't tell me. Just vague...some friction. He would have told me."

"Would he?" Quinn sipped his beer. "Even after all that with you?"

Will started a yes that was choked off. "I don't know. It was just harder to talk to him. After we weren't rooming together." Drowning, he set a hand on the table, reaching toward me, and I laid mine atop it, a safety line. "I missed him so much. Even then. He was still alive and I missed him."

"Me too," Quinn said.

If I had joined them in this booth having discovered them by accident, I might have tiptoed out to let them finish alone. Will smiled at me. "I've told you, maybe. How I felt like I knew him so well, but we only had this...part of each other, the part that was in the room. And then I get around people like you"—he turned to Quinn—"and you knew him a whole different way. That's a regret, not knowing him the way you guys did." He grabbed hold of the pitcher, shut his eyes. "Sorry, Leah, we're a little... You might need to drink more."

I examined him toward a diagnosis: exhaustion, too much beer. And if this was helping at all, he'd soon be unlikely to remember it. He went to refill his glass and I stopped him. "You have a test in the morning."

"Oh, shit. Yeah. I should go." To Quinn, he said, "If I fail this, they'll kick me out of school. And worse, Leah will be mad at me."

"I should go too," Quinn said. "I'll walk you that way."

"No, you guys stay. Finish that pitcher." Will stretched his eyelids wide, smacked himself in the face. "I can make it home."

Quinn didn't like it that I was blocking him from getting out of the booth as Will rose. From the seat he said, "Let's do it again. I'm serious."

"Definitely."

On impulse I said to Quinn, "I'll be right back. Keep my seat warm." He gave me a narrow look from the booth as I walked Will out past the bar and into the hall.

Threading his arms into his coat, he appeared groggy but competent. "Are you okay?" I asked. "I don't mind walking you home, even if you just want to talk a little. He can sit there and wait for me."

"I'll be fine. Sorry for the—" He waved a hand at the pub. "Man, that was intense."

"Quinn is intense."

He nodded. "Kind of spooky. He almost reminds me of Brantley. Just the way he talks, I guess. But it was good. He's a sweet guy." He pushed my shoulder, teasing. "You should give him a break."

Back inside, the jukebox had finally switched to the B-52s. I slid into Will's former seat. "You must be proud of yourself." Over the lip of his mug, Quinn gave me a perfunctory shrug-and-smile, as if this game were no different to him than the torment he'd visit on his brothers over some girl or vice versa. I pulled my beer into range. "Is it really that fun to poke someone who is already such a mess? He is *grieving*."

His open hand slammed onto the table, a crack so loud half the room turned to look. "*I* am grieving."

His fervor as much as the sound made me jump, left me gasping. And he was right; minutes before, I'd been there with him and had already let myself discount it, brush it aside. "I know. I know that, Quinn." He looked past me. I felt my own terrible act of betrayal, to take Will's side when Quinn needed me on his. Or maybe sex had ruined us. Once he'd manufactured pain just to get me to pet him, and now he wouldn't let me close enough. "I'm sorry." I took a shaky breath, suddenly fighting tears. "But you have to know he is falling apart. He's not stable."

"Oh, *wah*. I was so careful with him. You were sitting right there for the worst of it." His voice quickened into a growl. "I was helping him. He wants to talk, he is *dying* to talk. That's what's killing him, eating him. Don't pretend it's news. All those hours you spend with him, if you haven't gotten a confession yet, you're doing it wrong."

My mouth opened to object in ten ways; he leaned across the table, on boil. "He didn't even give me a chance to bring up the congressman, all that shit. And I don't know, maybe we forget all that shit. Because this is starting to feel very personal. Between the two of them and that room. Another pitcher, he'd be telling us all about it."

"Please. Another *beer* and he'd be passed out." He wasn't wrong, though, about the secret that pressed to be spilled, filed under *classified*, nor about the weight Will put on the room. "There are all kinds of secrets," I reminded him, "that get hidden in rooms, or that pass between roommates. And it wasn't just the two of them in there. You're forgetting Anna Vaughn."

"Funny, there's a name I didn't hear once all night."

With so much accusatory steam rolling off him, it was hard to escape the sense that he was scarcely seeing Will at all, only projecting what he meant to find. "Well, he says her name plenty to me, and she *really* hated Brantley. He would tease her in nasty ways, make her feel stupid. Say things that were vaguely mean to make her insecure. Kind of like you might do to some poor girl."

I'd not yet found occasion to bring this up, but as I spoke, it felt like more than a swipe, more even than the lightning awareness that Brantley had surely learned the trick from Quinn. It felt relevant, a clue. If torment of that sort was flirting, and Brantley had been an idealist, pining for what he couldn't have, could Will have meant they both wanted Anna Vaughn? Even if Brantley's true fixation was Will, pursuing Anna Vaughn might have been as close as he could come…

Quinn crossed his arms and broke into a fascinated grin. "Wow. You *really* want it to be her, don't you? All ninety-eight pounds of Anna Vaughn Whitacre went and threw someone off a bell tower. You just couldn't stand it, if it was him."

The slowing of his words, the epiphanic glint in his eye: *you just couldn't stand it* about three doors down from the evil scientist saying *let's try a little experiment.* That one insight, if he latched on, would compel him to push until he proved Will's guilt or made it so or drove him off the bell tower with the trying. I had to fight my voice into calm. "You're the one trying to *make* it him."

He softened with sympathy. "I get it, you know. Why you like him, why you want to protect him. I like him too. And sure, Anna Vaughn may have had something to do with it. But review your Shakespeare. Lady Macbeth wasn't the one holding the knife."

"There's no knife," I muttered, distracted, then reconsidered his metaphor, the *f* caught between his lip and teeth. "Will didn't *kill* him. If that's your idea, cold-blooded *murder*, you are way off in delusion land."

"All right." He sipped his beer, alarmingly mild. "You want to talk about something else?"

"Yes. Can we?" Here, at least, we'd come to a rare oasis apart from the usual spectators, half a pitcher between us and half an hour until closing. I worried he still nursed the wound I'd delivered earlier—so hard to tell, in any reaction of his, whether I'd really touched him—but he would recover sooner than I would from the remorse.

He refilled our mugs. I tried a lame lump of a question about his astronomy class, and next we'd balanced on a wobbly conversation about classes. If nothing else, I could bury his theories in small talk, make them equivalent to any other mundane happening in our lives.

By the time the pitcher was empty and our glasses nearly so, he had relocated to my side of the table and we were deep into a head-to-head on our remaining eleven, and who might or might not be on the pill, and whose business this was not, and the finer legalese of our deal including whether contracts were voided by ski bunnies in Colorado or merely at my whim.

"Now, we didn't have a rule about extracurriculars, right?" In a cozy slump against the tall bench back, he left inviolate the foot and a half of space between us. That he'd come so close, for ease of talk, and yet seemed content not to breach that space with even casual touch became maddening. It might have been a solid object between us, that space, its edges the very contours of our bodies.

"No rule. Provided you could handle two at once." Debbie, I'd named the ski bunny, because he wouldn't. Having dropped a few roundabout questions to the right Gammas, I'd become confident that she didn't exist. And could he really have forgotten me for a ski slope? So he had stopped calling with at least a little intent, because whatever was happening between us was too complicated, too scary. I could sympathize with that. Even if he'd wanted only to get rid of me, had gone running from my feelings and not his own, it was better than being forgotten. "And frankly, it's surprising, that you couldn't handle two. Pardon my curiosity. It's just, Debbie must be pretty special, to steer you around like that."

"The only one who steers me around is you, darlin'." I had to chuckle at that: either the most extravagant compliment he'd ever given me or some random piece of flirty banter he'd speak to any girl.

When we were kicked out at closing, he insisted on walking me home. A few steps down the path, he stumbled into the slushy grass. "Hey there, drunkie," I said.

"Well, I had to keep up a little." Squint-eyed, he took my hand. I frowned, irked at his proprietary ease along with the casual acknowledgment of what he'd done to Will, as if we were in cahoots. But I let him keep it. The better to steer him around with, perhaps. Not that I had too firm a conviction about who was steering whom.

"Quinn," I said as we ambled up the path, swinging our joined hands, "I have a vision of the future for you. You want to hear it?"

"If we're naked in it."

"Will could be a really good friend to you." He dropped his head back to groan at the sky, *Him again?* "Listen, please. He came tonight because he needs you. And you don't know it yet, but you need him too. You *will* need him, once you figure out you're wrong about him. I can promise, you truly are the two people on this campus who care most about Brantley. I happen to be the one person who knows it."

"Is that so."

"Yeah, it is. And what I want is for you to picture how you might look back on this later, once you realize you're supposed to be friends. All you might *regret.*" He made no sign of hearing, giving me some hope he had.

Benson was locked for the night. Quinn kept hold of my hand as I went for my key. "You gonna let me in."

I laughed, almost soundlessly since we were under a dozen windows. "Ain't no boys in Benson after hours." Ours was a cozy house with interior stairs and rooms all folded up close. Not even the seniors with their singles could sneak a boy in without three people noticing.

"Commons room," he said. "Probably empty."

"Uh, no. The proctor lives right next to it."

Under the glare of the security light, he set me back against the door, moved up into kissing distance and waited, like a dare. Then we were kissing.

Was this closer? Were we touching? Our tongues slid together and I wasn't sure he was within reach. *I should stop this*, I kept thinking. "Okay, I'm drunk," he said, with breathy, bashful guilt, having just spotted his own mouth engaged in unsanctioned activity. When I kept still and said nothing, he returned. Why, why? Because it felt good, because we were drunk, because why not, if it felt good and tomorrow the excuse could erase it.

12

FEATHERS V. IRON

Every year, in the weeks before Valentine's Day, the Pi Alphas set up a fundraiser table in the SPO to sell roses. The buyer chose red, white, or pink, and wrote out a message on a card, to be affixed by ribbon to a single long-stemmed bloom and delivered on the day by the new Pi Alpha pledges to the chosen one's door. My rose count fluctuated year to year, but I could expect a few: Jonathan, Vince, Emery, and Pem would never fail to send one apiece. This year I had two more, from Dex and Quinn, almost a bouquet. Most of them stuck with pink or white, except for Emery, who always went red. My other red one arrived with a card signed xxQ, no message aside from a pale green scrap of folded paper he'd taped to the card, which I knew immediately to be the note Will had written to Quinn along with his phone number that day in the SPO.

Buy her a rose, it said.

On a blustery day at the end of February, as I passed the chapel toward Stirling, I could feel the skin ache of some flu-ish illness coming on. From the bell tower came the wind-broken notes of a carillon melody I couldn't discern, whipped about like leaves. Up in the high cabin, I imagined, the carillonneur played with a space heater beside him, the fingertips of gloves cut off. My coat was buttoned end to end but the hood kept blowing down. Still, I was almost buoyant, eager to see Will, who days before had floated a solution to the least loved part of my life. "You can't wait tables another summer," he said. "That's crazy. You need an internship."

Paid, he assured me. Rockhaven even had programs to kick in extra for those that were lower paying but worthy. I'd heard of them in passing but hadn't imagined how they might apply to me. "Almost everyone ends up a congressional page," Will said, "but you can do all kinds of things. Maybe in publishing. Work in some field station identifying beetles! You can go overseas. Just find your interest and propose it."

He rattled off people he could talk to on my behalf, in politics, finance, nonprofits. At first, the prospect sounded overwhelming, prohibitive when I had to think about living expenses and transportation. But to spend my summer doing something interesting! Unable to stop dreaming the scenarios, I hadn't yet narrowed the options even to a field.

And how had Will become averse to my waiting tables? "Quinn talks about it," he admitted. Since the pub, they'd been out a few times without me, which drove me a little wild with worry and wonder. But I'd gained enough comfort with the idea to encourage Will in it, not by achieving any control over Quinn—who had gone scarce in my life since the pub—but by working carefully to build Will's guard, dropping hints that kept him alert to trickery while still allowing for a friendship I believed possible. Quinn had the capacity. He and Jonathan had even been cordial lately.

"Sounds like you have it kind of rough, really," Will added. "And stuck with shit tips because you can't serve alcohol?" But he didn't seem to know the context of Quinn's opinion.

I'd always felt some injustice in my lot, at least relative to the majority of my classmates, but hearing Will say it was like news. I did have it rough! To convince my father at age seventeen, I had martyred myself for the college cause, pledging real summer jobs toward my contribution. Real was waitressing, and if I hated it, that was the price. I was, in fact, supposed to hate it. It had never occurred to me that I could change my station.

The cross-country team ran by, flanked by two dogs. On the porch of Stirling in my hurry to get in out of the wind, I was stopped by the wall of a person coming out. "Ah, the study partner," he said, before I had finished realizing it was Dalton Gibbs. "Leah Gavin. I hear you're to thank for keeping Will with us."

"Um," I said, or something less coherent. My brain had turned to fizz at the inarguable fact of him, not only out of place—I liked to keep him, when in view, at least eighty yards distant—but seeming to block my way.

"We appreciate it," he said.

We? I didn't ask, while he was looking me over with curiosity, as if I were some other kind of animal than the one he'd expected. "You're welcome?" I said as I sidled past, and now we seemed like two people who had met in a doorway and knew how to tackle the problem. Nothing in this encounter was menacing enough to leave me rattled and hot with relief when I was inside and he was not.

Will's door swung open at a touch. He stood at the window watching Dalton go. He had never explained to me why I should stay clear of Dalton, or why he himself need not. Will didn't change paths to avoid him, as I did. Passing, they might nod like business associates or pause to exchange words in a way that appeared mutually agreeable. And though I'd come to account for a fair portion of Will's time, he had plenty of it left to spend on friends other than me, if Dalton was one.

"Close the door." Will sat on the window ledge, bent over his folded hands as if in prayer. "I have this idea. About the gown. I know you're not happy with me, for never wearing it, and you're right. You think I'm a coward—"

"Brantley's gown?" I stepped closer.

"Yeah." He sounded impatient, as if we'd been discussing it for the last hour. "And you're right, you've always been. I am a coward."

"Hold up." I held both hands spread, steadying, a few inches from where he sat hunched on the sill, rocking a little. "Why do you think I want you to wear it? I don't think I've ever said that. Is that what you want me to say?"

He lurched up from the sill, began to pace with his arms folded. "Well, I can't. It's just not a good idea, for me. And that's my fault. I accept that I... But it's *his gown*, his actual... I mean, it shouldn't just live in my closet, right? So I was thinking it should go to someone else." He dropped onto the love seat, hands curved alongside his face as if to peer into some future. "That I should give it to the Gammas, and then they can decide. Maybe Quinn could wear it. Or maybe no one wears it, but the Gammas could at least have it and be in charge of it and make the decision. Right?"

Too many questions banging around in my head, I stood beside him and asked none. I'd never petted him the way I did my other boys; it had never seemed my place, and in reaching toward him now I sensed how stroking those curls might make him jerk back, snap something between us. I let the hand fall instead to his shoulder. "I'm going to make us some tea."

He followed me to the island and took a stool, while I filled his kettle, turned on the burner under it, pulled two mugs from the cabinet and set one before him. "It's not a bad idea, right?" he asked.

"The initials on the gown," I said, as gently as I could. The innocence of his expression didn't waver. "Is it dangerous?"

"No." His answer was slow, puzzled. "It's just…initials. Not unless you—" He stopped, brow furrowed. "It's okay if it's someone else. There are just reasons I can't wear it. But it looks like any gown. So Brantley's parents"—his speech quickened, earnest—"if they had just given it to the Gammas in the first place, like they should have, it would be fine."

"Will. Are you sure about that?" Before he could answer, I clarified. "I don't think you should be. Especially where it involves Quinn. He's pretty smart."

Will pondered this, as cautious as I was. "He knows what they are?"

"No. I don't either, and I don't want to." This last had become very close to true. It was enough to know that what Brantley had taken pains to hide in the lake he had also stitched onto his own back for anyone to see. A taunt, perhaps, to that club he'd hoped to join and could not. And after his death, by intention or not, an artifact to be preserved. I didn't, shouldn't, want to know what it pointed to. Yet the words fell out. "It's some kind of code?"

"Code," he echoed, almost mocking. "The code is nothing. The code is idiocy, like your pledge book. Remember that? All that stupid shit to memorize that you weren't supposed to let out of your sight or breathe to another person, like it was state secrets?"

I nodded, straining to follow. Sororities had them too: great lists of arcana to commit to memory, though probably lighter versions than the frats. The birthday, major, and hometown of every active. The names and vital stats of the founders. He looked at me, more curious than wary. "How did you know it was code?"

"I didn't. Just a guess." But the word was too specific. "Brantley said something about a code once. To Quinn. But that's all. The word was in my head, I guess."

He nodded, no reason to doubt me. "Brantley, of course, thought it was a bigger deal than it ever was. Couldn't help himself, with stuff like that."

His manner tricked me into a minute's hope that it was all harmless, irrelevant, just secret society nonsense. I set his box of Lemon Zinger between our mugs. "What's the code for?"

"Nothing, anymore. Not like it ever did much, but it's been changed. Now it's just initials on a gown. Like anyone's."

If the code no longer held power, something did. I couldn't blot out the image of Quinn's notebook, those names. "So you'd give the gown to the Gammas because they wouldn't notice it was fake, right? Then it's safe." He nodded, uncertain. I kept my voice light, as if no more were at stake than Will getting in trouble for a pledge indiscretion. And maybe that was all we were talking about. "If you give it to them, they'll know. Quinn will figure it out. Whatever it is he shouldn't know, he'll know it."

Will's eyes rounded softly. "Okay." He nodded, thinking.

More than once, I had started to tell Quinn about the gown. I knew I was missing something, still, about how it mattered, something he would get on the spot or that we could sort out together. And maybe we'd land on some crucial piece that would turn him from his pursuit of Will. But now I understood why I'd held back. The gown was dangerous. And more so to Quinn somehow, once he knew of it, than it was to Will.

The kettle whistled. I dropped tea bags in our mugs and poured the water. Will with the tip of his spoon led the bag around. "Then I should wear it."

I took a seat beside him. He wasn't asking, though he had made me this voice—Brantley's voice—the one calling him a coward for not wearing it. "You have reasons for not doing that," I said. "I think they're probably good ones."

"They don't matter. Not really." He sounded bleak, and I thought the only way those reasons couldn't matter was if Will's life didn't matter. Very simply, clear-eyed and looking at me, he said, "I killed him."

The cold blade of the words was swift, more than I could allow to touch me, and the shield came up. "No. You didn't."

He looked down at his mug. "Maybe I didn't. But he'd be alive now, if he'd never met me."

I let out a breath I hadn't known I'd been holding, in a sense for months. He had not killed Brantley. Then I thought, *Of course not. You know this. You know him.*

"Did they kill him?" I whispered.

He didn't ask who I meant, only shook his head, no.

Then, what? He'd chosen a truth, convinced himself. The evidence was there in all I knew of him over our months together: like Quinn, he was torturing himself with doubts over suicide and what might have led to it. Letting Quinn torture him. What Quinn had to turn outward for relief, Will would turn inward. From nowhere a carping line out of *Franny and Zooey* popped into my head, something like *Buddy does everything Seymour ever did so why not this?* I had never seen it in my mother, if it had been there, and no one would say so if they'd seen it in Brantley. But I could see it plainly in Will, and how many people on campus would later insist he'd been the picture of well-adjusted stability? The gown was more than the locus of a mystery. It was cursed, monstrous. If he put it on, it would come alive at two a.m. and walk him up the bell tower stairs.

"Will," I said. "Listen to me. You can't start thinking that way. If he'd never met you—what does that even mean? You think he'd choose not to meet you? You know better." My voice had gone strident, breathless, not pausing even as he winced and shut his eyes. "And he'd be alive *if* a lot of things. Most of them under his control, not yours." I was on my feet, and he was blinking at me, listening. "Or...maybe no one's control. A lot of people in this world would be alive *if*. Sometimes there's just a truck where you don't think there's a truck. Sometimes the bullet lands two inches to the left. Or say you're out galloping where you shouldn't and your horse puts a foot into the one gopher hole in the whole entire field, and that's that." I wasn't sure what I was saying, where it was coming from. But it had drawn his attention from himself, and I barreled on. "Also a lot of people who are alive right now would be dead, *if*. Maybe you have a heart attack and it happens to be in front of someone who knows CPR. Maybe a shark is coming to eat you, and right then a fish starts to bleed somewhere, so it turns around. Maybe..." Maybe, I didn't say, you stumble on a high wall and someone is standing there who reaches out just in time.

I'd run out of words, stalled in a dizzy, torpid fatigue. "Was that about your mother?" Will asked.

I laughed at the way he'd perked into curiosity. And because it was what Jonathan would say. "The truck one, I guess." I dropped back onto my stool, drew the bag from my cup, and squeezed it. "She changed lanes into one. It wasn't raining, she wasn't drunk, she didn't have a stroke. It's possible she did it on purpose. I don't know. She didn't tell me a lot about what was going on with her. There was never enough money. She hated her job. There was always a man who was treating her wrong, or wasn't good enough for her. I was sixteen, not so great at paying attention, maybe."

"I'm sorry. You never told me."

I had meant to. For a long time, I'd been waiting to offer this story that would be somehow about Brantley, an opening to talk about
whether he might have chosen his own death. And how could anyone
make such a choice, to remove himself from a world like ours and let it
go on without him?

"I don't ever talk about it," I said. "It's just what happened. An accident, officially."

Will nodded, eyes lowered over his steaming cup. I felt a weak ce-
rebral burning helplessness, that I couldn't give him more, that I didn't
know what to do with this senseless love so vast it had almost no connection to him. Could my mother help me here? Did I get to put my
foot down and declare that no one else was allowed to die if I said
so? And what if I, the angel at his other shoulder, agreed with Anna
Vaughn, with Dalton Gibbs?

I said, "I think you should *not* wear his gown, Will. That is what I
think. Do you hear me?"

Later, when it was clear I'd been running a fever all afternoon, I
couldn't decide whether that heat to the brain brought my sense of
reality into question or made it more true, more right, than it could
have been otherwise. No question it granted me convictions worthy of
Joan of Arc, and one was that Will and the gown could no longer be
together. When I readied to go, I told him I was taking it, that I'd keep
it safe, that he needed to give it to me. And he did.

By evening my fever was undeniable. Sarah Beth, in fear of contagion,
went to bunk with her pals out in Clarkson, leaving me alone with anxious, fractured dreams. The gown, stuffed hastily into the back of my
closet, was a palpable presence, though I forgot if I'd put it there in a
dream or reality. Surely I had not committed this act, taken it against
its will. To do so would stoke its anger. I dreaded I'd open my eyes to
find it standing beside my bed with demands. At the least, it wanted to
be worn. Carrying it rolled and tucked over my arm across the quad, I
had felt it lean toward the bell tower, felt, too, the urge to slide my arms
through its sleeves.

Instead it slept where it was and infected my dreams. Will stood over
me in red sunset light, his toes past the edge of Roark's Steep, arms
open to the sky. "You can't fly," I warned him. "You don't have the
gown." "It's here," he said, and put on the gown, which some time ago

we had broken up its back into wings. It will be okay, I reminded myself, even when you see him falling. The falling is only the beginning.

I followed him into the black altitude of the bell tower. Ahead on the stairs, all I could see was the shape of the gown and its white-stitched initials, but they were warped and unreadable, spreading down his back farther than they should like a list pages long in Quinn's handwriting. Music blared, unreasonably loud—one of my inconsiderate dormmates, I thought. Every so often the needle shrieked to silence; the same ponderous chords started over. At the tower wall, as Brantley's face turned to me with tender intensity, I jerked awake, drenched and so unsure of reality that I reached out for an anchor, a human voice to talk me back to myself. If Sarah Beth had been there to wake, I might still have grabbed the phone and dialed Quinn.

My clock said 2:20. I listened to two rings before I found enough of my own clarity to hang up. I was surely a sorry specimen if I needed a minute's soothing and Quinn Cooper was the best I could do.

In the morning, on my way to Dr. Mathers' class, I saw Dalton Gibbs stopped behind the chapel, talking to Quinn. Had my brain been functioning, the sight would have sounded alarm bells. But I could handle little more than trailing my friends toward class, locating a desk, opening my notebook and my text: Emily Dickinson. I appreciated how often she was personally dying in her poems. A winter fly, dozy and fat, banged itself against the ancient casement window beside me but I couldn't get it open, and outside should have been the walkway parapet, a deep piece of courtyard lawn on which waited someone I needed to find, but I couldn't see through the glass.

"Miss Gavin." Dr. Mathers' face loomed close. Class had started and everyone was looking at me. Our professor, tall, narrow, and elegant in a pageboy the color of gunmetal, had taken up a stooped position before my desk. She set the backs of cool fingers to my forehead, so surprising a gesture that I sucked in a long, loud breath like someone about to scream. "What are you doing here?" she asked. "Child, return to your bed."

She straightened to full height, hands on her gowned hips, and scanned the other rows of students as if she had failed to appreciate what a pitiful wreck of humanity might lie before her, all of us afflicted with the same ailment. Turning back to me, she spoke with consternation and an air of discovery. "Some of your friends—you *are* her friends, correct?—will take you to it, and they will carry you if necessary, and they may instead decide to transport you directly to the hospital. You and you." Of the several volunteers I detected, her pointing finger landed on Dex and Pem. "Miss Dixon will take notes for you."

"We told her to stay home," Jenny objected, in a small mistreated voice.

I'd never missed a class in my life—if I could have formed an argument to stay, I would have. It seemed to take me ten minutes to fumble my books into my backpack, which Dex took up. Once we were in the hall, I felt just alert enough to be amused. "Now carry me if necessary," I instructed the boys, both too skinny for the task but who proceeded to scoop me up between them and then almost kill us all attempting the stairs. "No, y'all, I'm kidding. I'm not that sick. I can *walk*."

Since the county hospital doubled as our campus infirmary, a trip there didn't have to be for dire cause. But Vince had gone a week before, for the flu he'd surely given me, so I knew all I'd be prescribed was rest and fluids. Besides, the cultural norm at Rockhaven dictated refusing the hospital in all but the unavoidable instances, such as when grievously wounded in a cocktail-preparing mishap or required to report for hepatitis vaccination after dipping punch from the wrong cooler. Once, a girl had walked in with a backache from a sledding accident that turned out to be a spinal fracture, and even she had to be carted there by force.

The boys thought this might be one of those force-worthy situations, since they were in their element: a drama and project of the highest order, assigned by a venerable authority figure. In their minds they were already narrating the story for a lunch audience, complete with a full Mathers quotation, so I was lucky to talk them into returning me to my feet and letting me walk to my own bed.

For the next four days, hardly moving from bed, I struggled to sort lines of poetry from song lyrics, dream from reality. CONTAGIOUS WARD, Vince wrote on my marker board, and only he crossed the doorway to bring me his leftover cough syrup and ibuprofen, snacks smuggled from the dining hall, and presents from other friends. One of these was a Get Well card from Will. On the card's front, a sad cartoon bunny held a flower. Inside, Will made chipper offers of soup or bonbons or bedside reading—anything I might need, just call. No hint therein to feed the Will-centered anxiety that seemed the very substance of my fever, made worse by my inability to pin down a threat. Was it Quinn? Or was it only the gown, and Will safe if it was in my keeping?

On Sunday, upright enough to shower and then crawl down to the Commons cafeteria for soup and a sandwich, I returned to a message on my newly erased board: "L: Have you died yet? Q." Underneath: "Observatory, 10 PM."

Sunday night would be open lab for Astronomy I. Midterms looming, I felt weeks rather than days behind and meant to spend the evening deep in a book or two. But I couldn't concentrate, and at ten I set aside *Leaves of Grass* to walk over to the observatory, which perched on the roof of Hampsell at the back of the quad. I'd never been there, but tried the rooftop door. Inside was dark, unheated, lit a dim red. Beneath the nearest bulb, a boy I didn't know sat at a desk with a computer and logbook—the work-study attendant, I assumed. Across the room, beneath another spot of red, sat Quinn.

"I'm with him," I said to the attendant. He nodded.

No one else was there. While Quinn punched keys on a calculator, I adjusted to the red dark by wandering about looking at the telescopes and wall charts, beset with enough coughing attacks that he was surely aware of my arrival. Through the open aperture of the dome, the sky was a cloudless, star-salted black. I took a seat at a classroom-style desk beside his.

He entered numbers in his lab book, a penlight aimed over his work. "You look like crap."

"Thanks. Why is it all red in here?"

"Doesn't interfere with your night vision." He squinted to critique my sickbed look, sweats and glasses and no makeup. "I'm glad you lived."

"I'm glad that pleases you." I leaned to examine the near page of his lab book. *It's just applied math*, he'd drawl, whenever I harangued him about choosing the hardest major in existence. "Stellar parallax," I made out at the page heading. "That would be a great band name. Or title of my next poem. As long as it doesn't make me have to learn any physics."

"It's pretty basic. Just measuring the distance of stars using the relative apparent shift in distance as the viewpoint shifts."

"Um. Can you put that more poetically?"

"No." His gruffness was punishing me for something—had I forgotten what? But he sighed and said, "Cover one eye and look at this." He held a pencil vertically a foot before my face. I did as directed, beginning to adjust to the red dimness.

"Now cover the other eye instead. Now go back and forth. See it move? That's parallax. Now if I move it farther away...do it again." I did, focusing on the more distant pencil while moving my hand back and forth, one eye and the other. "The far one moves less, right? It's actually not moving either time. But by the amount it seems to move, you can measure the distance it is from *you*." The pencil snapped forward to pop the bridge of my glasses.

"Ow." Rubbing my nose, I nevertheless found myself mildly charmed by his effort, its lack of a detectable motive.

"Sorry." He gathered a breath, shook his head, began to vent. "Did you really pass out in class? Or is that more of Dex and Pem's bullshit, carrying you out of there? And they didn't even take you to the damn hospital? Why didn't you call me?"

Aw, you care, I didn't say, except with my expression. "It was just the flu."

He glowered. "A hundred and two fever, for three days."

And how did he know that? I spared him the question, knowing what checking with Vince where it concerned me would have cost him. "I did almost call you one night, actually. Had crazy dreams. I had this idea you'd tell me what was real and what wasn't."

He softened. "Such as?"

"Such as..." But all the scraps I'd felt so urgent to tell him had faded from their apparent logic. All but one. "Did I see you talking to Dalton Gibbs?"

"Maybe, yeah."

The chill came only now, the event clicking into reality. "Shit, Quinn. Why?"

My shock took him aback. "I don't actually know the guy. He just came up to me and started talking about, I don't know, Montgomery. My dad's law firm."

"What about it?"

"Nothing special." We were murmuring, maintaining privacy from the attendant. Though his gaze tightened on me, he seemed to be trying to remember. "He said he knew some people who knew my dad, heard it was a good firm. Heard business was tough down there. It was a thirty-second conversation."

"That's it? He didn't...want anything?" He shook his head. I fought an urge to grab him by the collar, to demand, *Think, what else?* I'd already said too much. I stood from the desk with a shrug, a dismissive "Weird," as if I'd lost interest.

"What?" He stood to face me, his suspicion only beginning. If a threat had hidden in the small talk, Quinn would have picked up on it. Right? And what had Dalton said to me? Nothing much, nothing I could locate menace in. But I remembered Anna Vaughn in the Benson hallway after Christmas saying *Quinn Cooper* at me—verifying?—and I remembered it for no clear reason except that whenever I caught sight of her lately, she was less likely to be with Will than with Dalton Gibbs.

She knew Quinn knew about the Order. She'd told Dalton.

All ninety-eight pounds of Anna Vaughn Whitacre didn't throw anyone off a bell tower without help. And any number of shadowy alums, congressmen or otherwise, would have needed an agent, someone on campus with access.

And of course, they would have needed a reason. Even if Brantley had their names, could he have been that dangerous to them? *They* didn't do it, Will had told me, but would he know for sure? Would he lie if he did?

"I'm just cold," I said. I made a casual turn toward the large central telescope. "Show me some stellar parallax."

"That was last week." He stepped up to peer into the scope's eyepiece, made some adjustments, then motioned me in. "Here's a poem for you." I took off my glasses to look, trying to hold myself still enough to see while my heart raced. In view was a great, variegated, silver-dollar-sized planet with a few perfect beads floating around it. "Jupiter," he said at my ear. "And the four Galilean moons. They're all in view right now. Look for the shadows on the planet's face. Io, Calisto, Europa, Ganymede."

"That is a poem." The beady moons—two over the planet's face, two against the night sky—almost seemed to move as I watched.

"You can remember the names because they're all the ones Jupiter fell in love with. Which tends to mean you're screwed forever, right?"

"That's beautiful." All of it, I meant, the names and the story as much as the sphere of Jupiter, dusty-looking like honed sandstone with its satellites brought so close. The myths escaped recall, the names attaching dimly to figures painted or sculpted in various attitudes of half-nude collapse, ravished and aggrieved. Three girls—Io, Calisto, Europa—and a boy, Ganymede.

"I'll show you something even cooler." He moved me aside to adjust the scope. "Have you been watching Venus? You can see it on the horizon." When I looked again, he'd backed off the view so Jupiter was half the size, the moons invisible. It shared the frame with a white burst of light. "The conjunction is in a few days. Venus and Jupiter will be only two degrees apart, which hasn't happened in a century."

"Is that your lab assignment?"

"No, I'm done with the lab. This is just cool."

While I looked a little longer through the scope, he returned to his desk. I followed so as not to have to call out my joke in the hearing range of the attendant. "Did Jupiter screw over Venus too?"

He chuckled, bent with the pen light aimed to write in his notebook. "I don't know. Isn't that more your area? The humanities and all."

"Guess I need to review. Do you know Walt Whitman's poem about the learned astronomer?"

Whatever answer he gave, I didn't hear it. Open before him was a page I recognized, with its ragged column of initials from Will's gown. But all around it were names he'd added since. The names of men. I spotted WHITACRE in block capitals, and above it, underlined, *Ransom Whitacre*, above which the tip of his parallax pencil was in the process of writing *Dalton G—*. Some bolt of light through my brain, unbound to thought or intention, made me clap a hand down onto his. I snatched the pencil. Next we were grappling for the notebook, but he didn't give it much fight, only stared at me, perplexed, as I ripped it away and clasped it with the pencil tight to my chest.

"Quinn," I said. "Don't. Please."

"Don't what?" He was deciding whether to find my behavior amusing, which made me frantic to laugh it all off somehow. Retreat. And I had nothing to give him for explanation. I was a burning knot of instinct, guided by Will's wry, mournful voice saying, *Thought he was smarter than everyone.*

"This." My eyes filled with tears. "I need you to stop."

"So Gibbs is one of them."

"I don't know that."

With a checking glance past me at the attendant, he stepped closer until we were eye to eye. "He is, and you do. Tell me, right fucking now, what you know."

"Nothing." Once again I was failing him in loyalty. "Look, I don't even know why this is freaking me out. This whole dumb secret club, it's probably nothing. But this"—I shook the notebook—"please. Just leave it alone. All I know is what you know, what you've always known. Brantley messed with it, and he is *dead*."

Quinn made himself straighten and relax, watching the attendant. "All right." He put his arms around me, both of us wrapped up around the notebook. I could feel a piece of the fear that was in me in him too, his mouth in my hair to murmur soothing things. To tell me yes, I'll stop, when he wasn't going to stop.

13

THAT FALLEN AM I IN DARK UNEVEN WAY

Over the next few nights, clear and cold and black, anyone who knew where to look could have witnessed the convergence of Venus and Jupiter. From the rampart of Hampsell as we left, Quinn pointed out the spot where I might find them later, a lovers' destined rendezvous above the Rockhaven trees. But I forgot to look. Had I remembered, I would have taken Will outside to show him.

After my bout with the flu, I found Will had tapped some new source of energy. He radiated good cheer. Taking charge of our catch-up midterm schedule, he imposed rigor with abandon: canceled my riding, banned me from other boys, took his phone off the hook and ignored knocks. A sign posted on his door directed all dorm matters to the APs. He knew more desk workers than I did and wrangled a sub to cover my work-study shifts. For a full week, we studied all afternoon, all evening, with hours blocked out for the classes we didn't share, a break for dinner at the pub or from fast-food sacks over our books in his room.

Our only fast food on the mountain, a Hardee's out by the interstate, didn't have a drive-through and wasn't exactly fast: you put in your order and sat to wait. Will favored it for the unlikelihood of seeing anyone there from school. Seated with him at a laminate four-top, I almost wished Quinn were with us, just for the clues about what he was up to, where his head had gone. Just to see him in clear, unfevered light. But better to keep him apart from Will, and better not to speak to Will of Quinn, nor of Brantley, nor of Dalton Gibbs, but only of literature, as if the violent grace of a Flannery O'Connor story were the greatest pressure on our two lives.

Will had a beard coming in, darker than the hair on his head and tinged in sunlight with teasing glints of copper. Anna Vaughn hated it, he said, hated his glasses too, which he wore often lately. I found his every alteration only a different kind of beauty. Idle across from me, while we mused over whether the Misfit was the devil, he picked up the foil ashtray from beside the salt and pepper shakers and began to fold down its edges with a thumb. The pattern was precise, crinkled like a pie crust, a twin to one Quinn surely now kept on his own dresser.

"That's destruction of property," I said.

"It's creation. For you." He handed it to me. "To remember me by."

So Will, not Brantley, was the crumpler. Or both were, one picking up the habit from the other. But surely the one Brantley kept was made by Will. Was Will aware of having played out this scene, maybe even in the same words, over a table with Brantley? His hazel gaze behind the glasses, though slightly elsewhere, didn't show it. I turned the metal disk like a dial on the table, knowing I would keep it, hidden in my desk drawer with other treasures.

On the drive back, the spring-like cast of the light through still-bare trees was pacifying, like Will's mood. So much Shakespeare tempted plots out of the air. As we dropped our angels at the gates, though, I was forced to bring up Dalton, as lightly as I could. "Is he dangerous somehow? I need to know."

"Why, did he talk to you?" The question was sharp, and he relaxed quickly when I assured him, no. "Tell me if he does. But you don't have to worry about him. He's just touchy, about outsiders. He doesn't understand why you're around so much."

Before I could be alarmed I was offended. "What business is it of his why I'm anywhere? Or—"

"It's not. He knows that now. I clarified the situation for him."

The Leah situation, apparently. "Okay. But say he were to talk to someone else, like Quinn. Out of the blue, asking about Quinn's dad and his law practice in a completely friendly way. Would you consider that a threat of some kind?"

As we parked in the Stirling lot, the blood had risen into his cheeks, a trace of the look I'd first seen when he argued with Dalton in the arcade. "Did Quinn take it for a threat?"

"No. He didn't." Squinting to read him—that anger meant a good chance he'd be going to Dalton with it—I added, "Not at all. It went completely over his head."

"Well, then it couldn't have been one, right? Dalton knows a lot of people. Probably just being friendly." He took up our dinner and opened the door. And he had a point, I supposed: a threat wasn't doing its job if it wasn't taken for one. His anger lingered, though, through half of dinner before I could soothe it away.

The next night I talked him into Maxon but decided never again, after I caught enough raised eyebrows or dirty looks from right-siders we happened to pass. Add to that the puzzled dozens who over the past months had dropped by his room on social calls, requiring introduction, and Will and I had become a kind of couple, the witch and her minion. If not exactly a scandal, we were no longer a secret.

"Fuck them," Will said. "Who cares what they think?" His newfound pleasure in stoking this sort of controversy seemed half his reason for insisting we study so much.

"Just spend the night," he urged me. "God, Anna Vaughn will hate that. Let's do it! Proctor's perk. You can have the bed. I'll put cushions on the floor."

I told him that would be taking diligence a little far, thinking mainly of fresh clothes, my own toiletries and bed. Hours later, against all intention, I awoke on the love seat with my cellular biology notes scattered around me and dawn light at the window. Will had draped a blanket over me and gone to bed.

When I was next in his room, my toothbrush stashed in my bag this time in case of accidental sleepover, he presented me with a bottle of bubble bath, a reminder of my refrain that someone ought to make use of his tub. Lavender and chamomile. And what if Anna Vaughn walked in while I was having a soak?

"She's walked in on worse." He murmured this darkly, then looked to see whether I'd believed it. "Kidding," he said.

He practiced no subtlety in banishing her from the room, though she turned up anyway. Head down on the love seat, I squirmed as she faked a breezy good cheer—"Well, I wouldn't *have* to drop by if you'd leave your phone on the hook"—and offered me an eyeroll at the hopeless illogic of men and then ticked off the bullet points of whatever business had brought her. While she restrained herself from ever calling our study time excessive, I couldn't fault her if she implied it with every word and look. Will, steeled from her knock to be pleasant, couldn't get all the way to warmth, and his mask of patience wore thin before he escorted her out.

Though she spoke in vague terms in my presence, I picked up from one such visit that she was anxious over the approach of spring break, pressing him to commit to plans. The instant she was out the door, he turned to me with one of his grand, light-filled grins. "Hey, want to go to Atlanta over break? I can introduce you to some nonprofit types, find you a summer internship."

And was he serious? Of course he was. We could stay at his house, he said.

As gratified as I felt to be his preferred companion, the extravagance of the offer—over the line, even for Will—freaked me out a little. It spurred me to cram in a couple hours at the library researching internships on my own, so that I could decide what I might really want to do. It forced me to face Dr. Crocker again, and in one visit to her office I came away with an application for a summer that sounded perfect, with a D.C.-based conservation fund that offered intern housing and was seeking candidates who had both a science foundation and writing skills. Dr. Crocker knew people there and would put in a good word.

In any case, my break was already spoken for: a road trip to Oklahoma with Vince and Jonathan that we'd been planning for most of a year, ever since Vince had learned he'd be getting a car. I might have tried to invite Will along, since he clearly needed plans, and a group trip would have been a less glaring target for the wrath of Anna Vaughn than a duo jaunt to Will's house. But Vince and Jonathan would never have forgiven me.

For days I resisted the call of the tub. Already I'd surprised myself with how much pleasure I could take in being inside while Anna Vaughn was out, creating a world with Will behind our door, and I was hesitant to bask too brazenly. I sensed the danger in giving in to decadence, forgetting appropriate caution—dangers that felt inherent in the room and our lavish seclusion, even in Will himself.

But soon enough, finishing a late paper on Emily Dickinson at ten p.m., I was done for, shedding clothes onto the bathroom tile and slipping into hot suds. Will, outside the door, read me lines of his religion paper to critique.

"'Traditional man requires the necessity of being orientated in relation to the Sacred...'"

I'd scraped an A-minus in World Religion back in freshman year, though I'd always felt a little lost. Will was grappling with Eliade's *The Sacred and the Profane*, which I hadn't been able to make much sense of until I'd replaced his abstract "Sacred" with the more concrete "Rockhaven." Outside of Rockhaven was nothing; inside was order and sense. One returned to the physical location, our mountain domain, cyclically, eternally, repeating its rituals in order to reconnect with the Sacred source—in Eliade's terms, in order to *exist*.

"Read it again," I called. His sentence was redundant, overly complicated, and I told him so. "How about 'Traditional man can be oriented only in relation to the Sacred.'"

"Mine sounds better."

I laughed. "No, it's just longer."

I heard him slump against the door. "How's your bath?"

"Wonderful." In an eerie flash I pictured Brantley soaking in the tub. He must have been bitter, wherever he was, not to be in my place.

Unless he was. When Anna Vaughn's voice reached me moments later, muffled, arguing with Will in the living room, another voice in my head, not my own, said *This bitch again?* I shushed it, trying to hear whether Will would be called to report my whereabouts. Whether Anna Vaughn would care at all, or merely steam ahead with her agenda, the idea of anything improper going on between us more ludicrous to her than it was to me.

Days later, on the path to the intramural football field, along which squadrons of jonquils stood boldly against the persistence of winter, I ran into Anna Vaughn. No real surprise: the Gammas were playing the Phi Os.

Thankfully, I was alone, as was she. "Leah! Aren't you studying today?"

"We thought we'd take a break." Midterms were upon us, but Will and I had caught up enough to be almost overprepared. Still, I found myself reluctant to give up our den. I dreaded facing the chaos outside, the people, even my friends with their manifold questions and demands. Today, for instance, was Quinn's birthday. To head off her suspicion over Will's absence, I added, "He'll be here. He wanted some exercise."

That she hadn't been apprised of the plan even when it was likely to overlap her own made me tense, but she went loose from the neck down with comical relief. "Oh, good. I was hoping he might decide to." Even now, she'd pretend he moved at her urging, but what did I know? Maybe he did. I'd gathered they would be spending the break as she wished, at a lake house with *other people*—a term Will shaded with enough bitterness that I guessed one was Dalton Gibbs.

"It's good you've got him studying." She turned to walk at my shoulder, half a head shorter than me, her face nested in the fluffy white cowl of her sweater. Khaki skirt, riding boots that would pass muster for a British foxhunt. Her steps were slow, her gaze on the path. "A routine like that, I think it helps with… Well, you must know he can be a little erratic. In his mood. Sometimes in his thinking."

Her simple, forthright manner, not merely friendly but seeming to confide, put me on guard. Instead of nodding along, I asked with measured blandness, "What do you mean?"

"Well, you know he's under the care of a psychiatrist." It wasn't a question. "What he may not come out and tell you is that—" She stopped in the path to choose her words. A shout from the IM field now and then reached us through a screen of trees. "Some of his treatments have been unconventional. Nothing too extreme, or shocking, once you know him. Warranted, for certain. And they're working. He's doing very well, comparatively."

My guard was throwing out coils of razor wire in defense of Will, smelling the lie in this carefully vague narrative. But to what end? "Comparatively?"

"You won't have seen him at his worst. I don't want to suggest he's *delusional* or anything like that." She had become almost jocular as she proceeded again on slow steps into the woods. "He's sensitive. Very, at times. Susceptible to…emotional ideas." She spoke this last with a *you know* of an eyeroll, as if Will's susceptibilities were all too familiar to us both. "I try to keep in mind that he doesn't always have the same take on reality that you or I might. Of things that have happened, for instance. His interpretations are easily skewed."

I kept my head down through this, nodding. Quinn's rant—*He's dying to talk*—echoed, because surely Anna Vaughn thought the same. She wanted to make me doubt something she thought he might have told me. Her analysis of him, though—sensitive, susceptible—rang true enough. I remembered the hypnotist freshman year who had glued his hands together merely by telling him so, who had summoned him wide-eyed to the stage for the remedy.

Will with that same credulous, haunted look saying, *I killed him*. But he hadn't been so attached to the idea that I couldn't unstick it with a word, fast as a finger snap, fast as the forehead tap with which the hypnotist caused the ones with glued-together hands to drop asleep in chairs. So maybe it was another admission that worried Anna Vaughn.

We had come to a broad stream that had to be crossed stone to stone in order to reach the playing fields. Some Gammas, arriving on our heels with the oversized beer cooler, set down their burden to rush ahead and hand the two of us across. "Such gentlemen!" Anna Vaughn exclaimed.

"They truly are," I said, though I doubted I would have been treated as such a damsel apart from her company.

"I know you won't mention any of this to Will," she murmured, her hand on my arm as we made our way up the bank. "It's nothing he wouldn't tell you himself, except that it upsets him to worry people. He wouldn't like to know we're talking about him."

"Of course." *You are*, I thought, *not me*. I felt suffused in a brief, pure rage that she would twist him this way behind his back for her own ends, that she should deserve any claim to him.

"Well, there he is!" We came through the trees onto the green where, in oblique afternoon light amid the players clustered at the far sideline, Will's fair curls made him easy to pick out. Out on the field, some Phi Os—no Dalton in view, thank god—spiraled the ball idly back and forth, waiting for the game to start. "Of course they're all in *shorts*," Anna Vaughn cried, "like it's actually spring!"

Will was talking with several guys. As I squinted to pick them out— Gammas, all—Anna Vaughn said, "We must seem an odd couple to you."

I mumbled some polite denial she smiled at. Her chin, as if drawn by a string, lifted by degrees toward Will. "I don't know if you've ever been in love, or in love this way. Not a lot of people have. It's like he's a planet, the only one in the field. As I am for him, even now, when he can't quite feel it. The force is like gravity." I blinked at her, the sunlight burning in her crown. "We don't choose this. It's not logical. It can be terrible at times, but it won't be broken, even if we both sometimes think we'd be better off. It just is." She turned to me, solemn. "Even now, you know, he and I, we're very lucky."

I nodded, unprepared to argue with such a speech even if I'd wanted to. To a point I understood, agreed. We took our leave of each other, I for the Gamma bleachers at the near end and she downfield for the Phi Os, bypassing Will. Odd she'd come at all but for the company of the few Phi O girlfriends she joined. Even I, not wenchy enough most days to spend good study hours in a Gamma cheer section, knew the Phi Os would not take the match too seriously. The Gammas had some athletes in their ranks—Quinn was one, when he felt like it, and Jonathan. But the Phi Os could send just enough of their second string to field a team and still expect to cream us.

As I headed for the cooler, I spotted Quinn, jogging over to greet Will with a shout and a slap on the back. Next Will was waylaid by more of Quinn's crowd and the younger ones who had attached to them, a small swarm of Gammas. Watching them, I felt a painful awareness that those sophomores had barely known Brantley, the freshmen not at all apart from the stories passed down in mythic light to pledges; yet these would be his friends now, were he alive. From my distant vantage, I restored Brantley to their midst, the yellow bandana from Quinn's photo around his head. Then I wondered if doing so would mean removing Will, at least to the other side of the field. The Gamma joy that bubbled about him appeared like the welcome for a long-lost member, or the brother of one. Better it went to Will, I thought, with illogical partisanship, in argument with my mental Brantley. Or maybe he would have felt the same.

By the time I'd worked my way through a few greetings and found a seat in the bleachers beside Mitzi and Carolyn, something bizarre had transpired. The two teams met at center field and had a discussion; then Will lined up with the Gammas. Armed with the scantest knowledge of football, I pointed. "What the hell is that?"

People around me, busy chatting, peered one by one into the field, murmured the news and their own questions. Mitzi cracked a laugh. "Fairness, I guess? It's a little more even that way, you gotta admit."

IM football was touch, since the players lacked helmets or other armor, but crashes happened regardless. What was the point of football unless you slammed other bodies, hit the dirt a few times? This game, though, was rougher than others I'd seen, and Will—smiling as he dodged his own brothers or rose from an accidental tackle—was getting the brunt. "God, they're pissed," I said, after an undeniable hit. "Are they *aiming* for him?"

The Gammas rallied around him, blocking valiantly with their slighter, ganglier, less coordinated bodies, and the first blood drawn was Quinn's. He played until halftime with a cleat-gash streaming down his shin, and then under duress came looking for the first aid kit. Even without the history between us, the Gammas manning the kit might have sent it to me by pledge, assigning me to perform the veterinary medicine as of old. But I doubted it. I was only an English major now.

"Happy birthday," I told him, soaking his leg with a sponge full of cold stream water I'd sent the pledge to fetch. He stood a level below me in the bleachers, his leg presented like a knight's token, propped between mine. To say these words was a reason I'd come to the game, in case I decided to review for my last midterm through his party that night; in case I forced myself to show up at his party and found him getting a lap dance from a stripper or judging his own private wet T-shirt contest, thus requiring me to leave before I could tell him happy birthday. From my first glimpse of him, jogging up to Will, I had tipped an inch in his direction as if my blood were magnetized, as if drawn by gravity. But surely only to say these words. To check him off my list and be released.

A beer bottle in hand and a fair buzz evident in his eyes, he lifted his lip over a fang. "That feels good."

Meaning, one might assume, my hand that wrapped his calf, but I said, "No, it doesn't, you freak. We call this feeling pain. It hurts." I dabbed the wound dry and swabbed it gently with alcohol, studying the skin's torn edges, the oozy exposed dermis of Quinn.

"You can admire my tan while you're down there."

In two days he was leaving for Fort Lauderdale, along with half a dozen of his more degenerate brethren and a few others recruited from outside the frat because, in truth, there were not so many Gammas who could keep up with a Quinn-Cooper-level debauch. On sunny, warmer days, the lot of them could be seen oiled up and arrayed over the Gamma house roof, trying for a base tan. Quinn, true enough, took a tan better than most. In swim trunks and shades, he might expect to draw some glances from long-legged state-school babes in bikinis before he even opened his mouth.

"You're in my light," I said.

He sat beside me, the shin over mine. "Want to know a secret?"

I did not, since I could surmise more than I cared to of what the trip would entail, and he had the vulpine look that meant my imagination was a poor second to whatever piece of the itinerary he was about to needle me with. But I sighed. "Sure."

He leaned in, filled my ear with hot breath, and ran his tongue around the circumference. Taken off guard by the zing of pleasure, I let out a shrieky laugh. A little late, I punched him in the shoulder. "Be*have* your evil self, please, so I can tape this."

"I know where your spots are," he said. "That's not a secret, though."

I weighed my chances that he might retain this receptive mood through the day, actually look for me at his party. But no. Quinn of all people, turning twenty-one, would want novelty, never mind whose ear he'd just licked. We'd all be lucky if he settled for a new girl or two, or three, rather than deciding he needed to go skydiving at midnight off Roark's Steep. He'd picked Fort Lauderdale with novelty in mind, cliché paradise for drunken coeds from half the states in the union but not many of us from Rockhaven before now.

Will banged up the bleachers that had emptied around us, a bottle in hand, looking flushed and happy. "Hey, sweetie," came out of my mouth, this name I'd never called him before, but it seemed instantly normal. "How about you? Are you wounded?"

"Nah." He slapped a paw onto each of Quinn's shoulders and shook them. "I think this guy took it for me."

"You'd do the same for me," Quinn said, so much warmth in his voice that I had to wonder what passed between them out of my presence. As I wondered always of boys.

Vince watched us from down by the cooler. When Quinn and Will returned to the field, he climbed up to sit beside me, arranged himself in twin position: feet on the next bench, arms folded, facing the field. "So you're in love with him?"

A typical Vince question, though less smirky in tone than his usual. With our trip approaching, I knew he and Jonathan both were feeling my neglect. "I'm not in love with him," I recited. "I'm just worried about him." Since I couldn't explain the multitude of reasons, I picked an easy, immediate one. "I think he needs to quit."

"Quit what?"

The game had started up again, and my gaze followed Will as if with it I could close him in a bubble of safety. "The Phi Os. Join the Gammas. Is that even possible? Look at him out there."

We watched Will fumble a catch and hit the grass. The Phi O who had tripped him up, purposely or not, offered a hand to help him up. "Pretty sure that's not possible," Vince said. "But I'm not talking about him, and you know it."

I needed several seconds to catch up, but then it felled me. Some things Vince just knew and you didn't argue. "Hey." He put an arm around me. "Oh no, that bad?" He added the other arm, wrapping me tight and rubbing as if to warm me, and we sat like that while I managed not to cry and we watched the game.

But why did it feel so devastating? Assuming the very complicated thing I felt for Quinn even shared a zip code with being in love, it was hardly a new predicament. Most of my life at Rockhaven had been spent in hopeless, pining, unrequitable love. As wounds went, it was the one I was most skilled at tending. I knew how to temper desire, play the buddy who stood by and even helped while he pursued others. I'd keep my place at his elbow and be better for it. He'd keep me in his life. Twenty years from now, we'd still be friends.

Later that night, well after his party had ended, he clarified the problem for me.

Not a real party, he'd said, *just some birthday booze*, so I went late, knowing none of my friends would show and I'd be at the mercy of his mood or circumstance. My odds of being glad I'd gone were low. But the instant he spotted me, he lit up, extracted himself from a mellow-looking sofa klatch of brothers to hug me and get me a drink.

"I didn't bring you a present," I said, suspicious.

He was all sex-eyes, pouring me a shot from his own beribboned bottle of tequila. "We'll see about that."

Ah, the eleven—and who was I kidding? All day, with no more intention than to privately mark the occasion of his birthday, I'd been wearing matching sapphire underwear, the only set that remained. Late as it was, with a midterm in the morning, and all my ranked objections besides, his twenty-first birthday would never come again. But I didn't trust so simple a desire in him, not on this day, with better targets in the room: virgins, strays from the broader campus, girls who were newish at the least. From an exclusive corner where we traded shots, I tried and failed to redirect his tenacious soft-eyed attention their way.

"I have something to show you," he said. "In my room."

"Mmm-hmm. Are you sure it isn't in your pants?"

"There, too."

Over a couple more shots he filled me in on the joke, which he swore under oath was his alone and not the party's at large: his wish was to mark the day with the loss of one of his few remaining virginities. Specifically, sex without a condom. And after a brief study, he'd determined I was the girl for the job.

"Wow, on that note. Time for me to go." As a motive, this one was so plausible I could stop looking for more. Based, of course, on his dumb idea that I was on the pill—which, I pointed out, as he whined sugared apologies and begged me to stay, plenty of girls were, if that was all he needed. I bet him a dollar I could find him one in the room.

But he turned down the bet, glanced in none of the directions I pointed, and poured me another shot. Those other girls, he explained, were not to be trusted—and in fact, I'd heard some of this opinion in the past, based on his father's wisdom that all girls were out to trap him with pregnancy. Quinn had never trusted a single one, not ever, and didn't plan to start now. "You, though," he said. "You're not them."

"But then," I said—not much later, in his room—"if, let's say, hypothetically, I were on the pill right now, getting near the end of my last pack, which is where I'd be if I were actually taking them, I'd have to trust *you*. That's a taller order."

"Is it? I know you. You trust me."

Thus far in my limited experience of such matters, I'd found nothing much more erotic than a boy saying *I know you*, in contradiction of my own words and most evidence, and being right about it. Probably didn't hurt if he and I were near naked in his bed when he said it. The condom, though, remained in question, and now that I felt the power it held, his lust ticking upward by the second, my impulse was to keep the trinket longer—more for pragmatic than selfish reasons. A means to regulate Quinn was a rare tool, one I'd be wise to save for an emergency.

But I couldn't be wise. I wanted too much to make him happy, this sappy, stupid longing. To be the one who could, even if it wouldn't last.

Worth it, he'd promised months before. For him, I'd assumed, though I'd never been convinced he'd feel it so much, a little membrane to be lost between us. But I felt it myself, the difference from *yes* long before skin met skin. He dropped down from his plateau of experience and became vulnerable, hesitant, boyish in the way he could never quite be when teaching me. He was with me. We were together, and if it was an illusion spun by our deceitful cells, I'd take it.

Then it was over, my token spent in a frenzy that scattered me. As if I had spent it on a ticket to a play, after which the lights lifted and the real world was restored and I couldn't fully remember why my face was wet. What I was crying for was gone, didn't exist; I was supposed to believe this, to smile and get up from my seat with everyone else and walk out of the theater. But I'd missed something. I needed one more act to understand. His warm, lithe body still against mine was a piece of that play already fading. Meanwhile reality crept in to berate me for wasting the token, all I had, and what if I had thrown away the power to save his life?

"Are you crying?" he asked.

I checked my face. "I didn't want that to be over, I guess."

He kissed my cheek, rested his mouth there. "Remember I said I had something to show you?"

I had taken this for a line. He clicked on the bedside lamp, rose on a hip. "Look here." I wiped my eyes and crawled up closer to where he pointed, above the head of the bed. In a gap between old party posters on the ochre weave of the wallpaper was an irregular brownish stain. He fit two fingers and the edge of a hand into its borders, withdrew them again. "That's my handprint. Your blood."

"Ew, Quinn." I was fascinated, though, peered closer to study it.

"It's your first time, undeniable. And ours. It's there forever."

Sacred space, I thought, while he snapped off the light and settled back on the bed. I laid my head in the hollow of his shoulder. "You could try washing it off," I deadpanned.

"I would never do that. Are you kidding me?" His randy vehemence made me picture small Gamma tour groups. What had he done with the sheets? But he ran fingertips over my back, and I felt, as unexpected as ever, his contentment in lying together, going nowhere. A one-off, a birthday present. I had permitted no thought of a *next time*, but now I wondered if there would be a way to make it happen again. To keep control of it. Ten remaining, by his count. On the other side of this one I had meant to allow, it seemed a wealth.

But between then and now lay Fort Lauderdale. "You want to give up condoms forever?" I asked, the lightest of pie-in-the-sky hypotheticals, and he answered in kind.

"God, yeah. Wouldn't that be nice."

With me, I wanted to say, but I wasn't prepared to offer so much. "Well, you'd better have a few boxes laid by to get you through the break. That's no place to explore your newfound freedom."

He kept quiet for a time. "Look, if spring break isn't a hell of a lot different than the last few months have been, I won't be needing any protection. I'm just not… I mean, it wasn't a plan." His hedging alarmed me. He seemed ready to confess he'd actually been screwing all over creation without a condom, and why, why of all people would I have trusted Quinn? "I mean, I flirt," he went on. "I've made some moves. I just haven't been that interested in anyone else, I guess? Go figure." He breathed as if he'd finished something difficult, while I was stuck sorting out *anyone else*. Other than whom? I might have bought Brantley, Will, the ski bunny, as easily as the answer in his fingers on my back. "So, I don't know. You want to come with me?"

"To…Fort Lauderdale?"

"Yeah, it's short notice. I can get us a bed, if not a single room. A couple other girlfriends are coming, it turns out, so it won't be that weird—"

"A couple other *what*?"

He spoke with a cringe. "Girlfriends? So maybe…" He gasped in disgust. "Look, just fucking face it. I'm pretty sure you're mine."

I sat up and looked down at him for a good half a minute in the scant lamplight that leaked through the bed's curtain. "Who are you? Are you being funny? Like a comedian, right now?"

"Oh, here it comes. Take a breath." He crossed his arms behind his head, regal. "Maybe I want to try something new. Is that beyond your belief?"

Unfortunately, it wasn't. *Quinn needs a girlfriend.* If I'd heard that twenty times, increasingly in the recent months, how many had he? The earnest among his brothers built for him a fantasy, and I knew, past his outlaw nature and the scorn he heaped on the edict, he was susceptible. At any moment, he might give in. Watching him chat up whatever pretty new thing, I'd even begun to brace for the days I'd have to suffer through, Quinn coupled, no matter the solace of implosion before long. But I had not guessed the girl would be me. I'd imagined it, perhaps, but then followed out the scenario through every possible variation to the disaster to come, so that now, met with his near-ingenuous hope, I could summon not a drop of my own.

"It won't work." I stroked his hair, already in soothing mode. "You know it won't. Just go to Fort Lauderdale without me. See what happens."

"You seriously think I can't control myself. All right. I know you've got plans with your boys. But I won't have much fun without you. That's just a fact."

Touching, his apparent conviction, yet oppressive. He meant to talk me into holding it for the two of us, like a table at a restaurant, while part of him went on making up his mind whether it was the place to be. "Well," I said, "it's good to have aspirations."

He chuckled. "God, you're killing me, Gavin. Ice in your fucking veins! Are you even a girl?"

I slapped him across the forehead. He laughed and said *ow*. "Part of your problem"—I was pissed, my voice shaking—"is that it's surprising to you a girl has a brain. Why I love you anyway, god help me, is a mystery, but you might as well know that as a *boyfriend*, I wouldn't wish you on my worst enemy."

That last I regretted as I spoke—over the line—and it tapped out his patience. He lifted himself upright but answered with less anger than expected. "Can't really say that, when I've never been anyone's boyfriend. Except maybe yours."

I tried to take that in, while he laid soft kisses along my neck. "Stop it," I muttered. His persistence struck me then as less like a bending to the general will than a twist on the standard Quinn. A girlfriend, after all, was uncharted territory, more novel than a string of one-night stands.

That, plus I was withholding it. Tempting him with something to chase. Was this control?

Or better: what if Quinn's girlfriend, heretofore nonexistent, turned out to be the person he'd listen to?

"I don't know why you think I'd agree to this," I said, a sentence chambered while I'd been seething, but by the time I spoke it, my tone had gone curious, the words like a cat toy I inched back from him.

"You have," he insisted. "Look where you are. Deny it." My arms were locked around his back, my face in his shoulder, and when had the sorcerer conjured that? "And I heard you. You said you love me."

"That is a whole different thing." But here was the problem I'd sensed for a while, same as he had, the one that had clobbered me on the bleachers with Vince. Deny it. I couldn't. There was no choice. Brantley Simms, closed up with his roommate, may have been forced to a similar precipice, a reckoning: that this was in every way wrong, unworkable, incompatible with social existence, that it couldn't happen and shouldn't happen, and yet somehow on its own it already had.

14

OF THOSE WHO FALL

By lunch the next day Quinn was ignoring my presence, to my cautious relief. I'd left Will in our classroom still working at his Southern Lit exam, and as I walked out of Maxon, I meant to swing by Stirling to compare notes. But I was caught up in a jubilant pack of my hallmates—midterms behind us, Polly and Kelsey gushing about their spring break plans—and followed them instead back toward Benson, the sun heating my shoulders. As we passed through the broad alley between the chapel and the science labs, the Porsche rumbled up from behind.

"Well, who could that be for?" said Mitzi.

"Hi, Quinn," Polly called.

To Mitzi, I said, "Her, probably." But with the Porsche crawling at my side, I gave the girls a jaded shrug and waved them on.

The car breathed warmly, a big cat at heel on a leash, its throaty vibrations radiating through my skin as though I were touching it. "Fine, I get it." Elbow draped over the open window, he peered up at me with *mea culpa* sincerity. "You're mad I didn't sit with you."

I strolled, puzzling that. "*Oh*, right. You think you're my boyfriend." With each step I slowed a little more to see if I could make him stall out. "And that would change where we sit? You'd probably want to hold hands everywhere too."

We might as well have been holding hands through the window. "I like that skirt," he said. It was the one he'd bought me: short, flared wool too warm for the springward turn the weather had taken. "Are you going to get in or what?"

I was not, but as a person walking a car I began to draw looks, and just ahead where the alley opened, boys in shorts flung a frisbee over the Phi O lawn. Not the place to take a stand, where someone in the vicinity of Dalton Gibbs might be reminded that Quinn existed, that he and I were in congress. Thus I found myself, after a short drive, at Alston Point, gazing over the pale valley from which rose the faint, miles-distant lowing of cows, while Quinn vanished down the rocky-stepped trail into the woods. *There went my boyfriend*, I thought grimly, intending not to budge.

When I caught up, he said, "I love you." His tone was accusatory enough that I could laugh it off, though I might have laughed harder had he tried to sound sincere. I wanted only his hands on me. Around us, the forest was an orgy of rustling sunlight and redbud bloom, foliage concealing precipices, and if I knew better than to fall for those words, *fall* was what our mountain called for, what it desired, and with greatest force, perhaps, in spring. Fallen I was anyway, in other dark, uneven ways, a slut who allowed her underwear to be peeled down in a well-traveled wood by a person not her boyfriend.

Unless he was, and pinned me even more publicly. Why must it be one of these two, nothing else?

I resolved to say no more about the impending break, to let it fall between us and do its work. Forgetting would come quicker if I managed to slip off down the road without his full awareness I'd gone. But the next day, as Jonathan, Vince, and I were fitting bags into Vince's hatchback outside Benson, Quinn sauntered up and stationed himself on a bench twenty yards distant.

"Oh, what hell is this now?" Vince muttered.

Quinn slouched with an elbow on the bench's back, his eyes blocked by the mirrors of his aviators. I said, "I'll be back."

Back, in my head and theirs, meant "in under a minute that will not involve any making out," so imagine everyone's surprise. In his presence, there was no option to hold back, no trying once our mouths met to be subtle or quick about it. When I separated myself, as I had to, to return to the rust-flecked yellow Ford Fiesta that would carry us into Oklahoma, it was like waking from hypnosis before an audience Quinn had chosen and arranged. My stunned mortification only just tipped the scales over my anguish at leaving him. Had the kiss not been still buzzing through me, I would have been clearer on the severity of my transgression.

The long goodbye got me banished to the back seat, where I waited the whole drive down the mountain and most of flat Tennessee for Quinn to fade. First stop: Graceland, then a motel for the night, another day or two to see the Ozarks and hot springs and any other oddity that caught our fancy on the way to free food and lodging at Jonathan's house. To Vince and me, all that lay west of the Mississippi sounded exotic. The boys had argued for a stop in my hometown on our way to Graceland, but I'd nixed it. The girl who had lived there wasn't me, and I didn't care to meet her again.

Stashed in various pockets and bags, I carried around a hundred and forty dollars. My allowance, I called it, skimmed from tips, near as much as Vince and Jonathan had been able to set aside from their own summer jobs and a little birthday cash. Once we reached the Pitts' house in Nichols Hills, we intended to play what we had left at the casinos—a vice Jonathan had never sampled, but Vince and I had inspired him with a fervor for the idea. Why not be a little bad?

"This is an Intervention," Vince announced over barbecue. At a shack just over the bridge, we'd ordered at the counter from a chalkboard and helped ourselves to beers from a case. He brandished a crinkled fry. "We are concerned with some of your recent behavior, to wit, whatever that was"—he checked his watch—"oh, about eight hours ago."

"I don't know what you're talking about," I said. Since Graceland, where the mood had been standard-issue silliness and Elvis the topic, I'd grown truly a little forgetful, or at least hopeful the boys had chosen to excise the mishap from memory.

"Well, here's a hint. It involves sticking your tongue in Quinn Cooper." He aimed the name sidelong at Jonathan, who was too busy picking onions from his sandwich to corroborate. "How long has *that* been going on?"

"Oh, come on," I said. "Wouldn't it be more fun if we just pretend we didn't see the very unfortunate thing?" I took an aggressive bite of sandwich. *We talked about this*, I said to Vince with my eyes, and his said, *No, we talked about a feeling, not an act.* I said, *Jonathan doesn't want to talk about it*, and he said, *Too fucking bad.* I said, *But*, and he said, *No buts, young lady, you know better!* I said, *Who are you, my dad?*

Vince glared. "We're worried about you. Now sit there and tell me you don't know why."

"I know. And I appreciate your concern. This is not intentional. It's not even a *this*." A glance from Jonathan seemed enough like participation in the *we* that I forged into it. "I've told him it won't work. It's just one of his stubborn, terrible ideas, and I'm going along with it, sort of? Because..." I doodled in ketchup with a fry, and here came, out of reasonable and authentic despair, a buoyancy I couldn't fight. It was spring break, I was on the open road with friends I loved. There was a cold beer in my hand, bought with my own money, and out the window tiny white petals were blowing loose from a tree limb just as they had along the perimeter trail below Alston Point. "I couldn't even tell you why. I have no good answer."

"God, you love him," Vince said, slit-eyed. "I might need to puke." Jonathan's hands were under the table, biceps gathering for a grip on his thighs.

"No, I'm *confused* by him. And mostly just when he's in front of me. My brain goes all static."

This was honest enough that Vince laughed. "You're such a girl! I had no idea."

I clutched myself in theatrical pain. "That's not even the crazy part. He's on the road to Fort Lauderdale with this idea that he's going to be faithful, and I kind of *believe* him. But only because I told him he wasn't capable, and you know how he can't stand being told what he can't do."

"Faithful," Jonathan said, his hands gone still without my help.

The proximity of the word to Quinn was enough to question, but I said, "There's nothing to be faithful to. I've told him twenty times."

Jonathan selected a fry and ate it. Then another. "So you already slept with him, right? Was it the night of the formal, or just this week? We have a bet."

He was straining for a casual, ribbing humor, as if our friendship were based in this sort of confrontation and we weren't still virgins to each other. But in our lexicon, it was an air strike.

"Jonathan." I blinked hard, met his eyes. "If I had slept with him, why would he still be interested in me?"

This took half a minute for him to parse in full. It was a wry no, or it was a yes that required him to think through the *why*, within which lay all that might have been Jonathan's. "Restroom," he said, and left the table.

I nodded. "Well, this will be fun. Maybe I can catch a bus back to Rockhaven."

Vince gave me a sidelong squint. "So did you? Sleep with him?"

"Not now," I said, hurt by Jonathan's attack and that "bet" reference. *Can you just be on my side for once?* I'd learned to stop saying this to Vince, who too readily fell on the sword. Many times, he'd commended me for calling him on his failures and had sworn new resolve that our friendship could and should be equal to any that didn't suffer from our unfortunate gender difference. But he could never really get there.

He set a hand on my arm, tilted his head toward the restroom. "He'll get over it. I think he could see where that whole thing was headed."

"Oh yeah? Where? Which way did you bet?"

He wouldn't touch that. "Look, you've seen me through this kind of mess enough times. I'm aware you can't stop your friends from making *apocalyptically* bad choices in love. You just wait it out."

Later, looking back on the whole hellish trip, these were the words that returned and resonated. That Vince could draw a level comparison between his past foibles with girls too pretty for him and my own apocalypse, call both the same mess, both love—it rebuked me for ever questioning our friendship or his capacity to grow into it.

In the moment, I took in only the kindness. "How did y'all see this coming if I didn't?" My own question made me consider the wider angle. "Do people *see* this?"

"Where do you think you live? Everyone sees everything."

Vince and I traded off driving, since Jonathan had never gotten his license, kept from it by his parents for a reason he called overprotectiveness and we suspected was an actual reason. When I drove, Jonathan sat in the back. The two of us barely speaking soured all our impressions of Hot Springs and the Ozarks. We persisted with our idea because no one would call it off, exploring listlessly by day and then driving about until we came upon a dumpy roadside motel, a room with two beds. What he most wanted was to remove himself as he would on campus, but in perpetual close quarters with Vince between us and me lobbing bland, please-pass-the-salt sentences his way, we ended up in fights of the sort we'd never had. No small factor was my new disenchantment with what I'd always taken pleasure in, my status with them as special-for-a-girl. I liked being her, the girl they would include on such a trip even over Pem, but I was tired of the concessions I made to maintain their approval. I was tired of the work of always guessing and then being what they needed. A road trip made me especially tired of tending to my hair and face and clothes, shaving my legs, checking the mirror to make sure I looked cute enough to serve as their accessory. There had to be a limit, past which they could take me as I was or not at all. Though I went on skirting a direct answer about what Quinn and I had done or planned to do, I refused to apologize for it.

The running argument was mostly calm—teary, exhausting attempts to drag each other toward reason—with blowups at odd moments. In the parking lot of a Waffle House, when I made an offhand remark about Quinn ruining our trip, Jonathan launched a surprise defense: don't blame Quinn, who had never turned a girl into a piece of trash who didn't want to be turned. "You mean who didn't start out as one," I snapped back, my rage infused with a backlog of hurt over never being good enough for him, while his at me was so twisted up in religion it was hard to feel the jealousy, the love he didn't know how to handle or place if I wasn't his mother or his sister or his bride.

Any girl, he said, who would link herself to Quinn in a public way was soiling herself worse than the slut he took into the woods, since she was choosing with open eyes exactly what she would be. "Vince and I will have to listen to what half the frat will be saying about you. And Pem, Dex, all your other friends will hear it too. And we can't even defend you. Because why would a person we cared about do something that disgusting? Or even let people think it."

Vince, enlisted from both sides, said, "I don't know that the talk would be so bad, necessarily. But he's not wrong."

"Maybe y'all should do something about that system." My honest defense was that I wasn't choosing anything. That how you feel about a person isn't a choice. That I hadn't intended anything that had happened so far or that might happen in the future. I might have added, but didn't, that my current fixation made more sense than all the ardor I'd poured into the sea of Jonathan, none of it, ever, rational, nothing near a decision.

This was the trap into which I'd fallen, and even now it's hard to see the way out I might have missed. I had allowed a ruinous accident to occur. I had chosen that much. But I could not choose a middle ground in which what I did with my own body and with whom was no one's business but mine and that person's, not subject to anyone else's labels or constraints. I knew where I lived. It was everyone's business.

The Pitts' neighborhood was the kind both Vince and I knew from our own childhoods, the scraggly edge of a ritzy suburb, their '60s split-level just barely in zone for a good public school and the limit of what they could afford. Once we arrived, Jonathan warmed at the surface, not willing to let his parents guess at any strife. The three of us had formed a unit for a few of the Pittses' campus visits, and their habit was to tease us all with the belief that I ought to be the girlfriend of one or the other boy. If possible, they were more religious than their son but didn't share his standards for feminine perfection, since they were not too cryptic about wanting me for a daughter-in-law. It had been their obvious approval that had first alerted me to the horror I would feel if Jonathan ever decided to agree. At our first dinner in Nichols Hills, we were each grilled individually about our love lives. When I tried to demur, Jonathan said, "Leah's got someone new." "No, I really don't," I said, and he didn't push it further. In fact, it was the same conversation we'd performed for his parents twice before, though Jonathan had both times named the boy he'd decided I was chasing. He was always ten percent right and ninety percent wrong.

I matched his cheerier tone, hoping we could at least fake our way through the remaining few days. But as soon as we left the house on our gambling trip, he closed me out, talking to Vince as if I weren't in the car. In all our road-trip bickering he wouldn't ever say, *We're done.* I pushed him on it a few times ("If you don't want to be my friend anymore, you don't have to be"), but I must have known I was doing it to call him back, make him retract and apologize. Freezing me into eternal oblivion fell within range of his ability, but he would never, not in his worst mood, make the decision and say it. Watching him from the back seat on the way to a casino, my old dependable ardor felt dulled to near nonexistence, and I wondered if I would have to be the one. *We're done.* Not yet, not yet, but someday. There was a limit, surely, to what I could make room for, the too-many fervent and wrongheaded convictions that didn't seem to mellow over the years, the table of topics we couldn't discuss so full I couldn't fit another onto it. And maybe I'd lost him anyway, and he would never again be the tenderhearted boy who would crawl onto my bed for nothing but soothing.

At the dim, smoky casino, I didn't feel like sampling much. A couple of slot machines, more than enough of watching my money sucked away for nothing but some noise and flashing lights. I wandered about watching them at different games or sat on a bench with a book. Jonathan kept returning to a blackjack table where the dealer was a handsome middle-aged Native American with a thin ponytail and a bolo tie. "So, um, what kind of Indians are at this casino?" Vince had goaded Jonathan in the car. "Maybe your *dad* will be there."

"Shut up! Maybe yours will."

"Mom, no!" Vince cried. "I thought you loved the mailman!"

But Jonathan at the blackjack table gave no thought to the man before him, not the idle what-if, a squint at a cheekbone. From across the room, I knew this. I could have taken comprehensive exams in Jonathan. He didn't have the dreams I did of belonging elsewhere. His brain wouldn't waste energy on what blood might brush against his in a casino in Oklahoma. He acknowledged his parentage only in gratitude to God for placing him in the correct life. I could not have wished him less contentment, only that he would now and then feel his displacement, his loss. That we could have been orphans together.

For more than an hour, I'd been parked in a corner with *The Second Coming* when I heard voices rising from the blackjack table. The dealer was confronting Jonathan, demanding to know what his problem was, calling on him to hit or stand, the second voice not Jonathan but a fat guy in the next chair, yelling—"Hey, no, hey"—and waving a pointer finger as I settled a hand on Jonathan's shoulder. He had a queen and a six. I leaned between him and the dealer. "Sweetie, you want a card?" His gaze moved on a slow drift along the table's edge. "Hit him," I told the dealer.

"There's something wrong with this guy," the fat man told the dealer. His chair was a wheelchair, I noticed, and oxygen tubes ran from a tank into his nose.

"There's nothing wrong with him," I told everyone. "He's fine."

Vince arrived, took up position at his other side. "Hey, buddy, look at that, you won!" But I didn't stay the few seconds more it took for him to blink back to the room, slowly collect his chips. I turned and went for the door before Vince's sentence had finished.

We had seen him go absent for briefer spans, eight or nine seconds— just long enough for us to be positive it was happening—and pick up a conversation where he'd dropped it. Longer meant he would return quiet, stilled, assessing his own mysteries; then Vince and I would help him out with the words: "Tired? Me, too. Ready to go home?"

When I went back inside to check on what seemed a long delay, they were cashing in their chips. "Where'd you go?" Vince asked, and I shook my head, unable to answer. In the car, after half a dozen tries from Vince, Jonathan turned to look at me. "Leah?" All I could do was cover my face with both hands to block him out, pull up my knees and wait for the car ride to end. By then I had gathered a few words and an offhand tone to keep them from tending me: I'm fine, just going to lie down for a bit.

If staying curled in a ball until I was back in my own bed in Benson had been an option, I would have been happy to try. But the only way to make them leave me alone was to answer when they tapped at the door, to go down to dinner and say, "Yes," and "Thank you," and "This is really good."

"Jonathan had an episode today," Vince said to his parents while we all ate. "Not a bad one. Just kind of spaced out for a minute." This was less a report on Jonathan than on me. He was attempting to account for my quiet, which I suppose gave him the excuse to speak as if we all knew about episodes, and allowed Jonathan to accept it.

But Jonathan knew, of course; his parents knew. His doctors knew. It was a mild form of epilepsy—we learned this over dinner—no cause for much worry; nothing to do but watch for changes, maybe don't operate heavy machinery. Vince and I had not exactly believed the secret ours alone, only that we must guard it.

His parents nodded about the day's incident, having seen worse, as we had. "We know you two are looking out for him," his mother said— perhaps the most surprising news of the evening, that Jonathan had told them we knew. She spoke this to me, tenderly, so confident of my awareness of her son's problems and my alert attentions that she wasn't sure why I was upset. It was as if I'd broken a protocol, forced us all into this slightly uncomfortable acknowledgment for no clear purpose. The topic had turned to dessert before I had to excuse myself or else cry in front of them.

He let up on me then. He came to my room, turned all remorse and affection and long eloquent speeches on friendship, reiterations of letters and talks I knew by heart. How many times had he promised we'd always be friends? He had made me doubt him often enough, but never so far that I couldn't stay by his side in a seizure, unsure he'd want me there when he returned. I'd never pictured a future in which I was no longer the person allowed to go to him at all, by my own decision if not his. And I kept remembering how, in the casino, I had paused in my rush to the table. I had looked for Vince first.

For the rest of the trip, Jonathan was warm and repetitively reassuring, yet no less intent on finishing the unfinishable argument. On the drive back to Rockhaven, he was still bringing it up, trying to reason me back from the precipice of ruinous sluthood for my own good.

"I love you," I replied at every salvo, until I was doing it in sing-song. "I'm not fighting with you. New topic." If he objected to the music I chose or a lunch stop I suggested, I'd warble *I love you* or *I'm not fighting with you*, until the two of them had to pick it up. A year later, we'd still sing-song to each other in the dining hall over whose cookie was that. *I'm not fighting with you*. When people asked what was so funny we'd say, "Road trip from hell. You had to be there."

With all the ruckus he caused, it was strange how little of the trip I spent thinking about Quinn in any actual way, dreaming him up in my bed or pondering what beachy flavor of intrigue might be keeping him amused. To get him back into the box he'd escaped from, a necessity, but I had come no closer to a plan. And at the farthest end of break, Sunday two a.m. and Sarah Beth's bed across the room still empty, I woke to the music of his pebbles plinking my window.

My vanishing roommate had spent three-fourths of the year thus far "over at Wells'." "Bye, going to Wells'!" Wells Naylor was a brash, buxom, life-of-the-party senior in Sarah Beth's sorority. Most of Sarah Beth's stories began "So we're at Wells'," though they spun the wheel for outdoor settings I'd never heard of—"So we're out at Crying Rock"; "We're over by the old quarry"—and involved a fairly stable cast of seven or eight girls and boys, many of them independents, who out-cooled the rest of us without effort. They all seemed to have a special talent in acting or music or painting: Sarah Beth had a beautiful singing voice. Perhaps this group had never cared much about their social status, but they'd never had to; most of us wanted to be them. Outside of class they wore mismatched rags and baseball caps and laughed with such abandon while flinging each other through representative landscapes that the yearbook photographer just followed them around. They glittered in sunlight and flushed rosy in the snow, the effortless beauty of good genes and karma.

Sarah Beth didn't turn up until Monday afternoon, having spent the break with Wells at Disney World. "Just you and Wells?" I asked, gathering books for an escape to Stirling before Quinn could pop in to delay me. "I thought it was the whole gang."

"We decided just us." She drew out the *s* in a way that made me stop and look at her. "Oh," I said. She nodded, and I said, "Oh." This was how I became the last person on campus to find out my roommate had a girlfriend.

It was also the entirety of our conversation about it, though "going over to Wells'" acquired new connotations. Tapping the grapevine, I couldn't get any detail beyond *Oh yeah*, that's *happening*. It was like Anna Vaughn and Will breaking up: headline news but unthinkable, too delicate for gossip. No telling what got said in the nastier frat-house corners, but people I came across did not joke about it or disparage them or speculate salaciously or refer to them as a couple. Yet there was an atmosphere of vague alarm about the matter that hadn't surfaced for the Renaissance clubbers' more demonstrative display. Sarah Beth and Wells were widely known and liked, private school girls from good families. Within the space that expanded around them, by no more than seemed a deference to their privacy, they didn't even hold hands. They merely refused, in the face of scandal, to keep apart or conceal their happiness. We at Rockhaven didn't know what to do with such behavior in their set. So we pretended not to see it.

Or most of us did. "I hear your roomie's out licking pussy," Quinn, at my door, more or less shouted before I could get a hand over his mouth or close him inside.

"You cannot talk like that on my hall!"

"Well, that's what they do, right? And what about you, rooming with her all this time? Do tell. You'd better hope lezziness isn't contagious." Etcetera.

His tone was jolly, and I waited for it to turn. If anyone was going to head the pitchfork mob, Quinn had an outside shot at it. In truth, this coupling confounded him. He knew it should piss him off, but he couldn't make up his mind whether lezziness counted the way faggotry did. For a while, he'd poke me with references—"So how are the dykes?"—but mainly to annoy me. I was squeamish in the way of the campus: unwilling to hear possibly hurtful words spoken of people we liked.

But sooner than expected, he got bored with the topic. "I'm just glad she's got somewhere to be," he said. "My girlfriend's got a single!"

"You don't have a girlfriend."

True, over the week or two since break, I'd been easily snared in the dreamy rush of contact and allowed him to nuzzle and grab-ass in public a little more than befitted close friends. I let him take my hand, briefly, when few people were around. True also that he knocked near-daily at my door, and alert dormmates might notice how often he went inside and the time that passed before he emerged. But I wouldn't sit with him in the dining hall before dessert. I wouldn't hang out with him at the Gamma house for more than a rare hour if there wasn't a party. With some strategic dodging, I caused now and then a whole day to pass without a word between us.

"I'm too busy for you," was my refrain for most restrictions, and this was true. I was far too busy to indulge even half of my own cravings for the sight of him or any degree of touch. Since boys who visited to loll about on my bed had always taken my time, I tried to hold Quinn to some similar amount of it. But my resolve was weak. I dropped riding altogether and began to steal time from Will, an evening and then another.

"You never come to my room," Quinn complained.

"That's because you're always in *my* room."

He and Chip had a long-standing system for crashing on a senior's sofa down the hall whenever the other wanted privacy. But the arrange-ment—one I'd unknowingly put into effect twice—made a dorm-wide spectacle of whatever girl was in there. Plus there was the problem of the bathroom. Quinn rolled his eyes and listed girls who had all but moved into their boyfriends' rooms in other dorms, who shared a hall bath with the boys, no big deal. But I could sort his examples into either the unofficially married or the sluts who would be kept around for a month or two before being excommunicated in eternal shame from that wing of the dorm. Of the two, no question I was the latter.

When I let drop that I was "seeing someone, sort of," Sarah Beth leapt to provide me with advance schedules of when she'd be away. "You can have sleepovers!" she prodded, gleeful in conspiracy. Most nights now she spent out at Clarkson, the funky, out-of-the-way dorm converted from the old day school where Wells had a single, leaving Quinn and me with luxurious hours of evening vacancy. Still, I sent him out promptly at midnight. A sleepover was sure to involve sneaking him into the hall bathroom, a dicier prospect than the reverse and enhance-ment of the story I already didn't want to be part of.

Quinn joked about keeping me in my place as if it were his idea, and he likely spun it that way for his friends, though he soon noticed that being coy about our status granted bonus cachet. Everyone saw us whispering together, ducking away together. Everyone was interested. "You," he would say from afar while standing with his friends, pointing, crooking the finger. "Come here." He'd whisper in my ear, smile, and send me away. Or beckoning from a Gamma sofa, he'd pat his lap, and when I seated myself there in an easy slouch he'd proceed to tell his friends how cold I was, too good for him, he could never have me. When my own friends interrogated me, my efforts to put them off—"I don't know," "A thing, maybe?" or "None of your business"—were too often undermined by my unruly blushing grin.

This kind of evasion drove Rockhaven out of its mind. People demanded a definition. Was it just sex? Was it more than just sex? In what way was it more than just sex? Never mind that neither of us could have given an honest answer if we'd tried. Quinn was off his usual seduce/score/annihilate program, while I appeared to be not the prude I'd been pegged for. We looked, caught in providential glimpses, like two people in love. But in that case, why didn't we sit together in the dining hall?

In the end, we envied Sarah Beth and Wells, but for different reasons. I wanted to be that kind of couple, granted special license to carry on in private while the world took pains to look away. Quinn merely envied their freedom to share a bed without anyone's fuss over the damn hall bathroom.

In the yearbook for that year is a black-and-white photo of us, taken at a picnic prior to an outdoor production of *As You Like It*. We have staked out a prime spot off to one side, a slab of lichened rock lifted like a tongue a few feet above the slope of lawn where most of the audience is seated. The lawn itself, with the forest at its back, will serve as the stage; the actors, some on horseback, will come and go by the broad, garden-groomed paths of Bishop's Walk. In this central campus wilderness, *pastoral* in the Shakespearean sense, we are comfortably elevated, our rock no more precarious than most of the plateau that held us all in the sky on its flat palm. Yet anyone looking at the uncaptioned photo, a tight shot from a low angle, might assume us to be perched on a cliff over a ravine.

I am tucked inside Quinn's bent knee; he is propped back on a hand, speaking to Will beside us. His other hand might be on my neck; this isn't clear. Because sunlight bleaches my face half featureless, I appear to be a pretty girl. Quinn's eyes have a canny shine, his mouth twisted with its usual sly humor, though the quality of light grants him its own benevolence; it blanches his pocky scars and softens his hollows. In T-shirts, shorts, and sneakers, we three are a jumble of limbs, skinny in the astounding way of youth; even Will, at the cupped shadow of sleeve on his upper arm, is softer, newer than I recall. His eyes, like mine, are cast down. Our lashes shape prominent crescents. Our smiling lips are parted—we are listening to Quinn—though Will seems about to speak. He and Quinn tip toward each other as if their foreheads are magnetized. Quinn's attention, like the camera's, is given over to Will, who absorbs seven-eighths of the light's beauty like a Renaissance angel and doesn't need any of it.

Quinn was drawn to pretty things, I often thought, in my insecure, adolescent way, but I understand it in finer terms, looking back. We were all drawn to pretty things. Quinn had to keep moving closer. He wanted possession, full knowledge, mastery, a trophy to keep. It wasn't conscious, his desire to destroy, but it drove him.

More than ever, I had to work at keeping them apart. It was hard, when for events like Shakespeare on the lawn, Quinn naturally wanted to go with me; Will was more interested in going if Quinn would be there; and I was less fretful over looking couple-ish when Will was along. And we had fun together. Credit the power of pillow talk or Will's own unassailable sweetness, but Quinn's conviction loosened, as I'd hoped: not even the master of persistence could go on thinking Will Oliver a murderer. Now and then, as we passed whole light-hearted days clear of the topic of Brantley, I could be lulled into forgetting that Quinn had other suspicions.

"Just be *gentle*," I told him.

"I'm not *hurting* him." Like parents with opposite styles: we both loved the baby, but I wanted to coddle it and he wanted to play rough.

Quinn began taking Will to the weight room or out to run trails, Will's preferred exercise. Then there was the universal catch-all for masculine privacy, "fraternity business." Big concession on Quinn's part to let me deduce that the business in question *might* involve hypothetical scenarios for Will's deactivation—not to join the Gammas, but perhaps to allow for some informal shift of association. "Then it's not fraternity business, is it?" I pointed out. "Anyway, it was my idea. You wouldn't be talking to him at all without me, so don't pretend it's too sensitive for my ears." An argument that might have cowed one of my more reasonable friends had zero effect on Quinn, who could answer without a mote of dissimulation that I was wrong, that it did not involve me at all.

During my own private hours with Will, Quinn would drop by with a six-pack, and how could I turn him away when gravity had its way with me, drawing me toward him just as Will was drawn to the beer? "He's not my boyfriend," I told Will, ducking as Quinn went to kiss me, then inching my back up to his chest on the love seat while the three of us talked.

"We're just friends who fuck," Quinn said, for an elbow in the ribs.

"You'd better not be saying that to *other* people. Will knows better than to believe you."

"Isn't she cruel?" Quinn popped a beer tab, musing about how he could next mortify me. "That's what happens when you channel Brantley Simms."

That he should not throw around Brantley's name willy nilly was restriction number one on the list. I looked to the ceiling for strength. "Why do I need him when I've got you right here?"

To Will, Quinn said, "Do you have an inner Brantley? Leah does."

I tried waving this off. "I sometimes think of him here with us, that's all. Listening."

Quinn helped my tale along. "Speaking. Asking questions. Offering opinions."

That's just my inner Brantley, I'd tell him whenever I blurted something overly cynical from within Brantley's purview. For instance, that Will had spent spring break at some lake house with Anna Vaughn having his brain washed.

And maybe Quinn had a point, that Will wasn't poised to fall apart at a few words, a name, a notion of mine that I'd deemed too intrusive or cute to mention but couldn't help, while under leopard sheets, giving away to Quinn along with every half-safe fragment of myself that surfaced as if he were a vessel I could fill.

"Like what?" Will asked.

"He's not so crazy about your girlfriend," Quinn said. "Or is it Leah who doesn't like her?"

"No, we're chums now. She and I have long conversations about the meaning of life."

"Brantley doesn't like her," Will confirmed.

Quinn pounced on the tense. "Ah, you do have an inner Brantley! I don't, which seems a shame. Maybe it's this room. Is he here now?" His tone was respectful enough that Will and I exchanged a look, checking with the other for the answer. "He'd like this pad, wouldn't he? Except for Leah being in it all the time. She kind of wrecks the whole vibe."

"Brantley likes me just fine," I said, dead calm, daring a challenge from either of them. Maybe it had begun in the fever I'd suffered, the gown stashed in my closet, but I felt this as truth: without quite believing in ghosts, I'd become partly attuned to a presence I called Brantley. He had things to say. He understood I was protective of Will, favored me for this. More than in the room, he lived in Will's mind, held sway there, a place where I'd become some means of their communication—this much was I trusted. At times I sensed his jealousy of my flesh, my life, so close to Will's, but he forgave it and let me be; I was no threat. Anna Vaughn could not have been much of one either, yet some portion of Will's antipathy for her, which he never could explain, must have come from that lingering emotional fog of Brantley. I felt it too: he wanted her gone.

And how did he feel about Quinn in this room? No denying that when Quinn spoke to Will, he sounded—not in voice so much as diction, syntax, patterns of association—more like Brantley than I ever would.

"The funny thing," Quinn said, "is if we could really bring him here, talk to him, he could just tell us about that fall. Right? What does he say, Will, when he talks to you?"

To my three sips, Will had emptied his can. "He doesn't exactly talk. And never about that. It's not what he cares about."

The specificity implied gave me a shiver of anxious vigilance. Quinn took it in with a nod. "What he cares about. That's what matters now, isn't it? That we find a way to give him what he wants. We can honor him that way."

"And then you go and change the subject," Quinn said, stretched on his back atop my bedcovers, listing my crimes. In these semi-clandestine visits, permitted as rarely as I could stand it, I'd come to expect a rapid nakedness for both of us, achieved with minimal assistance from me. But aside from a swath of beach-tanned belly where his shirt rode up, we were both fully clothed, and he was deep into my secondary infractions, subsidiary to the principal charge: I was hiding something from him. He was sure of it.

Sarah Beth's tape deck, primed for noise cover, played softly beside us, the upbeat final notes of *Life's Rich Pageant* flipping to *Fables of the Reconstruction*, surreptitious and strange, while I puzzled over how to get our clothes off by some novel route. Slower, better. In his usual hunger and haste he forgot to prod me anymore to say what I wanted, and I would have felt stupid, crazy, suggesting we kiss for an hour in disheveled formalwear while his hand played between my legs. The pleasure I knew how to attach to myself was mostly his. If he felt good, I did. And if he directed the action, I reasoned, a quick conclusion must be what pleased him. But I knew it had become too much the same; it would bore him soon, or already had.

He heaved himself up against the wall. "I need this, you know. It's not his goddamn heart on a stick. It's an answer. It won't hurt him to tell the truth."

"You don't know that."

"There, see? He's the one you love." Past his head, a second Quinn eyed me from the wall's photo collage with carnivorous intent—literally posing for the camera as the Big Bad Wolf—his cheek resting on the hair of some virgin in a cheap strapless dress who was laughing with her mouth wide open and looking in the wrong direction. "If you loved me, you wouldn't keep things from me."

"I might if I were trying to protect you."

All his tension eased into a smile—he wasn't even surprised. I shook my head, mad at myself, denying the truth before he spoke it. "Even so. You've been wanting to tell me."

Every sweet hour he had spent thus far in my room had been marred at its edge by my awareness of the gown in the closet. The more I worked to forget it, wanting to believe I denied him nothing, the louder its presence spoke, until I began to wonder if the voice was Brantley's, asking to be let out.

So I made him promise to stay calm, to take no action without me. Then I told him, as simply as possible, about Brantley's gown. That his parents had given it to Will. But Will couldn't handle having it in his room, so I took it. I lifted it from the closet to carry like a sleeping child to the bed. There I sat at Quinn's side, containing him with our backs to the wall as I spread the gown's initialed scapular over our knees. "This is it. It's what he was wearing."

Quinn set his hands on it, at either side of the initials. Just having him beside me, taking it in, made my own thoughts start to click. "He wanted it to be seen?" I said. "He thought it would be, if he died in it?" I was surprised by my readiness to think suicide. It was where Will's desolation had left me, whatever the Order might be. And wearing it had always been the choice that spoke.

Quinn shook his head. "It *was* seen. He was wearing it, all over campus. For how long, a week? Two weeks? It's why." His breath came in soft bursts. "They took him up there and threw him off."

They could not mean Will, only faceless others. They, who would make Brantley answer for his offense, had marched him up the tower steps, wearing the gown... "Not wearing it," I said. "If it was something they wanted to hide, they would have taken it."

"Right." He nodded, puzzled. "Then, what? He's not going to kill himself just to...expose them."

"But you think there might have been other reasons."

"Like he was a fag, you mean?" Quinn's fingertips hovered over Brantley's initials, and he tipped his head back hard into the wall, began to knock the cinder block in dull, punctuating thunks. "The problem was he couldn't just keep his stupid mouth shut about it. He could have messed around on the sly. But he was having some goddamn awakening, and it wasn't going to work, with the frat." His head dropped forward before I had to intervene. "He had to shut up. Or they'd kick him out."

"Would you have been one of them, doing the kicking?"

"I don't know. Probably."

To argue that Brantley could have lived his life outside the fraternity crossed my mind, but Quinn would never grant the premise. I wasn't sure I would either, not when everyone would know the charges. To leave school, that would be his option. Unless outside of Rockhaven was nothing. "But they hadn't yet," I said. "And Emery told me he seemed okay, at the time. Not unhappy."

"It was the gown. Because...we all saw him that night, you know. He was at the house right before. There was a meeting about him."

The meeting. In piecing together events, I'd understood "the Brantley situation" had been discussed in his presence, that what had been said haunted Quinn. But I'd never imagined it taking place that very night. The story we all knew had never included a meeting.

Quinn went on, his voice airless. "That's why the coat and tie. He knew it was about him, he'd better fucking dress for it. I told him he disgusted me. But he was my brother. I told him that too. The whole thing, it wasn't that rough. He had support on his side." Jaw gone slack, he drifted, dazed. "A couple of the guys even tried to go with him when he left. He said no, he had something to do. He seemed fine. Two hours later… I swear, no one saw it coming. I sure didn't. But when he goes up there in the gown, how do you not think he must have done it himself?"

I remembered how the Gammas had all agreed to stop talking about it, to call it an accident. How many of them secretly believed suicide? "But you thought the Order," I reminded him.

"I did. I guess I wanted another reason, like a ceremony where people would wear gowns at two in the morning." He breathed a laugh. "God, if there was one, that would have been the highlight of his life. I'd sort of forgotten the gown since then. And this idea I had, that Will would have tricked him up there, telling him he was getting inducted, then push him over."

He spoke the notion like something long discarded, absurd, while I was picturing Brantley leaving the house with plans past midnight. A ceremony, highlight of his life, a pure Brantley *reason* to wear a gown at two in the morning. "But not Will," I murmured. "Someone else."

Quinn gave me a narrow look. "Not the Order. Like you said, they wouldn't have left him with the gown."

My fingers went to the initials, reading them like a Ouija board, seeking the boy who had chosen to sew them there. What did he want? He wanted to be with Will, to help Will escape, or to join along with him. To show his own frat they couldn't make him feel less worthy. Climb the ranks, thumb his nose from a more secure berth. He *thought he was smarter than everyone.* Could flaunting the stolen code have been some warped effort to impress them? "How about this," I said, too restless to sit. I stood before my desk, while Quinn turned onto the bed's edge, the gown furled across his lap. "They tell him he's getting inducted, trick him up there. But they're going to kill him. When he knows it, he jumps. Before they can get the gown. It's his only way to get back at them, to take it with him."

This sounded to me, as I spoke it, crazy, far-fetched, but Quinn sank back, solemn. "Holy shit."

Because his doubt receded, mine surged. I followed the gown to the gravel path, the same one I had walked past in the fogged-in dark on my way to the radio station, before the ambulance arrived. "But they could have just taken the gown from his…"

"Right," Quinn said. He'd followed it there too; we stood together over the gowned corpse, the fog moving in. "Unless they freaked out. They didn't mean to kill him. They meant to scare him, and he took them seriously?" He pushed the gown aside, rose to his feet. "Or… say they put him on the ledge to scare him, and something went wrong. Then whoever got him up there, they just flipped out and ran. Like any of us would."

This, I had to admit, was credible, far closer to the Rockhaven I knew. *None of us would do such a thing*. It was still true. Even the Order was us. "An accident."

A calm elation suffused me, but Quinn wasn't done. "Had to be more than one of them, to scare him that bad. Will was one. He was fucking there."

"No. No way." My instant rejection came from fear, but then I was sure of it. "How many are in the Order, on campus? Must be half a dozen, at least. Guys, according to you. And I'm guessing some big, athletic ones. They wouldn't need Will, and they wouldn't want him. He loved Brantley. They knew it. Will was the *problem*."

"Damn. You're right again," he said, unsmiling. "And now we're in my territory. Because when you've got a problem like that in the ranks, a *loyalty* problem, the thing to do is devise a test. Will probably had to run the whole event. They need him to make a choice, the Order, or his little friend."

"He'd choose Brantley." I drew back to the bed's edge, sick with foreboding. "Will never wanted to be in the Order." Quinn, with a doubtful look, crossed his arms, sat back on the desk edge. I said, "Obviously he doesn't talk about them. But he's basically told me. *Brantley* was obsessed with them, but Will never wanted any part of it. Like he hates the Phi Os, but worse."

"He doesn't hate the Phi Os. He's still one of them, isn't he?" Quinn pondered. "You know who doesn't hate the Order? Fucking Ransom Whitacre's daughter. She'd be a bit of motivation. Wouldn't you agree?"

"Not enough." But that was a lie, when Will and Anna Vaughn were still together, when he wouldn't divide himself from this girl he loathed more than he could account for. And I remembered, too vividly, Will's obsession: being there, reaching out in time, catching hold of Brantley before he could fall. They hadn't meant to kill him. Will hadn't meant to.

"Does our friend happen to have one of those mystery keys to the tower?"

"Not that I know of." But who, if not Will, if keys followed privilege?

"Let's find out."

15

WHAT IN THE MIDST LAY BUT THE TOWER ITSELF?

Ask a Rockhaven student, perhaps an English major not yet prepped for comprehensive exams, to identify Childe Rowland. The quickest correct answer, at some other school, would call him a hero from medieval folklore, one who later lent his name and tower to a poem by Robert Browning. We at Rockhaven would more likely leap to Browning's source, *King Lear*—where Rowland is all but irrelevant—for Shakespeare formed the scaffolding of our very souls.

"Childe Rowland to the dark tower came," says Edgar in the guise of a madman, Tom O'Bedlam. Narratively, the line has no meaning, no context; it serves only as a sham indicator of madness. Edgar has assumed his disguise after his brother has falsely charged him with the attempted murder of their father, Gloucester. Thus unrecognized, Edgar meets his father on the heath where Gloucester, blinded, is seeking a cliff's edge from which to jump to his death. Edgar—as mad Tom—takes his father's arm as if to assist him to that end.

Here, he says, jump. Dark comedy that there is no cliff, no void to receive the blind man's fall.

On Good Friday, Dr. Macintosh released us ten minutes early. From Polk Tower came the sonorous, slow bonging of a single bell. "Where are we going?" I asked, my head still on the heath as I followed my classmates over the foggy quad. "Way of the Cross," Pem said. We stopped at the edge of University Avenue for one of those arcane Rockhaven liturgical practices that tended to happen under my radar and could be startling to come upon unprepared. Up the center of the road, cloaked in fog, came the bent form of a young priest, a full-sized cross hefted on one shoulder. Behind and around him, a solemn clot of people in street clothes walked in attendance, some with a hand beneath the cross's long post or at the squared-off arms. The one who bore it wore black vestments but no crown of thorns, and he did not stagger in agony beneath his burden.

Beside me, Will sat on the friable rags of his gown, his sockless loafers in the street. As the procession passed, he stood and joined its tail; I almost did as well, thinking we were all meant to. In front of the chapel, the cross was lifted erect. A man's voice intoned what seemed a prayer, lost beneath the unwavering boom of the bell. The cross continued on its way and was raised upright at the chapel steps. Will disappeared in the crowd around it. By the time it passed coffin-like through the great doors, the faithful trailing, most of us were drifting away toward lunch.

"I didn't know Will was churchy," Jenny said, as we heathens walked toward the Commons. I could only shrug for an answer, unsettled at the thought of Will in a pew, facing the cross's final station. Too fragile, too undefended, for all that heavy suggestion. No telling how the voice of God would come to him, especially when he went seeking it.

In the SPO after lunch, as my friends dispersed with their mail, my mind remained anxiously elsewhere. Purely subliminal, whatever cue made me stop, back up, and return to a bulletin board. Tacked at the center amid fliers for club meetings, fundraisers, lost and found items was a marker drawing on white paper. An eye, inside a spiky thistle flower, inside a Celtic cross, inside a circle. I had never sketched it out as Quinn had so often, after we'd teased it from the ashtray's stamp of sealing wax, but I knew its every element as if I had.

Above, in bold letters, were two words: "Recognize this?" Below, in smaller print: "SPO 680."

I yanked it down from the board, as if I could keep it from being seen. My friends had gone out the door, but I hadn't noticed Dex lingering behind to pop up at my shoulder. "You recognize that?"

"No…"

"They're all over," he said. "As of today, I think. Some game?"

"All over *campus*?" I looked around, heart thudding: at least one photocopy tacked on every board in sight. My immediate instinct, to get them down, was checked by the need for discretion. "SPO 680. Who's that?"

Dex rounded his eyes. "A mystery, I presume. Let's look."

I snatched his sleeve as he started toward the mailboxes. "They might see us!"

"So?"

His amused unconcern emboldened me somewhat, plus there were few others around. We went along the walls of boxes, scanning until we found 680. Bottom row, back wall. Only numbers identified the boxes, so I had to consult my memory of where I'd seen people stand in the room to collect mail. It wasn't Will's. Not Quinn's. I didn't remember ever seeing Dalton or Anna Vaughn at a box, turning the dial. I couldn't call to mind any particular person crouching at this spot where Dex did now, peering through the glass while I kept nervous watch on the room.

"Empty," he said. "So it's someone who's been here today. We've all got fliers." He stood, while I squatted to look as well. At the other side, a mailroom worker passed, the shadow falling oddly. The nearby slots, many of which held fliers and mail, all showed a piece of the mailroom through the other end, but not 680. Something blocked it.

"What's with the interest?" Dex asked as I stood. "You know what that thing is, don't you? Are you going to write to 680? Are you going to disappear into some kind of cult? And then will we have to band together to break you out and deprogram you? That sounds fun. Do that."

Saying goodbye to Dex, I went into the bathroom to wait him out, then crept back to collect the other copies. But who was I protecting, hopelessly, and from what? It smelled like bait in a trap, for Quinn if not me—and what were my chances Quinn hadn't seen it yet? Or maybe it was nothing so sinister, only posted by some innocent soul who had come across a piece of evidence, as Brantley once had.

At the mail window the student worker, a prickly, self-important girl named Janine, was rolling down the metal gate to close for the weekend. "Wait," I begged. Keeping my voice low and an eye on the students who passed in and out, I asked whose box was 680.

She sighed, disinclined to help me. It took some work to talk her into paging through a clipboard list. "No one's," she said.

Not possible, I wanted to argue, but to produce the bulletin as proof seemed unwise. "Then…what do you do with mail for that box?"

"Mostly trash it. Depends."

If that was true, the message couldn't be bait. And unless it was a misprint, it couldn't be real either. But it had to be something. Janine stood with her hand on the gate, done with me, while behind her, another student worker, a girl in heavy eyeliner whose name I didn't know, was stacking crates, shooting furtive glances my way. I appealed to her over Janine's shoulder. "Why would there be just one box in the middle of a row not assigned to someone?"

Janine snipped, "I'm sure it was assigned, and then that person left."

"Or died," the other girl offered, before Janine shut the window.

For a stunned minute, I wanted to run straight to my sounding board, Quinn. Fliers that directed messages to a dead boy? Fliers *from* *Brantley*. And wasn't it exactly the message he'd post, having copied the code onto his own back? The symbol needed airing as well.

If his ghost was now finishing the work, he'd waited a long time to go about it. I was more ready to ascribe it somehow to the living Brantley. For instance, fliers he'd left to be posted had been mislaid for a year and a half, then posted in error—some weird mix-up that allowed him to persist from beyond the grave, dragging secrecy into the open.

Wherever he was, he was smiling. It was a good joke on the living. *Bad idea,* I told him in my head. *Did you learn nothing?*

But then I had to rethink the accusation. By now I took enough cues from my inner Brantley to know that if I was worried, he was too. It was Quinn's inner Brantley, the one he pretended not to have, who was grinning with such keen satisfaction.

Recognize this? the sign repeated on half the campus boards I could think of to check. I flew from one to the next, ripping them down.

That afternoon, rain fell on all the lavishly decorated cars of seniors who had completed their comprehensive exams. It fell on the trail ride once we were headed home, on the chapel where Will contemplated the resurrection. Walking to dinner at twilight, I found him on the wet path outside the chapel doors.

"What happens," he asked me, "if we can't believe Jesus was raised from the dead? A man of flesh, who died and was buried? Sealed behind a stone."

I glanced up into the great bloomed rose of stained glass over the chapel doors, as if for the answer he'd missed. "We go on with our perfectly human lives. You've been reading too much Faulkner."

"You don't ever feel like you need to know? For sure?"

"Not even a little." A breeze blew over us the damp reek of pear flower.

"Brantley was an atheist." Will swallowed. "Is that awful? To say so? Maybe he wasn't, really."

"You think God will hear, you'll get him in trouble?" I hooked a hand through his arm to take him home, hoping he'd not seen the fliers but wondering, too, if they were his own doing. If my confiscation of the gown had thwarted his urge to wear it, he might have found another way to let Brantley speak.

"A stupid joke," I told Vince, who demanded to see what he'd caught me grabbing from the board in the dining hall foyer. I balled the thing and refused.

The gesture had become automatic, so that the next night, when I spotted a flier atop Will's kitchen island, I snatched it up. To hide from whom? Not Will, clearly. Not Quinn, who had come in at my side. "That looks familiar," he said. With an alert air of discovery, he turned to Will. "Is it Brantley's? I've seen it before. Part of his investigation into a certain secret society?"

Will, dull-eyed, said yes, it was Brantley's.

Then I was sure: Quinn's handiwork. To some degree he was taking up Brantley's fallen lance to go on jousting at the Order. But why point them at SPO 680? They would presumably uncover the owner but wouldn't know it on sight, nor hear Brantley's voice speaking from every wall, the way Will would.

"I've seen these all over campus," I said. "So it's somebody else's investigation now."

"Maybe," Will said, meaning *maybe not*. Maybe a ghost could use a copy machine? Resurrection after all.

"All over campus?" Quinn asked me.

I had to restrain my sarcasm. I couldn't let him hurt Will without a fight, but I couldn't be disloyal either. It was a hard line to walk. "Yeah, I guess it's someone else digging after conspiracies, thinks it all a game. Shall we go?" I didn't want to go, our evening's excursion too much under Quinn's control. A Black Saturday vigil, he'd called it, conceived on learning how Will had spent his Good Friday.

Behind us came a tap at the open door. Before I could turn, Will had snatched the flier and tucked it under his *Complete Shakespeare*. Anna Vaughn. "Well, the gang's all here," she said, with forced cheeriness. "Hi, everyone."

Will, too much tension in his jaw, nearly growled, "What's up, Anna Vaughn?"

She sucked a breath in pained surprise. "I just came to get you for the party." Her glance shifted to each of us, assessing the situation. "We can...all go together if you like. The Phi O party?"

"Yeah, y'all," Quinn echoed, as Will went past Anna Vaughn and out the door, "the Phi O party? Maybe we should stop by, on our way." He had, in fact, already argued for our making an appearance.

We were all outside, Anna Vaughn calling Will's name until he turned to answer from halfway up the walk. "Sorry, we have plans."

She stalled behind us in the porch shadow. "Can I come?"

The question stopped me in the path. It delivered my first pinch of remorse over being among the chosen, though it must have been clear to her by now that I wasn't the one hurting her, was hardly involved. Before I could think, I said, "Why not? Guys? She can come, right?"

Already I was arguing in my head with Quinn, who stood with Will beside the Saab: *I'm sorry, but you saw her face!* I wasn't sure bringing her was wise at all, though I sensed her presence would disrupt Quinn's agenda, whatever it was, far more than I could.

"We're going to talk to Brantley." Will said this distinctly, evenly, and I gaped at him, because this was not any part of the plan we'd discussed. His gaze didn't move from Anna Vaughn. "Is that what you'd like to do? Would you like to come with us and talk to Brantley?"

She looked woozy but steadied herself, said, "Yes."

Will took it in, remained unmoved. "I don't think so. Coming, Leah?"

He and Quinn opened their doors. Anna Vaughn took three marching strides as if she meant to force her way into the back seat, then stopped, hands out, like a signal to herself. "Be careful, please," she whispered—to me, I realized when she added, "Watch him. Keep close."

She could have followed us easily had we been crossing the quad to the bell tower, Quinn's much-pressed plan. Perfect spot, he said, for a Black Saturday vigil with a couple sixers, if only one of us had a key. But Will swore eight times he had nothing of the kind, so we'd settled for an alternate location off the southern end of the domain: Hangman's Bridge, a sandstone cliff with a passage eroded through its center big enough for a train.

Why not the cemetery? I'd suggested dryly. Quinn dismissed the notion as morbid. For Will and me—as I supposed it—any alternative to a Phi O party sounded preferable, even getting loaded while seeking Christ on a rock named for a form of execution.

Quinn intended for us to camp at the top, but once we found our way out onto that crooked finger of rock, he had to concede it was too narrow and irregular for comfort. So we descended by a steep path in disconcerting darkness, gripping saplings for balance, to the stone amphitheater floor beneath. Caves opened in the cliff at our back, and all along the valley past the arch of the bridge, bluff dropped away into treetop. From somewhere below the canopy came the crash of falling water, etching out, as it struck, a deep, clear pool popular with skinny-dippers. I had not yet found the nerve to join one of those post-midnight expeditions, though back in warm weather when we'd been only friends, Quinn had made a hard run or two at talking me into it. It was his favorite after-party, Quinn the faun who had introduced the spot to half the Rockhavenites who could claim to have been naked in its water. If Will and I escaped it tonight, we could thank the nip in the air.

Quinn had offered to bring the beer. Instead he produced Solo cups and a liter of Maker's Mark, capped in its blood-red sealing wax. "Brantley's favorite," Will said, almost ironic with unsurprise.

Quinn agreed. "Pretty sure it's what he was drinking his last night. A bottle went missing from the house."

For me, girly that way, he'd brought a can of ginger ale as a mixer. Why had none of us brought a flashlight? Why were we there at all? Because our Lord was dead, sealed in his tomb, and we must wait on him somewhere.

But it should have been the tower. A shame, not one of us with a key. "Brantley would pitch a goddamn fit," Quinn said, with a ceremonial lifting of his cup. "Who gives out keys, and on what grounds?"

I thought of those Edelman soirees Brantley had attended. Gourmet dinners at a professor's house, sipping brandy and smoking weed. *Once or twice*, Will had said. *His kind of scene*. Brantley had been as trim as the other boys, not unhandsome with his surfer-blond forelock and heavy-lidded eyes. Yet I pictured how he'd have to beg Will to take him again after that first time, somehow too eager, too loud, too gauche, too Brantley, to be one of the chosen on his own. So close to the fence, he saw better what he was missing.

While I sipped, Quinn and Will set about knocking back their cups and refilling with heavy-handed pours. They took a notion to build a fire, and soon had a little one popping in the kettle of rock we sat around, me between them. Quinn had tried to leave me home on the ground that he had man-things to discuss with Will that would only bore me. I'd defied him to try. No, really, I said. *See if you can bore me.*

And he intended to, with *honor*, that snore of a Rockhaven gentleman's topic. How shall we be Men of Honor, let us count the ways. Yet even in Quinn the continuing dialogue was not pure pretense. When he spoke to Will of the proper intricacies of fraternal divorce, he was speaking—earnestly—of honor. When Will with a stern word or look shut Quinn down for saying something too crass about me, he was serving *in loco fraternis* as my brother, Quentin to my Caddy, looking out for my honor. In Faulkner's South, I had not much honor left to fuss over, nine-tenths of all that could be called mine already lost to Quinn. Yet in admitting females to the ranks of its gentlemen, Rockhaven granted us some semantic access to the larger, more nuanced question. In theory, we mattered as much, and sometimes even in practice. When Jonathan—unreformed upholder of the patriarchy though he was— spoke of how we all might hope to be remembered after death, he was speaking largely of honor, and he meant me too.

Will was writing a paper that touched on it for Southern Lit and should have been eager to join in. But he didn't look up from the fire, as if the topic were a sore spot and private. "It's just integrity. Being true to an ideal."

"Doing the right thing." Settled back on his rock, Quinn rubbed an ankle over mine, the most he'd touched me in a week. Our last time having sex had been some days before I'd shown him the gown. Perhaps we had run out our allotment. "That sounds easy enough. For most of us."

"I think it's a smokescreen," I said, meaning to sidetrack Quinn at any opening. "The people who valued it above all owned slaves. How do you convince yourself that's honorable?"

"But that's the difference between honor and morality," Quinn said. "All they could do with slavery was try to claim it was God's will, the Bible says so. That's why morality is such a load of horseshit in the first place, because you just arrange the law how it suits you, then figure out how to blame it on God. Honor, though, is about what's fundamentally right. You can't apply it to slavery."

"It was applied," Will said, a sleepy lull of bourbon in his voice. "Honor was in going to war for a way of life, for what was yours. Defend your brother and your neighbor and your womenfolk, but also your property and the system that allowed it. Dying for that was called honor. You're just talking about what ought to be called property."

Quinn grinned. "Well, ain't you a regular ole Beauregard. Go on, recite 'Ode to the Confederate Dead' for us."

Will shook his head. "I promise I could not."

"The grave, the grave," Quinn tried, "the moldering, ravenous grave. With a spider in it."

I laughed, then tried to get Will started on Stevens' "Sunday Morning" instead. Quinn spoke over the top of me. "Well, what have we left then? 'Thou shalt not lie, cheat, or steal' is just some restrictions. Give me an ideal worth living up to."

He meant for Will to answer. I said, "Loyalty."

Quinn blinked at me. "That's what you think?"

"That's what *you* think."

"Okay." He sucked his teeth. "And what are we loyal to, or who? It would have to matter that we choose someone worthy."

I caught back a laugh. "Isn't that like choosing who you love? It's not always someone who deserves it." This was pushing too near the line—even Will looked askance, curious to see where my own loyalty would land. I steered for neutrality. "Like your frat brothers. You don't exactly choose them. But you pledge loyalty to them anyway. They're your people."

I could expect Quinn to bristle anytime I mentioned fraternity, so far beyond my ken. But as I'd handed him something that suited his needs, he gave it a nod. "Like family." He turned to Will. "And in rare cases, you might need to remove yourself from family."

Will stared into the fire, chin resting on his cup. "Choose better?"

"Or be true to the friends you know are true. Even if they're dead." Quinn leaned to tip the bottle into Will's cup. "That's what tradition is about, right? Honor your dead. Be someone worthy of that honor."

"Do what Brantley wants, you mean. Trash all my living friends... burn it all, leave it all..." Will's voice creaked with misery, beginning to slur, and Quinn set a stopping hand on my knee as if I would speak and wreck it. It was a strange moment, both of us poised in a breath-caught silence that was part love and part hunger and part fear of what he would say next or what he never would. "For what," he said, "what?"

"For honor," Quinn said softly. "Hell, for your sanity. If you have something to set right in the world, you find a way. It's hardly ever the easy choice. But ask yourself, since I think we three can agree that Brantley *is* here with us: is that the kind of principle he would stand behind?"

Will nodded, his face open and anguished. *Stop this*, I told myself, but Quinn was leading so gently, and I wondered if he might, after all, be right. That we were gathered in the presence of, among other entities, a wound that needed lancing. That Will would be relieved, grateful.

"Would he want you to tell the truth?" Quinn asked. "And I mean what you know about what happened to him. Just to us, right now?"

Will grunted, looking ill. "I doubt it."

Quinn drew back, unready for dissent. His voice remained lullaby soft, almost disinterested. "Keeping their secrets. That's what he wants? Bullshit. You know better. Why, Will? Why do you protect them? I don't think you even want to."

Will's face hardened at the word *them*. "They don't need protecting. And that's not even it. I told you."

Quinn looked at me, quizzical. I could only shrug.

"Told me what?"

"It's not what matters."

Quinn folded hands over his mouth. "Okay. So it's not the truth that will set you free." I felt him reading Will's body as it slumped back into assent. "Then it's something else. Something he wants." His voice was tightening with frustration. "There has to be a way to honor him, do right by him. I'm *trying*—"

He snipped the thread of his sentence, but I could finish it. He was trying, now and always, in his merciless way, to do right by Brantley. Every missile had been launched some time ago at that target. "How many of us still even try," he went on, calmer, "to live by ideals? Courage. Sacrifice—there's one nobody's up to these days. Sacrifice, on behalf of love, brother, country, a true friend. It's sad." He and Will had locked eyes and looked ready to fall into the fire, meet each other there. "We, on this goddamn mountain, who mean to live by honor. We all just go on, as if we have no blood on our hands. As if the atrocities of history belong to other people, there are no connections, nothing matters but our own pitiful lives, our stupid futures. We sit here talking as if honor still matters…"

The sobbing catch in his voice—did he fake that? "Okay, drunkies," I said. "I'm calling for a new topic." I'd spent a portion of the night picturing Anna Vaughn seated with us, wondering how the conversation might have turned in her presence. It could have been worse, I supposed.

"Good idea." Will set down his cup. "Y'all pick one while I take a piss."

He lumbered up and off into the dark. Before I knew I was on my feet, I was trying to follow, into a sudden blackout where I stumbled hard. Quinn, at my side, caught me. "Whoa, there." His breath quickened toward a laugh, both of us peering into the unrelenting dark. He hollered after Will, "Don't fall off a cliff!"

"God, please. If you care about him, or me, even a little—"

"Shhhh. It's okay." Behind us, the firewood cracked. Tenderly, like a favor, Quinn said, "I'll go."

I made a serious grab for him but he was already leaping down the trail like a deer. How could his feet still be under him? But we both knew my night vision was worse than anyone's; I couldn't follow more than a few steps. Straining to listen, I picked out a voice, later another, indistinct, mingled with the pop and hiss of fire, the rustle of leaves and rush of the waterfall below. I screamed their names two or three times apiece.

They were gone long enough for me to gather more sticks for the fire, refresh my drink, contemplate the remainder of the night I might spend attempting the walk back along the highway or losing my way in the dark. How much would they worry to find me gone? Assuming they returned at all. And what did I know of Quinn and his limits, unmonitored, the whole dark woods he knew well at his disposal?

Watch him. Keep close. That Anna Vaughn might have Will's interests at heart, might know him better than I did, seemed somewhat less doubtful. The fear in her eyes on the lawn of Stirling, at least, was now my own.

But then came the approach of scuffling steps, their voices—Quinn laughing, Will telling him to shut up—long before they emerged into the firelight, conjoined at the shoulder, Quinn's under Will's. "He fucking fell off a cliff," Quinn crowed, and it was some time before I understood he wasn't joking.

Like a good Rockhavenite, Will refused the hospital. Nothing broken, he swore, just banged up. In his room, we eased his sweater over his head and edged his T-shirt loose of abrasions that oozed over one shoulder and down his back. Comically stoic, he lamented the torn sweater, accepted a shot of bourbon for medicine. From the bottle's remains, Quinn poured us each a last, good-sized drink, then emptied the rest into a dish cloth to apply to Will's wounds. I found him a fresh T-shirt, and we dressed him between us. Still it was an hour before I noticed his awkward left-handedness, the right curled to his body, and made him show me. Two broken fingers, I decided, drunk enough by then to splint them myself with half a pencil and scotch tape like the only medic in the wilderness.

The story Will told: he'd walked a few steps off the trail toward a tree he meant to grab hold of, its trunk a hand's span in diameter. He could see it clearly, see the near-level plate of stone it seemed to grow from, the same he could feel beneath his feet up until he looked down. And there was nothing. Not stone, not tree, only black.

He'd fallen a dozen feet at most, Quinn promised. To Will it had been five times that, but soft, the landing almost easy. He wasn't sure he was on the ground at all or how much time had passed before he heard Quinn calling from the ledge.

"I had such a strong feeling," Will said, "that we were in the wrong place for a vigil. Or I was. Which is how I felt in the chapel. I needed to be alone. In the woods, that's where I started to hear him. In the trees, the waterfall, in my head. And I was walking where I was supposed to, like being called. I don't remember falling. I'm not sure I did. Only that I was *caught*. And set down. I mean, I shouldn't have lived through that, right?"

By this *he*, I took him to mean Brantley and Jesus both. One in the form of the other. Earlier, Quinn would have snatched at such a string to draw it out, but he'd gone gentle, penitent, his head in my lap. "Bourbon set you down, brother." His voice was all molasses, the humor in it wondering and grateful. "You got caught by alcohol. If you'd been sober you'd have fallen like a china doll and smashed into little bits. Instead you went all loosey-goosey, and here you are."

"So we should all drink more," I quipped. "For safety." The booze in our cups, buzzing in our heads, nipping bacteria from Will's torn skin, was the same Brantley had used to replace something near two-tenths of a percent of his blood volume, and it most certainly had not caught him in its tender hand. It was, in fact, the only known perpetrator.

Will, reading my mind, said, "Depends how high your rock is."

Sometime after we noticed his broken fingers, after I splinted them, Will—in pain, intensely drunk—began to talk to Brantley through tears, saying, *I'm sorry, come back*. Quinn and I, almost too drunk to remember this, shushed and tended him and scooped him into bed, then passed out there catawampus beside him, three in a row. In some daylight hour of Easter morning we rose in righter minds and drove him to the hospital.

16

OVER THE TUMBLED GRAVES, ABOUT THE CHAPEL

After Will's fall, we were all sickened in some lingering way. In the hospital waiting room we hardly looked at each other or spoke. Torpid on painkillers for the ride home, Will declined our offer to help him into Stirling. "I'm so tired," Quinn said, and when he dropped me off we didn't exchange a glance. I was ready to be alone. Later, once I'd slept and showered and eaten, I felt content to be back in my own room, embarking on the *Henriad* with only the voices in my head to serve.

Young Prince Hal hanging with his frat bros in the pub—one more pitcher, one more game of quarters. Why not? He's young. But comes a day when destiny requires one to break with the companions of youth, even the sweet, the valiant, the true. Even Falstaff, though to banish such is a friend is to banish the world. "I do," says the prince, still in his cups, with a king's succinct resolve. For now, a play between friends, but a cold stiletto of promise. Doubt me? "I will."

Monday afternoon, Anna Vaughn knocked at my door, wanting my account of the accident. I was on my bed, book open in my lap. She shut the door at her back, her first time in my room. I told her I knew only what Will had told me, same as he'd told her: that he'd gotten up early to run trails and tripped. She seemed willing to believe this story, which matched Will's habits and befitted his injuries better than the truth. Like any of us, he preferred not to have his name chiseled in Rockhaven's eternal tablet of cautionary tales for overimbibers on rocks.

"Do you believe him?" she asked. "That it was an accident?"

"Anyone can trip," I said. "You ever tried running these trails? I'm surprised it's the first time—"

She went on as if her question hadn't finished. "*Having* been with him the night before, as I was not, and witnessing his state of mind. You can believe in accidents?"

Her worry was intense, and though I wanted to reassure her, I could feel a thickening of the atmosphere, an anger that dimmed and clouded my vision. I almost choked on words I meant to make comforting. "I think if he wanted to hurt himself he could have tried harder."

She gasped. "You don't get it. It won't be like that. It will be like... this. An impulse, a moment..."

"What happened to Brantley?"

The question came out with the same half-strangled force, fully intentional though the intention did not seem all mine. She looked at me with fear. "You know," I said. "An impulse, a moment. Was *that* an accident? Was it because of you?" The grip at my throat loosened; oxygen seeped back into my head. God, he hated her. He wanted me to seize hold and break her, while I remained fidgety with the wish to soothe. "You know what happened to him," I went on, as if certain. "Maybe you're the one who has to say it, if Will can't."

"I don't know what you're talking about." Her face began to crumple. "I don't know what he told you, but this has nothing to do with...him."

"With Brantley. And nothing to do with you, either."

"Will is sick," she said, near inaudible. "That's all. I'm just trying to help him. I love him."

I searched her anguished face, her pale blue eyes gone lilac, dewy. Ophelia. However vividly Will played the part of Hamlet, I'd always believed him the other prince, Hal, with his secret time capsule of resolve. When the moment arrived, he would turn on his temporary loyalties and set the kingdom to rights without a flinch. But I had begun to doubt it.

"It was an accident," she insisted. "If he thinks otherwise, he's just wrong."

And should Brantley, that moody essence come to room with me, be more trustworthy? She was alive, still clinging by her nails, and if Will dropped the battle she'd end up Anna Vaughn Oliver, still a double dactyl and more fancifully tripping than the original. It was plenty to hate her for.

"Shh," I told him, after she had gone. I fetched the gown out of the closet for a tête-à-tête, but it only hung on its hanger, an insentient piece of cloth.

As the week went on, I saw Will only in class, Quinn when he dropped by my emptied table in the dining hall, as if to prove nothing had changed. He hadn't seen Will for more than a passing minute—Will with the middle fingers of his writing hand braced together so that he struggled to take notes with the left. It all felt ended, not just our threesome but the intensity of what I'd shared with each, as if Will's fall had answered a question or at least knocked us loose of our obsession. Would it matter, if the truth never emerged like Christ from the tomb? If we all just shook ourselves free and went on with our human lives?

One night, because Quinn had told me to drop by the Gamma house, I found him on the dock with a girl. Or missed finding him. Emery intercepted me before I could head that way, told me her name, some Pi Alpha freshman whose face I couldn't picture. Doing what? A shrug was honest, I supposed, for what anyone in the house knew of specific actions on the dock. But no chance it was innocent. If it might have been, Emery would have warned me and sent me down, or come along for support.

I left the house, telling myself fourteen things on rolling repeat as I walked home through the dark. That I knew nothing for certain. That I had witnessed no part of a transgression to charge him with. That we weren't a couple. That I had no claim on him, wanted none. That we could go back to being friends. That I would just ignore him forever. That he would be sorry. That I should set his car on fire. That I should pretend nothing had happened, ever, between us. That he had intended for me to catch him with some random girl because he didn't know how or didn't care to do the talking part of breaking up. That to break up was not possible because we were not a couple. That the frog should not be surprised when the scorpion acted on its nature. That we had been so happy, for minutes at a time, a fact that in no way justified ever having pictured a happy end. That it shouldn't hurt so much more intensely than what I'd been carefully prepared for.

I made it as far as the cemetery, where I collapsed on some moss and sobbed for long enough to feel ridiculous, my tears watering some Confederate soldier's grave. Or a bishop's, a former vice chancellor's. Scattered about in these grounds there must have been a few of us, too—boys at least, grown to wealthy men whose last wish had been to stay forever. The nearest stone was lichen-spotted in the dark, weathered to unreadable.

Brantley Simms, buried near Charleston, hadn't chosen his resting place. Wouldn't he have chosen our mountain? Wasn't his grave in the earth at the bottom of Polk Tower? We all knew the spot. A decade or two or twelve in the future, those who followed us might still know it.

As soon as I was able, I picked myself up and shuffled home, glad to escape discovery. It was a warm spring night, plenty of us out walking between dorms and frat houses, the library, the pub; and Rockhaven wasn't the kind of place where those who heard a girl crying just walked on past.

The next day a thick envelope arrived in my SPO box, with a return address in Washington, D.C., a radical adjustment to my summer plans, and more. My life was changing. The stipend Will had helped me find wouldn't quite match what I'd make in a summer of waiting tables, yet I felt overwhelmed with riches. A job that asked for an education and particular skills, that might provide a measure of respect in return and even some adventure, if not a path to a post-grad life, was worth many times the stipend amount.

Will was with me when I opened it. We still walked to the SPO after Southern Lit, at the somewhat hobbling pace his injuries required, still talked as if we'd study together though our schedules weren't lining up well. I'd seen him once at some distance kiss Anna Vaughn on the cheek. "Well, of course," he said, about my internship, and hugged me gingerly, the tendrils of his legacy falling all around me.

He seemed to know about Quinn, having read it in my face, in the tea leaves—unlikely he could have heard the rumor so quickly. Had we been a real couple, half the campus would have heard by breakfast. Maybe if we'd been a couple, he wouldn't have done it: cheating on your actual girlfriend in front of your mutual friends wasn't something you got away with at Rockhaven, though he might have liked to be the first to try. For the ten-to-twenty percent of campus privy to that romp on the dock, I pretended, as the week went on, that our mad flirtation had burned out some time back, had been half a joke in the first place. Us, a couple? Never.

It was Spring Party Weekend, and the campus turned its attention to the work of maintaining a three-day buzz, rumpled and red-eyed yet dazzling enough to secure a date or two to the spring formals. I made myself go to a few parties. I even scored a pity date to the Gamma formal, with Emery.

I expected Quinn to avoid me forever, if not crush me to dust under his heel. Instead, looking at least a little authentically miserable, he came at me with excuses: that if I wanted exclusive rights I should say so, etcetera. I told him to go to hell. In the midst of a soggy Omicron band bash, I shouted a mild and weary speech on how we were really only friends in the first place, that he should consider our friendship a milestone in his personal growth, and maybe we should just concentrate on that. Then we adjourned to our separate corners to concentrate on that.

Missing him, missing Will, feeling loveless in the hullabaloo, I communed more with Brantley. Whenever I had to hide away from light-hearted others, arms crossed over my wound and cheeks burning with hurt too tender to share with the living, I felt Brantley beside me in the same posture. We had devoted ourselves to these people who so easily forgot us. We no longer mattered. They threw us aside and went on.

So what happened next was, you could say, not entirely my decision. The gown had proven docile in my care, asking little, and Brantley's company gave me permission one evening to try it on. Scary as a dare at first. But considering myself in the mirror, I felt calm enough, then more substantial inside it. At a glance, I looked no different. It draped me in the same black as my own, though its cotton was denser, softer, more pleasing to the touch. Set aside its stitch-work and all it had seen, and it was just a gown. *Looks good on you*, Brantley decided. *Wouldn't it show them?*

I didn't intend to entertain that suggestion, but the next morning, dressing for class, I reached for it instead of my own. *Yes*, he said, and *yes* as I put it on, so that I didn't pause to consider the repercussions. Wearing it felt like a duty, one I'd not been brave or sure enough to take up before now. Or I had simply waited like Hal for the ordained time. *I do. I will.* Was there a question? One breath, and I slung on my backpack, marched out the door.

"What's up with your gown?" Dex said, still on the Maxon steps as we left breakfast for Dr. Mathers' class: Huck Finn, "The Open Boat," *The Awakening.* With the Civil War behind us, Romanticism had given way to Realism.

"That's not your gown," Jenny said. With Pem and Emery, they converged behind me to gawk at the initials, until I had to come clean with whom it belonged to.

Dex looked at me like I was a stranger. "That is not okay."

And he was right. The Brantley in my head was not the boy who had walked these grounds with us. I was standing in front of his brothers wearing the gown he'd died in as if it were nothing. I had to scramble for a lie.

Will, I told them, had asked me to wear it.

"He wants it to be worn," I added, on firmer ground when not specifying the *he*. "It's too hard for Will, so I said I would. Not forever. Maybe just for today."

This placated them enough that we could at least go on walking—class awaited—while they asked squeamish questions about the mending and laundering and Brantley's parents, the inclusion of his initials and a date no gown yet bore. None of them paid any mind to the initials lined up above his.

When I joined Will for the last class of the morning, Shakespeare, I found myself jumpy and shy, keeping my back to him. Though I needed his awareness, in no small part because I wore it in his name, I felt scorched with the new shame of overstepping where I had no business. It occurred to me that he might be really angry, not that I had taken a risk but that I'd presumed to don a sacred vestment I was not worthy of.

When class let out, as my crew headed toward the Commons, Will drew me off in a stealthy turn, so they didn't notice us cut away into the sunny quad. Twelve days since his fall, and he still couldn't walk with even steps or at a normal pace. His less injured arm draped my shoulders, his head down as if to dodge the eyes around us.

He ushered me through the nearest door, at the side of the chapel. Light spilled through stained glass into the aisle outside the pews, where the statues of saints and dignitaries looked on from their recessed vestibules. "What are you doing?"

"It wants to be worn." My own steadiness, the hot core of resolve, surprised me.

He held out a hand. "Give it to me."

I took a step back. "Why? You can't wear it, and Quinn"—his name made me swallow a wince—"can't wear it, but I'm no one, I'm just a girl—"

"You don't understand. You think you do, but you don't."

"So explain it to me." The gown gained more weight, closed itself in a hug around me.

Arms wrapping himself, Will turned his eyes to the rib-vaulted ceiling. "You don't have to give it to me. Just take it off."

After some hesitation I did, folded it over my locked arms. I found myself assessing his posture, his injuries, thinking I could fight him off if he made a grab for it, though he still gazed up into the arches. If the ceiling could slide open like the observatory dome, would it show him the face of God, or only the bell tower?

He said, "Meet me here, tonight. Midnight."

"I won't bring it."

I wanted to tell him why, but he was already stepping away. "We don't need it. Just put it away. Bury it."

Bury it where? I thought, watching him go. But Brantley, at my side, seemed pleased.

That afternoon, as I dozed off over my cell bio text, the ringing phone startled me into semi-alertness. "Don't hang up," was Quinn's greeting. He waited until I let go a breath. "Did you mean what you said?"

My head was still with the gown, though I didn't think he could know I'd worn it. What had I last spoken to him? He must have meant my oddly sincere-sounding promise of our present and future friendship.

I said, "That depends."

He wanted to talk, in person. "Come to my room."

I told him I was quite able to imagine all the girls lined up on his bed without walking in on the act, thanks. If he wanted to see me, he could do it in a well-lit public place, and buy me dinner while he was at it.

"Am I the kind of friend who buys you dinner?"

Though his flirty purr made me want to smack the phone, I had to recognize that for him to even feign interest in a girl he'd just screwed over was unprecedented. "For now, plan on being that kind of friend."

Driving down the backside of the mountain in the sunset-at-seven light of spring, warm enough that we inched down the windows, I tried to relax, to feel normal beside this friend. He took care to make himself tolerable: grinning and talkative, aviators flashing as he rounded tight curves at speeds just crazy enough to make me shriek. He left no room for anger, almost none for hurt. Though his physical presence rendered my armor near weightless, uncertain, I found I could exist in two bodies: the one that leaned toward him like a reflex, the other that sat back in the cool enjoyment of knowing him too well to budge. I tried out an image for myself: the one girl he'd keep, ever, who would be able to call him on his bullshit while safe in her own perfect immunity. The prospect made sex seem a trifle I wouldn't mind watching him toss to others.

As we tapped the Porsche's roof through the back gates, "Green Grow the Rushes" was playing, and next it would be "Stay Up Late"—still Brantley's tape. If every good mixtape told a story, Quinn had this one more than memorized. He meant to free the songs of bondage, but surely he only drove that story deeper into his own head—the story, at least, that he was able to hear, told in the voice of his own Brantley. In snatches of every song, I still heard half a conversation with Will, no matter that Will himself may never have heard this tape. Ten bucks' worth of "Stay Up Late" on the pub jukebox couldn't torture him the way Quinn was torturing himself.

In the valley, our fanciest eatery was the Pizza Hut, where I craved a particular double-crusted deep-dish spinach pie that Quinn objected to on concept alone but agreed to share with me. My love for this unlikely concoction—a freak of the '80s—was based entirely on one charity slice from a year before that I'd been dreaming of ever since. On his legit ID he ordered a pitcher. When we had the booth to ourselves, Hall and Oates playing on the jukebox, he began to deal out papers onto the red-and-white checked table mat.

Until that instant's rush of dread and elation, I had let myself believe he would drop it. But how could I have? He would never drop anything, ever, not until it was good and dead.

"I got their name." He pushed a flier into my hand, THE ORDER OF THE THISTLE printed across the top in 36-point drop-shadow type. "Don't ask. The less you know."

Below, a paragraph addressed to "Fellow Rockhavenites" began, "We've all heard rumors of a long-standing secret society on our campus…" Under the paragraph was the hand-drawn symbol, beside a column headed "Founders?" that listed the names he'd extracted from the code. In the voice of an unspecified "we," the flier accused the Order of murder. It threatened to name other members, including current students, unless a satisfactory account of "the incident in question" was printed in the campus newspaper within the two weeks that remained before summer. It was signed SPO 680.

The other papers were variations. The second, an identical-looking flier, was more specific about the incident, naming Brantley as victim. The third was composed as a letter to the Order. He wanted my help deciding: a flier on every bulletin board, or the letter sent privately? He liked the flier for its public aspect, the swelling of a campus collective in the know, but there was danger in being caught while posting it. The letter had the virtue of discreet delivery and the likelihood of swifter, cleaner results, being entrusted to a single target.

"I assume you don't mean Will."

He shook his head.

So, Dalton, a name I didn't care to speak even in a booth twelve miles down the mountain. "He'll know it's you. Or us."

"Won't matter." He gathered the papers to shake at me with a rageful pleasure. "There's a lot of *us*, you see, who hold the evidence now."

Our pitcher arrived, and he stuffed the sheets into his backpack before I could make a choice. "Listen," he said, and launched into an hour-long ramble that seemed at first unrelated: about me, about Will, about his own shitty behavior—for which he seemed to be apologizing, by an oblique route that threaded back over and over through Will and the regret he'd come too near. While we put away the pizza and the beer, he kept circling back, trying again to say what I already knew at least subliminally. "I had to put myself on restriction," he said—this still wasn't quite it, though close—"with him. Which meant getting rid of you." Yet no justice, no truth, and not even me to talk it through with had turned him restless. Hence, the flier, or the letter, or something else he'd not yet devised... It was hard not to think, as he tried to explain himself, that he'd gone digging again just for the excuse to talk to me.

"You want to make something explode," I said.

He opened his hand across the table. It was such a forthright, comradely gesture that I gave him mine. So often I had to take his better nature on faith, I the sole believer in my crackpot religion, mooning about for these stray glimpses of what he kept so well obscured: the struggling, ethical person.

He squeezed my hand. "Let's explode something."

The alignment in our impulses brought a flush of heat. The two of us teamed had actual power, and maybe we'd gotten into bed only by seeking that charge in the wrong place. Part of me felt ready to do anything he asked, even go on chasing the grand conspiracy in our midst, for nothing but the erotic high of unfolding secrets with him. Didn't I know it already, how little we'd find there? The answer was meeting me in the chapel at midnight.

I told him I'd think over his plans, the course of action. We could get together the next day and hash it out.

Outside, the spring peepers shrilled, pervasive, a tinkling multitude of tiny bells all around the parking lot. Windows cracked, we drove back up the mountain, the breeze of our speed set against the stillness of stars in the blue-black bowl above. We were quiet, listening to Echo and the Bunnymen, "The Killing Moon" as ever the follower to "Stay Up Late." I pointed at the crescent moon, bright enough in its slenderness that it seemed to light our mountain ahead of us. He looked, nodded.

Fate, up against your will. And that was the end. Silence.

Quinn looked at the tape deck, looked at me. He pulled over to the shoulder and popped the tape. It came trailing broken thread that he ripped loose of the gears, folded fast against his belly as if to stop its leaking. A semi lumbered past—less likely to kill us, I supposed, going up than down. He'd betrayed me, so I didn't touch him, though maybe I wouldn't have anyway. How many times had he admired me for being the coldest girl he knew, when I'd wanted only not to smother him into running?

He opened his door, walked around the car and a few paces off the road until the jagged wall of rock stopped him. Passing headlights lit the cassette in his hand, the unspooled ribbon that dragged over the grass. For half a minute, he stood facing the rock, then let the cassette drop. He didn't watch its fall, didn't note its landing.

And what are you going to do? a voice asked me. I'd promised him friendship, and it struck me as possible, however unlikely, that I'd become what Brantley had once been, his closest friend.

Until we pulled up at Benson, near ten o'clock, Quinn held silence—so strange to hear nothing in that car but the engine. "So, tomorrow. After dinner." His voice was quiet but normal enough. "Come to my room. I promise to behave."

I had expected he might break down, want to talk for another hour or two. "Quinn. Are you sure you want to do this? Aren't you tired of it all?" He seemed so now, if not before, or at least ready to listen to my suggestion. "Maybe the tape...it was a sign. Time to stop."

In a languid slump against the headrest, he rolled his head to face me. "Brantley didn't break my fucking tape. I broke my fucking tape. You English major dork."

His gaze was only sad and fond, so soft that I touched his face, then leaned in and kissed his cheek. Getting out, I paused before shutting the door. "I'm sorry you broke your tape."

Until the last minute, I'd thought I might tell him my plans, bring him with me to the chapel, for his company if not for something to give him. It was briefly disconcerting to end up alone. Two hours to go, I gathered books and hiked to the computer lab, figuring some work on a paper would keep me awake. At the screen, concentration eluded me. Brantley hung over my shoulder, dictating lyrics to a song that lay split in two on the roadside halfway down the mountain.

Under blue moon I saw you...

What was a "Killing Moon," anyway? Spinning the song up in the radio station, I'd pictured it full, the killing done by its light. The slaughtering of pigs, perhaps. Or maybe tonight's sickle was the more likely shape.

Five minutes to go, I stepped into the deserted campus. The moon hung over the tower, deepening the shadows of gothic buildings as I made my way toward it. The breeze smelled of honeysuckle. Childe Rowland was not a girl. Girls were not permitted these adventures, unless they stole them. In a Shakespeare play, I'd have gone disguised as a boy. On stage I'd have been a boy, disguised as a girl, disguised again as a boy. But Childe Rowland was not a character in a Shakespeare play. The one who came to the dark tower, summoned, was one of us.

Midnight. Not two a.m., as it should have been. But he didn't object. *Midnight, of course. Go on, go.*

Picturing that night, I had not imagined Brantley entering the sanctuary, passing over marble tiles before crucified Christ into the south transept. But that was where the door was. That was where I waited, though Will had not mentioned the tower, and I did not think of its door as being on the inside. I didn't know the door before me was the door. *It's open*, Brantley said. But it wasn't. We had to wait for Will, who had the key.

When Will arrived, he seemed unsurprised to find me in that spot. "You want to see it, I guess."

"I've never seen it before."

And so he opened the door, and we went up.

17

CHILDE ROWLAND TO THE DARK TOWER CAME

October 19, 1986: The day of his death—though technically it is the day before, not yet midnight, when he ascends the many turning flights to the slender balcony. Half drunk from an emergency frat meeting—concerning, in large measure, himself—he carries a third of a bottle of Maker's Mark pilfered from the house, tucked into his backpack between Eliade's *The Sacred and the Profane* and the fat padding of his gown. Before climbing the last flight, clammy with anticipation, he removes the gown and slips it on over his coat.

The air feels cooler this high, the wind nipping with small teeth. It pushes the hair from his forehead and sings along his temples, ripples the gown behind him. The moon is close, just past full, and scraps of cloud scud over it. Below the ledge, treetops rustle. Moonshadow slips over campus parapets and terraces like some eely creature. If one had to choose a final night of one's life, a place from which to take in its tableau, the tower's midnight edge would not be the worst.

To the great heavy door below, he does not have a key. But since he has passed through, he is either a ghost, or someone has arrived ahead of him. Will, he assumes, but he might be wrong. All he knows is that he has been summoned here for a reckoning, and it wouldn't cross his mind to refuse.

"It was just a place to meet," Will said. "For a while, after he moved out. It could have been almost anywhere, any number of spots. But he liked this one."

We climbed slowly, Will ahead on the narrow stairs, gripping the rail in his good hand. In the dim cavern, the bells hung in iron solemnity, smaller and smaller as we climbed, unmoved by the breeze that gusted around us. His bruises or his dread stopped him often. When we passed through the final door onto the balcony, his breathing came heavier than mine. "I haven't been up here since then," he said. "Watch where you step. The pigeons nest right on the ground."

I had so vividly pictured the balcony wall—a low, flat ledge on which a daring person might sit, or stand—that I was shocked to find it crowned in close concrete spires, bulbous along their edges like cartoon Christmas trees. Or maybe angels. I might have squeezed myself a seat between two, but not with ease or comfort.

"This shit is awful." Will laid his good hand flat to a spire. "These weren't here before. Added last summer, I heard. A safety measure for drunks. But they won't stop anyone who means it." He seemed to consider how he might hoist himself, maneuver between them if need arose. "Here." His hand brushed along a spot where the spires attached. "We used to sit here. On the ledge, I mean, and just look out at the campus. Always after midnight, so no one would catch us. It was crazy. But we thought we were immortal."

He led me around a corner past dozing pigeons to where the roof of Maxon became visible between spires. "This." He pointed to a spot in the former ledge. "He was standing here when he fell. I can't even touch the place now."

"You were here," I said. "Only you and him."

He nodded, leaned against a spire with his face and body as if it could embrace him. "We were kind of having a fight, I guess. That night. About the gown. About…I don't even know."

"Maybe you should start from the beginning," I said.

He pulled a flask from his hip and offered it. As he spoke, I understood this was a story I already knew. He merely smoothed out what he'd told me already or revealed in flashes, what I'd gleaned in other ways. He filled a few gaps and narrowed my options, but was anything he said a surprise? Very little.

The mistake had not been Will's alone. But he should have known better than to tell his roommate, of all people, a secret of that magnitude. Brantley, along with his utter lack of discretion, was ruled by a brainy arrogance that made him unyielding in his naiveté about the social strata. Well past their fraternity initiations, he still smarted over being denied a Phi O bid.

"Get me in," he prodded, when Will let slip that he was being considered for membership in a club so elite no one knew it existed.

The Order: even that false, generic name should never have been in Brantley's possession.

It should not yet have been in Will's. But Will had his own spiller of secrets, Anna Vaughn.

Between their beds in the first week of school, he and Brantley had gone deep into the topic of girls, starting with what perfection might consist of and where it divided between the ones you wanted to sleep with and The One you might marry. Brantley shared Will's notion that The One awaited, already chosen by destiny, and the trick would be in recognizing her, then winning her. They each had found possibles in the past, like Brantley's ballerina with whom he'd had two conversations before she went off to Julliard. Will had been imagining his own since he was ten, a girl who was sweetly composed and wise and certain of herself, certain of him. Beautiful, of course, but modestly so, and of no particular appearance, dark or fair, tall or short; he had to remind himself that she could materialize from any crowd in front of him. Every girl he came across, he idly assessed—was it her? He didn't expect to meet her, though. He pictured these college years as free, his life unserious until a later time that would always lie a year or more ahead.

Anna Vaughn was one of a half dozen girls already tagged by his picky frat brothers as special, a glimmer at the edge of a room or in the seat near his in English for three whole months before she clicked into place: this was her, the very one he'd been describing for Brantley back in August. Something about the way her expression opened in his presence, her air of having known him from birth; they knew each other and he'd just forgotten. Had it been possible, he would have delayed her, caused her to appear in his senior year and ideally five minutes before graduation. But he couldn't risk it. Already in the Phi O house, where no one had yet managed to touch her, tipsy arguments were springing up between random pairs of brothers over which one would be marrying Anna Vaughn Whitacre.

"I'm scared to death," he confessed to Brantley, once he'd asked her to his winter formal. But the fear evaporated almost from the first minute; she made it all so easy. They were simply together, with the affirmation of everyone around them as if it had always been so. Before Christmas, he was in love.

She, of course, had been in love longer. If you are Anna Vaughn Whitacre, do you expect to simply choose the boy who will be yours? Probably. But she'd had to stalk him for a time, count his dirty blond curls from a distance, along with me, along with twenty others stationed around an auditorium or some reception lawn, his reticence fueling her certainty. I respected her for that. Will had good looks and money, but so did others—older money, a more sanctioned, less brazen style of beauty—and his personality, while undeniably magnetic, would have marked him as an oddball around the Phi O house. A girl like Anna Vaughn would need a keen discernment and a spirit of independence to settle on him so firmly. She'd need confidence, as well, in her own power to refine him.

When she took him to the Highlands over spring break to meet her family, Will had not guessed that he'd be auditioning for her father. He and Anna Vaughn were at a giddy stage, but so sure of each other that he forgot to bother with questions about marriage. He paid little attention to her list of mild complaints and corrections, feeling no need to impress her, and Anna Vaughn was too infatuated to push. This was the sort of nonsense that Ransom Whitacre had a nose for, and over several nights he took Will aside, out to the night porch overlooking the lake with glasses of bourbon.

"You strike me as a very fine young man," Ransom said—no surprise to Will, who had spent his nineteen years thus far striking everyone, parents in particular, as a very fine young man. "But that's not going to be enough. I know my daughter. She's all gaga right now but it won't last, not unless you find yourself some ambition."

Ransom was big on connections, on the power that accrues through knowing the right men, and few bonds, he contended, were stronger than the ones made in school. "Oh, *Daddy*," Anna Vaughn would chide him when he pushed some similar notion over the dinner table, in the living room. "Leave Will alone with that. We're freshmen!" But Will soon detected how father and daughter worked as a team. Their closeness made him uncomfortable at times, the way she massaged her father's shoulders and kissed his bald head. She was his youngest, his favorite, the only one who loved him enough to attend Rockhaven, and he had no sons. He had plans for her.

His closeness with his daughter was such that he slipped her information he should not have about the attention he was sending Will's way, in the form of the Order. And she, as incautious in her love as her father, told Will.

So were not Ransom Whitacre and his daughter as much to blame?

In any case, Will hadn't planned to tell Brantley. But he'd been unsettled by the news, and super-secret societies, their existence or not, was a hobby of Brantley's, as was smoking pot, an indulgence the two of them shared at a level of privacy that bordered on the erotic. *Only with you*, Brantley said, in keeping with the campus culture of puritanism about nonalcoholic drugs; and Will, who accepted the rare joint a frat brother might produce, didn't smoke in a regular way with anyone else or in any other place than on the floor between their beds, Will's between their backs and the door in case anyone should burst in past the button lock. In that position and state they fell into long, late conversations, candle-lit so no one would see their lights on, voices low and clapped into silence if a knock came at the door—even Anna Vaughn, calling, "Will!" He heeded Brantley's headshake, held silence until she was gone.

After he activated with Phi O, one of the senior brothers began to take him aside and give him inscrutable pledge-like assignments. This, he was told, was not fraternity business and was not to be mentioned to anyone—not his brothers, not Anna Vaughn.

"Like what?" Brantley was dying to know. Smoking, Will found it impossible to deny him a few details. He was to buy a copy of a certain book and deliver it to a certain place. He was to memorize a sentence and deliver it at a certain time to a certain person. His instructions: don't ask questions. Perform tasks in the open, but don't let anyone suspect you.

This went on for weeks, until school ended, and then he was given assignments over a summer spent in part with Anna Vaughn's family. He began to resent the apparent collusion between Ransom and his daughter, their murmuring together about the strings they pulled to make him twitch. A college buddy of Ransom's came to visit, and Will felt himself being displayed like merchandise. Membership would ease his path in life, bring him bounty and power, but who were all these puppeteers to assume he wanted these things? Maybe he wanted to read Donne under a tree, become a modest scholar of English literature.

"Let's mess with them," Brantley said. He was half stoned, joking, but the idea began to solidify into obsession. "I'll bet that's never been done in the history of Rockhaven. Let them know you don't need them. You rule the rulers."

"Maybe later I can get you in," Will had offered once. But Brantley had come to doubt that, and now Will did too. Recently he'd been taken aback by the loud and general dismay within his own circle at the news that he meant to keep his freshman roommate another year. What was he after, some kind of good citizen award, charity credit?

"Be nice," Will would mutter to Brantley at Anna Vaughn's knock. But Brantley's version of *nice* tended toward an assault of genuine-seeming friendliness that pried into private matters, hinted at secrets he knew (about her, about the Order), or disguised kernels of possible insult. Anna Vaughn would attempt all manner of polite response in a matching tone of sincerity as she attempted to parry thrusts she couldn't fully see.

As sophomore Advent semester began, Will and Anna Vaughn were chafing over two issues, The Order and Brantley. Anna Vaughn had lost her sense of humor—or had Will failed to notice that she never really had one?—and picked at him constantly over his lack of seriousness about his impending induction. Did he not grasp how rare it was for the Order to pursue someone so young? Did he think they wouldn't drop him in a second if Will hinted the kind of disdain he'd once or twice shown her? When he complained of being watched, she said, "Well, of course. Everything you do from here on comes under suspicion. And right now, I'd say the most damning element is your roommate. I assume you know what people say about him."

"No, I don't. What do they say?"

Anna Vaughn preferred not to speak the answer aloud: that Brantley was considered by some to be gay, and in love with Will, and that Will was even suspected of possible reciprocal involvement, if only by Anna Vaughn herself. Too many times he'd ignored her knock without a satisfactory account of his whereabouts. She responded by knocking less, asking less. If he was doing something, she wanted him to get it out of his system before she had to know.

And nothing was really happening, nothing, at least, that they had to call by a name or refer to with words or think about much regardless of how it escalated, until the day, long after they'd stopped using much free time to smoke, when Anna Vaughn walked in on them. They'd become careless with the lock, careless even with the latch—she claimed the door had been open, leaning shut against the frame. Will could have explained away what she'd seen—just showered in a small room—but the crossing of his two worlds shocked him awake, left him unable to form a real denial. When she insisted he petition for a room change, he agreed.

Brantley sulked and blamed Anna Vaughn, her snooping and controlling nature. If Will wanted to nix certain activities, fine, but did he have to move out altogether, because the Queen of Sheba snapped her tiny fingers? As much as Will regretted what he'd put Anna Vaughn through, he began to feel worse over the loss of the room, the damage to the friendship. For this reason he made his second big mistake. Eager for forgiveness or at least the crafty spark that had gone missing in Brantley, he offered up the second best enticement he had.

One day he showed Brantley a note. Communiques from the Order came through the SPO, folded in a complicated series of envelopes. He was not to open them in the presence of others, was to memorize them and incinerate them behind the dining hall.

Brantley snatched it up, awestruck and alert. "Code. Lord, they've taught you the secret code already."

"You won't crack it. It's uncrackable."

In under a minute, Brantley had the gist of the message's intent—a location and time for a meeting. It was a pleasure to watch him work, to answer his yes/no questions in the sudden ease that opened between them. A ratified genius, Brantley had been calling himself since receiving his notice that he'd be gowned in a few weeks, and they were joking over it, Will reaching for the note, when Brantley took another look. "Oh, wait. MH, as in MPH, from the list of founders and dignitaries. That's your key?" And he rattled them off, every number and letter in order.

Once, weeks before, Will had recited it just to impress him, the string so void of meaning that a single recitation seemed safe. One look at Will's face sent Brantley into ecstasy. "God, did I get it right?"

This was when Will's dread was born, though its source remained unclear. So-called secrets, empty enough to be entrusted to a new recruit, were a step toward any initiation, a test of commitment and loyalty. Fraternities threatened their pledges with similar injunctions against leaking pledge-book contents, which hadn't stopped Will or Brantley, a year before, from messing around with it in the privacy of their room, slipping random pieces of their frats to each other in a contest of who had the stupider shit to memorize. The illicit thrill of it. And then Brantley, over the bathroom sink months afterward, would out of nowhere recite a random piece of Phi O nonsense he'd preserved all that time, just to freak Will out. Beneath the sink that Brantley spit toothpaste into, nearly choking on his grin, the earth didn't rumble. The ax of fraternity hadn't yet fallen onto Will's head.

So he could hardly have been surprised at Brantley's skill, nor could he justify any great fear of the repercussions. He'd broken the sacred law of a club he didn't want to be in. Perhaps it was the shadow of Ransom Whitacre, his future father-in-law, that made the Order seem serious, real. All Will's life until now had been play, his mistakes correctable—even, especially, the ones he'd made repeatedly with Brantley. But he'd been feeling more and more that the Order was rushing him toward a swift end of that free time. He had to be one of them or not, to make a choice.

Brantley was watching him, going quiet. "Will. Seriously. Do you want to go through with this?"

"Of course. Why wouldn't I?"

Brantley shook his head, seeing it now. "All that elitist bullshit. It's not who you are. They can't *make* you be that."

"Maybe it won't be so bad," Will tried. "Like the rotary club. We'll be helping the less fortunate."

"Right. Or you'll be sacrificing babies. Man, I think you're missing an opportunity. You could *investigate*. Do an article for the paper. Before you're in, before you're implicated. Or, let's be honest, brainwashed. Next you'll wake up naked and covered in goat jizz and there's a baby on the end of your spear."

Will laughed, unsure if it was funny. He'd seen enough of the Order not to expect anything crazy, though what it *was* he couldn't yet see.

Without telling Anna Vaughn, he withdrew his room change request. A week later, they received notice that it was happening anyway, Brantley being shifted to a larger room with a junior. Had the Order made that happen, or only happenstance? And what would Brantley's removal mean for the two of them? However it might help with the problem of temptation, now a mere hour in the same room would be picked up on Anna Vaughn's radar as suspicious. With their separate fraternities, they hardly crossed paths otherwise, never shared a table in the dining hall. And though they might choose to disrupt the seating establishment— itself a suspect act—no talk compared to the talk in a shared room.

Unless a room might be rivaled by the bell tower. Will's key was not to be used except on Order-related business, but he felt fairly certain the members would not make use of the tower at times he was not aware of—they met in more clandestine places. Brantley, like most of the student body, had never been up. After he moved out, they arranged meetings there, alone in the night sky. They brought bourbon and drank it on the balcony ledge, their feet dangling over the campus far below, feeling like princes of the realm.

"We shouldn't be doing this," Will said, the week they were both playing hooky from rush. They would too easily be caught, he meant. But if no one caught them, then what? An end had to come somehow.

Brantley gazed off over the wall, peaceful and inattentive. "It's this school, the whole fucking south. It's people like the Order, you know. The old guard. The best they can do is hold us back ten years. Change comes. Look at the women we now find ourselves subjected to."

At the time Will didn't know that over the past weeks, all Brantley tamped down in his presence, trying not to express, had been finding its verbal outlet at the Gamma Chi house. Yet he perceived the traces: that *us*—that was new—and Brantley's voice growing louder on it, testing the limits of what might carry to passers below.

Then Founders' Day arrived and Brantley was gowned with dozens of others. His Gamma Chi big brother performed the honors, up at the front of the chapel, Will too far back for more than a glimpse. Brantley's parents came up for the day, and Will found them on the quad afterward to say hello. He gave Brantley a congratulatory hug and made a point to stand for a time, doing the parent-chat with a friendly arm around Brantley or a grip on his shoulder, despite Anna Vaughn shooting him looks from the other side of the quad. Brantley seemed uncomfortable, and Will assumed he knew the reason, while the very thread of the code went undetected on the gown under his hand.

Five days later, the Order called Will to account. It took them that long to spot and verify what Brantley had been wearing all over campus. Surprisingly quick, Will thought, considering the time he himself had spent looking at Brantley, if from a distance, without ever noticing.

Dispatched to deal with the problem he'd created, Will sent Brantley a note, decreed the meeting. He arrived early as usual and left the door unlocked behind him. Brantley showed up soon after, half trashed, still in the blazer and bow tie. And the gown. He was actually wearing it. "Are they here?" he whispered, his face a mask of stagey dread. "Around back? I assume there's punishment."

"What the fuck are you thinking, pulling something like that?"

"It's a *joke*, Baldrick," Brantley said in a slithery whisper, close to slurring. "And they fucking deserve it. I did it for you, you know."

"How do you figure?"

"Leverage. They can't hold shit over your head when I've got shit over theirs. I have more evidence in other places too. You want out, it can happen."

"And if I don't?" Will's first inkling of attachment to the Order came as Brantley offered to relieve him of it. And what wasteland would that make of his future? What could Brantley offer in its place?

"I'm sure you can fix it," Brantley said. "Just work the Will Oliver magic. If you put it to them the right way—"

Will scowled. "You have an inflated idea of my influence, when I'm not even *in*. *Now* I'm out. At best. And you're on the tracks in front of a train."

"Like me," I said, before he had to. "The Leah situation."

Was I still so very sure he wouldn't throw me off the tower? We sat with our backs to the inner wall, passing his flask, and he'd have a hard time hurling me past those spires, if he took a mind to become other than my Will.

His mission on that night of October 19, besides securing the gown and arranging certain follow-up conditions, had been to impress upon Brantley something near what he meant to impress upon me. He knew the Order better now, if still little about those men who made up its ranks outside the gates. Their power on campus was as vast and unseeable as God's, if they felt a whim to use it. Their hands worked the machinery that could withdraw a scholarship, arrange for honor code charges, dismiss a student from school. They could hire and fire professors or administrators at will. But their alma mater rarely called for action of that sort. It could run itself. They had bigger things to run out in the world. In business, in politics, in finance, even in marriage and family, the Order arranged success where it chose. It arranged failure when necessary, as it always was, for someone. If the Order wanted to punish you, reward you, set you up or knock you down, that would happen.

But within the student body, the Order was not the Order. Until graduation they were only, in equivalence, the pledges, tasked with proving themselves worthy of active status. If secrets got loose, they would be held responsible. Keeping shit in order was their job. The real danger was not the men outside but these boys, gazing on the prospect of their own future power, who couldn't be sure which infraction might lead to exile.

"I'm less worried about you," Will admitted.

"Because I'm a girl?" We were talking about young gentlemen, after all. I didn't have to meet any of those grown-up members of the Order to know that, whatever casual carnage they might perpetrate in the name of business, they were gentlemen to the bone. They would not pass a week without using the word in conversation. They would speak it on their death beds if fate permitted.

At my back, the tower stones were maybe the same that had touched the white thread on the gown's scapular the night Brantley had worn it. What did we love if not tradition?

Will said, "I'd like to promise you that's true. But these days. I don't know anymore."

In Brantley's case, before they met on the tower, Will had, in fact, worked the magic. He had negotiated a solution, simple and humane, that would guarantee Brantley's safety and possibly even correct his own misstep. Brantley was to hand over the gown, then confess to everyone who would listen that it had been a fake, that moreover he'd been called before the vice chancellor and threatened with expulsion if he didn't retract his joke. His story would be that he was a liar, a show-off who spit upon a beloved tradition for his own aggrandizement, and that he was sick with remorse. If he did this, if he remained forever after meek about his crime and clear of the Order, he might escape reprisal.

"Because they say." Brantley shook his head, handing Will the bottle. They had been passing it for an hour or more, and it felt noticeably lighter. "Already it's true, then. What they want is theirs, and we fall in line. Maybe this should be when somebody stands up to them and says no."

Brantley climbed onto the broad ledge, the footing steady enough though wind buffeted the gown, jerked it wildly sidelong to twist about one leg. "Come up. It feels great. Really, this is something you should experience."

"Brantley. Come down, please."

"If they want me to stop, I want to see them." His voice lifted over the wind, loud enough to be heard below. "Tell them that. I want to talk to them. They can give me a bid or I'm making some damn noise. How about that?"

Will made the grab for him, his first emotion rage. That Brantley wouldn't listen, that he was up there dangling Will's future over the edge besides his own safety. Will wanted to drag him down so he could hit him.

"I wasn't thinking clearly," Will told me. "I didn't mean to push him. But I was so mad at him right then. I think I just wanted it over, or something."

We sat on the cold stone floor, his flask empty, the moon between two spires. It must have been nearing two a.m. "But you didn't push him."

He grunted, almost amused. "So you get to decide?"

"You made a grab for him." I held out my flat palm between us. "The gown, it was right there. You didn't miss. You grabbed it, didn't you?" With my other hand drawn back inside my sleeve, I set the empty cuff across my open hand as he watched. "You remember that, feeling the gown in your hand? So you could pull him down?"

As with their bedroom, they had become entirely too comfortable with what they shouldn't be doing on the bell tower at night. They forgot it wasn't their private princedom, that they needed to be careful. This much of the error Will felt as it was happening. The rest, those seconds, he had replayed through so many variants that they were covered over, gone forever.

A fistful of gown in his grip—was it the back, or a sleeve? He meant to drag Brantley down from the wall. That piece of black cloth had blown into his hand, the only real handle, but also what he had come for. Surely Brantley felt it too, if only for an instant: that what they were struggling over was as simple as the possession of this object. Pulling—aware of the danger though not sober—Will felt it slip loose at Brantley's shoulder. An inch, maybe, but reflexively he let it go, the ledge too precarious for a tug-of-war, and then, so fast the thoughts overlapped, he knew he needed to do the opposite, grab two-handed and yank.

But before he could organize the movement, Brantley yanked back against nothing. And still he was standing there, at the edge of balance, the gown back in place and a grin shaping, gamely playful, about to chide, while somewhere in the dark, a foot met air. Will saw the awareness register on his friend's face. And then he was gone, Will stomach-down on the ledge where he'd been propelled by that last, too-late impulse to grab him back.

He recalled, later, pieces of the aftermath. He knelt in gravel, inches from the heap, afraid to touch it and calling Brantley's name in a voice that found no volume, calling still when he knew. Through darkly spangled vision, he could see Brantley's open eye above a brokenness of his face. The pale initials at his shoulder. He remembered locking the tower door. He remembered unlocking it again, wiping prints from the handle with his shirt. He carried away Brantley's backpack and the bourbon bottle, burned them together days later in the woods. He didn't remember deciding to leave Brantley there and go back to his single room. He sobbed and woke the next morning from no real sleep, remembering more of it than he wished he did.

For a time after, in his own mind, he succeeded in erasing himself from Brantley's fate. Brantley climbed the wall, carelessness an inborn trait; ergo, Brantley could have done it without him. At the funeral in Charleston, packed with Gamma Chis and the Gamma girls, he could not escape the conversation these weepy and shell-shocked mourners would not stop having, in which they speculated over how it had happened. Dissecting the fall became a way to undo it, to alter the steps that had led Brantley to that place.

He'd driven to Charleston alone, though Anna Vaughn had offered to come. She'd arrived at his room crying from the news and made herself available as his twenty-four-hour nurse, urging him to talk about it. She was good that way, a natural counselor. He knew her well enough to spot her little deceptions—she didn't have many—and it was clear she remained unaware of the gown, unsuspicious of his own involvement or the Order's. For that reason, as she tended him through weeks of sometimes prostrating grief—numbness and silence—he all but forgot about the Order. What had happened, after all, had so little to do with them. He went to class, tried to keep up, and found slim space in his head for anything else. His body showed up for lacrosse practice, but day after day the coach sent him out, until he was placed on a strongly advised leave of absence. He'd be standing in the second-floor library shelves, on the vice chancellor's lawn, with no idea how he'd come there or where he'd been going.

A few weeks after Brantley's death, Will was inducted into the Order. They rallied around him with condolences, grieving with him, disturbed that his task had come to violence but taking its necessity as a given. "A terrible accident," they called it, with rigid insistence, though no one asked him what had happened. No one questioned the tower, as if its purpose were assumed. No one told him, in so many words, that he had more than proven his loyalty, nor that he would be rewarded with what he very much needed even if he didn't know it yet: their protection.

It was December before he confessed to Anna Vaughn, around the time his mourning—in the form of insomnia, spaciness, general lack of affect, and specific lack of interest in her—had passed what she considered a reasonable expiration date. Her surprise lasted less than a minute. He sensed, in fact, her relief at the news, its offer of a better cause for his mental state than the one she feared. This foe she could fight. She became very calm, told him he had not been on the tower that night and must never say otherwise—not to her, not to anyone. Out of love, out of some unrelinquishable vision for her life, she colluded with the Order to cover his crime and form about Will a cushioning ring of watchfulness. With their assistance, she arranged for his Atlanta psychiatrist. For a time, he tried to believe they were right, that there were steps by which he could recover and become normal, but belief ebbed, until his only focused desire was for them all to go away and leave him with Brantley in their room.

"It was the only way," Dalton said to him once, trying for comfort through a measure of candor. "Not that anyone would have suggested it, or wanted it. But it's fixed, and I doubt it would be otherwise."

Statements like this worked on him in strange ways. A push, a wish for a slip—so extreme a solution could not have occurred to him. Yet when it was done, he had thought more than once, *it's over.*

It's over, the Order all but said, patting his back. Now, for the well-being of all concerned, let us not speak of it or think of it ever again.

18

DOWNWARD TO DARKNESS, ON EXTENDED WINGS

As much as to hear Will's story, I had climbed the tower to see the place where Brantley had last stood. And that launch pad, the ledge, was gone. He didn't like it. He didn't like change, of course—none of us did. Worse, the spires thwarted his deepest impulses. Even now, he wanted to climb up. The happiest moment of his life: Will seated beside him on the balcony wall, their feet dangling over campus, invincible together and half over the edge.

So many songs to encourage a fall, any end with you.

Come up, he said. You should experience this. He'd meant to show Will they could survive it.

We peered down through separate gaps between the spires, joined at the hands. Will's calm reminded me of the one I'd felt in him on Roark's Steep, as if high places made him less likely to end himself than when he stood on solid earth.

"I thought you'd hate me." His cheek, like mine, rested against the grit of concrete as he considered our interlocked fingers. "Take his side."

"This is his side. I'm on it." That Brantley would give anything to be standing where I was, holding Will's hand, was not quite speakable even now. I added, "He doesn't blame you, you know." I was still ready to blame Anna Vaughn, if in a different way than expected. A girl less accustomed to getting what she wanted would have seen Will for lost, given him up. Instead, she made him change rooms. She had called us all to the tower.

But to blame her was to blame Will. Instead I said, "He took a risk. And it was stupid. If he could be here, he'd tell that."

"Now we'll argue about what a dead person wants." Will sighed, near seeing the humor. "Please. Tell Quinn. I can't. Let him decide, okay? You're not to be trusted with this sort of judgment." He squeezed my hand—meaning that, I supposed—and dropped it. If I loved him blindly, could I be blamed? It wasn't all my love. "Promise me. He needs to understand, or he'll get himself hurt, in more than one way. You know he thinks it was his fault. I keep trying to tell him. But I'm a coward, like Brantley says."

"When did he say that? About what?"

Will's brow folded in searching thought. "It's what he meant. A hundred times."

"You think he still means it." He wouldn't meet my eyes, wouldn't say the same voice told him, *Choose me.* But for Will left alone in the world, did that mean *jump*, or *confess*, or *trash them all, free yourself?* "So come with me. To tell Quinn. We'll do it together."

"You'll do better without me. Just make sure he understands it wasn't him, and it wasn't the Order. He can take it out on me however he needs to. I'm ready."

He rolled his back to the wall, arms stretched languidly over his head. Saint Sebastian awaiting the arrows. Part of him craved martyr status, one of the few not in his reach. He was stacked to his neck in privilege he couldn't shed. Yet he was less of a coward than he let himself believe. His bravery lay dormant until these rare instances when it awoke in its peculiar form, and he cliff-jumped blind into the dark. He enacted the fall, while anticipating the hand that would catch him.

It was a lot to expect of Quinn. I suppose he knew that well enough to entrust Quinn's handling to me.

In the shower after my last trail ride of the spring, then dressing for dinner, my head was a jumble of what I would say to him. Mitzi and Carolyn's door hung open, and I let myself be drawn onto a sun-covered bed to chat about dorm assignments for the next year, and spring formals, so we were running late for dinner by the time we descended the Benson stairs. Below, in the commons room, our proctor stood hands on hips, talking to a middle-aged man—not maintenance staff, no one who belonged in a girls' dorm. The proctor lifted her face to mine, lifted her finger and pointed.

All I could think was that one of those men had come for me, and if I did not descend one more step, the dorm could keep me safe. But it was worse than the Order. It was my father.

I'd hardly listened when my aunt had mentioned he was driving this way, might stop in for a visit. My father didn't do visits. I'd seen him only once since my mother's death, when I'd been brought to spend that first Christmas with his family, almost certainly at the insistence of Gretchen, his wife. If not for the women involved—my mother, now Gretchen and my aunt—pressuring him with the fact of me, he would not have been in my life at all. He would not have been here in my dorm, hands out in the *hug your old man* gesture neither of us in our rare lifetime encounters had ever cared for.

He was heavier than the man in my head, jowlier, with less hair. Mitzi, Carolyn, and the proctor had vanished. I was strolling at his side, into the parking lot, because I didn't know what else to do. Run? I was one of those Rockhaven students whose father, so he said, had come to *take her to dinner*—the kind of scene I sometimes caught in a glance from a window that required me to suppress my envy. But my father didn't do dinners out, with anyone. My father considered fast food too steep and contact lenses a luxury item. Getting into his dirt-colored, fender-smashed hatchback, I felt only fear. He'd come to tell me there was no more money. I'd have to find it elsewhere or quit school.

We ended up at the Rockhaven Inn, our mountain's version of fine dining. Tales of the place, which I passed by regularly, were all I knew, from those anointed students who had crossed the threshold in the company of a parent. Even for those of us with money, it ceased to exist otherwise, as if its portal vanished without the key.

"You've never been here?" my father asked, holding the door for me.

"Only people with parents go." It pleased me a little to say it, to see the twitch in his eyebrows, looking away.

I didn't spot another student in the dining room, filled with well-dressed, middle-aged people—alums, I supposed. Out the window beside our table, golfers made their way in sunset light over the Rockhaven course. The menu was placed open in my hands, glued to hinged, narrow boards. "Nice place you got here," my father said.

"Yes," I admitted, feeling an unexpected flush of guilt. Really, who was I, to need such a celestial glow on my manicured golf course? Did the beauty of gothic buildings cause me to learn more? This man with his ancient wreck of a car, a spray of moth bites in the shoulder of his off-brand polo, had granted it sight unseen. He hardly knew me.

He ordered the cheapest entre, baked chicken, so I did too. We made halting small talk about my half-siblings. *His kids*, I thought of them, never able to feel much kinship.

"Big plans for the summer?" he asked. "Rosie told us you got some fancy job in D.C.. Environmental something agency?"

"It's just an internship."

"She made it sound like an honor."

"Kind of, I guess. It's competitive."

He raised his water glass. "Then, congratulations. It's good news, right? I wish you'd tell us these things. We want to know what's going on with you."

"It doesn't pay that well," I said, determined to get it over with. "I have a subsidy but it's not... It might be less than I can usually make."

"But something, right? You can feed yourself up there? How will you get there?"

I'd posted a sign seeking a ride on the message board, though DC would be trickier than Knoxville, which a good quarter of the school drove through.

"I'll chip in for gas," I added, though I hadn't thought of this expense. "Or I can take the bus."

He smiled and nodded. The father I knew should have pointed out the flaws in my plan, lectured on my lack of financial foresight.

"Okay, please, just tell me why you're here," I said, poking at the peanut butter pie he'd directed the server to set in front of me, after I'd said I didn't need any dessert. "Is Aunt Rosie sick? You need me to take care of her? It's okay, I can get out of the internship, if—" The words *family emergency* formed in my head, the key component of the regrets I would send to the conservation fund. I'd heard the phrase used to excuse classmates I'd envied even when it meant tragedy. To have a family emergency was to have a family.

"Rosie's fine," he said. "Everyone's fine. It's just... Let me have some of that." I slid the pie toward his poised fork. "I didn't think you'd last here. Chipping in like you do, making good grades, and I guess it's harder than other schools. Don't suppose you've found that rich husband yet?"

I frowned. He frowned too. "Sorry, not why you're here, right? You're doing something on your own. I'm proud of you. That's what I'm trying to say. And Gretchen, she's real proud. She feels like your mom, you know? We know it's not been easy on you to...to lose your mom like you did."

Only when we were walking out the door did he give up his true reason for coming: the dirt-colored hatchback in the parking lot. "It's old, but it's had a tune-up. New tires, new brake pads, battery, master cylinder. Should get you to DC and back. Maybe last you a few years past college, who knows. It's a stick, though—can you drive a stick?"

The little Chevy, as we stood beside it, blossomed into a beauty, with its artfully battered seats and bohemian paint color, the rakish head-lights set in an adorable snub nose. My whole life could fit inside it, go anywhere. I could hardly speak to thank him. He accepted a hug. "We just really thought you could use it."

Sweet, a quality I'd never thought of near my father, but his pleasure in his gesture and its subterfuge was undeniably so. They had driven two cars; Gretchen had taken the other to visit a friend in Chattanooga and would be back later, as they were staying at the Inn. She could see me for breakfast if I was free. While I dimly took this in, a person approached out of the darkening lot whom I expected to be Gretchen. But it was Quinn, materializing with arms open and an oozy "Heeey!" as if he and I had agreed to meet here. Before it occurred to me that he could not be here by coincidence, he'd caught me in a chummy chokehold, while greeting my father with the crisp *Hello* he might use on a stranger accosting me in a parking lot.

I spoke some jumble of words. "Dad, this is Quinn. Who is here, for some reason. My friend Quinn. Cooper, Quinn Cooper."

"Boyfriend," he said, two smooth syllables slowed to last almost through the handshake he extended.

I looked at him askance, but he wasn't talking to me. "We're friends," I told my father flatly. Quinn only shrugged and smiled down at me. I couldn't help laughing at the bizarreness. "What are you doing here?"

"Night golf." He tightened the arm across my collarbones. "You didn't tell me your"—he paused—"*father?* was coming to town. To see you? That's new." Friendly, he offered the joke to the man before us. "See, *we*, I mean me and Leah's other friends, we didn't even think she had a father! We know she doesn't have a mother. Anymore. But, well, you probably know all about that."

"I do," my father said. "Know that."

"And Leah's an adult, barely. Oh, right, she's not even twenty-one! But close enough." I went slack against him, still perplexed but helpless in gratitude for whichever of his demons had brought him here, even a couple years too late. If only to bash some rival male, it counted that he knew his evidence. "Old enough to get by without a parent, for sure. But nice of you to come by."

My father tried to smile, to match the small-talk mood Quinn was miming, but I could see he was wounded. I would have to apologize over breakfast. (When I did, the next morning, my father said, "No, I understand. Your friend had a point. He was being protective. I'm glad you have friends like that.") And best not to prolong an encounter involving one's unsocialized pit bull in hopes it might be persuaded to play nice with the other dog. "We have to go," I said, pushing a shoulder into Quinn's fight-rigid torso. "Sorry, Dad, I forgot, but we're super late for a thing." As we moved off, I called back that it was great seeing him, and thanks again, and I'd meet him and Gretchen for breakfast in the morning.

Not fully out of earshot, Quinn snarled, "I fucking hate that guy."

He didn't know that guy, I might have reminded him, even by my report. "Shush. He came to give me a *car*." Aloud, the words sounded nonsensical.

"A car. Why?"

"I guess he had a spare one? And I need one. I think he feels bad." My father lingered under the streetlight by the entrance, waved when I turned. I waved back. Getting into the Porsche, I felt oxygen-depleted, on the edge of hyperventilation. "I have a car." And there was no bad news with it: I was going to DC, I would return for senior year, in my car.

Quinn let this sit on his scales of judgment. "Where is it?"

"It's mine, so be nice to it." I pointed it out as we drove past. He swallowed his opinion but kicked some Porsche rubber at my father as we circled by.

With distance down the parkway, my shaken life eased back into place. "What the hell? How were you even there?" But I could have guessed: Mitzi for the news. He'd tried the pub first, then the Inn on his way to the Hardee's.

"To save me from what? Dinner and a car?"

He was still pissed. "Don't be a wuss, Leah. Don't let him off the hook. He hasn't earned it."

"Mm, good point." The purl of the engine, the tires against the road, strange sounds in his car with its speakers silent. Other cassettes were scattered on the floor at my feet, but I didn't pick one up. He pulled off the road and killed the engine. Outside was stillness, cobalt sky over the etched black of forest, and before us, lights strung along the ground like a fairy path. The tiny Rockhaven airport: like the seminary or the Inn's dining room, a place I'd known of only by report.

"It's nice here at night," he said. In his spare hours he hung about the airstrip the way I'd once haunted barns, hoping for someone's largesse. A few planes sat out from the hangars on the tarmac, and he named their breeds, owners, and salient features as I would with horses.

"You know I've never been in a plane," I told him.

"Christ, you are a bumpkin. Well, I'm going to fly you somewhere. How's that? I'm going to be your first."

He may not have meant to mess with me until he hit that last word, may not have conceived of kissing me until the word mixed with the limp ease that lingered in my mood and brought it into reach. Before he could move more than an inch toward me, I laughed and got out of the car.

He followed. In the farther of two hangars, a figure moved behind lighted glass. "Someone must be landing tonight," he said. "Or Frank is behind on paperwork."

I walked past the runway's edge, out between the rows of lights. At the end of that swath cut between trees hung the crescent moon. I felt him at my shoulder an inch back. "That photo on your wall," I said. "The one from Shake Day. Brantley being thrown into the lake."

The runway asphalt, as I sat on it, radiated a portion of the daytime heat. He sank down beside me and glanced back at the office. "We're not supposed to be out here."

"A plane will land on us?"

He tipped his face to the clear sky, grown dark enough for a few stars. "I guess we'll see it coming. What about the photo?"

Once, I had taken it down from his wall to examine under light, had said only, "He looks happy." None of the Gammas wanted to admit their sacred water was lousy with pathogens, that any break in the skin could land a swimmer in the hospital with meningitis or worse. No one swam by choice, nor could be called eager to enter that water except, on some level, a pledge being thrown. Quinn couldn't remember who had snapped that airborne shot. The hazy bodies of brothers, the arms that had tossed him, even a grinning set of teeth, could be seen behind him, but none clear enough to identify. Brantley himself was minimally blurred, eyes open, mouth open. Nothing touched him, though the lake soon would.

"He doesn't look like he's falling," I said. "He could be rising. Either way he's still in the air, in that photo, forever."

I wasn't sure I'd made sense, but Quinn nodded. "Is that beautiful, or just fucking creepy?"

Time for him to land, then. I sat back on my hands and watched the sky. "I talked to Will. It wasn't the Order who killed him. Nobody did. Will was there, but you know that already. We've known it, I think. He feels guilty because he couldn't stop it."

Since he kept his head down and waited, I went on. How they'd been arguing, about the gown, the Order, but mostly about them. The two of them. "I think they were in love. But they didn't know how to say that, or think about it, or *be* that. They didn't even know how to argue about it, so they argued about the Order. But it was just an accident. He fell, that's all."

Quinn did not lift his face for any of these revelations, but as I began to ramble further, he set a hand on my knee. "You're saying no one else was there. And they didn't send him." Dark had deepened. I didn't need light to see Quinn's face. "He can say anything now. Whatever happened, he was the cause. And he covered it up, all this time."

"You should go to him," I said. "Get him to tell you all of it. You know he wants to. I think you're the one he's been wanting to tell."

"Because he thinks I'll kill him."

Yes, I thought, *and no*. "Because you'll decide what justice is. How he can atone."

He peered up into the constellations, pricking into visibility, for the plane that would land on us. "So, your idea of justice? You plainly have one."

"Only what you've been saying all along. What would Brantley want? What would give him peace? He was your friend. How he felt about Will… I'm really only guessing about that. But you knew it. Didn't you?" I had to take his silence for an answer. "Even if there was a struggle up there and…if Will caused it. Would Brantley forgive him? Go on loving him, want him to be happy and protected? I say he would. You have to consult what you know about Brantley and decide what you believe."

In the far hangar, the light had gone out. A barred owl began to call, while Quinn mused on what he knew of Brantley, of love and its capacity.

By way of more evidence, he asked, "Do you still love me?"

Not a fair question, I told him.

That summer in DC, in my conservation-fund mail cubby, I collected postcards from Jenny and Pem, letters from Dex and Vince, and the thickest packets, as always, from Jonathan. One night during finals, he and I had spent seven good study hours hashing the ineluctability of romantic attraction (re: Quinn, also Jonathan's heartbreak and determined optimism over another year without a girlfriend), so by summer we were back to ourselves. Quinn didn't write, no matter how I disparaged his comparative poor showing whenever he placed a late-night call to the townhouse I shared with four other interns. A recent Cornell grad named Edgar roomed beside the kitchen phone, and since I'd let drop that he was cute, Quinn called more often and later than he otherwise might have, for the pleasure of waking this strange male, of then making him wake me.

As usual, nothing from Emery. Near the end of July, though, I found in my cubby a postcard from Paris, signed *Yours, Will*.

Later, in the fall, I would hear rumors he'd been hospitalized briefly at the beginning of summer for an accidental overdose of sleeping pills. I didn't question the adjective. *Accidental* struck me as the way in which Will would take too many pills. Those who repeated the rumor seemed to trust it too, Will being one of our beacons of stability despite the recent irregularities in his social life and the fact that he did not return to school. Anna Vaughn had attended his bedside.

When his postcard arrived in DC, though, I knew none of this. The card bore the image of the church of Saint Michel des Batignolles: a red brick bell tower, topped in a golden figure of what seemed an angel brandishing a sword.

Dear Leah, he wrote with a bleeding black pen, *Greetings from the 17th arrondissement near the banks of the Seine! AV and I are house-sitting for a friend of her dad, a fourth-floor walk-up with a balcony garden and a cat that hates us. Every day I ride a bike to buy a loaf of bread! In our travels (Spain, Belgium, Germany, Switzerland) we stumbled on a cool study abroad program, credits may transfer. We're talking about staying on, maybe a full year. AV says I need a break, and she's probably right (as usual!). The air feels different here. Hard to imagine going back. If they let me into this pr. it will be thx to you. Forever grateful and hope you will visit if your life allows.*

The print became hard to decipher as space ran out. *Yours, Will* had crept below the address. His language struck me as edited, not quite his own though in his handwriting. I wrote him back on a tissue of blue aerogram, in loose script to keep it short, aiming toward fluff since I pictured him handing it over to Anna Vaughn before he had read it himself. I asked about the study abroad program, for which he'd not specified a country. I filled him in on the joys of my internship, on my housemates and our outings around DC, and thanked him for his help in bringing me there. My townhouse was prone to romances, and since both he and Anna Vaughn might enjoy the news I mentioned Edgar, my summer boyfriend, half a secret and plainly a fling. *Boyfriend,* in fact, was an inaccurate term for the manically energized being who snuck into my bedroom past midnight and begged without the first kiss to go down on me, a request I found incomprehensible at first; who flirted madly in spurts that I judged to exceed the amount he flirted with others; who eventually kissed me in the dim corners of populated places, and only in our final week held my hand.

Will never wrote me back. Or maybe, in the end-of-summer transit, his reply had been lost.

My housemates, winsome thick-lashed Edgar included, were city-dwellers who attended big northeastern schools like Georgetown and SUNY and Brown. They found me exotic with my southern accent (they informed me I had one), my tiny, oddly appointed school and the fact that I'd never been to a city bigger than Knoxville. They were smart, funny, turbocharged, refreshingly unneedy people. I loved them and was a little afraid of them, for the speed at which their talk spun through easy references to current national and foreign affairs in particular, the goings-on of the big wide world. Quinn, in their midst, would have come off as provincial. One night, to entertain a visitor, we all went out to a gay bar, where I gawked big-eyed and dumb from start to finish, having deduced the existence of such places but not like this, with its regular door on a regular street we could all enter like any other. My housemates, by contrast, had all been to gay bars and had openly gay friends; their schools had gay clubs and gay class presidents and newspaper editors. *The air is different here,* Will wrote of Paris, and maybe he had needed to go that far. Picturing him in my DC house, I doubted the influence could have cracked through the layers of expectation he'd been raised into, like most of us at Rockhaven.

"You never talked to Will?" I said to Quinn, in one of his kitchen calls. I'd been sure he would corner Will before we left campus, and that whatever story he extracted would lead him to doubt mine. He pretended flirtatious motives for these calls, but I could feel a deeper restlessness that kept him awake.

"I couldn't," was all he would say. "I should tell the fraternity. But it would damage Brantley's memory. And what good would it do?" I was surprised by his reflectiveness, moved by his confusion. He'd grown up a little, in the time I'd known him.

Once we'd returned to school, though, Quinn had constructed a wall behind which he sealed Brantley, Will, the tower, and me. He was mostly civil, but distant. His primary mode of engagement was to treat me as if I were pursuing him endlessly: "God, here she is again—surprise. Can't get enough." On a good day he was wearily patient; on a bad one I was a troll who couldn't take a hint, even as he instigated almost every encounter. "You don't fool me," I would tell him—and to an extent it was true, that I could talk myself out of feeling hurt when I factored in the pain that drove him. I learned to avoid him. When he drank enough, the wall cracked, and he would drag me out to the Gamma dock to spill a torrent about Brantley and Will. He would come on to me, aggressive and pleading, then call me names when I refused. When he apologized, I helped him seal the wall again.

This I still called friendship, however hard he made it, as if the word alone could keep it true; in his gentler phases he called it that too. Years later, when he'd grown more temperate, he would say of senior year, "That was after you refused to be my girlfriend and I was just pining for you all the time. You were always so pleasant to me and so cold, an impenetrable fortress." I told him he was wildly misremembering, on multiple levels. I didn't accuse him of rewriting history to soften it, which had to be partly intentional, a way of flirting and assuaging his guilt at once. Or maybe only of apologizing.

That Dalton had graduated the previous spring and Will was no longer with us, nor Anna Vaughn, allowed for the walling. Without Will in my life, and with only rare, violent bursts of Quinn, I returned to the fold of my friends and nearly forgot the strangeness of junior year. It surfaced in stories of events I had missed, when Jenny would say,

"That was when Leah had other things to do." The interlude saved our
friendship, I suppose, giving her a reason to regret my absence, and by
senior year it had all come to feel like something that had happened
long before, half a dream, the way summer in DC seemed once I was
back on the mountain. Those who had done a junior semester abroad
had similar feelings, I learned, after reconnecting with my freshman
roommate, back from London and assigned the room next to mine.
Here was one of the very first people I had met on the mountain, with
whom I'd chatted amiably on our first night as freshmen, side by side
in the dark, feeling we had little in common, turned at last into one of
my closer friends.

In my single on the top floor of Paschall—a new dorm for every new
year—I made up the bed with my leopard-print comforter, collaged the
walls in three years of party fliers, photos, a pair of Picasso posters
inherited from a graduating senior. I left Jim Morrison rolled in my
closet. Knowing he glowered in there made me think of Will admiring
him freshman year—his sole visit to any room of mine—and of Will's
own belongings, stowed in the basement of Carlson, the dorm at the
back of the Gamma lake where he'd been assigned the standard-sized
single he'd requested before deciding to leave us. Some other petitioner,
surely, had been moved into his room, while down in the basement dark
his framed print of Blake's "The Fall of Man" leaned against a dusty
box marked *Oliver*, communing with spiders, awaiting his return.

And did Brantley wait too? I no longer talked to him. Though he
would never fully leave campus, he clung less closely with Will gone. It
was October before a whisper nudged me to bring out the gown, folded
away in one of my own boxes. Any Rockhaven gown demanded pres-
ervation, and handiwork of his called for double. But this case might
be the exception.

Without taking time for doubt, I worked at it with nail clippers,
snipping loose all the stitched initials but the final set. Then I folded
it into a bag and knocked at Quinn's door—not with any enthusiasm,
since the day before, as I'd passed by his snickering cluster of Gammas,
he'd glanced back at me and hushed them: "Wenches are listening." *A*
wench might have sounded far-fetched enough to be amusing, but he'd
reduced me to one of the rest.

He was still in Lower Gilchrist, three doors down, another year of
netherworld mildew and moaning pipes on the claim he didn't care

enough to look elsewhere. But I knew better: he enjoyed the cachet of hanging with the jocks who tended to congregate on the hall. He and Chip had turned it into their personal drinking club, would now and then go on tears about having it recognized in the yearbook like the Dragoons. If Quinn couldn't be Gamma Chi pledge master, he'd appoint himself to the office in Lower Gilchrist.

PiL pounded through his shut door, which he opened shirtless. I stood under the assault of chanted anger on repeat until, put upon, he went to the stereo and turned it off. His room, twice the size of mine, was half as big as the one he'd shared with Chip, less redolent of old beer. That I'd found him alone in it was difference enough.

"I brought you something," I said. "And I want something in return."

He made a smarmy guess at what. I had to step him back and specify: the photo. His new walls, though, hosted no shrine to Brantley, few photos at all. No splash of red among them that might be my dress.

Maybe they were all piled together in the drawer beside his bed, from which he produced the one in question and allowed me to hold it. The boy who flew from the dock's end in fearful delight already looked younger than I recalled. And he was, in a way. He had become younger than us.

Quinn removed it from my hand. "Better have something good."

He was being gowned in a week—by a Gamma, no question. Asking me to do it would not have occurred to him. I passed him the bag. "It's not mine to give you," I said, as he lifted the scapular, pinched between thumb and forefinger. "But Will isn't here. You can wear it or not. Do what you think best."

He thumbed the space above Brantley's initials. "I took them out," I told him. My intent was as honorable as I knew how to make it: to satisfy tradition, to preserve what I safely could of the gown and give it a proper home. But also, I just wanted to give him something. The photo was to keep him from knowing it.

He crumpled gown and bag together and pitched them aside to the bed. I had to stop myself from going to it, smoothing it, maybe gowning him on the spot, if only to cover the distraction of his too-bare torso with its visible obliques. Quinn eyed the remaining set of initials with a queasy expression. "He didn't sew that, I guess."

"His mother did."

"So give it to his folks."

"You can, if you want. But they gave it to Will."

He was quiet for long enough that I was halfway to the door when he said, "I'm not giving you the picture. You'll have to do better."

"Keep it," I said, but he chose not to hear, was on his feet shouting after me.

"You've got no right to even ask for it! It's just some weird souvenir of something that never involved you in the first place!"

Even as I slammed the door, blinking back tears, before he came out and wailed my name, I was aware I was being goaded to stay, to argue, to kiss him, to do anything but leave. But he wasn't wrong. I went home to Paschall past the bell tower, wishing Will had left me the key. Then again, what if he had? To jump from such a place would feel presumptuous, a claim of too much belonging.

A week later, the photo arrived in my SPO box. Only when I had it without a fight did I realize I couldn't add it to my wall collage, couldn't judge to which of us it most belonged. But he'd given it to me, and that counted for something. Without Brantley to consult, I tucked it away inside the rubber-banded roll of Jim Morrison and lost it for years. Quinn, for his part, put the gown behind the wall, or at least he didn't wear it until the day of our Baccalaureate and then graduation. Among the Gammas the story circulated that yes, they were Brantley's initials, added by Quinn to his own gown so Brantley could walk with us.

Until our senior yearbooks arrived, I'd forgotten the bleak misery of leaving his room on that day in October, the brilliance of the fall afternoon he sent me into. How many times at Rockhaven, while surrounded by beauty, had I felt myself outcast beyond hope, a pretender failing to pass amid the chosen? Brantley calling me ugly in the dining hall could not have been the first nor the last, only the rare event not obscured by subsequent happiness. And that one stuck fast only because he died, so that it became what I had to remember him by.

I had forgotten, for instance, that after leaving Quinn's room I hadn't walked past the bell tower but stopped in its shadow, unable for the moment to drag my sorry self farther. I dropped down on the lawn beside the walkway, wondering if I'd make it to the end of the year, if it was too late to transfer to UT. Overhead, the trees turned their final reds and golds for others, the ones who strolled in perpetual sunlight while I curled on my side in the grass, trying not to cry.

I had checked, prior to this collapse, to make sure no sunlight dwellers strolled near enough to take note of my pathetic heap. Yet I wasn't down a minute before there came a rasp of approach. I told myself to get up, look normal, but my body didn't respond, so I was relieved when the rasp became the panting of a spotted hound called Clara, who belonged to Dr. Mathers. She stepped past to inspect me from a few feet off, tail sweeping, then flopped down in support of my fine idea. Out of the blue sky, a yellow leaf drifted down to join us. From some vantage I didn't see, the campus photographer took our picture.

Many years later, classmates would report they had thought of leaving school at least once, like those stories you hear of happy-seeming people who have considered suicide. "We all did," one or two claimed—far from true, but still a comfort to learn that others had been gripped with the impulse. Most of us, the ones who didn't leave, had landed in the place we belonged.

Even Will, who after sophomore year had yearned to sever what bound him to the mountain, who could have gone anywhere he pleased, had returned. Like that line out of *Gatsby* about life starting all over when it gets crisp in the fall: we all, on some level, felt our fall return as a bright cleansing, a beginning, the opposite of itself. Yet for some, more than wisdom, more than beauty or nostalgia for the pleasures of youth, the lure of our mountain domain was history.

I return now and then, tapping my roof at the gates to release my angel. I visit with students to talk about the internship program I administer in grant writing, and I stay with Vince, professor of history, who keeps the tiny cabin behind his house in fresh sheets for me. It is otherwise his children's playhouse. He and his wife and I worry together over Jonathan, alone after his own wife—a sweet beauty who had seemed equal to the challenge—left him for a less complicated man. We worry about Pem, who is stingy with the details of his bout with cancer. We worry about Jenny, whose husband is a brutish lout we all hate. Nobody worries about Dex, who married Mitzi of all people, a shockingly perfect match, and made a killing in investments, nor about Emery, who married a Phi O no one had ever witnessed him speak to while in school, and with whom he opened a test prep company in Boston. By the time we received his wedding announcement, twenty years on, we'd all become more enlightened members of a new world— newer for us than for others. It's heartening, though often disorienting, to hear my classmates speak with their revised assumptions in place.

I suppose some of them worry about me—still unmarried—though the only one who says so is Jonathan, who still can't accommodate the idea that women exist who don't want that. When I tell him I believe myself happier than any of us, he thinks I'm acting brave. He can't grasp how another night of no one's expectations, pure freedom to do as I please, can still make me giddy. Hanging out with couples who seem to love the duo adventure, like Vince and Donna, does not make me pine for a partner. Communing with their intelligent, interesting children does not quicken any dormant desire for my own. If a husband would demand more energy and attention than I'm prepared to spare, how much more children? The whole enterprise strikes me as a raw deal. I'd rather give what I have to friends or the occasional boyfriend, then be free to curl up with a book and a dog in the sunny window seat of my own house.

I've never met Quinn's wife, Tamara, an anxious-looking woman who doesn't, after all, come from money or play tennis. A base rat, he called her when they first met—he was stationed in Tampa, just out of officer training—and I'm surprised they're still married. He's gained enough self-control not to insult her to me but has never seemed to consider her bright or interesting. I imagine she survives him on the energy of hating other women—me, for one—blaming them for transgressions he has not yet committed, that she intends to stave off with her special powers. Didn't we all think it would be different with us? If I don't hate her back it's because I'm grateful to her for filling a slot he needed filled, kids and a tidy house, while he cheats on her all over whatever country they're stationed in—Germany at present. For years he's been on the verge of a discharge, wanting to try other work, and they keep upgrading him into cushier foreign berths.

My gratitude to her is no joke, though I know myself well enough to be confident I could not have ended up in her place, that even for him there was always a limit to what I would give up. And admittedly I'm guessing, about the tidiness and infidelity. I read it between the lines of soulful instant messages from Ramstein whenever he's struck with a late-night mood. Our congress is well off to the side of cheating—I'm more like a therapist—but whatever it is, the internet has made it easier. We speak only of friendship but veer from "I'll love you forever" to "What are you wearing?" and though we haven't seen each other in fifteen years I've come to count on him turning up at my hospice, ninety-five years old and rocking angrily in a bedside chair, demanding to know how dare I die on him.

Then again, don't we all think we'll be that one?

Anna Vaughn can be spotted now and then on the mountain, with her husband whose triple names I've not once called up correctly, a Rockhaven grad two years ahead of us. A Phi O, I'd bet my life; Vince cannot confirm. Though they keep a weekend house near Calla's View, I had not glimpsed her in my visits until our twenty-fifth reunion, when I landed half-drunk at a party near the football field, at the home of my old Southern Lit professor, where I was waiting for the bathroom when she came out.

At a glance it was her, the cut and color of her hair hardly changed and somehow still in style. She needed several seconds to recognize me, and then came her pageant smile, the burr of pleasure in her voice, even a squinty bit of teariness about the eyes for very old friends. From her absence of wariness or concern, I could already detect the stone and mortar of her own wall, behind which certain elements of our shared history had long ago been stashed in unmarked boxes.

We made the usual small talk. I told her I lived in Atlanta, working as a grant writer for conservation groups. She ran a financial-sounding business with her husband in Norfolk; two kids, the elder headed to Rockhaven, early admission. I was transfixed by the visible lines beside her eyes: if this woman could forgo plastic surgery, then wrinkles must now be permissible. She wore a brown belted dress with a drapey shrug I vaguely wanted and tall boots. It wasn't her reunion year, of course, since she'd returned to graduate a year after us, but one might assume that she, like her father, never missed a Homecoming.

"And Will," I said, buzzed enough to ask, as another person went around us into the professor's bathroom. "Do you hear from him?" We all knew Dream Cone had folded many years before, not much else. But then my cohort had never been the ones in the know. Even Vince, now the faculty advisor to Gamma Chi and member of more than one drinking society to which professors were invited, would never be one.

"We lost him," she said.

I thought she meant he had died. But there was an ironic quirk in her mouth as she slouched against the wall with her stadium cup of scotch. "I think he's still in the French Alps? He discovered mountain-climbing. It's what he does, as far as I know."

"Wow." Beneath her blithe summation must have lurked a welter of pain. My attempt to picture Will, wherever he had landed, involved a pick and a blizzard, a bushy beard tinged reddish and threaded with ice. "I sort of thought he'd be, I don't know, in politics by now," I blurted, though it wasn't true. Climbing an alp in France seemed one of the few reasonable ways to imagine him not dead.

"I know, right?" She sighed, bright and fond. "He would have made a great senator. Can you imagine? The scandals would just"—lips pursed, she stroked a hand through the air—"slide right off him."

But he was no longer that person, she implied, when I pressed her on whether she talked to him still, could put me in touch. She gave me a shuddering head shake on both counts. "Trust me." He had become someone beyond what we, on our puny plateau, could imagine. Seconds later she summoned her façade, gushed over the joy of seeing me and excused herself.

I stopped to refresh my drink and chat with my former professor, and then walked alone up the road, under the gorgeous dying of the leaves. Back at the reunion tent beside the football field, my friends waited. Not everyone had made it, but Jenny had come—thankfully alone—and Pem, Dex and Mitzi, Vince of course, and dear Jonathan, who had turned up to surprise us after sending his regrets. Some people you know you will keep in your life.

Past dark, on the porch of our rambling rental house, the boys bring out the guitars. We stay up most of the night singing the old songs, recounting the stories distorted by time, by better wishes more powerful than truth. At our age, we declare, we should no longer have secrets; yet reunion makes us young enough to pry each other loose by means of "I Never" and Solo cups.

I Never: had a crush on Leah.

I Never: fooled around with Jonathan.

I Never: fooled around with Will Oliver.

The one whose turn it is to speak the line will sometimes inform on himself, but most will say something true, aimed at another. Anyone for whom the statement is untrue must drink. Two things I learn, or discover afresh: we all had crushes on each other, and everyone seems certain Will and I were getting it on. They know I'd drink if it were true, Will needing no protection from me in this group, and so they vary the question: I never kissed, never groped, never saw naked, never took a bubble bath with. To please them I drink to the last one and don't explain.

I Never: helped cover up a homicide.

Were this offered—and it's not—I'm unsure I'd be summoned to drink. But a discomfort surfaces in these confessional gatherings, a reminder of the part of my experience on our mountain they did not share, the secrets I keep still. I wonder if even honor might be expendable for those we love. Or if honor needs a new definition. I have come to realize—*nel mezzo del cammin di nostra vida*—that our capacity to love new people does not increase forever. We spend some vital and disproportionate portion of it in our youth, on attachments that mark us more deeply, hold us fast however far we go. We are not all here on this porch, yet I might say I have never loved anyone in my life, and never will, more than I love these few.

While composing our porch circle of random chairs, I purposely miscounted and dragged over one extra. Beside it, on a wicker table, I've set a clean cup. No one but me knows who sits in the empty chair. Had events taken another turn or two, he might be seated there in the flesh, deciding whether to drink or hold his secrets, rewrite history in the name of love. It's not beyond imagining that by now we could have been friends.

ACKNOWLEDGEMENTS

First I want to thank everyone I loved as an undergraduate or knew in some way or encountered in passing, who inspired this book. The Sewanee English department carries particular weight in the composition. The words of professors—Bill Clarkson, Tam Carlson, Bob Benson, Doug Paschall, Gil Gilchrist, Brown Patterson, to name only a few—are lodged in some deep part of my subconscious along with so many all-but-lost memories I wish I could excavate and relive. If there were a hypnotist who could take me back to correct all my strangely distorted recall, I would hire that person for any amount. I hope this work of fiction, on the other hand, benefits from my radical misremembering.

Deepest gratitude to my extraordinary writers group who lived with this book from conception through the five years of its gasping genesis, helping me to see it more clearly: Susan Rebecca White, Peter McDade, Beth Gylys, and Jessica Handler. And to my readers in the later stages—Jennifer Haigh, Suzanne Van Atten, Lauren Cobb, Buck Butler—I'm indebted for your energy, time, and expertise. Special thanks also to my agent, Mitchell Waters, who keeps me going with his belief in the work.

This book was begun and also concluded at the Hambidge Center, a place close to my heart. Parts were written as well at the Virginia Center for the Creative Arts, Rivendell (sadly gone now), and South Porch. Without these nourishing work spaces, I can't imagine how I would get by. Thanks as well as to Georgia State University, for generous grants of time and travel funds.

Lastly, I want to thank my family, especially my parents, who believed in this book and who allowed for its existence in more ways than one.

www.ingramcontent.com/pod-product-compliance
Lightning Source LLC
Chambersburg PA
CBHW050528110726
47899CB00005B/1635